a chilling look at the Vampyre theme. Rising horror author Darren Speegle gives us a new long fiction piece spanning both history and time; Nicholas Kaufmann sends his vamp after some small town kids; the talented Mercedes M. Yardley shows us how love can often be more a taking than a giving; well-known horror personality Gary Raisor debuts his brand new novella, which returns to his characters Steven and Earl from *Less Than Human*; and finally, Gene O'Neill offers a tribute piece written in the style of the great Tom Reamy. You're really in for a treat with this one, and be sure to check out the blurbs of praise we compiled to commemorate Tom's work—featuring Gregory Benford, Al Jackson, Howard Waldrop, and more!

For our nonfiction, we have a fascinating new article on vampires in New England by K.H. Vaughan. Donald Tyson in his column Murmurs in the Dark explores how occultists in the past have dealt with vampiric lore. Mike Davis in his Weird Reflections column gives us a list of some recommended Lovecraftian reading, and also the amazing Laird Baron in his recurring column The Black Barony discusses the use of vampirism in horror fiction and film.

We have two new columns we're happy to present in this issue, the first a new dark poetry section which this time features the work of Stoker award winning poet Linda D. Addison. In the second new column, K. H. Vaughan has cooked up a Dark Arts feature with an interview showcasing the legendary Kathe Koja and her

Dracula installation. Yours truly has written an article about Stephen King's *IT*, in which I analyze King's famous novel in terms of psychoanalysis and ritual magic. Richard Dansky and Robert Morrish deliver some great new interviews, including one with S.P. Somtow, and another with Ken Hite and Justin Achilli. There are two new horror film features by Colleen Wanglund. And don't forget the tribute section for Tom Reamy!

What more could you want!

So come, rise up from your graves, but please don't track any gravedirt on the carpet, mind you, and have a seat by the crackling fire. Let us explore what it means to be living, yet dead…

— *Aaron J. French*
Editor-in-Chief

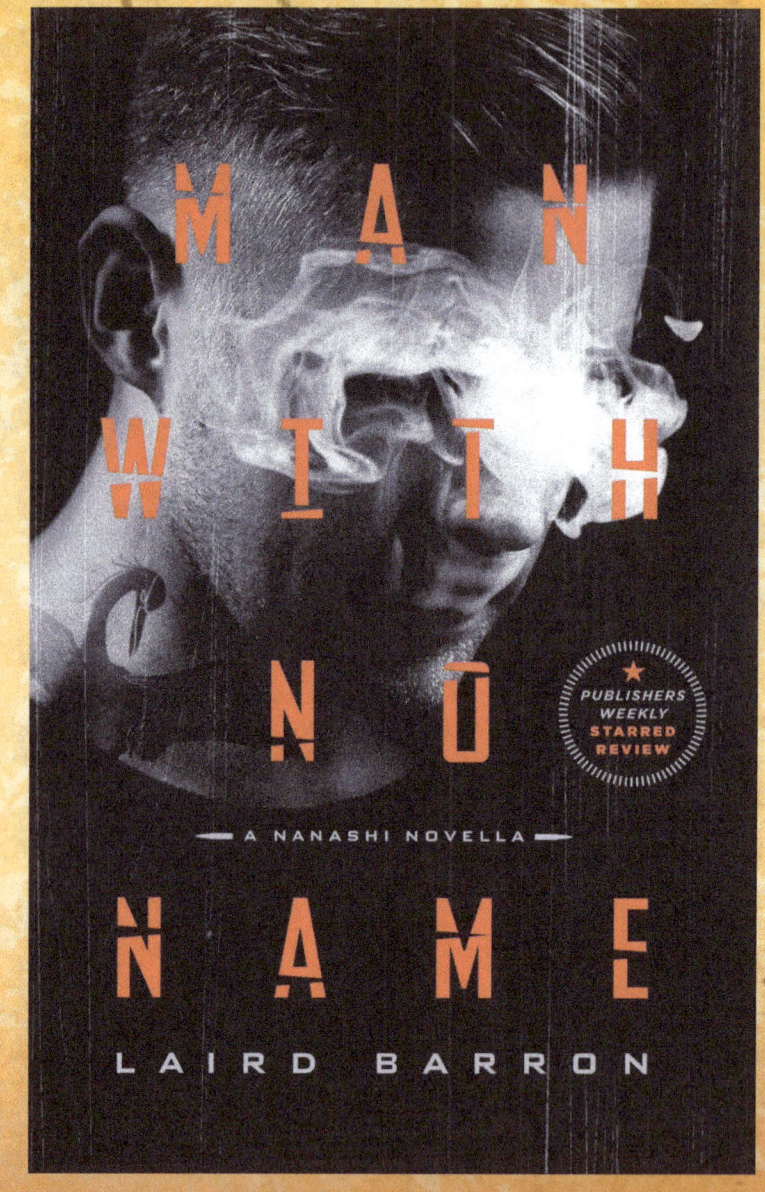

MAN WITH NO

— A NANASHI NOVELLA —

NAME

LAIRD BARRON

PUBLISHERS WEEKLY STARRED REVIEW

Nanashi was born into a life of violence. Delivered from the streets by the Heron Clan, he mastered the way of the gun and knife and swiftly ascended through yakuza ranks to become a dreaded enforcer. His latest task? He and an entourage of expert killers are commanded to kidnap Muzaki, a retired world-renowned wrestler under protection of the rival Dragon Syndicate.

It should be business as bloody usual for Nanashi and his ruthless brothers in arms, except for the detail that Muzaki possesses a terrifying secret.

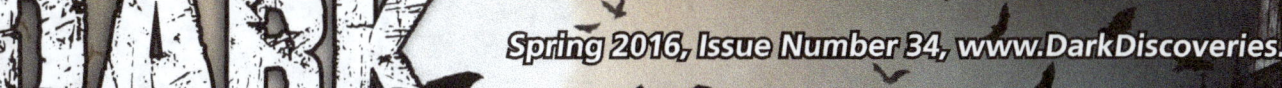

DARK DISCOVERIES

Spring 2016, Issue Number 34, www.DarkDiscoveries.com

Publisher
JournalStone Publishing, LLC

Editor-in-Chief and Art Director
Aaron J. French

Contributing Editor
K. H. Vaughan

Assistant Editors
Russ Thompson (Senior Submissions Editor)
Stuart Conover (Assistant Reviews Editor)

Layout and Design
Paul Fry

Contributors

Aaron J. French
K. H. Vaughan
Laird Barron
Chelsea Quinn Yarbro
Gene O'Neill
Mercedes M. Yardley
Gary Raisor
Darren Speegle
Nicholas Kaufmann
Colleen Wanglund
Mike Davis
Donald Tyson

Robert Morrish
S.P. Somtow
Ken Hite
Justin Achilli
Richard Dansky
Gregory Benford
Al Jackson
Howard Waldrop
John R. Little
Linda Addison
Kathe Koja

Founding Publisher and Editor
James R. Beach

Special Thanks

Wiley Saichek
S.P. Somtow
Michael E. Bell
Tom Reamy
Ken Hite

Justin Achilli
Gregory Benford
Al Jackson
Howard Waldrop
John R. Little

Contributing Artists/Photographers
David Watson (front cover photographer)
Denise Daniel (cover art)
Greg Chapman (pg 29 & 61)
Steve Santiago (pg 9 & 99)
Luke Spooner (pg 37 & 77)

DARK DISCOVERIES
(ISSN 1548-6842) is published (Qtrly) by
JournalStone Publications
439 Gateway Dr., #83, Pacifica, CA 94044

FICTION

Lauren, with the Fall of Night by Darren Speegle — 37
A Faint Scent of Musky Lime by Gene O'Neill — 99
Night's Ivy by Mercedes M. Yardley — 29
Things Heard in the Dark by Chelsea Quinn Yarbro — 09
Whatever Happened to Solstice Young? by Nicholas Kaufmann — 61
Bad Blood [Part 1] by Gary Raisor — 77

FEATURES

Stephen King's IT: A Conjuration of Childhood Fears
by Aaron J. French — 69
A Tribute to Tom Reamy — 95
Searching after Dark: An interview with Chelsea Quinn Yarbro
by Aaron J. French — 05
Featured Film Reviews by Colleen Wanglund — 24
The Vampires of New England by K. H. Vaughan — 33
Dark Poetry by Linda Addison — 59

COLUMNS

Weird Reflections by Mike Davis — 53
The Black Barony: Drain Me by Laird Barron — 55
What the Hell Ever Happened to… S.P. Somtow by Robert Morrish — 91
Playing with Vampires: An Interview with Ken Hite and Justin Achilli
by Richard Dansky — 105
Murmurs in the Dark: Vampires in Western Magic by Donald Tyson — 16
Dark Arts: Kathe Koja by K. H. Vaughan — 74

REVIEWS

Hellnotes/Horror World Reviews — 108

Editorial

Welcome to issue #34 of *Dark Discoveries*. We're thrilled to feature nothing but good old-fashioned vampires this time around, with our theme being Vampyre. Continuing on with the new trend of placing one of our authors on the cover, this issue you'll find the amazing Chelsea Quinn Yarbro gracing the front. Here at DD, we're excited to be working with Quinn for this theme. To our minds, few authors have written so skillfully about vampires and history. She ought to be considered an expert on the subject!

While we love traditional vampires, common to the horror genre, we did not limit the theme to merely this well-known image of them. In fact, we encouraged our authors to explore vampirism in a variety of different ways: from psychic leeching to soul sucking, to money grubbing, to cannibalism, to mind draining; you name it. These concepts can be portrayed in the light of vampirism, which, perhaps, is why the bloodsucker mythology has struck a chord with readers for so long.

Feasting, immortality, man/woman as half beast, etc., even zombism. These too contain elements of vampiric lore. And because the mythology of vampires is just that—a *mythology*—some of the authors have drawn deep in archetypal wells of human consciousness to spin their tales. The result makes for some unnerving, and really rather haunting, reading.

The main feature of any story dealing with vampirism has to do with a form of theft. That is, something has be stolen from one entity by another, in order to nourish or prolong the wellbeing of the thief. In the conventional vampire setting, the thief is the undead vampire, and the victim is the unwilling human being, who is robbed of blood in order to sustain the livelihood of the vampire. Lately, as we have seen (think *Twilight*), the human being is not always so unwilling. But actually this may have always been the case; think also, for example, of Lucy Westenra in *Dracula*.

But this dynamic of thief and victim can be played out through a variety of scenarios. A virus that is parasitic to the physical body is a case of vampirism. A vodoun priest keeping a dead person zombified and dead-but-alive for one purpose or another is acting as a vampire. My own contribution to this issue deals with Stephen King's *IT*; in the article, I try to show that Pennywise haunting the minds of the kids in the novel represents psychic vampirism. The complexity of this theme, which all too often is displayed in simplistic terms (I have to cite the *Twilight* book again in this regard), is why we've chosen the alternative Vampyre spelling for the cover. This form suggests something old, archaic even, something infinitely alien to the normal day-to-day experience of human life. It hints at something much, much darker, and deeper.

On, then, with the content of the issue.

We are pleased to feature a new interview with Chelsea Quinn Yarbro, as well as a new story from her which takes

Searching after Dark: An interview with Chelsea Quinn Yarbro

by Aaron J. French

Photo courtesy of Charles Lucke

Aaron J. French: Could you start by telling our readers a little about your personal biography—what drew you to dark fiction, how did you get your start, etc.?

Chelsea Quinn Yarbro: I was born and grew up in Berkeley, and lived there just over 29 years after my divorce. Even when I was little, I knew it was a very intellectually stimulating place. I learned to read early (age 4) and developed a taste for 19th century literature. My Finnish grandfather told me Finnish folktales when I was a kid, and many of them—like a great many folktales the world over—are cautionary tales, with gruesome consequences for those not heeding the warnings in the story. I found them deeply satisfying. By eight, I was hooked on grand opera, and big, complex emotions are the heart of opera, even in the comedies. Making the step to horror literature was easy.

AJF: To what extant do you prefer writing horror versus, say, fantasy or science fiction, or any of the other genres you write in? You employ a number of pseudonyms, as well, to handle all this. Is it difficult to balance?

CQY: To answer back to front, writing in multiple genres is easy—it keeps

CHELSEA QUINN YARBRO

HAUNTING INVESTIGATION
a Chesterton Holte Mystery

"This diverting and involving story will leave readers both satisfied and hungering for more..."
— Pamela Sargent, author, *Earthseed* and *The Shore of Women*

me balanced. What's hard is doing a steady diet of any single genre. What I like about horror is that it is flexible—you can do a horror story in almost any genre, including comedy (although Edmund Keen was right: dying is easy, comedy is hard)—and it is filled with ambiguity. In horror, things are seldom what they seem, which is a wonderful advantage to structure. I find westerns to be the most fun, but I wouldn't want to have to do two of them in a row. And my current new mystery series, which takes place in 1924 has a ghost for a main character: the first novel is out—*Haunting Investigation: a Chesterton Holte mystery*. I just turned in the second book in the series—*Living Spectres*—and will be doing a proposal for the third this next week. Pseudonyms, for the most part, are the result of publishers wanting to "brand" each genre, and pen names are the easiest way to do that.

AJF: We want to know how you got so good at implementing erudite historical research into your novels. The historical elements are particularly well done. What's the secret?

CQY: The simple answer is research.

The more complex answer is to find material contemporary to the period of the novel, which gives a flavor as to how the people going through that time and place saw themselves. Once you have the basics of the period and place, get the mindset, you have a running jump on the feel, which is essential to keeping your reader in the story. It also means that your sense of the time will be inclined to favor the literate, which is inevitable.

AJF: There's often a strong current of spiritualism and other esoteric themes in your work. We love that kind of stuff at *Dark Discoveries*. Could you tell us a bit about your interest in this field, and also how it relates to your relationship to the weird fiction author Robert Aickman (we're a big fan of Aickman's as well)?

CQY: My interest in the occult is related to my worldview: many people see the world as basically rational with occasional outcroppings of irrationality; I see the world as basically irrational with a thin veneer of rationality spread over it most of the time, so it figures that I would be drawn to occult studies. Incidentally, I do not believe in the supernatural. I think that if something is happening, no matter how strange, it is natural, but part of *natural* that we do not yet understand. I have a fairly extensive collection of books on the occult, and it's no secret that I read cards and hands. By the way, I had the pleasure to meet Robert Aickman on two different trips to London. We spent most of those two meetings talking about opera. I know he had a reputation for being something of a ladies man, and while that may have been true, I never saw a sign of it, but then, I might not have been his type.

AJF: The theme of this issue is vampirism. You're most well-known for your Saint-Germain epic, which features

vampires as well as Le Comte de Saint-Germain. Could you tell us how you researched the subject of vampires and how you wove it into your novels? Were you influenced by Stoker? Rice?

CQY: The first five Saint-Germain novels were a kind of experiment as to how far the vampire paradigm could be pulled to the positive and still have a recognizable vampire, and it turns out, it can go quite far—although, for the sake of full disclosure, I have written some very negative vampires in my time. I began in the winter of 1971 to play with the possibilities by taking the Stoker model and working with that, removing all the religiosity and instead, investigating the blood metaphor, which is pervasive in vampire lore. After delving into all manner of vampire folklore, I decided that blood was a metaphor for intimacy, and went with that; it's still at the heart of the series. And I thought about how a vampire could actually fit into society, while remembering my Italian grandmother's admonition "No one ever got old being stupid," which, while demonstrably not true, is a good guiding principle when writing about such an ultimate outsider as a vampire.

AJF: Your Saint-Germain series began with the first book *Hôtel Transylvania* in 1978 and has gone on to feature many more follow-ups. Could you give our readers a picture of where this series began and how it has developed over the years?

CQY: The first five novels (*Hôtel Transylvania*, *The Palace*—not my title—*Blood Games*, *Path of the Eclipse* and *Tempting Fate*) were the starting place for exploring the lives of women in history through the lens of a compassionate vampire. With the obvious exception of *Tempting Fate*, the books were based on the claims of the real man: he said,

when he first arrived in Paris in 1743, that he was four thousand years old, and kept his longevity by drinking the Elixir of Life, and said he had been in Renaissance Italy, in Imperial Rome, and had left China when Jenghiz Khan's Mongols had invaded. After doing nothing more with him for about eight years, I came back to the series after writing the three Olivia books, and I'm still at it, still keeping as accurate to history as my research will allow, and still writing about the lives of women as seen through Saint-Germain's eyes.

AJF: Le Comte de Saint-Germain is very well-known in both historical and esoteric literature. What led you to choose that name/character, and how did hope to utilize the background associated with such a person? Perhaps you could tell us something of the historical background of this figure?

CQY: I've read extensively about Saint-Germain, and I used his extravagant claims to mine for story information. He was remarkably long-lived for the period, but his claim for being between 3,000 and 4,000 years old and still looking to be in his early 40s is a trifle hard to swallow. He was an alchemist, but then, so was Isaac Newton. He traveled widely, which, while not common in the eighteenth century, was not wholly impossible. He spoke over a dozen languages. Quite a remarkable fellow and, for my purposes, irresistible. I have a brief essay about him as part of the Afterword to *Hotel Transylvania*, if readers want to explore more deeply.

AJF: What kind of readers tend to be fans of your Saint-Germain series, and do you have any interesting anecdotes about meeting them or things they've said?

CQY: I have a fuzzy grasp on my fans and readers—and there is a difference between them—and there are a couple of them I've been known to duck into men's rooms to avoid, but generally they seem to be a fairly diverse lot, pleasant people who know the difference between fantasy and fantasize. But let me repeat what I've been saying for more than forty years: please do not write fan fiction about any of my characters—if you do, and I find out, I will be contractually obligated to sue you. Write your own stories about your own characters.

AJF: In 2014, you were named Lifetime Achievement Winner of the World Fantasy Award. What was that experience like?

CQY: It's always nice to get a public thank-you, which such awards are, and my ego loves it. It's good to know that there are people out there who think reading my work is a worthwhile thing to do. But I often remind myself that awards do not in any way change the words on the page, and receiving an award, lovely though it is, does not magically improve the work(s) in question.

AJF: The past few issues of *Dark Discoveries* have focused such subjects as Secret Societies (#29) and The Occult in Dark Fiction (#32). In a similar vein, we'd love to hear anything you would share with us about your Messages from Michael series. I know you like to keep those separate from your fiction work, but that sort of thing is very interesting to us at DD.

CQY: I've been toying with the idea of doing a fifth Michael book. I have loads of material, and the group is generally for it, provided, of course, I conceal their identities, which I am glad to do. Does that mean the group still exists? Yes, it does, and before you ask, it is still closed; I'm not at liberty to bring new members into the group. Both our mediums require privacy, and I think they're wise to do that. I've thought so ever since the time, more than twenty years ago, when I received a death threat from an earnest young Mormon about doing Devil's work and explaining why he had to shoot me because of it.

AJF: Yikes, that's scary. Let's change the subject! Do you see your later novels as any different from your earlier ones? How have you seen your Craft evolving over the years?

CQY: Don't ask me; I have no idea. I'm sure that there have been changes, but since self-consciousness is deadly to fiction writers, I go out of my way to avoid it. I know a couple academics who could probably tell you the answer, but I can't.

AJF: What projects do you have on the horizon? More Saint-Germain Cycle novels? Anything else?

CQY: A novelette is on the burner, science fiction. I'll be doing the third Chesterton Holte mystery, and working on finishing the 28th Saint-Germain. A small theater-cum-Holmesian group in Jackson (the county seat of Amador County, up in California's Gold Country) will be performing a Holmesian play I wrote for them a couple of years ago in May and June; a novella-ized version of the play will be up on the Internet sometime in March. Check my Facebook page (Facebook.com/AuthorChelseaQuinnYarbro) for more details.

JANUARY 2015   DECEMBER 2014   NOVEMBER 2014   NOVEMBER 2014   NOVEMBER 2014   OCTOBER 2014

DOUBLE DOWN V AUGUST 2014   WWW.JOURNALSTONE.COM   MAY 2014   Special Edition JULY 2014

JOURNALSTONE
YOUR LINK TO ARTISTIC TALENT
WWW.JOURNALSTONE.COM

CHELSEA QUINN YARBRO

Things Heard in the Dark

The trouble with insomnia, as Terry Pinkerton's mother had often said, *is that you don't get enough sleep,* and Terry was forced to agree, having gone six nights of post-surgical pain in an elevated bed placed next to the window in the apartment living room which provided a view of the outside and easy access to the TV; at hours like this one—three-seventeen—a favorite old film came to mind: *Rear Window.* Terry could not help feeling a bit like Jimmy Stewart, only without the binoculars, and the view of a small, woodsy part instead of an apartment house across a courtyard. The lack of sleep had given Terry a skewed sense of the world, which leant a kind of surreal glamor to the street beyond the window; things shimmered and shook in the night and the sounds that he could hear were often strange.

Ordinarily, the television might have been on, and one of Terry's large collection of classic films would be running; that way Terry could have almost ignored the gnawing ache of the healing incision. But the upstairs neighbors had complained about the noise, so after ten p.m., Terry was left to sit in the dark, staring out at the park across the street. Every movement brought forth a chorus of twinges and aches, so Terry tried to move as little as possible; when the pain sharpened, it was more difficult to doze, let alone sleep, and that was the case now.

On impulse, he picked up the phone and punched in a number from memory, teeth gritted. After eight rings, a sleepy voice said, "Doctor Wilson."

"It's Terry Pinkerton, Doctor."

There was a pause. "I gather you're awake." The doctor sounded more resigned than annoyed.

"That I am; I'm also hurting," Terry agreed. "What do you recommend I do about it?"

"First, don't double up on the pills; you could have a bad reaction," came the sharp response. "I'll give you an appointment in the morning, and we'll see what we can do to adjust your dosage."

"That sounds like a good start," Terry said. "But what am I going to do tonight?"

The doctor sighed. "For now, I'm sorry, but you'll just have to endure it. If opiates did not act as stimulants for you, this wouldn't be such a problem. I'm sorry, but that's what we're up against."

"Why? It doesn't make any sense, does it?" Terry demanded. "And don't tell me genetics."

"We've been through that before," said Doctor Wilson with deliberate patience.

Now it was Terry's turn to sigh. "Okay—it's genetic. Big f-ing deal."

"It is. Your case is complicated."

Terry wanted to shout, but spoke softly. "I'm getting really spacey. I can't think. About all I can do is stare out the window, since I have the TV off, to spare the neighbors the noise."

"I'll make sure you can get some sleep in the morning, Terry. Be at my office by nine-thirty."

"Kyle doesn't arrive until then; would ten do?"

"I'll call him at seven and tell him to get there early. It's his job to get you to appointments." The doctor yawned. "Nine-thirty. My office."

"I'll be there," Terry promised. "If Kyle's on time." Kyle usually was, but he did not like having to show up early.

"Good night, then," Doctor Wilson said, and hung up.

Terry pummeled the pillow that was supposed to help ease the pain, but did not. "Damn. Damn, shit."

The old pendulum clock in the hallway chimed three-thirty, a muffled sound that caught Terry's attention more than usual. "It's three hours until dawn, more or less," Terry announced softly, to hear something other than the soughing of the wind. The night seemed longer than usual, its deepness heightened; sounds were sharpened and distorted; swaying trees seemed to be moving their roots as well as their limbs. Terry felt edgy, which had to be on account of the lack of sufficient pain medication, which by now was only doing a half-assed job and undoubtedly contributing to the sensitivity he experienced.

There was a flicker of movement on the edge of the park—or perhaps it was only a hallucination. Terry squinted, searching for the source of the movement. No, it was not a trick of the mind, there was definitely something there: for an instant, Terry saw a tall, lean figure with a long, faint shadow, but then it vanished among the trees.

He sat up as much as possible and blinked. "Must be a dog on the loose. A Great Dane, maybe." Staring down and waiting for the animal to emerge, Terry began to realize that the movement had come from above the trees, not under them. "Couldn't be a dog, not up in the trees. Or a bird—too big for a bird. There are no more pterodactyls, or pteranodons, or whatever they call them now."

Very faintly, there came a kind of crooning cry, too melodic to be an animal, too feral to be a person.

"What the—" Terry said more loudly.

The sound went on, wistful and seductive, caressing, like a wild heart crying out in loneliness; Terry listened, hoping to identify the source of the eerie near-music; the sound rose and fell in seductive ululation, now louder, now softer, as insinuating as a lying promise. Several minutes of this ticked by, and Terry was about to fall back against the therapeutic pillow when someone came into sight on the street two storeys down—probably a woman by the length of hair—hurrying toward the park; Terry could tell that she was following the sound like a hound on a scent.

He leaned toward the window to watch.

The woman hesitated at the edge of the trees, but as the weird cry soared, she moved forward, into the shelter of the poplars and larches, and the sound stopped, only to be replaced by what might have been a stifled scream, and a shaking of one of the saplings near the street.

Terry could not move any nearer the glass without falling out of bed, which was vexing, for now it was clear that something unusual and possibly dangerous was happening in the dark shelter of the trees, like the large, clawed, smoking footprints that follow Dana Andrews in *Curse of the Demon.* He stared and stared, willing his sight to penetrate the leaves and branches, but without success.

After a while, the woman staggered out from under the trees, her hands clutched to her neck, each step more unsteady, until she fell onto the grass, convulsing.

For the second time that night, Terry reached for the phone, this time dialing 9-1-1, and waiting nervously for the operator to answer.

"Emergency. Which service do you require?" The voice sounded almost bored, or half asleep.

"In the park at Seventeenth and Redmont, there's a woman on the grass. I think she's injured," Terry said, hung up, then went back to watching.

Four minutes went by before a police car pulled up at the corner and two uniformed men got out; one was large and stocky, the other whipcord thin. They shone their flashlights about and quickly located the woman; the thin officer knelt down to examine her while the other used the device on his shoulder to call for help.

In less than three minutes, an ambulance arrived, lights blazing and siren yelping. It parked behind the police car, and another two men emerged, both in white jackets; one was blond, the other swarthy. They rushed toward the policemen and both of them took the place of the thin policeman beside the woman.

Suddenly the woman spasmed, shrieked raggedly, and fell ominously silent.

Terry watched in fascination, awareness of pain relegated to secondary but persistent importance.

The cops went into the woods, flashlights and pistols at the ready, leaving the EMTs to deal with the woman.

The fair-haired EMT went to the ambulance and brought a stretcher out, and a case of what Terry assumed were medical supplies. The two EMTs went rapidly to work on the woman, the darker of them removing thick bandages from the case, the blond preparing a neck-brace before they very gingerly moved her onto the stretcher, securing her with belts before they lifted the stretcher and made for the back of the ambulance, and put her into it; the darker EMT hurried around to the driver's side, while the fairer climbed into the rear with the woman. The siren came alive again, and the ambulance rushed away.

A little bit later the policemen emerged from the woods, their transmitters crackling.

Terry listened intently to catch a few words of their report.

"No . . . nothing . . . blood on the ground . . . scuffle . . . couldn't find . . . attacker," said the beefier policeman.

"Need CSIs here," said the other, his voice louder and more strained than his partner's.

". . . tape off," the first said. "Mark . . . victim fell." He paused, then responded, "We'll have it ready in ten minutes."

"We'll be waiting for backup. Tell them," said the other.

For the next forty minutes, Terry watched the CSIs scour the grass verge and then go into the woods, their very large, very bright flashlights marking their progress through the trees as they sought out the site of what was being described among themselves as a wild assault, where they set up to gather evidence. Another squad car arrived, and two more policemen—one Asian, one of mixed ancestry—took up guard positions as the CSIs departed, laden with boxes and bags along with their equipment cases. Now there was yellow tape stretched among the trees and a sprayed outline on the grass where the woman had fallen.

Terry heard a faint sound of a radio from the cruiser.

". . . unknown assailant . . . no description . . ."

The Asian policeman returned to the car and there was a quick exchange via the radio that Terry could not work out; his partner came out of the woods and the two had a quick, quiet conversation.

Terry could hear nothing of what they said to each other, and was quickly distracted by movement in the trees at the far end of the park.

A figure, long and cloaked, appeared to be floating out of the woods, drifting like an enormous leaf on the rising breeze, but against the direction the wind was blowing.

Now Terry was fully awake and engaged in what was happening. Leaning dangerously beyond the bed, Terry tried to follow the progress of the inexplicable thing even while trying to believe that this was something conjured up by all the films and stories that had held his attention for the last six days. Surely nothing like what was out there could be real. But there it was, sailing along at tree-height, the hem of its garment flapping like rudimentary wings— like a bird of ill-omen, thought Terry, trying to remember which movie he'd watched with such a bird in it.

For a minute or two, Terry lost sight of the figure, and was beginning to feel relief that the vision was gone, when something rose in front of his window, and within the long folds of a dark hood, Terry saw a bone-white, emaciated face spattered with a dark substance that looked red as the lamplight shone upon it through the glass.

There was a kind of purr mixed with a growl, and then the musical wail that had first caught Terry's attention. The figure lingered a few seconds, peering straight at Terry, then wafted away.

"Bela Lugosi," Terry whispered, and thought that Lugosi did not fly in *Dracula*, but turned into a mist.

The cry resumed, despairing and carnal, growing louder and softer, like the motion of the waves on the beach in *From Here to Eternity*, only more scary than sexy. Mixed with alarm, Terry felt a yearning, more intense than anything known before. Without being aware of it, he reached out, overbalanced, and fell to the floor in a welling of agony as two stitches tore.

***

By dawn, Terry had managed, after long, painful effort, to sit up, but was then too exhausted to do much more than pant; the ordeal of such a simple thing was worrisome, which only made him more determined. After trying to stand up by pulling on the blankets, all Terry had achieved was to drag them onto the floor, which provided a kind of cocoon to rest in. For the first time in hours, Terry slept.

The doorbell sounded, and then the door opened, as Kyle Melton let himself into Terry's apartment. "Hey. Terry?"

Terry came enough awake to moan; almost at once, Kyle appeared. "Shit, what did you do?" He bent to lift Terry back onto the bed. "Doc Wilson called. You got a nine-thirty appointment downtown."

"I know," Terry muttered.

"I'll put something on for breakfast and then sponge you down," Kyle said as he picked the blankets up off the floor and began folding them. Kyle was in his mid-thirties and had combined his training as a physical therapist with a Masters in social work, and spent his days caring for those recovering from surgery at home; he had a steady but slightly distant manner, and was efficient at most things, including making sure his people took care of themselves. "And I'll redress the incision; that bandage looks pretty awful." He set the folded blanket on the folding table next to Terry's bed.

"Thanks," Terry said. "I felt like an idiot after I fell. I thought I was better balanced in my bed."

"How'd you manage to do that? I thought you understood about the risk of falling." He inspected the remaining two blankets and put one of them back on the bed before tossing the other onto the nearest chair.

"I didn't mean to," said Terry.

"I didn't think you did; you gotta be more careful; the pins in your bones need to stay put," said Kyle, bustling into the kitchen and raising his voice to be heard as he filled the kettle with water and set it on the stove. "Tea or coffee this morning?"

"I don't care."

"Coffee it is," Kyle declared.

Terry tried to stretch, then gave it up as a bad idea. "Will you hand me the remote before you do? I want to catch up on the news."

"Something to take your mind off things?" Kyle asked as he retrieved the remote from just under the bed. "You gotta put a tie on this thing."

"Yeah," said Terry, turning on the TV and pressing down the numbers for the city's best news station. For a time, everything was about politics and the tricky international situation, and next there was a report on the antics of the latest rock band, but at last, the irrepressibly perky young woman who did the local news took over, reporting first on a boisterous protest at city hall, and then taking on a more somber tone.

"Police are asking for anyone who might have seen a savage attack on Nancy Monroe, a night nurse at Joseph Palmer Memorial Hospital, who was found at the edge of the woods in Redmont Park early this morning; the attack on Miss Monroe is estimated to have occurred sometime between three-twenty and three-forty. Miss Monroe was taken to Palmer Memorial where she is listed in critical condition. We'll put up the tip line and email address for—"

Terry changed the channel to a rerun of *Wiseguy*, and waited for Kyle to bring the coffee. Terry's appetite had vanished.

***

After two hours in Doctor Wilson's office being monitored by his nurse to make sure that Terry had had no adverse reactions to the analgesic that the doctor had administered, and that the new stitches were not tearing, Terry and Kyle left to spend another hour at the pharmacy to fill a ten-day prescription for the same medication as the one he had received in Doctor Wilson's office.

"No refills," the pharmacist informed them as he handed over the small packet. "If you need more, we'll need to get your doctor's approval."

"Noted," said Kyle as he helped Terry out of the chair.

"Remember, no grapefruit at all with this."

"We got it," Kyle assured the pharmacist.

By the time they got back to Terry's apartment, Kyle was out of sorts and Terry was exhausted. Kyle helped Terry into bed, saying, "You rest up. I'll have lunch ready by two-thirty."

"Good. Wake me up if I'm asleep."

"Right you are. I'll do laundry while you rest. Do you want the TV on or not?"

"Put on the first season of *Buffy*; it'll take my mind off things," Terry said with more hope than certainty while trying to get comfortable, and very nearly succeeded. "That new stuff really takes the edge off." As Kyle went off, Terry began to get drowsy, and during one of Giles' explanations of the dangers Buffy faced, finally slept.

"That's what the pill's supposed to do," Kyle remarked, and went to unload the disc.

***

Although a bit groggy, by nightfall Terry was reasonably comfortable, feeling warm and cozy while watching out the window. Kyle had made a chicken stew for dinner and there was more of it in the fridge. The stitches in Terry's back had subsided to a remote kind of soreness that was less than the discomfort from sore muscles. Terry was half dozing for most of the evening, not very attentive to what was on the TV. Watching the eleven o'clock news, Terry pricked up a bit when there was an announcement that the nurse who had been so brutally attacked in Redmont Park—Nancy Monroe—had died of her injuries; Terry thought about *Some Like it Hot*, and mused in a muzzy sort of way that Monroe seemed to be a jinxed name for women, and then, more sensibly, considered placing a second call about the attack, this time to the police, but after a period of consideration, decided not to. Anyone taking the amount of medication Terry was would not be deemed a very reliable witness, and, Terry had to admit, who could blame them? If that white-faced creature ever came around again, Terry might take the bull by the horns and contact the cops, but until that happened, there was no reason to report anything, certainly not anything so weird as a floating figure in a cloak. With that thought as consolation, Terry went solidly to sleep.

***

The next night, he woke up abruptly in the wee smalls, and fumbled to check the time on the cell phone. Two-forty-eight. Terry felt wide awake and filled with restive anticipation. How could the pill have worn off so soon? He was not so much in pain as consumed by prickles. Was this some new kind of reaction to the painkiller Doctor Wilson had prescribed, or something else?

From outside there came that weird cry again, haunting and sensual, disturbing in its wordless implication. Terry moved, very carefully, to the edge of the bed and peered out into the night. A mist was forming, making it hard to see the street clearly, let alone the park, but there was a fluttering shadow that descended into the trees—that much was certain. Terry went cold. What was out there, and what was it doing? Tempting as it was to think of the floating cloaked figure as a special effect somehow escaped from film—possibly *Doctor Jekyll and Mister Hyde*—Terry had to admit that this could not be possible.

This night, it took almost half an hour for someone to answer the call: an angular youth dressed all in black came slouching toward the trees, his black-dyed hair at odds with his pale skin. He carried a small flashlight, and its narrow beam flitted beneath the trees, then went dark; a few minutes later there was a moan that came out of the center of the park, and another sound that was similar to eating watermelon at a picnic, as well as a kind of trembling that made the very trees seem enveloped in terror or ecstasy. Ten minutes later, the shape emerged from the crown of treetops, slipped past Terry's window, and continued on into the thickening fog to be lost to sight.

***

The police did not converge upon Redmont Park until shortly after dawn, in response to the cell phone alert from a morning jogger that there was a body at the picnic tables. This time there were five officers, two men in plainclothes, and a half-dozen CSIs searching the taped-off park for clues and evidence. A cluster of news vans were relegated to the convergence of Seventeenth and Redmont, where a few of the more determined reporters were interviewing each other until the police were willing to talk to them.

Terry watched well into the morning, stopping only when Kyle filled the bathtub and called to him. After the gymnastics of the bath, Terry went back to bed, staring out to see what more had happened in Redmont Park. The news vans had departed, and only three uniformed policemen were left on the scene with the CSIs, to keep gawkers from entering the crime scene. After an hour or so, Terry turned back to the TV, and asked Kyle to put in *The Fall of the House of Usher*.

Kyle left at four in the afternoon, while Terry was sleeping, leaving a pot of turkey soup simmering on the stove, confident that its aroma would wake Terry before six, although he also set the alarm on the stove to buzz then, as well.

***

It took Terry almost half an hour to prepare a simple meal of soup, a lettuce-wedge salad, and French bread, all arranged on a bed-tray so that there would be support and warmth to accompany the food. He carried the bed-tray into the living room, set it on its folding legs, and climbed back into the covers to dine. In the middle of dinner, he heard a sharp tap on the door, and very reluctantly got out of bed, made sure the bathrobe was fully closed, and tottered to answer the repeated knock. Opening the door with the clamshell guard still on it, he looked out and saw two men in inexpensive suits and very sensible shoes,

with police badges hanging from lanyards around their necks. "Just a minute," Terry said, and closed the door to disengage the guard, then opened the door properly. "Come in. I was wondering if you might show up."

The two plainclothes policemen exchanged glances as they came into the apartment living room. "You're ill?" the older man asked.

"Recovering from surgery. I'm Terry Holland, gentlemen. Please sit down."

"I'm Detective Tate, and this is Detective Ostermann," said the older man, a fellow with salt-and-pepper hair and a lugubrious expression. He made a grimace of a smile as he plunked himself down in the loveseat that served as a sofa in the small room; his partner was at least a decade younger than Tate, a tall, sharp-faced African-American with a keenly inquisitive manner, who moved about the room, taking note of all he saw.

"What can I do for you?" Terry asked, and got back into bed. "I'm just finishing dinner."

"You go right ahead," said Tate. He went on less cordially, "Have you been following the news?"

"You mean the murders in Redmont Park? Yes, I have," Terry answered before taking another bite of French bread.

Detective Ostermann took the lead. "We're talking to everyone on the block whose windows face the park, to find out if anyone has noticed anything that might be useful to our investigation—any strangers hanging around, or anyone behaving suspiciously?" The tone of his voice was dubious; he had noticed the array of prescription bottles on Terry's folding table. He took out a smartphone. "Do you mind if we record this?"

"Go ahead," said Terry.

Ostermann stopped and directed his stare at Terry. "So, what have you seen? With your bed so near the window, you've got a great view."

"I don't know what to tell you. I saw the police and the ambulance arrive two nights ago, and all the fuss last night. It would have been hard to miss." Terry had some more soup. "I was kind of groggy."

Ostermann nodded. "Commotion woke you, did it?"

"I was dozing before then. I was pretty sore."

"How long since your operation?" Tate asked.

"Eight days. I had a bad fall and messed up a couple of ribs and three vertebrae," Terry said, almost apologetically.

"Sounds painful," said Tate, coming as close to sympathy as he could.

"I'm told it will be better in a few days," said Terry. "For now, I nap a lot."

"But did you see anything—that you remember?" Ostermann asked.

"Nothing specific, but I'm taking a lot of medicine just now." Terry felt uncomfortable at not being more candid, but knew that the police would doubt whatever was volunteered. "I did see a woman go into the park night before last, sometime between three and three-thirty. I wasn't quite awake."

Tate leaned forward. "Did you notice anything about her?"

Terry tried to be more forthcoming, but withheld the least believable details. "She had long hair. She went in under the trees, and a little while later, came out again, stumbled, and fell. A short time later, a squad car pulled up and two uniformed policemen got out. They found the woman, and summoned the ambulance. I guess you know the rest better than I do."

"How well did you see this woman?" Ostermann asked, more sharply than before.

"Not very well, I'm afraid. I couldn't tell you what she looked like, aside from the hair."

"Did you notice anyone else in the park?" Tate inquired. "Was there anyone about before the woman appeared?"

"You mean aside from the police and the rest of them? That was after; before them, I don't think so." Terry finished the soup.

"You don't think so?" Ostermann challenged.

"I fell out of bed and pulled some stitches loose. So, no, I can't say for certain that I saw anything more than what I've told you. I was lying on the floor until eight in the morning." Terry took the last piece of French bread. "I might have seen something at the edge of the park, or I might have confused it with movement in the trees while the police were putting up tape. That was afterward, too. Sorry." Terry recalled the baleful stare of the cloaked figure floating outside the window and suppressed a shudder. Mentioning that would surely make the two cops believe that Terry was drugged, nuts, or both.

"What about last night?" Ostermann pursued.

"I'd got some new pain medication yesterday. My memory's a bit fuzzy about yesterday afternoon and evening. You can check with my doctor, if you like; he'll confirm that. Or Kyle Melton; he's my caregiver and physical therapist. His card is on the refrigerator."

"I'll get it," said Ostermann, and made for the kitchen.

"I assume you know that there was another victim last night?" Tate said while Ostermann got the card.

"I found out on the news, this morning. It's a bad thing, a very bad thing." Terry glanced toward the window. "I suppose you'll have police in the park all tonight, just to be safe?"

"That's the plan," said Tate. "But if this killer has the brains God gave a cantaloupe, he'll stay away."

Terry nodded. "What about the other parks in this part of the city? What about Ramsey, and Twelve Oaks?"

"We're setting up patrols in both of those, and in Elias Whitney. We don't want another murder." He said this with a tight smile.

Terry nodded. "It makes me nervous, thinking about it."

Ostermann came back with the card. "I'll call him later today. Do I have your permission to discuss your situation with him?"

"Go ahead," said Terry, reaching for the napkin. "If he has doubts, tell him to call me."

Tate stood up. "We may be back tomorrow or the next day. It depends on how our investigation pans out."

"Please let yourselves out. I'll put the latch on when I take these"—Terry indicated the tray and its contents—"back to the kitchen."

"Do you want some help?" Tate asked in an automatic way.

"Thanks, but I should take care of it myself, or so Kyle tells me." Terry shrugged.

The two policemen exchanged glances again, but let themselves out without further comment.

Terry waited until the door was closed to get up and lift the tray, folding up the legs before carrying it back to the kitchen.

***

All through the night police cars and news vans came and went around Redmont Park. Terry watched them until it was certain that nothing more would happen there before morning. After taking another pain pill, Terry sank into slumber, and paid no attention to anything until Kyle arrived at nine-thirty to begin his day with Terry.

"How did you sleep?" Kyle asked as he came over to take Terry's blood pressure, pulse, and temperature.

"Fair," said Terry. "There were a lot of people in the park. I drifted off around two."

"There's been no news about another murder, at least

not in Redmont Park." Kyle made notes on his notebook and emailed them off to Doctor Wilson. "You need to rest more, Terry. Your pulse is on the fast side."

"Yeah, I thought so, too."

Kyle lifted the blankets to check Terry's feet. "I'm going to give you some exercises to do in bed. Nothing strenuous, but you need to keep your muscles working. And I'll clip your toenails; they're getting a bit long."

"In the tooth?" Terry asked, trying to make a joke.

"Sponge bath today, real bath tomorrow," Kyle said without amusement. "Try to get a good eight hours tonight. You'll regain your strength more quickly. You need to start doing more than making up a dinner tray. What about taking a walk around the apartment a couple of times a day?"

Terry offered a salute. "Yes, sir."

***

For the next three nights nothing much happened aside

from the police patrolling Redmont Park. No disturbing howls disrupted Terry's sleep, no cloaked figures flew by the window, no one was attacked. Terry took to watching *The Great Escape* for excitement, and *The Scarlet Pimpernel* for relaxation, and wondered if there really had been a cloaked figure in the air outside the window.

On the third night, there were fewer policemen in the park, but Terry saw that Tate and Ostermann were among the plainclothes officers keeping watch on the place. "Something's changed," Terry murmured, and decided to go into the bedroom and fire up the computer. "There ought to be something online." Moving carefully up the flight of five stairs, Terry took almost eight minutes to reach the bedroom where the computer sat on a mission-style desk. After logging on, Terry went to email, which was full of get well notes from friends, associates, and family; answers to them could be postponed. Terry switched over to social media and began looking for reports on the two murders in Redmont Park. After twenty minutes, there was a posting on the We're Local chat group that startled Terry: *There's a story going around Palmer Memorial that says*

the body of Nancy Monroe has disappeared from the morgue. The cops have been around, asking questions, but so far, no other news. An orderly did say that the body was gone, but so far the hospital administration is denying the report. This was followed by a flurry of posts, some suggesting everything from Satanists to necrophiliacs to vampires as the cause, the rest skeptical, a few to the point of derision.

Terry read the first post three times over, and then sat still and thought. The body of Nancy Monroe was gone. What, or who, would account for that? Or was it as simple as the police wanting their pathologist to do the autopsy and did not spread that about? It was hard to believe that anyone would want to steal so gruesome a corpse as Nancy Monroe must be. No doubt Tate and Ostermann would have their hands full now.

With muscles trembling, Terry climbed back into bed and took a pain pill, as much to still the turmoil of thoughts that demanded attention as to lessen the hurt from the incision, which by now was beginning to itch. Lying back, Terry took a last look outside and noticed that

Tate and Ostermann were nowhere to be seen. "Probably questioning people along the street again," and with that, lapsed into a deep sleep.

***

Around midnight, Terry was abruptly wakened by a sharp knock on the door. Not quite fully awake, he struggled out of bed and staggered toward the door, saying, "Pretty damn late for the cops to come."

The tap was renewed and a melodic voice said, "Terry Holland?"

"Other cops," Terry grumbled. "They're working in shifts." After disengaging the clamshell latch, Terry opened the door, and blinked.

There were two lean, cloaked figures standing just outside the door, both with pale, skull-like faces; the taller of the two opened his mouth and gave the haunting cry that Terry had heard on the night the first murder took place. Feeling bewildered, Terry said, "Yes?"

The taller of the two shoved Terry back into the apartment with one cold hand. "We're here to claim you."

"Claim?" Terry repeated, more confused than ever.

"You're a witness," said the second in a soft, feminine voice. "We can't afford to have witnesses."

"But—" Before Terry could say another word, the two cloaked figures were lunging forward, knocking Terry to the floor.

It was like something out of a bad 50s horror film, thought Terry as the taller figure bent over his supine body, ravening; in less than a minute, Terry lost consciousness, and shortly thereafter, life.

***

While waiting for the pathologist's van the next afternoon, Ostermann and Tate stood in the living room of Terry's apartment, trying to make sense of what they saw.

"Okay," said Ostermann at last. "I was wrong about Holland."

"Might have been a scout, or some other kind of accomplice," said Tate by way of consolation.

"No. The surgery was real. No way Holland could have got down to the park and killed those two," Ostermann conceded. "The killer must be working alone, after all. I wish I could figure out how he got past our guys on the street."

"That doesn't make our job easier," Tate remarked, and turned away from the pool of drying blood that spread out from the ruin of Terry's throat. "The guy's got a thing about throats, doesn't he?"

"Yeah," Ostermann sighed. "Almost makes you think it was some kind of vampire."

In answer to this suggestion, Tate punched Ostermann in the shoulder. "No going off the deep end."

Ostermann shrugged. "Just saying," he said, and opened the door to the CSIs.

Le Vampire, lithographie de R. de Moraine, tirée des Tribunaux secrets.

MURMURS IN THE DARK: VAMPIRES IN WESTERN MAGIC

By Donald Tyson

In recent movies and novels the vampire, with his boyishly handsome face, his charming manners and sparkling aura, has reached such a level of romantic absurdity, it may come as a surprise to learn that the vampire is treated quite seriously in the modern Western occult tradition as something both real and dangerous.

Here, I will examine what prominent magicians over the past two centuries understood the vampire to be. It is something quite different from the sparkling high school students of the *Twilight* series of movies, or the sexual sophisticates in the novels of Anne Rice, and bears little resemblance even to Bram Stoker's iconic character, Dracula, which served as the prototype for the evolution of the modern vampire in pop culture.

But before turning to the vampire as understood by Western occultists, it is necessary for the purpose of comparison to look at the historic figure of the vampire, which reached its maturity in eastern Europe during the 18th century. It was from this vampire folklore that Stoker drew his literary masterpiece, *Dracula*.

Historical Accounts

Three centuries ago, the common rural peoples of eastern Europe had no doubt about the vampire's reality. They believed the vampire to be a reanimated corpse, usually the corpse of a person who had recently died. The vampire returned to those he or she had known or loved during life to feast on their blood. The victims of these nocturnal visitations quickly sickened and died. When the grave of the suspected vampire was dug up, the corpse in its coffin was found to be filled to bursting with fresh blood, and showing no signs of decay. Indeed, the corpse appeared alive, but in a kind of stupor or trance.

Jean-Baptiste de Boyer, Marquis d'Argens (1704-1771) related in volume four of his letter-novel *Lettres juives* (published in six volumes, 1738-42) an historical incident that occurred in the fall of 1736 in the village of Kisilova, in what is now Serbia. A 62-year-old man died, was buried, and three days later appeared to his son, asking to be given something to eat. His son fed him and he disappeared, but returned two nights later, again asking to be fed. The following morning the son was discovered dead in his bed.

That day, five or six other people in the same village fell sick, then died one after the other.

The local magistrate knew about the spectral appearance of the man's dead father, because the man had told this wonder to the people of the village before his death. Two commissioners and an executioner were sent to the village in response to the magistrate's report.

> They opened in the first place the Graves of all who had been buried in six Weeks. When they came to that of the old Man, they found his Eyes open, his Colour fresh, his Respiration quick and strong, yet he appeared to be stiff and insensible. From these Signs they concluded him to be a notorious Vampire. The Executioner thereupon, by the Command of the commissioners, struck a Stake through his Heart; and when they had so done, they made a Bonfire, and therein consumed the Carcase to Ashes.
>
> (D'Argens, *The Jewish Spy*, Vol. 4, 1766, p. 123)

D'Argens went on to relate the appearance of a vampire five years earlier in the village of Medreiga. A man named Arnold Paul (or Paole) was killed when he fell beneath the wheels of a hay wagon. Thirty days after his death, four others in the village died in a way usually attributed to vampirism. It was remembered that Paul liked to tell the story that as a young man he himself had been the victim of a vampire, but had driven the fiend away by eating some of the vampire's grave earth and rubbing his own body with blood. Forty days after Paul's death, the villagers dug up his grave.

> His Complexion was fresh, his Hair, Nails, and Beard were grown; he was full of fluid Blood, which ran from all Parts of his Body upon his Shroud. The Hadnagy or Bailiff of the Place, who was perfect at the taking of him up, and who was a Person

well acquainted with Vampirism, caused a sharp Stake to be thrust, as the Custom is, through the Heart of Arnold Paul, and also quite through his Body; whereupon he cried out dreadfully as if he had been alive. This done, they cut off his Head, burnt his Body, and threw the Ashes thereof into the Saave. They took the same Measures with the Bodies of those Persons who had died of Vampirism, for fear that they should fall to sucking in their Turns.

(D'Argens, *The Jewish Spy*, Vol. 4, 1766, p. 125)

Alas, the efforts of the bailiff of Paul's village were not successful. The vampirism had spread, and broke out again five years later. Within three months, seventeen persons died of vampirism. It was determined that before his end, Paul had sucked the blood of cattle, and that when people ate the flesh of these beasts, they became vampires. A great digging up of the graveyard was undertaken, and out of forty corpses, seventeen were determined to be vampires. Stakes were driven through their hearts, their heads were cut off, and their bodies burnt to ashes, then the ashes scattered in the river.

In concluding his letter concerning these events, D'Argens raises the vexing question of how the vampire is able to go out from his grave and return to it, even when covered with six feet of earth. He says that either they go out physically, in which case they must be visible to the eye, or they go out in a more subtle body that is invisible. He asserts that when the victim of a vampire cries out for help, and others rush to the aid of that person, no vampire is ever seen. From this he concludes that whatever goes out from the grave, it is not the body, and he supposes it must be the soul, which in some manner carries the blood back to the body in its coffin.

This question of how the vampire leaves and returns to his coffin beneath the ground is of some importance in the occult theories of the vampire we will examine a little further on. It is, indeed, a puzzling matter for those who view the vampire as a corporeal being. In movies the question is usually side-stepped—the coffin of the vampire is seldom buried, but rests in a cellar or vault. However, in actual historical accounts of vampirism the coffin is almost always buried.

The French satirist Voltaire (1694-1778) wrote in his *Philosophical Dictionary*, which was published in 1764:

There were *broucolacas* [vampires] in Wallachia, Moldavia, and some among the Polanders, who are of the Romish church. This superstition being absent, they acquired it, and it went through all the east of Germany. Nothing was spoken of but vampires, from 1730 to 1735; they were laid in wait for, their hearts torn out and burnt. They resembled the ancient martyrs—the more they were burnt, the more they abounded.

(Voltaire, *A Philosophical Dictionary*, Vol. 6, 1824, p. 306)

Types of Vampire in Occultism

Now that we've established the general nature of the vampire, as it was understood by those who lived in eastern Europe during the 18th century and actually believed in its existence, we can turn to the vampire of modern Western magic. To the occultist, vampires are creatures that sustain themselves on the vital energy of living human beings. Several distinct types of vampire are recognized by occultists. I will list them.

1. The risen astral bodies of human corpses that continue to lie in their graves.

2. Spirits created, intentionally or unintentionally, by strong human desires and emotions.

3. Other hungry spirits not created by humans that prey on human vitality.

4. Living (or seemingly living) humans who, intentionally or unintentionally, suck the vital energies from others.

Eliphas Levi

A good place to begin is with the works of the great French occultist, Alphonse Louis Constant (1810-1875), who adopted the pen name Eliphas Levi in his numerous books on magic. Levi has been called the father of modern magic. His writings exerted a profound influence over the French, English, and American occultists of the late 19th and early 20th centuries.

In his 1861 work, *La Clef des Grands Mystères*, translated into English by Aleister Crowley, Levi gave as his Axiom XI:

When one creates phantoms for oneself, one puts vampires into the world, and one must nourish these children of a voluntary nightmare with one's blood, one's life, one's intelligence, and one's reason, without ever satisfying them.

(Levi, *The Key of the Mysteries*, 1959, pp. 170-1.)

Occultists believe today, just as they did in Levi's time, that strong emotion, particularly fear and anger, coupled with strong physical urges such as desire or revulsion, can create independent spiritual entities. This creation may be done deliberately, by a process of intense visualization, as happens when a Tibetan magician makes the spirit-servitor known as the *tulpa*, but it can also occur spontaneously.

Once created, these shadow entities seek to sustain themselves by drawing vitality from living human beings. The vital energies of the body are believed by occultists to reside in their most concentrated form in the blood and semen. This is why freshly-spilled blood was so often offered as a sacrifice to pagan gods in ancient times, and

place, and these human remains would be less alive in a sense than a mere animal. Dead persons of this kind are said to be identified by the complete extinction of the moral and affectionate sense: they are neither bad nor good; they are dead. Such beings, who are poisonous fungi of the human race, absorb the life of living beings to their fullest possible extent, and this is why their proximity depletes the soul and chills the heart. If such corpse-like creatures really existed, they would stand for all that was recounted in former times about *brucalaques* and vampires.

(Levi, *Transcendental Magic*, Part 1, 1979, pp. 126-7)

why some forms of magic, such as the system taught by the artist Austin Osman Spare (1886-1956), are empowered by a deliberate ejaculation of semen.

Religious mystics, such as Christian contemplative monks and nuns, sought to control their emotions and desires in large part to prevent the spontaneous and unintended budding forth of these vampiric entities, although you will read little about this in the writings of the saints. Magicians and witches, on the other hand, sometimes deliberately created these entities to be their servants. The witch's familiar spirit is such a being. It may exist either as a free spirit, or as a spirit bound into an object such as a mirror, or into an animal such as a toad or cat.

The Soul hovering over the Body reluctantly parting with Life

Witches were reputed to feed their familiars on the blood of their own bodies, by allowing them to suck on small blemishes in the skin known as "witch teats." The blood of the witch both energized the familiar spirit and bound it to the witch. Witch finders of the 16th and 17th centuries in western Europe used these skin blemishes to identify women (and more rarely men) as witches.

Drawing upon the mystical Jewish doctrine of the Kabbalah, Levi speculated about another form of occult vampire in his *Dogme et Rituel de la Haute Magie* (1854-6)—a living person who, due to some great emotional shock, has lost his soul, leaving his body still apparently alive.

When the human soul suffers a greater strain than it can bear, it would thus become separated from the body, leaving the animal soul, or sidereal body, in its

This idea that the soul could depart and leave the body still living, but hungering for the life force it lacked, which the soulless body then sucked out of other human beings who associated with it, was a popular theme in modern occultism. In another place in his book, Levi explains what happens when actual death occurs, and the soul leaves the body.

Nothing can enter heaven save that which comes from heaven. Hence, after death, the divine spirit which animated man returns alone to heaven and leaves two corpses, one upon earth, the other in the atmosphere; one terrestrial and elementary, the other aerial and sidereal, one already inert, the other still animated by the universal movement of the soul of the world, yet destined to die slowly, absorbed by the astral forces which produced it. The terrestrial body is visible; the other is unseen by the eyes of earthly and living bodies, nor can it be beheld except by the application of the astral light to the translucid, which conveys its impressions to the nervous system, and thus influences the organ of sight so as to make it perceive the forms which are preserved and the words which are written in the book of vital light.

When a man has lived well the astral body evaporates like a pure incense ascending towards the upper regions; but should he have lived in sin, his astral body, which holds him prisoner, still seeks the objects of its passions, and wishes to return to life. It torments the dreams of young girls, bathes in the stream of spilt blood, and floats about the places where the pleasures of its life elapsed; it still watches over treasures which it possessed and buried; it expends itself in painful efforts to make fresh material organs and so live again.

(Levi, *Transcendental Magic*, Part 1, 1979, p. 120)

Here we have the basis for the occult conception of the vampire, and also an explanation as to how the vampire of European folklore can feed on the blood of the living, yet still remained buried six feet beneath the ground in his coffin. It is what Levi calls the astral body, which is not made of physical matter and can fit itself through the finest of screens or the narrowest of cracks, or indeed through solid matter itself, that rises from the terrestrial body, or corpse, and seeks the blood of the living. This astral body then carries the blood back to the terrestrial body in its coffin.

We also find in Levi's division of the corpse into terrestrial and astral bodies an explanation as to why the vampire was reputed to cast no reflection. It is not the physical eye that perceives the astral body, but a psychic perception. And although this psychic perception may make the astral body look perfectly solid and real, yet it is apparently unable to cope with the complexity of a reflection.

H. P. Blavatsky

The founder of Theosophy, Madam Helena Petrovna Blavatsky (1831-1891), in her monumental 1877 work *Isis Unveiled*, quoted the belief of the French spiritist and mesmeriser Z. J. Pierart (*d.* 1878) that vampires are human bodies buried while in a state of catalepsy, which was believed to require almost no air to sustain itself (see Pierart, *Revue Spiritualiste*, Vol. 4, 1861, pp. 61-2, 104-5). It is their astral forms that venture forth from the grave in search of fresh blood with which the body may be sustained.

So long as the astral form is not entirely liberated from the body there is a liability that it may be forced by magnetic attraction to re-enter it. Sometimes it will be only half-way out, when the corpse, which presents the appearance of death, is buried. In such cases the terrified astral soul violently re-enters its casket; and then, one of two things happens—either the unhappy victim will writhe in the agonizing torture of suffocation, or, if he

had been grossly material, he becomes a vampire. The bicorporeal life begins; and these unfortunate buried cataleptics sustain their miserable lives by having their astral bodies rob the life-blood from living persons. The ethereal form can go wherever it pleases; and so long as it does not break the link which attaches it to the body, it is at liberty to wander about, either visible or invisible, and feed on human victims.

(Blavatsky, *Isis Unveiled*, Vol. 1, 1877, p. 449)

The link alluded to is the famous silver cord that is supposed to connect astral travellers with their physical bodies. The mesmerist Pierart believed the body to be still alive in the true sense. He divided the vampire into a cataleptic physical form and an astral soul that wandered from it in search of blood. He does not appear to have made the threefold division of Levi into a divine spirit that immediately leaves the corpse at death, a physical corpse, and an astral corpse. But then, he did not really believe that vampires were dead. He believed that a cataleptic could lie in a sealed coffin for many days, yet still be capable of

To the Aryan Theosophical Society of New York with H P B's & H S O's good wishes London. October 1888.

awakening to conscious life if exhumed from the grave.

Blavatsky presented this viewpoint of Pierart without commenting on it one way or the other, but a leader of the Theosophical movement, Henry S. Olcott, wrote an essay devoted to the topic of vampirism, in which he laid forth very clearly what Theosophists were taught concerning the nature of the vampire.

Henry S. Olcott

It is noteworthy that in his essay on the vampire, Olcott quotes Levi concerning the threefold nature of man—that on death, a divine spirit rises at once to heaven, leaving behind it a terrestrial corpse that lies inert in the ground where it is buried, and an astral corpse that lingers near the grave for a time until at last it dissolves into the soul of the world.

Olcott does not wrestle with the matter raised by Levi of the divine spirit that leaves the body upon death, or sometimes even prior to the physical extinction of the body. In his examination of the vampire, Olcott deals only with the lesser two bodies, the physical corpse and the astral corpse. However, it is significant that he quotes this passage from Levi where the higher spirit is mentioned. He was certainly aware of the concept of a higher essence that was wholly divine, and had nothing to do with the lower bodies of man, yet was the essential principle of a human being, without which a man could not be considered truly human.

According to Levi, when this higher spirit departed, what was left might continue to live and think and talk and function in society, but it was in the truest sense dead. That is to say, a being composed only of the elementary body and the astral body could give the illusion of life, but could never be completely alive, because the divine spark had been lost. These unfortunate individuals became living vampires, forced to prey on others for the higher vital force that was missing from their own natures.

Olcott wrote in his essay:

> During life it is the body which develops and nourishes the astral body; in the case of vampires the process is reversed, for the corpse, being confined in its coffin and by the superincumbent soil, cannot walk about, so the double, being an entity of the "Fourth Dimension," hence not impeded by either coffin, tomb or grave-soil, is free to move about in search of its blood-food, and to transmit it by sympathetic psychical infusion to the cadaver, now become its mere dwelling-convenience.
> (Olcott, "The Vampire," in *The Theosophist*, Volume 12, 1891)

Olcott gave five truisms that he had observed over the course of his study of the vampire. These factors appear again and again in older historical accounts of vampires, even when those accounts are centuries apart in time and come from widely separated countries.

1. The vampire elementary always attacks the robust;
2. The signs of the obsession are invariably nervous prostration and anæmia, and usually a slight puncture over the jugular vein;
3. The corpse of the suspected vampire, when examined, appears well-nourished with healthy blood, and presents the appearance of one in cataleptic sleep, rather than of death.
4. If a pointed stake or weapon be thrust through the heart, the corpse cries out and often writhes in agony;
5. If the corpse be cremated, the vampire ceases to trouble. I have found no exception stated in this respect.
(Olcott, "The Vampire," in *The Theosophist*, Volume 12, 1891)

When considering the implications of these five truisms, Olcott reached a definite conclusion, which was foreshadowed by Blavatsky in her *Isis Unveiled*. He wrote: "All these are indications that our problem has to deal not with a dead, but with a half-dead, person: in short, that the defunct is in catalepsy or some other form of suspended animation. The phantom which sucks the blood of the living, appears to the eye, creates noisy and other phenomena in and about houses, and disappears when the corpse is burnt, is an astral, not a physical shape, a body of sublimated, not one of concrete, matter..." (Olcott, "The Vampire," *Theosophist*, Vol. 12)

Cataleptic Vampires

The 1920 German film, *The Cabinet of Dr. Caligari*, gives a very good account of what was believed about cataleptics by Theosophists. The cataleptic in the film, a young man named Cesare, spends almost all his time lying in a coffin in a near-death condition from which he cannot be aroused by normal means, and is insensible to pain. Only the dominant psychic bond of a mesmerist is able to awaken him, and when awakened, Cesare is shown to have supernatural strength, abilities and perceptions, including the gift of prophecy.

To Theosophists, the vampire was a person in a cataleptic trance who had no mesmerist to awaken him; a person assumed by his relatives to be dead who was buried in a coffin under six feet of earth, yet who sent forth his astral body each night in search of fresh blood. This view was derived from Blavatsky's *Isis Unveiled*. Olcott wrote, "The unqualified affirmation of the theory that the vampire corpse is the hibernating cadaver of a *somnabule*, was made by Mme Blavatsky in *Isis Unveiled* (i 449, *et seq*), and supported by a sufficient body of testimony." (Olcott, "The Vampire," *Theosophist*, Vol. 12)

Olcott was a staunch proponent of cremation for the corpses of the dead. Burning the corpse broke the link between the physical body and the astral body, and prevented the formation of a vampire. In the conclusion of his essay he alludes to the two types of living dead—the *somnabule* or cataleptic who becomes a vampire, and the unfortunate who is buried while in a state of trance, and awakens briefly in his coffin only to suffocate to death.

> To conclude our analysis of this painful subject, it is most evident that too much care cannot be taken to ascertain beyond doubt the actual and complete death of a person before committing the body to the grave—if that senseless, unscientific and revolting custom must be preserved. One shudders to think of the untold agony that must have been felt by thousands of victims of ignorant hurry to put the body out of sight, who, awakening too late from a state of trance, found themselves screwed up in a coffin and buried under six feet of earth, without the least possibility of succour. ... Of course, I need hardly explain that, while cremation is a sure preventative of the return of the vampire *somnambules* to plague the living, the chances of premature disposal of the body of a half-dead person are equally serious as in the case of burial. If the trance be deep, it is quite possible that the unfortunate subject might not recover the use of his bodily members in time to save himself from being burnt alive.
>
> (Olcott, "The Vampire," *The Theosophist*, Volume 12, 1891)

Although Olcott makes very clear here the two kinds of premature burial—the unfortunate but perfectly normal person mistakenly buried alive, and the *somnabule* who turns into a vampire—he is not at all clear in defining the distinction between the two. To my mind it can only be the presence or absence of Levi's divine spark of spirit. If death comes to the person buried alive before the divine spark leaves the body, the death is natural, even though horrible; but if the divine spark leaves before death comes to the physical body—perhaps because the higher, divine spirit left years prior to death due to the inclination of the person for vices and gross physical indulgences—then a state of catalepsy may result in which the astral body leaves the grave to gather blood to nourish the physical body. At any rate, this is the best I can make of this distinction, which neither Blavatsky nor Olcott deal with in any definitive sense.

Sexual Vampires

I must briefly mention a particular type of vampire, the *lamia* of ancient Greek mythology. This inhuman spirit came in the form of a beautiful woman to solitary men traveling alone on dark and lonely roads. The spirit seduced the men and drew forth their vital energy in the form of their emitted semen, draining them so completely that they died.

This is a form of sexual vampire, of which the Babylonian demoness Lilith is the archetype. Sexual vampires are usually spirits that can derive the vital force they need from semen rather than from blood. They visit men who lie sleeping alone in their beds and induce erotic visions in order to provoke emission of their seed. Frequent wet dreams are evidence that a man is being preyed on by a sexual vampire. Another sign is a deep lassitude while awake and a disinclination to do anything.

Flying Rolls of the Golden Dawn

The concept of the psychic vampire, both in the form of an inhuman spirit and in the form of a living human being, was a common feature in the teachings of the Hermetic Order of the Golden Dawn, an English occult society founded in London in 1888. There was a rumour floating around that the head of the Order, S. L. MacGregor Mathers, had once sent a vampiric spirit to plague Aleister Crowley. Whether or not that rumour has any basis, in a teaching document of the Order that was known as a Flying Roll, the procedure used by a member of the Golden Dawn, John Williams Brodie-Innes, to banish a psychic vampire from his ailing wife, is presented in detail. Brodie-Innes wrote:

> My wife had suffered a severe attack of influenza; her recovery was followed by great exhaustion, an exhaustion which ultimately I came to share. I considered this exhaustion, which seemed more than natural and it came to me that this was the obsession of some vampirising elemental. I seemed to hear a voice say 'cast it out.'
>
> (Brodie-Innes, Flying Roll XXXIV)

Using the magic he had been taught, he burned incense and traced pentagrams of fire and earth upon the air toward the east, while vibrating on his breath various divine names of power.

> As I drew the Earth Pentagram I called up the foul thing that had troubled me to manifest visibly before me. As I did so a vague blot, like a scrap of London fog, materialised before me. ... I saw, at first dimly, 'as in a glass darkly,' and then with complete clarity, a most foul shape, between a bloated big-bellied toad and a malicious ape. My guide spoke to me in an audible voice, saying 'Now smite it with all your force, using the Name of the Lord Jesus.' I did so gathering all the force I possessed into, as it were, a glowing ball of electric fire and then projecting it like a lightning flash upon the foul image before me.
>
> (Brodie-Innes, Flying Roll XXXIV)

This exorcism was successful. Brodie-Innes and his wife were troubled no more by this vampirising spirit. The Golden Dawn was a Rosicrucian magical order that relied extensively on the power of the Hebrew names of God and the name of Jesus in its rituals. The name of Jesus is believed by Christians to be more powerful than any other name in exorcising evil spirits.

I should mention that the image Brodie-Innes saw was only a symbolic representation of the entity that troubled his wife. He saw what he expected to see—something horrifying and disgusting. Such spiritual creatures have no real forms of their own. They derive their forms through interaction with human intelligence, which clothes the spirits in whatever shapes seem most appropriate to the unconscious mind.

In Flying Roll V, Dr. Edward Berridge gave an account of his own encounter with a psychic vampire, and four other accounts of how he had helped other people deal with similar situations. The Golden Dawn response to psychic vampires was to attack them with magical energies designed to destroy them, or build magical barriers that acted as shields through which they could not reach.

I'll set down here Berridge's experience, as told in his own words.

> A few years ago, I noticed that invariably after a prolonged interview with a certain person, I felt exhausted.
>
> At first, I thought it only the natural result of a long conversation with a prosy, fidgetty, old gentleman; but later it dawned upon me, that being a man of exhausted nervous vitality, he was really preying upon me. I don't suppose that he was at all externally conscious that he possessed a vampire organisation, for he was a benevolent kind-hearted man, who

would have shrunk in horror from such a suggestion.

> Nevertheless, he was, in his inner personality an intentional vampire, for he acknowledged that he was about to marry a young wife in order, if possible, to recuperate his exhausted system.
>
> The next time, therefore, that he was announced, I closed myself to him, before he was admitted. I imagined that I had formed myself a complete investiture of odic fluid, surrounding me on all sides, but not touching me, and impenetrable to any hostile currents.
>
> This magical process was immediately and permanently successful. I never had to repeat it.
>
> (Berridge, Flying Roll V)

Dion Fortune

No member of the Golden Dawn wrote more about vampires than Dion Fortune, who went on from one of the later incarnations of the Golden Dawn to found her own occult school, the Society of the Inner Light. Her short story, "Blood-Lust," the first in her 1926 collection of stories titled *The Secrets of Dr. Tavener*, is based on the vampire. In her introduction to this book, Fortune wrote that "Blood-Lust" was "literally true," and claimed that it had been toned down to make it fit to print. In the story, a young man recently returned from the First World War becomes obsessed by a spirit that instils in him a craving for freshly spilled blood. The spirit is seen by the young man's fiancée, who describes it: '"I have seen it," she said; "it is like a wisp of grey vapour that floats just behind him. It has the most awful face you ever saw."'

When Dr. Taverner and his associate confront the spirit to drive it away from its human host, its form becomes clearer. "We could see it quite clearly from its flat-topped cap to its knee-boots; its high cheekbones and slit eyes pointed its origin to the south-eastern corner of Europe where strange tribes still defy civilization and keep up their still stranger beliefs." Fortune's vampire was the blood-thirsty astral body of a soldier in the German army with a knowledge of black magic, who had sent his astral form to obsess the young English soldier and feed through him when the black magician lay on the point of death.

In her fascinating book *Psychic Self-Defence*, published in 1930, Fortune makes the useful distinction between vampirism and parasitism. "Vampirism, as generally understood, is a very different matter, and we shall do well to reserve the term for those cases wherein the attack is deliberate, applying the term parasitism to the cases wherein it is unconscious and involuntary." (Fortune, *Psychic Self-Defence*, Weiser, 1979, p. 58) By Fortune's definition, the elderly man who sucked the vital energy from Golden Dawn member Edward Berridge would be classed a psychic parasite, rather than a vampire, because he was not consciously aware of what he was doing.

Fortune shines more light on the incident of vampirism described in her short story, "Blood-Lust." The real-life mentor in magic she called Dr. Taverner in her stories gave his opinion of the affair.

His opinion concerning the case, though there was no means of obtaining independent confirmation of this, was that some Eastern European troops had been brought to the Western Front, and among these were individuals with the traditional knowledge of Black Magic for which South Eastern Europe has always enjoyed a sinister reputation among occultists. These men, getting killed, knew how to avoid going to the Second Death, that is to say, the disintegration of the Astral Body, and maintained themselves in the etheric double by vampirising the wounded. Now vampirism is contagious; the person who is vampirised, being depleted of vitality, is a psychic vacuum, himself absorbing from anyone he comes across in order to refill his depleted resources of vitality. He soon learns by experience the tricks of a vampire without realising their significance, and before he knows where he is, he is a full-blown vampire himself, vampirising others. The earth-bound soul of a vampire sometimes attaches itself permanently to one individual if it succeeds in making a functioning vampire of him, systematically drawing its etheric nutriment from him, for, since he in his turn is re-supplying himself from others, he will not die from exhaustion as victims of vampires do in the ordinary way.

(Fortune, *Psychic Self-Defence*, Weiser, 1976, pp. 60-1)

If you suspect that one of your friends or a member of your family may be the victim of a vampire, Fortunes writes, the best way to determine it one way or the other is to examine the body of the victim very closely, using a magnifying glass, for small puncture wounds that resemble mosquito bites. If the person is being drained by a vampire, clusters of these needle pricks will be discovered, but they are so small they are often invisible to the naked eye alone. "The places to look for them are around the neck, especially under the ears; down the inner surface of the forearms; on the lobes of the ears; about the tips of the toes and, in a woman, on the breasts." (Fortune, *Psychic Self-Defence*, p. 62) Happy hunting.

FEATURED REVIEWS

BY COLLEEN WANGLUND

Priest (USA, 2011)
Directed by Scott Stewart

Based loosely on a South Korean *Manhwa* (comic, manga) created by Hyung Min-woo, *Priest* combines the American Western genre with dark fantasy and horror. It gives a unique and interesting perspective on the classic vampire story while highlighting humanity's willingness to give up their rights to a higher authority—in this case the Catholic Church—in the name of safety and survival. The film reunites director Scott Stewart and actor Paul Bettany after the 2010 film *Legion*.

In an alternate timeline, a war was waged for centuries between humans and vampires. Both the planet and population were decimated but eventually the war ended with most of the vampires wiped out and the remainder contained to reservations far outside the walled cities that remain. Some humans also live in communities outside the walls away from the totalitarian theocracy of the Church.

In order to fight the vampires, the Church established an elite army of Warrior Priests, seeking out and taking people of all ages from their homes because of certain abilities they possessed and training them to fight. After the wars the warrior class was disbanded, keeping their vows, but unable to fully reintegrate into society. Priest (Paul Bettany) is told by Hicks (Cam Gigandet), the sheriff of a wasteland outpost, that Priest's brother and sister-in-law were attacked and killed by vampires and his niece Lucy (Lily Collins), who is Hicks' girlfriend, was kidnapped. Priest asks the Church to reinstate his authority to find her but is denied by Monsignor Orelas (Christopher Plummer), so he goes off on his own. Priest and Hicks go to one of the reservations where vampires live with familiars—humans infected with a disease that makes them slaves to the vampires. They discover that most of the vampires are now ensconced in a hive where Priest and other warriors fought a fierce battle during the wars. Priest and Hicks reach the hive where they are joined by Priestess (Maggie Q) who tells Priest that she along with three other Priests were sent after him to bring him back. The three make a horrifying discovery at the hive and head to Jericho, a large independent city, but they are too late. Jericho has been decimated and the three Priests crucified. Not only does Priest have to rescue his niece but he must now save the humans from a resurgence of the vampire population headed their way

by train and led by a mysterious man in a black hat (Karl Urban) who is apparently the only human-like vampire.

What I liked about *Priest* was its concept of vampires. They are not even remotely human. They are more like the monsters you would expect them to be. Their hives are like those of termites and their hierarchy is similar to that of bees. There is a queen, guardians, and worker drones. They look like giant mutated bats and hang out in cocoons. When a vampire bites a human and infects them, the human becomes a familiar, not a vampire, aiding the vampires during the day. And these vampires aren't as vulnerable to sunlight as in accepted lore. These vampires are more like cave-dwellers and only photosensitive. They are not the usual undead human with charisma and charm and good looks, luring in unsuspecting victims. Black Hat seems to be the exception and very special. And these vampires want to take over the world.

While it is not explicitly stated, the Church that runs the lives of the remaining humans living in walled cities is clearly meant to be the Catholic Church. The warrior Priests have all taken the same vows of poverty and chastity, and the weapons they use are typically fashioned out of familiar Catholic icons, such as the cross (the Priests do not use guns). The Church rules through a totalitarian theocracy with many of the human population willingly giving up any freedom for the veil of safety. Many humans have left the so-called safety of the cities for smaller outposts and towns in the wasteland to make their own way, and many have been successful. For years they have been told that the remaining vampires have been contained on reservations, but we find out that is not the case. One huckster trying to make a buck (played by Brad Dourif) by selling a fake elixir that keeps the people safe from vampires is also informing Black Hat about the arrival of Priest. To his dismay, he receives no compensation and is instead turned into a familiar.

Priest is a very dark film, set in a post-apocalyptic dystopian world flavored with a bit of cyberpunk and sci-fi Western. It is violent, gory, and seems to have a hopelessness from beginning to end. And in typical dystopian fashion, the powers that be don't see the danger staring them in the face, even when confronted directly by Priest himself, with everything he has learned. Priest is obsessed with finding his niece Lucy but makes clear his intention of killing Lucy if she has been infected. Hicks, on the other hand, has no intention of harming Lucy and threatens to kill Priest should he try to harm the girl when, and if, they find her. Hicks is young and a little trigger-happy, but he is learning from Priest as they travel

to the hive and then Jericho. Priest lived in obscurity and poverty since the end of the Vampire Wars and he is clearly a broken man and somewhat damaged soul due to PTSD. Going to the hive brings back memories of the loss of comrades, but also shows us the deep connection between Priest and Priestess. He may seem almost invincible while fighting the vampires and eventually Black Hat, but he is vulnerable and at times, it shows. The reason for his obsession and vulnerability become clear when Priest, Priestess, and Hicks come up with a plan to stop the train headed for the city and when the true identity of Black Hat is finally revealed.

While many critics panned the film as being too cliché, I rather enjoyed it. And though it only loosely follows the original Korean manhwa, the actual plot of *Priest* is similar (an homage?) to the classic film *The Searchers* (1956) directed by John Ford and starring John Wayne and Jeffrey Hunter. The vampires here, however, don't even come close to the Comanche tribe and Priest doesn't have quite the emotional range as John Wayne's Ethan Edwards. I found the ending to be a bit abrupt but it also seems to be setting up for a sequel—a restart to the Vampire Wars, perhaps? I'm not much for sequels but would welcome a violent and gory film tying up the story a bit. I love the visuals of *Priest*, but the CGI vampires leave a bit to be desired, though they aren't terrible. I would have also liked to have seen more in the vein of the political climate, as it appears to be a key part of the story. I've always liked Paul Bettany and Maggie Q. Yes, it has its clichés, but it deviates from some typical Western vampire lore. It's an entertaining film and I do recommend it, if only for the unusual and intriguing way the vampires are portrayed and the well-choreographed fight scenes.

From the Director of OLDBOY and LADY VENGEANCE

A **PARK CHAN-WOOK** FILM

WINNER
CANNES INTERNATIONAL
FILM FESTIVAL
JURY PRIZE
2009

Lusting after
Simple Pleasures

"Chan-Wook's vampire
opus is unlike anything
you've seen before"
★★★★
TOTAL FILM

"Both emotional &
shocking, THIRST is a
stunning vampire movie"
RICH CLINE, RADIO 5 LIVE

THIRST†

18 CONTAINS FINE USE OF VERY STRONG LANGUAGE AND STRONG BLOODY VIOLENCE Where's it on?

Thirst (Korea, 2009)
Directed by Park Chan-wook

Written, produced, and directed by Park Chan-wook (The Vengeance Trilogy), *Thirst* uses the core story of Emile Zola's 1867 novel *Therese Raquin* as inspiration with a few added twists. It is a vampire story but more a tragedy involving a heartbreaking love triangle and a pious man's existential crisis, and though it takes its premise from Western literature the film does break away from some Western vampire conventions.

Thirst stars Song Kang-ho (*The Host*, 2003; *Snowpiercer*, 2013) as Sang-hyeon, a Catholic priest who administers to the sick at a local hospital. He volunteers for an experiment to produce a vaccine for the fatal Emmanuel Virus, with which Sang-hyeon is infected but survives with a blood transfusion. The doctors cannot explain how the priest survived and made a full recovery from the deadly virus, but the local parishioners believe it to be a miracle and come to see Sang-hyeon as a healer. The congregation of his church grows by the thousands as more and more people hear about Sang-hyeon's miraculous recovery and

seek his perceived power of healing, including the priest's childhood friend Kang-woo (Shin Ha-kyun).

Kang-woo, who is ill and frail, invites Sang-hyeon back to his home which he shares with his wife Tae-ju (Kim Ok-bin) and his domineering mother Lady Ra (Kim Hae-suk). Sang-hyeon finds himself attracted to his friend's wife, but being a priest, pushes the thoughts aside. To his great horror, Sang-hyeon discovers he has become a vampire as he finds himself in dire need of shelter from the sun. It also becomes apparent that unless the priest drinks human blood, he relapses to the viral illness (though he has no fangs). Sang-hyeon cannot bring himself to suicide, but attempts to stem the need for human blood by stealing donated blood from the hospital.

Sang-hyeon finds himself back at Kang-woo's house and not only irresistibly drawn to human blood, but to his friend's wife Tae-ju. Sang-hyeon desires Tae-ju so deeply that he kills Kang-woo, believing that his friend was abusing his wife. He then kills Tae-ju when she asks him to out of guilt, but he then feeds her his blood because he does not want to be alone. She proves to be a ruthless killer, but Sang-hyeon still believes in finding other ways to acquire blood instead of killing. After all, he is still the same man he was morally when a priest even though he's finding it harder to ignore his animalistic desires. He comes to the only conclusion, which is to protect others from the monsters that he and Tae-ju have become.

While maintaining some of the conventions of Western vampire lore, Park's priest/vampire is overall a bit unique. There is no explanation as to how Sang-hyeon actually became a vampire, but he is the only one in existence and will die from the Emmanuel Virus if he doesn't feed on human blood. He is a devoutly religious man and is able to maintain an ethical standard by stealing blood from the hospital as opposed to resorting to senseless murder, or murdering only when he finds it necessary. Tae-ju, on the other hand, becomes what Western audiences would expect from a vampire. She is a monster who has no problem killing to feed her hunger, or giving in to other base needs. Being the good man at heart that he is, Sang-hyeon makes a decision that will change both his and Tae-ju's lives forever.

As with Western vampire films, Christianity is ever-present in *Thirst*. It is not seen in those tools used to traditionally kill vampires. There are no crosses or holy water. There is, however, Sang-hyeon's deep faith in his religion. He would remain a priest if it were possible, but he soon learns that it isn't. Sang-hyeon is fighting urges that he'd never experienced before and it is a battle between good and evil within himself. Tae-ju gives in to her urges, having no problem killing anyone. She believes she is now a superior being and the rules don't apply to her. She abandons any pretense of morality she may have held prior to becoming a vampire. Sang-hyeon is alarmed by her behavior and tries to fight her. He is also alarmed at his own internal struggle between what he knows is right and what being a vampire is turning him into. He is a man in crisis. His faith and moral code lead him to the recognition that he and Tae-ju are monsters and must be destroyed. He also has seen what his ability to heal has done to those around him—the selfishness of his peers and congregation, seeing the priest as merely a means to an end. This is also seen in the breakdown of his relationship with Tae-ju.

While *Thirst*'s main characters become vampires, the film is not really *about* vampires—or the supernatural. Vampirism is akin to a medical condition. Sang-hyeon was infected with a deadly virus and then given a transfusion. If he doesn't drink blood, he will die from the initial virus. He then passed this virus onto Tae-ju. The film is more about the struggle within oneself between the light and the dark sides of the human soul. Sang-hyeon and Tae-ju each view their condition differently based on who they were prior to the change. He was a pious priest with a strong moral standard. She hated her husband and mother-in-law and conned Sang-hyeon into killing her husband when she realized that he was attracted to her. She had no problem using him to get what she wanted, and even after her conversion to a vampire that dark side of herself could not be contained. Tae-ju reveled in the killing of another human being. She craved the hunt and attempted to emasculate Sang-hyeon because he only took blood if the victim was willing or through stealing from the hospital's blood supply. Tae-ju thought Sang-hyeon was weak. At one point in the film, the two vampires fight over rooftops. The very thing that brought the couple together is now driving them apart. It is heartbreaking to watch the deterioration of the relationship between Sang-hyeon and Tae-ju, as well as watching Sang-hyeon struggle with his former self and what he has become.

And this all makes for a fascinating look at the human condition, with a twist. I thoroughly enjoyed Park's film and his unique take on vampires, and his use of modern evangelical Christianity, which has become a bit of a trend in Korean films over the last decade or so, regardless of genre. He doesn't use an in-your-face approach; it's more subtle. *Thirst* has some gory and striking imagery, which Park Chan-wook is known for, but it is not scary. It's not a typical horror film. It is also not as shocking as any of the films in his Vengeance trilogy, but it is still a very good film and one worth seeing.

JournalStone's DoubleDown Series Continues
Number VIII in the series of flip books

Coming April 22, 2016

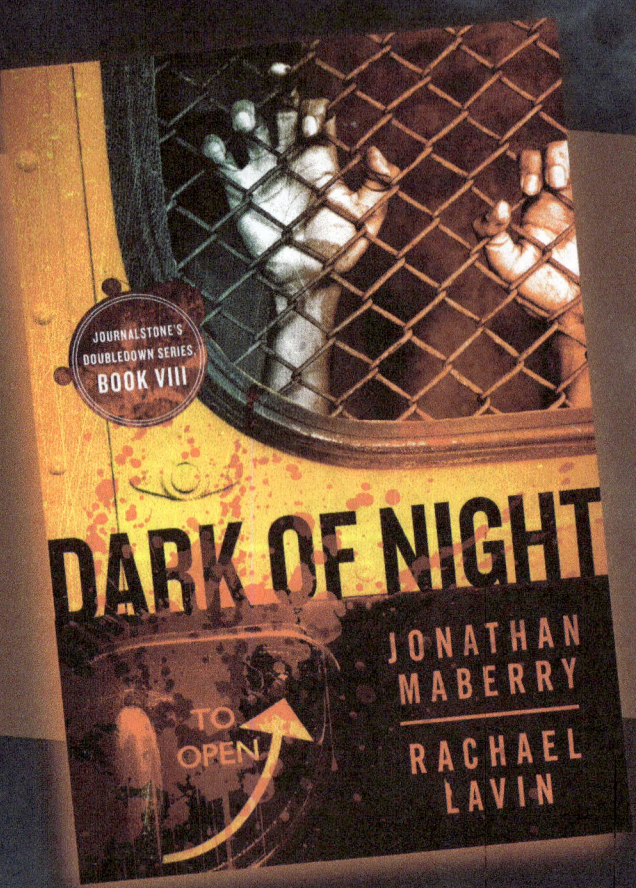

Three heroes who have survived the apocalypse are in a deadly race to save a busload of children from ravenous zombies and ruthless human scavengers.

In the midst of a midlife crisis, Todd is haunted by Chloe, the lover who died after their relationship ended. When Chloe escapes Hell in search of the peaceful rest that has eluded her, a demon named Samael is on her trail and she needs Todd's help.

Night's Ivy

Mercedes M. Yardley

Christopher wasn't a dreamer. He was a good, solid man with a good solid job, and he didn't believe in things like whimsy and love at first sight. At least he didn't until the night he met her.

He was standing in line for the opera. It wasn't something he particularly enjoyed, but his sister gave him tickets every year for Christmas because it gave him something to discuss with his boss. So he went without protest and even took notes when necessary. Then he went home to take something to alleviate the pain that startburst over his eye.

This cold January night started like any other. He stomped to keep warm and chuffed a bit, perturbed at seeing his breath dance in the freezing air. Then a woman knocked into him, and everything changed.

"Oh, please excuse me," she said, and when she pushed her glistening hair out of her face, he saw her eyes somehow managed to shine even more. "I'm so terribly sorry."

"It's all right," he said, but she had already cried out and dropped to the ground.

"I've lost my ticket," she exclaimed, and Christopher knelt beside her at once.

The cement was icy and his fine trousers were getting wet, but he didn't care. What was an uncomfortable wet stain when this dear woman's ticket was concerned? He scrabbled around until he saw a piece of quality paper, and took hold of it.

"Here you are," he said, presenting it to her.

Her smile lit up the sky. Her eyes became moons.

"Thank you so much," she said, and clutched the ticket in her beautifully gloved hands. They knelt together in a sea of beaded dresses and pressed suit pants, as the stars glittered down on them.

"Your lipstick is applied perfectly," Christopher told her. It was deep and red and reminded him of blood and rubies. Exquisite in color and spread expertly from corner to corner of her mouth. "Too many women think they can wear red lipstick, however they can't put it on correctly. But you…"

She laughed and he pondered being embarrassed, but what he said was true and precise. Nothing to be sorry for.

"Let me help you up, my love."

Christopher looked to see who spoke. It was a hardened, corpselike man in a suit two shades poorer than Christopher's. He drew the woman to her feet, but his eyes never left Christopher's.

"Thank you for the assistance," the corpse said icily.

Christopher stood and fixed his tie.

"It was a pleasure," he answered, and the man turned away, holding the woman's arm tightly. She smiled at Christopher once again, dazzling him with more than her diamonds, and then leaned her head on the man's shoulder.

The opera was as operas were. Christopher tapped his foot impatiently and congratulated himself for refusing to check his phone messages. When intermission came, he fled gratefully for the lobby. When his boss appeared from the theater, Christopher was immediately at his side.

"Mr. Edstrom. What a delight to see you here,"

Christopher said warmly, and shook his boss' limp hand. "How are you enjoying the performance so far?"

"It's quite divine," his boss began, and then launched into speaking about the exquisite tone quality of the soprano and the complexity of the storyline. "And the costumes," he gushed. "Don't get me started."

Christopher did indeed get him started, and while Mr. Edstrom clapped his hands in glee at the jewel-tones used in the garb, Christopher caught the delicate sheen of something ethereal in the crowd.

Her hair. The woman from the ticket line.

He was not a boorish man or the type to stare, but he stood and watched her with unusual intensity. She picked her way through the forest of people like a doe through a glen, her date guiding her. Right before she disappeared into the theater, she turned and met Christopher's eyes from across the room.

He gasped and then coughed quickly to cover it up.

"How right you are," he told Mr. Edstrom, and they

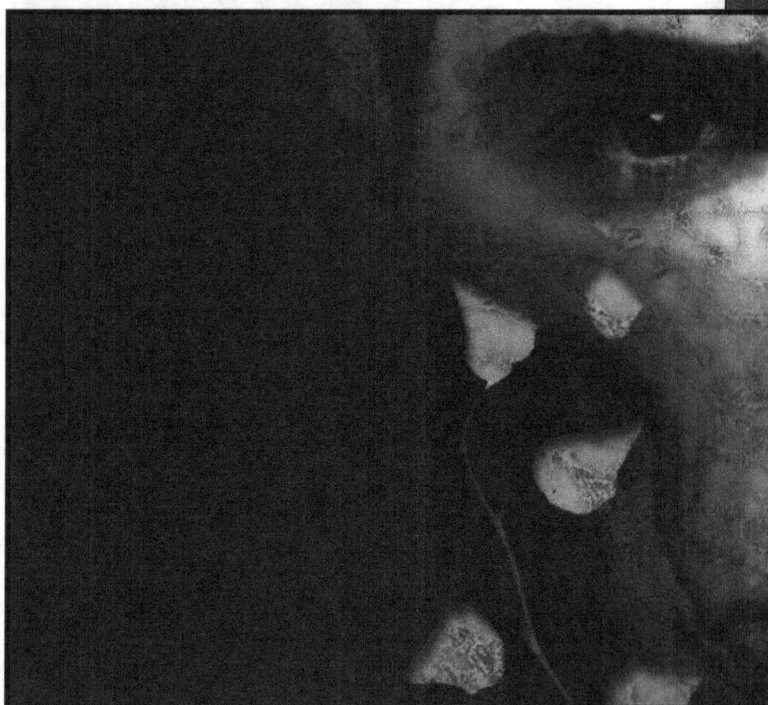

made the usual required pleasantries and disconnected.

Since he had already given mouth service to the boss about this particular opera, Christopher allowed his eyes to glaze over for the remaining half. Every now and then he searched for the woman with shining hair, but then he flopped back into his seat and stared at the ceiling. The decorative walls. The evil villain or do-gooder or whoever was swooping obnoxiously around the stage at the moment.

And then it ended.

Ah, the play ended, but the downward spiral of his life was just beginning.

He gathered his coat and gloves. Dressed wearily. Proceeded to walk out into the bitter cold.

"Sir," said a voice just behind him. He spun around.

Those eyes. That hair. The perfectly outlined blood red lips, sinful in their lushness. Her lips curved into a smile that nearly made Christopher groan in the sweetest of ecstasies.

She leaned close and slipped something into his coat pocket, and then disappeared into the crowd. She was most likely returning to her lonely corpse. He imagined she'd spoon-feed him some old man's soup before tucking him into his casket for the night.

He reached in his pocket and pulled out a business card. "Ivy," it said, with a phone number scrawled prettily underneath. Best of all was the deep, blooming lipstick kiss that promised all of the adventures he could handle.

Christopher smiled. And the very next day, he called. Ivy answered, and he was lost.

***

Ivy's name fit her perfectly. When she threw her arms around Christopher, she wound around him in impossible ways. He was a tall, straight tree, her hero, and this made

Christopher feel useful and needed.

"I'm needed at work," he told her. They were sitting on the couch, her feet on his lap. He rubbed them gently while speaking. "I'm fairly integral to the entire thing. But people? That's a different story completely."

She snuggled up to him.

"Oh, darling, I knew I needed you from the moment I met you."

"You did?" He was delighted.

"I did. I was so very unhappy with dear old Mr. Frowny Face, but I didn't think I deserved anything better. Why, he sucked me dry! And then I bumped into you…"

"It was like fate," he said.

He felt her lips curve against his ear.

"Something like that," she said.

She moved in quickly, her elegant clothes soon hanging beside his, her shoes overtaking the closet. His perfectly acceptable, prim apartment became a palace of pink and gold pillows.

She owned a horrid little dog that gnawed at his Versace and peed on his Italian loafers. The mutt made her laugh so hard that she opened her red mouth wide, and that was worth it all, right there.

"Will you take me out to dance?" she asked him. Christopher rarely danced, but he said he would. They danced all night and Ivy would sleep during the day. Christopher seemed to get no sleep at all.

"Would you take me to see the stars?" she begged. The light pollution made that impossible in the city, so Christopher drove her out into the country. They stayed in a little bed and breakfast, and he ate pretentious muffins that he abhorred, but Ivy sighed dreamily.

"I would so love to dine somewhere new," she said, and Christopher obediently dressed into his tuxedo and took her out. They ate tiny portions of something mediocre, but the lightbulbs flashed and Ivy blushed demurely with the attention. Christopher looked at her lovely skin, flushed with joy, and he quickly downed another glass of wine.

That night she nestled up beside him, her wondrous hair spread out on the bed like fabric, or gold, or diamonds, or all manner of precious things.

"Be with me forever, for eternity," she whispered before falling asleep. Christopher gulped and tried to think of something witty and yet heartfelt to say, but she was already slumbering.

Forever is a long time, came to mind. Or perhaps *Maybe we should see how the next, say, three or so months go.* But at the same time, his heart screamed, *Yes, oh yes! Let us be immortals together.*

Christopher's traitorous heart couldn't be counted upon to protect itself. It was so very new when it came to this thing called love, and didn't understand that love shouldn't hurt so badly, shouldn't drain a man dry.

Ivy wanted and Christopher gave. It was very nearly like opening a vein, but instead of blood he gave money, and time, and gifts, and his good sense. He came home when she called him at work.

"I'm frightened," she would say, and her lovely skin would be a terrifying shade of alabaster. "I think there is a mouse/ghost/intruder/certain gloom of loneliness in the house."

He would comfort her and she'd bury her face into his neck, fitting her mouth ever-so-nicely over his jugular, clinging to him as an Ivy would.

Mr. Edstrom requested a meeting.

"Now Christopher," he said, and somewhere in the back of Christopher's mind, he was delighted that his boss remembered his name this time, "we need team players. Are you or are you not a team player?"

"Of course I am, sir."

"I'm not seeing the dedication to this company that I expect from you. You can't keep leaving whenever the mood strikes you. Do you understand?"

Christopher opened his mouth to say something, but was interrupted by the ringing of his phone.

Mr. Edstrom raised an eyebrow.

"I'm sorry, sir," Christopher said, and reached down

to silence it.

Ivy. Her name flashed on the screen. She was home and frightened, or lost and afraid, or perhaps she was being abducted right this very minute!

"Christopher."

Mr. Edstrom's voice held a dangerous note of warning. Christopher's finger hovered over the silence button, but he was suddenly buried under an avalanche of fear. There were so many possibilities concerning his clinging Ivy. Perhaps she cut herself badly and was bleeding. She was overcome with hopelessness and took all of her depression medication at one time. She found another man, or perhaps the old corpse had returned to take her back.

The thought of her old lover with his skeletal hand around her dainty wrist was what broke him.

"I'm sorry, sir, but I need to take this. She knows only to call in an emergency."

He bolted from the room and down the hall. His hand shook when he tapped his phone.

"Ivy? What's wrong?"

"Why hello, darling!" She was fairly purring. "I went shopping and found the most charming dresses. One is yellow and one is blue. Which color, do you think, my love? Or both?"

After being let go from work, Christopher started drinking more heavily. He'd sit at the bar, studying his formally immaculate nails, and tried to ignore the phone in his pocket.

She left messages.

"Christopher! The puppy did the most delightful thing. I have to show you."

"Darling, I'm worried about you. You…you aren't mad at me, are you?"

"It's lonely and you aren't home and I'm frightened. Where are you?"

"There's another woman, isn't there? Someone younger and prettier than I am. That's where you are right now, isn't it? Oh, Christopher! How could you?"

"I'm sorry. I'm sorry for everything. I love you, and I thought you loved me. I must have been wrong."

"By the time you hear this, I'll be dead."

He rushed home. He always rushed home. He held her and consoled her and watched whatever new trick or heard whatever funny story or appreciated the newest shiny bauble. He did whatever she wanted. Christopher held her while she cried and ducked while she threw his most precious mementos at his head. He told her she was the only woman he loved, and tried not to choke on the "love" part, but attempted to say it with conviction.

"Oh, Christopher," she always said, and wrapped herself too tightly around him. He strangled on her desperation and woke up in bed, choking on her lustrous hair. It had worked its way into his mouth and nose, tendriling down the neckline of his shirt.

He disentangled himself and slipped from his tiny corner of the bed. He tripped over the stupid dog who nipped at him, drawing blood on his ankle. He staggered to the bathroom and turned on the light.

The man in the mirror blinked back at him. Cheeks hollowed from stress, hair graying rapidly. The skin of his eyelids had gone papery and fragile. He'd lost weight and his night clothes hung on him almost comically.

Where was his zest for life? Where was his excitement? While his cheeks had never been rosy, by any means, they held color once. He had become nearly cadaverous.

Ivy, with her beauty and neediness and searching hands, had buried herself so deeply inside his skin that she was eating him from the inside out. She sucked the dreams and spirit and passion from his soul. The energy from his body. The desire from his loins.

The next morning, she threw her arms around him and he learned into the hug. It was a taking hug, not a giving hug, and Ivy received the comfort she sought from him. He almost felt her pull the wellbeing from his body.

Christopher felt cold and alone. He settled deeper into his dry husk of a body.

"Darling, I miss you. Perhaps we could do something tonight. Would you like to go to a show?"

A show sounded lovely.

"Do you mind picking up tickets?"

Of course he didn't.

Tickets were purchased and Ivy swirled around in a new dress. Her hair fell in radiant waves that reminded Christopher of the first time he saw her, back when he was young and energetic and full of undiscovered hope. Christopher slipped on his pants and cinched the belt two holes tighter than usual. He hung the jacket over his shoulders like dressing a scarecrow. He combed his sparse hair with shaking hands.

They stood at the entrance of the theater. Ivy glittered and spun, full of excitement and stardust and vitality that didn't belong to her. Christopher stared at the ground and shuffled alongside her dutifully.

"Oh, I'm so sorry," he heard her exclaim. "Please forgive me. Goodness, where is my ticket?"

Christopher froze, afraid to look. He finally forced himself to turn around and saw Ivy nose-to-nose on the sidewalk with a handsome young man. The man had dark, radiant skin and the finest of hats. Money, health, and enthusiasm fairly dripped from him like blood. Christopher ached to feast on his vivacity himself.

"Ivy."

Christopher held out his withered hand. Ivy and the man exchanged significant glances, and the man handed her a ticket.

"Thank you so much, sir. Now I really must go."

"Not a problem," the man said, and discreetly eyed Christopher. Christopher stood silently, knowing exactly what the man would see. A corpse in the moonlight. A cadaverous sugar daddy who knew when he was beaten.

Ivy's lunar eyes were unusually dreamy during the show. She inconspicuously took out a card and scrawled something on it. In the hubbub of intermission, she scurried over to the radiant young man and slipped the card into his hand. They both smiled.

Christopher smiled, too, for the first time in a long time. He sighed as he felt Ivy's fangs unfasten from his throat.

He could breathe again. His rusty heart began to beat. His blood flowed.

THE VAMPIRES OF NEW ENGLAND

BY K. H. VAUGHAN

AFRAID OF A VAMPIRE.

The Dead Suspected of Draining the tality of the Living.

Providence, R. I., March 23.—A horr suspicion has been put to the test in city. The wife of George T. Brown of consumption about eight years ago. years ago the oldest daughter succum to the same disease, leaving the other m ers of the family in apparently

It is a lurid tale.

Readers of the Providence Journal awoke on March 19, 1892 to the headline: *Bodies of Dead Relatives Taken from their Graves*. After the deaths of Mary Eliza Brown and her daughters Mary Olive and Mercy Lena of consumption, husband and father George Brown faced a grim choice. His

EXHUMED THE BODIES.

Testing a Horrible Superstition in the Town of Exeter.

BODIES OF DEAD RELATIVES TAKEN FROM THEIR GRAVES.

They Had All Died of Consumption, and the Belief Was That Live Flesh and Blood Would be Found That Fed Upon the Bodies of the Living.

Providence Journal headline of March 19, 1892

only son Edwin was also tubercular and, despite spending months in the dry elevated air of Colorado, had returned home in failing health. There was nothing to be done but wait for the inevitable. Edwin too would die, unless…

Folk tradition in rural South County Rhode Island held that when consumption ran through a family, it was due to the influence of the deceased, who fed upon the vital essence of their kin from the grave. The only way to stop this supernatural visitation was to exhume the bodies of the dead and examine them. If any should have blood in their heart or liver, the organ must be removed and burned, and the ashes consumed by the living. Only this could break the curse.

Desperate to save his son, Mr. Brown took the advice of his neighbors and, according to the Journal, went to the small family plot on Shrub Hill in Exeter. There, with the family physician and a few other in attendance, he participated in digging up his beloved wife and daughters. Mary Eliza and Mary Olive were well into decomposition, but Mercy Lena has been buried only two months before. Her liver was well-preserved (if dry), but her heart was filled with dark, clotted blood. The organs were removed and burned on a nearby rock. There is no record of whether

Edwin ate the ashes as prescribed. He died a short time later on May 2nd at the age of twenty-four.

Mercy Brown was not the first New England vampire, but she is thought to be the last on record. Reports of this type can be found in newspaper clippings, private journal and letters, and even public records from Colonial times, peaking in the 19th Century. Mercy Brown is referenced in H. P. Lovecraft's *The Shunned House*, Caitlyn R. Kiernan's *So Runs the World Away*, and inspired the book *Mercy: The Last New England Vampire* by Sarah L. Thompson. The 2015 film *Almost Mercy*, directed by Tom DeNucci and starring horror legends Bill Moseley and Kane Hodder was also inspired by her story. It has even been suggested that Bram Stoker based the character Lucy Westenra from the iconic novel *Dracula* on her. An 1896 newspaper clipping describing the incident from the *New York World* was found in his papers and Lucy and Mercy both wasted away and died at nineteen. Dracula was published in 1897, perhaps time enough to revise the manuscript if this theory holds true.

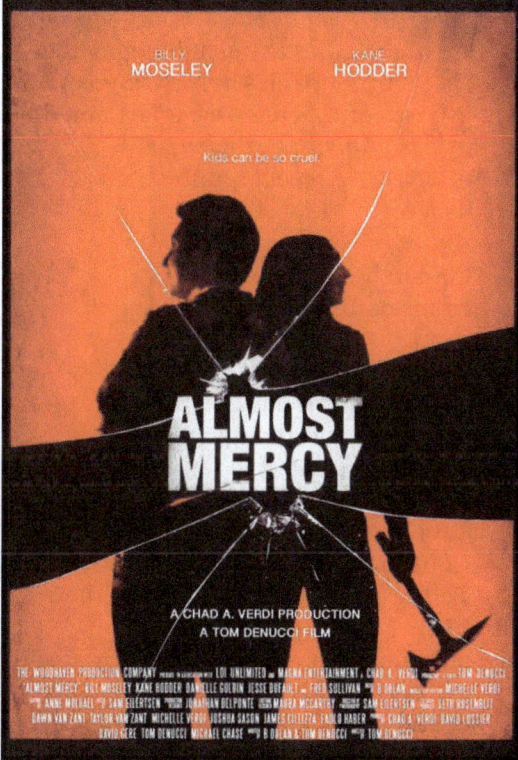

In 1981, Dr. Michael Bell, Consulting Folklorist for the Rhode Island Historical Preservation & Heritage Commission, drove down to an isolated farm at the end of Sodom Trail in Exeter to interview Lewis Everett Peck. Peck, 52, was a descendent of the Brown family, and confirmed that his mother and grandmother acknowledged the act. As a child he was warned away from playing near her tombstone or the rock where her heart was burned. In family lore, it was "an awful thing that had to be done." Over the years the story has grown, with dubious press reports adding detail and labeling her a "vampire," a term never used within the Brown family or the community. Puff pieces around Halloween have led to teenagers and supernatural investigators hunting for Mercy's grave. Her headstone was stolen in August 1996, but recovered. Peck expressed frustration at the misrepresentations and vandalism.

But was Mercy Brown a vampire? Did the events happen as described, and how common was the practice? The internet has much to say about Mercy, although much of it appears to be copied from website to website without research. A number of books and academic papers have been written on the issue. Dr. Bell provides the most scholarly investigation of the subject. He confirmed twenty cases throughout New England between 1793 and 1898 in his book, *Food for the Dead: On the Trail of New England's Vampires* (2001). By the publication of a 2012 *Smithsonian* interview he counts 80 cases as "just the tip of the iceberg."

Vampire panics in New England appeared exclusively in cases of tuberculosis, a fact noted by George R. Stetson in *The Animistic Vampire in New England*, published in *The American Anthropologist* in 1896. Research by Dr. Bell confirms this trend. Tuberculosis is one of the world's deadliest diseases even today, with one third of the global population infected and 1.5 million deaths in 2014 (Centers for Disease Control and Prevention). Today it is treated effectively with antibiotics, although resistant strains are on the rise and many people who are infected are asymptomatic carriers of the disease. But in the time of Mercy Brown, there was no cure. Victims who became ill grew progressively weaker. They developed pallor, which is why the disease was sometimes called The

White Death or Great White Plague. In the end, they would be wracked with coughing, producing enormous quantities of bloody sputum. In the absence of a cure or effective treatments, people turned to folk remedies and environmental treatments such as rest in the thin, arid air of Colorado. The cause of tuberculosis was not known until Prussian physician Robert Koch successfully cultured and identified *Mycobacterium tuberculosis* in 1882. Even then, treatment with antibiotics was not available until after World War II.

It is not as strange as one might think that people might have attempted cannibalism as a cure. Medicinal cannibalism was practiced in Europe until the 18th century in the form of corpse medicine (Bethge; Dolan). Human fat, flesh, bone, blood and mummified remains stolen from Egypt were prescribed as curative, a practice that peaked in the 17th century. This tradition may have taken root in New England as well. Puritan poet and physician Edwin Taylor (1642-1729) included "Mummy" in his formulary of potential treatments (Gordon-Grube). Even today, some people engage in ritual cannibalism for alleged health benefits. The eating of the afterbirth (placentophagy) is on the rise in the United States. People with chronic or terminal illness will often reach for cures that are unproven or speculative when medicine fails.

It is fair to suspect that knowledge of folk remedies made of human remains may have come to New England with European immigrants. Although newspapers of the time suggested these incidents are due to the ignorance and moral deficiencies of rural degeneration, the practice may have crossed class boundaries and been viewed as a reasonable, if unpleasant, response to a horrifying and tragic circumstance. The moral outrage expressed in accounts may reflect the same urban-rural prejudices illustrated in the film *Deliverance* more than objective reporting.

It could also be that these stories are pure fabrications written for mass consumption: the "redneck porn" of the era. The question, remains: how often did this ghoulish (at least by modern eyes) practice occur?

Although Dr. Bell believes there are 80 confirmed cases and possibly hundreds more, there is very little direct evidence. The only case with physical evidence comes from Griswold, CT, a rural township near the RI border. In 1990, an unmarked burial plot from before the Civil War was discovered by children playing in a gravel mine. Twenty-nine sets of remains were recovered by authorities. A single set was found in an unusual position within a broken coffin: the skull and thigh bones were placed on the ribs in a position resembling the Jolly Roger and the ribs broken. Forensic analysis confirmed that this damage had been done five years after death and that he may have been tubercular. This individual, identified as "J. B." from the initials on the coffin may have been desecrated as defense against an outbreak of consumption.

Unfortunately, the identity of J. B. has not been established, and there is no record of how or why his skeleton was damaged (although it was clearly intentional). An 1854 press report describes a scene similar to the exhumation and burning of Mercy Brown in nearby Jewitt City, CT, suggesting that the folklore existed in the region, but documentation of the so-called "Jewitt City Vampires" is lacking. The closest bona fide documentation of the use of corpse medicine to thwart consumption comes from a cryptic note in the records of the Town Counsel of Cumberland, RI from February 8, 1796: Mr. Stephen Staples petitioned the counsel for permission to disinter the body of his daughter Abigail "in order to try an experiment on [her sister] Lavinia Chase." The Counsel approved his request, but the nature of the experiment is not known. This leaves little solid evidence behind.

Bell, more than any other researcher, has attempted to supplement old newspaper clippings with genealogical research, archival research, and interviews, and claims only those cases that he believes meet his standard of evidence. He acknowledges that stories may have been altered or smoothed over the years, perhaps even to conform with modern legends. Even as Dracula may have been influenced by the case of Mercy Brown, retellings of the Mercy Brown story and those of other so-called "vampires" seem to have been influenced by

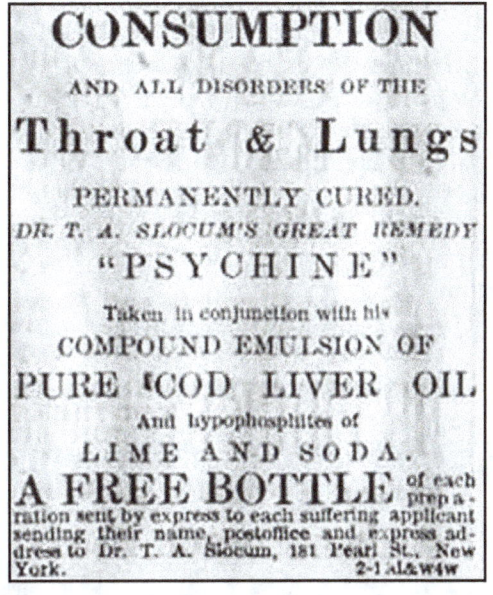

Dracula as well. Bell seems convinced that modern media is only interested in sensationalism when it comes to these stories: television programs edit interviews with experts deceptively and newspapers run Halloween features that suggest that Brown is a vampire in line with the Dracula legend.

Yet he pulls back from the possibility that the news accounts of the 18th and 19th century may have been every bit as sensationalistic and driven by headlines. For example, accounts of the Hatfield-McCoy feud of the late 1800s were highly dubious in terms of journalistic standards. Even if some details of newspaper stories can be cross-referenced with birth and death records, that doesn't confirm the facts reported in the accounts. Urban legends are still reported in news outlets with some frequency today, despite greater ability to verify stories. Indeed, Bell begins to question the veracity of some of his "confirmed" cases. Given the absence of headstones and official records, he would have to "conclude that many of the cases considered to this point did not happen" (FFD p. 210). And yet the stories persist, and continue to grow, a process accelerated by the internet.

The case of "vampire" Nelly Vaughan (no relation to the author) almost certainly started as a rumor at a local Rhode Island high school and, indeed, the particular grave selected may have been completely arbitrary. The inscription on her headstone "I am waiting and watching for you" and her death in 1889 at age 19 (like Mercy Brown and Lucy Westenra) may have been suggestive to adolescent minds. There is no record of her being identified as a ghost or vampire until the 1970s, and Dr. Bell's research suggests that this urban legend does not predate the 1960s. As the case became popularized, additional details and ghost sightings were added. Over the years, thrill-seekers and paranormal researchers chipped away at her headstone for souvenirs and even attempted to exhume her more than once. Due to the repeated vandalism of her grave and damage to the cemetery in general, she was exhumed and re-interred in a secret location.

When I was a teenager in Worcester County there was the legend of the "Spider Gates": an abandoned cemetery with wrought iron gates in the shape of spider webs. If you went past the last gate (between seven and nine, depending on who was telling the story), you would never

come back, although what exactly would happen to you was never clear. Perhaps this was an allusion to "going all the way" sexually. In reality, the burial ground in question is a functioning Quaker cemetery on private land. There is only one set of gates (at the entrance), and they look more like wagon wheels with curving spokes than spider webs. No credible news source records any strange activities there. Yet paranormal tourists have become so common that the owners have been forced to issue a policy statement on such visits and a plea to allow the families to mourn in peace, and for their dead and monuments to be left undisturbed.

As intriguing as the Vampires of New England are from a cultural or folkloric standpoint, it's likely that the story of Mercy Brown is no different than that of Nelly Vaughan or the "Spider Gates." Patterns in folklore can just as easily reflect cultural trends or the perceptions of the viewer as they can actual fact, especially when there is little, if any, verifiable evidence. These vampires could very well be no more than fantasies built upon the dust of history. Whatever grain of truth remains is probably lost to time, inseparable from the myth surrounding it.

References

Bell. M. E. (2001). *Food for the Dead: On the Trail of the New England Vampire*. New York: Carroll & Graf.

Bethge, P. (2009, January 30). Europe's 'medicinal cannibalism': The healing power of death. *Spiegel Online International*.

Centers for Disease Control and Prevention (2016). Tuberculosis. http://www.cdc.gov/tb/default.htm

Dolan, M. (2012, May 6). The Gruesome History of Eating Corpses as Medicine. *Smithsonian*

Gordon-Grube, K. (1993). Evidence of medicinal cannibalism in Puritan New England. "Mummy" and related remedies in Edward Taylor's "Dispensatory". *Early American Literature*, 28(3), 185-221.

Rondina, C. (2008). *Vampires of New England*. Dennis, MA: On Cape Publications

Tucker, A. (2012, October). The Great New England Vampire Panic. *Smithsonian Magazine*

Tucker, A. (2012, October). Meet the Real-Life Vampires of New England and Abroad. *Smithsonian Magazine*.

Lauren, with the Fall of Night

Darren Speegle

One

GLIMPSES
June, 2013

We were still fighting when the bouncers, clutching the backs of our shirts, opened the door and threw us out into the wet cobblestone street. It was late, even by German standards, and Trier's Old City was quiet, with not a soul around to see this senseless display of barbarism. Or so I thought when I finally ended the thing by punching my attacker in the throat as he pounced on me where I'd fallen trying to escape his latest flurry of blows.

He sat on his ass now, clutching his throat with one hand and waving me off with the other. All the fury he'd displayed inside the club had been replaced by genuine fear for his well-being as he gasped and gulped for air. Suited him right, I thought, fucking with someone with a bum leg. What had we been fighting about anyway? Some woman? *His* woman? Had he thought I was hitting on her? Who knew, maybe I had been. I was pretty drunk. Drunk enough not to recognize who was with whom on the wild dance floor that had nonetheless accepted a cripple like me.

My attention was diverted by an abrupt blast of the music coming from within the club. The face of one of the bouncers appeared again at the entrance, shouting, *"Raus hier!* Go home or we call the Polizei!"

I was turning back to the German in the street to call it a truce when I saw her. She was standing just at the edge of the halo of light surrounding one of the streetlamps, the swirling rain obscuring her features within the frame of her matted dark hair. She was more than a silhouette though; I could see enough to tell that she was a young woman, probably in her mid-twenties. Moreover, it was evident that she was watching us, or more specifically *me*, where I'd risen, in spite of the pain in my bad leg, to a standing position above the still recovering German. A protracted moment to let the certainty sink in that we had made mutual contact across this drizzly void and then she was backing up, now turning and moving away briskly into the dark.

How like the Trier night to produce such oddities, I thought. And extended a helping hand to my fallen opponent. Which, to my slight surprise, he accepted in the proper spirit.

***

"Hell of a way to start a vacation," I said to the taxi driver as he deposited me at the steps of the footbridge that crossed the narrow Kyll River to my residence. Perhaps a bit unsettled by my appearance, that and the alcoholic stench I must have given off, he'd waited until we were almost to our destination before inquiring about my injuries.

"You're vacationing at home? Not going anywhere special?" he said politely, taking the euro notes from me.

"Special? Look at the place where I live, man." I motioned across the river to the watermill outlined in the dawn's early light against the backdrop of the valley's fir-covered slope. "For me, this is like a fairy tale."

"Yes," he smiled. "Yes, I see what you mean. Enjoy yourself, friend. Here's my card, should you find yourself needing a cab again."

I thanked him and, acutely aware of my aching leg, climbed the steps to the bridge. Halfway across, I stopped and leaned against the wooden railing, admiring the picturesque valley of the winding river. Indeed the setting *was* like something out of a book, particularly now, deep into spring's foliage-rich reign. It had been by pure luck that I'd walked into the Housing Office on the very morning they'd posted the rental. Like many of the U.S. installations in Germany, Spangdahlem Air Base was rural and depended on available rentals in the small surrounding villages to house its personnel. While there seemed to be a reasonable number of such properties, they also seemed to be regularly snatched up almost immediately. I knew this from my first stint in Germany, when I worked as a contractor shipping vehicles back to the States. This time around it had been wonderfully easy compared to what I had gone through then, when I was on such a tight budget after my divorce that Lady Luck couldn't have intervened if she'd wanted to.

Not that I hadn't earned my current favors. Having spent six years in Iraq and Afghanistan as a defense contractor, often living in a tent and *always* working twelve hours a day, seven days a week, I felt I deserved whatever glimmer of a smile came my way. I'd of course been paid handsomely for my civilian services in the logistics arena, but I'd also given a lot of my soul in the process. When you whore yourself out to the highest bidder for wars—particularly one of them—with which you do not morally agree, that's how it feels. Like you're selling your very essence. And what's worse is that you're doing it under the watchful eyes of the real casualties, the soldiers, who are neither paid handsomely nor have a choice in the matter, but who do their diligent duty without complaint.

A balance to strike, for sure, as I now tried to strike a match against the canyon's breeze. Failing once, then again, I returned the cigarette to the crumpled pack. Shoving the pack in my pocket, I left my thoughts to drift with the rising, silvery breath of the Kyll River and continued the limp to my abandoned flour mill, stuff of drunken songs.

While I wasn't singing as I descended the steps at the end of the bridge, I was drunker maybe than I'd realized. I slipped on the wet wood and would have crashed against the steps behind me had I not managed to grab the rail for support. When I'd corrected myself, I saw something. Saw and heard it simultaneously. Movement in the boughs of the trees above the mill's roof. And not a minor disturbance as a squirrel or a bird might cause, but a significant one, as though a monkey was shuffling around up there.

The shuffling turned to passage as the source now moved from limb to limb between the trees, offering the merest glimpses of itself as it put distance between us. That I was the cause of its retreat, I didn't doubt. The flashes of… fabric? human hair… were a little harder to swallow. But I was sure, as it disappeared into the forest, that a human form was exactly what I'd seen. A lithe, wet-haired woman of a form. An almost revenant sort of form. The sort of form a concussion might conjure up out of lamplit cobblestone streets.

I rushed, as far as my leg would allow, to my front door, fumbling with the key as I tried to fit it in the lock. But there was nothing to be afraid of, finally, as I was back inside my house and the Grimm monsters relented to the fairer fairy tales. I tried to sleep, and when that didn't happen in a timely fashion, I wrote. I did that when I wasn't serving the cause. I wrote short stories and novels and sometimes slept with them.

***

I woke tasting old liquor and a sourer something from my dreams. My face ached almost as much as my leg, which itself vied with the place inside my skull for the honors. Recovering the memories gradually, I touched the swellings around my mouth and eye. Fuck. Had she done this to me? No, that wasn't right. It was the dude in the club—what was the name of the place? Something subterranean… *The Vault*. Yes, that was it. A place you had to use a spiral set of stairs to exit while some cat with a woman problem tried to beat your face in even as the bulls were escorting you out.

Jesus. Had I been a part of that? A thirty-two-year-old man acting like a member of the university set thronging the fire hazard of a place? But as my head continued to clear, I knew that yes, I had indeed been a part of that. That and more if you let your nightmares creep in. If you let yourself try to reconcile what you thought you had seen with what had actually occurred. Had there been a woman in the street watching you when you were thrown out of the club? Entirely likely. Trier had its indigents, its crazies, its voyeurs, like all cities of any size. Had this same woman been in the trees above your house? Now who was crazy.

I went to the bathroom and splashed water on my face before looking at myself in the mirror. When I did, I nearly recoiled from my reflection. The lump on the side of my head was bigger than a golf ball, while my upper lip sagged puffily over the bottom of my mouth. My cheekbone had been split open, and a wide swath of blood had dried on that side of my face, joining the blood around my nostrils and mouth in a grim mosaic. Finally, the eye on the opposite side of my head from the lump was bruised and bloodshot. I was a living, breathing grotesquerie, something fit for Trier's torture museum.

Oh fucking well was about all I could say as I treated the wounds to the best of my ability, washing off the blood, applying Band-Aids where needed, butterflying the cut on the cheekbone, placing ice on the lump around my temple. I sipped coffee and Goodies for breakfast, rice soup for lunch, then slurped buttered noodles for dinner. Watched a lot of CNN and BBC, slept some, watched some more TV, called the guys from work to tell them I wouldn't be breaking all the known protocol of the universe by spending a segment of my vacation with their sorry asses after all, and then zonked out for the long haul on the sofa with the TV buzzing in the background.

I woke sometime around midnight to find her sitting there in the armchair adjacent to the couch, images from the flat screen flashing across her watchful face.

***

It took a while, some seconds anyway as the shock tried to wear off, before she finally spoke. I'd been able to manage only the obligatory "Who are you?" during the strange interim. It was that question she seemed to be circuitously responding to now.

"Lauren. French father, German mother. Heidelberg. Do you remember her, Roderick? Is it Roderick still? Or have you reverted to Rod?"

I swallowed. "Rod will do."

"Yes. And I suppose it's always done. I supposed it then, when she shared the experience of you with me, and I suppose it now looking at those fading dreams on your face. Roderick, you told her, would better serve the writer you aspired to be. Readers wouldn't take to Rod. It wasn't intellectual enough. Write down to earth, you said. But be above it. Have command. It's the way you saw your reader seeing you. Isn't that so?"

"I suppose."

"But that never played out, did it, Roderick? The reviews of your small press releases criticized you as being too above your work. There was too great a distance between yourself and your readers, the critics said. Oh, it was dazzling prose, mesmerizing even, but you put your reader too far away from what was going on. They couldn't relate. Couldn't participate. Couldn't empathize. Didn't care really beyond the poetic lines, the hallucinatory images, the disturbing nature of the content as revealed by your fabulous words. Style over substance, isn't that what it was, your attempt at writing? No story. No real experience as it came to other people's experiences. For you not only wrote above the salad you were treating them to. You lived above it. You always have. You have *always* witnessed your world from aloft, haven't you? It's your way of dealing with the mundaneness, the frivolity of it all. Are we together on this?"

As I looked at her, searching for any answer but the truthful one, my shock had turned to despair. For there were no answers. Whoever had sent her, whatever they were up to, their grasp of me was as perfect as anyone could achieve in a pool of strangers.

"I don't know what you mean… I don't know you. I don't know how you can know me."

"But that's just it, Rod. I *do* know you. I am the one person in the world who has lived aloft with you. Who has understood your way of seeing things. It's why I am here. It's true that I had never experienced you until Lauren. But I have now. You come with the highest recommendation from her. Are you aware that she died with you? That she gave the blood of her heart to you?"

"I have no idea what you're talking about. Who is Lauren? Who are *you*?"

As she leaned forward, it seemed her face finally came out of its shroud of mist. Her eyes were large and bright, with irises of the deepest brown. This face, with its otherwise delicate though unafraid features, touched something in me. Something from another time. Some other history. "We know you, Roderick Lachance. You partied with us, when we were all so young. We lit each other up in our drug-induced euphoria. Ah, to be young again, right?"

It was coming to me. At least to that suggestible part of me. This woman had power. She created where perhaps there was nothing. "When did I know her? Know you? I get that it was in Heidelberg, but when specifically?"

"When you were reeling, Rod. When you were reeling from your divorce. When you returned to the place you had lived in your youth when your father was in the service. When you returned to Germany and went to Amsterdam every other weekend, supplying yourself with drugs for the long sleepless nights. Do you begin to remember now?"

"I could remember a lot better if you hadn't broken into my house."

"I didn't have to break in. You left it open."

"That's impossible. The door locks automatically."

"There are many ways to enter a house besides the front door."

I looked at her. "If you're you, you mean."

She smiled. "Then you do begin to remember."

I sighed. "If you'll just give me a spark… anything…"

"Branden Apartments. 2007. You lived there for a time, surrounded by Heidelberg University students. Lauren, a graduate student, lived next door to you. She invited you to a party at a place off the Walkplatz. A pre-party, actually, for the real attraction—the Vampire Ball at the Heidelberg Castle. You were high when you answered the door, and you'd remain that way for a week. Think on it, Roderick. And when you're ready, call for me. I'm never too far away."

With that, she rose and with what might have been a slight bow, was out of the room and gone.

Two

RECURRENCES
February, 2007

The knock comes just as I am lying back on the bed in my shorts, amazed by this transformation a little magic dust has inspired. The cat in Amsterdam called it a substitute for the real thing, but I think he lied for the sake of the sale. I'm not the type, he must have recognized when I asked for ecstasy, a drug of a wholly different ilk. At least I think that's what I did. Who knows now, with the door seeming so far away, the knock so inconsequential.

But whoever it is, they're persistent. A woman's voice has joined the rap of knuckles. *Rod*, she calls. *Rod, are you home?*

It's Roderick, I want to say, but haven't the inclination. Easier just to get up and go there now that she's added this layer to it. Truly, my body floats, while the idea of speech seems cumbersome. It's the least of two evils simply answering the door.

"Yes," I manage in spite of myself as I hold the door open and try to get a fix on her. I've met her once or twice, it seems to me. But I can't recall when or why. I can't recall circumstances at all except as they pertain to my current state.

"Hi, Rod. Are you okay?"

"Adjusting," I said, feeling freer even as I do. What's it been, five or six minutes since I snorted the stuff? Yes, I'm beginning to cope a little better now, thank you.

"It's Lauren. You remember me, right? I mean we don't talk much, but we live right next door to each other. I feel like we should know each other."

"It's a pool of strangers," I say.

"What is?"

"Humankind, of course. Never mind, come in. I'm just lazing about the place, wondering when someone will knock."

It's a trick of words. "Pool of strangers." "Lazing about the place." My own, previously used words. Something to hold on to as I continue to come into it.

"Nice place," she says as she enters the studio and I close the door behind her. "The art makes it different than my apartment. Smaller… and yet, less cramped somehow. Does that make any sense?" She turns to look at me.

"You wouldn't believe how much," I reply. I'm feeling I can command my situation now. With every moment that passes, my high and I are coming to better terms with each other. It isn't a matter of whether it controls me or I control it. It's a harmony thing. Balance. Is this how Keith Richards, Lou Reed, Iggy Pop, Kurt Cobain felt?

"This is a da Vinci print, isn't it? Wow, I'd not have guessed you could incorporate it into a student's décor. The matting is fantastic."

"Actually, I'm not a student. Though I do happen to do some part-time work at a picture framing shop to make ends meet. It's what we call French matting. The strips of marble paper, the gold outlines. The small frame inside the matte is called a fillet. The cut-outs in the corners I do with a cheap little device with a blade that cuts at a bevel. Learned it in the States, where I bought art for a chain of shops."

She shakes her head. "The more you talk about it, the more interesting it becomes. Where are you from in the States? When we talked in the hall a week or so ago, you said you were from America, but I don't think you said where."

"No?" Did we talk, actually, or are you in a dream like I'm in? "Louisiana. Mardi Gras land."

Her smile grew. "That's an amazing coincidence. I'm actually here to ask you if you'd like to go to a Fasching party."

"And what makes you think I know what Fasching is?" I say in a teasing, though genuinely curious way.

"Um, let's see… you wrote about it in your story *Fasnacht for the Damned*?"

It settles on me now. She read the article in *The Heidelberg American*, which provided links to a couple of my online publications. A fan. How strange, considering I can count on one hand how many of those I have. And here is a German one.

"I'm delighted to hear my work has reached a wider audience," I say for lack of anything better.

"You're pretty good, you know." She smiles. "And now that I hear you're from Louisiana… that's just a bonus for a half-French girl."

"Yeah?"

"My father's from Nice."

"But you knew my name was Lachance if you read my work…"

"Yes. But most Americans have European names. Made no connection."

"So you're half French and, I'm assuming, half-German. Where does this perfect command of English fit in?"

"Both home and school. My father taught English and insisted I speak it at home. And I, myself, am an English major."

"You make me feel ashamed that I haven't yet fully cracked Deutsch."

"Don't. German is so throaty it would drive anyone crazy."

I smile. I like the girl and I'm on my game now. A Fasching party sounds like something I can embrace. But…

"Costume?" I say.

"It's not obligatory at the party. But if you're coming with us to the Vampire Ball at the castle afterward, you might at least put on a monk's robe or something."

"Like with sandals? It's kind of cold outside for that, isn't it?"

"Don't worry. We'll fix you up."

Will you indeed, I say to myself.

"We can do it now, if you like. My friend Gabe's been part-timing at a costume shop."

I chuckle. "You have this all planned out, do you?"

She smiles in turn. "Really, I hadn't thought that far ahead. I'm a little surprised you don't already have plans."

"What? I'm Captain Carnival because of a story I wrote? Give me a few minutes to shower and put on some clothes."

***

I can't remember her face as I knock on her door. It's been at most a half hour, yet I can't visualize her, can't feel the essence of her. It's like I'm wound up in a mystery, and everything outside me constitutes the mysterious. I've never even considered attending Heidelberg's Vampire Ball for that very fact—that it is a costume party, an affair for non-identities. Too close to home for me normally. But now, because of the drug, I revel in the notion.

Is she aware that I'm high? Does she care? I wonder as I wait for her to answer. Does it at all matter?

No, I decide as the door comes open and there is that face I couldn't recall. Behind its smile it seems something I should remember for the future. But I know I won't. I pass through this life as a shadow even when I'm straight. The props, the comers and goers, they are even less solid than me. Being among them is like being among one's toy cars as a child. They have features, color, they are distinct, but it's the world you create of them that is real, not the objects themselves. I don't know, perhaps that's the writer talking, I think as I follow her into her austere environs.

Gabe's here, and he's obviously gay. There would

be some relief in that if I needed any. That I don't says nothing for his having found himself in the wilderness. He is still a magnificent specimen in the pool of strangers. He still commands his road in a way that the rest of us, save for those of us on our substances, cannot. I resist the temptation to kiss his hand, knowing it would not be normal. That it would be unbecoming of an invitee.

"Let's just take a look at *you*," he says, admiring something in me, perhaps my lazy build. "Yes, yes, I think Lauren is right. You will do best in the simplest garment. A monk it is for you then. Sandals for your cold feet, I'm afraid. Don't worry, we'll rub your feet for you if need be, isn't that right, Lauren?"

She blushes. "Gabe, it's not necessary to tell him I told *you* about our conversation."

"No worries," I say. "I like the idea of a foot massage."

As we laugh, Gabe says, "*Do* you now?"

"Back off tiger," Lauren says. And winks at me.

They put me in my robe, and it is a great feeling being in a single article of clothing, with only my underwear beneath. I forget that it is February, don't even bother wondering why they didn't cover the garb I had on. Maybe she does know the state I'm in. Maybe they both do, bless them.

As I ponder that and the nothing it represents, Gabe, as if in my mind, produces a tray on which rests a powder very similar to the one that has freed me tonight. I'm tempted to call it cocaine, just of a slightly different hue, but I know it is not. They've come for me full-throttle, whether knowing what I've been up to or not. To our collective credit, we merely snort it as I did before, no more. It's a secret and secrets are kept without marks. When it is done, when the full effect has taken hold, Gabe slips into his outfit, a vampire's. Lauren applies his makeup. And then he, hers. When he's finished I ask her what she's trying to be—for she still wears the black tube dress she was wearing before.

"A whore, of course."

"Of course," I say, letting it all float out there in front of me.

"Let's do it then," she says. "Maybe you'll find fodder for your next story tonight."

***

The pre-party is in a school-lunchroom-sized common area as opposed to the private apartment or suite I envisioned. "The old Paracelsus Music Hall," Gabe tells me. "The building's owner rents the place out now for smaller events." And a small event it is, with a few dozen people occupying a space that could easily accommodate a few hundred. We are mixing with them almost upon the moment of our arrival, Lauren or Gabe introducing me to people whose faces I will not remember, but whose costumes I sense will continue to flash on my retinas as the night progresses.

"Welcome, my American friend," says one of them, ghost-kissing my cheeks in the European way. "Rod? Isn't that short for Roderick, a Germanic name?"

"Is it?" I say. Any previous knowledge is overshadowed by the use of my name in its long form. The authorial form.

But I won't get into that. I won't be the conversation piece that perhaps Lauren wants me to be.

But Lauren needs no help impressing as she sweeps among the small crowd, playing a game she seems at once to love and to despise playing. She seems pale to me, almost ghostly in her contrasting black dress, her severe makeup. As though playing the part of the whore must involve a self-sacrifice of blood. Gabe, meanwhile, is almost absurd in his depiction of the vampire. While it's no doubt intended, it's hard not to feel as though one is on the Nosferatu set with him, in his abrupt and dramatic visuals. Indeed, where do these light effects come from in so open a space? But now I see Master Phantasmagoria up there in his booth above. It's Halloween here at the old Paracelsus Music Hall.

"Come, let's get a drink," Lauren says.

"Is that wise?" Roderick asks.

"Oh? Is this your first time on smack? Could have fooled me."

Indeed.

We pass through bodies, occasionally offering something of ourselves to the curious or polite soul who inquires. The more I watch her, the more I realize Lauren is not a social butterfly. The part she plays is either expected of her or is for some other's benefit. Let that someone, I think, not be me.

The drink is strange to my mouth, but I have no reaction otherwise to it and so continue to sip as we float deeper into the mix. It occurs to me that Gabe is no longer with us and I ask Lauren where he has flown off to. "Wherever they do," she says, and smiles. Which sets as strangely on me as the flavor of my drink on my taste buds.

"Is there more to this thing than drifting?" I ask. "Shouldn't we be participating in some activity?"

"Like what?" She turns to me. There is a weird, almost dangerous something in her eyes.

"Hey, cool down, sister. It's dancing I had in my mind."

"Is it?"

"Yeah," I say hesitantly. "I think so."

She puckers her lips, scanning the group that's congregated here. None of them are dancing. Nor, it hits me, would the somewhat eerie music that seems to come from Master Phantasmagoria up there be conducive to such. Says Lauren: "I haven't danced in at least a year. I lost interest somewhere along the way. It just seems so…"

But suddenly she is doing just that—dancing to the strange vibe permeating the place. It starts with a slow, rolling motion of her arms, then extends to her hips and legs as she calls up some sinewy, erotic thing out of herself—the only thing that can possibly meld to the sound that now finds its way into focus at the expense of the surrounding conversations, the pattings and the kissings of the hall's anonyms. A moment to absorb and now I am there with her, feeling it out with my body, with the blood that flows through it, the ghost that inhabits it. Conjuring the snake out of myself, slithering in the naked air.

"Christ, you two," comes Gabe's voice from out on the skirts of it. But I ignore him. I'm performing the serpents' ballet with her. It's more than a dance; it's a story, some ancient story that only twain, synchronous bodies can tell.

"Enough," comes his voice again. Now more forcefully: "Lauren, behave yourself!"

Though my eyes are closed, I feel her obey. And as she does, so do I, dissolving into a puddle on this random floor in this place that is fit for neither of us.

As I look up at him out of the melt, I see something resembling wrath in his eyes.

He disguises it with a grin. "There will be plenty of opportunities, Roderick, at the Vampire Ball."

"Opportunities?"

"To lose yourself."

I exhale. "As though it's any of your fucking business."

"Someone must," he says, gesturing to the rear corner of the hall, where I'm almost sure I see her fall from some higher place before slipping into the passage that, according to the sign above the doorway, leads to the toilet.

***

Being a Louisianan, I have been to many parties in my life. Mardi Gras. The New Orleans Jazz Festival. Wild impromptu beach affairs in Daytona, Fort Lauderdale, Panama City, Florida. And that's just my younger years. Add in the raves in Amsterdam, the Love Parades in Berlin, the Rock am Rings in Nuremberg, and I'm a grizzled veteran of such experiences. What can one Vampire Ball in admittedly one of the most imposing castles in this land of imposing castles give to such a body of memories? That remains to be seen as we present our tickets and are admitted into the fray.

I'm feeling unnerved now, but in a pleasant way—if that's possible. Something happened in the Paracelsus Hall that I cannot quite reconcile in my borderline delirium. It was to do with physics, of that I think I'm sure. Physics or reality, if the two can be separated. Lauren became a slithering, then a falling thing. Gabe became the thing that keeps the dangerous defier of physics, of reality, in check. Or was it all an opium dream? Something devised by Morpheus to keep his own reality in question. I like to think it's that. That the heroin takes care of itself and we just play in the little pools it spills.

The Vampire Ball is a wondrous thing in this historical place. In my right mind I might find discrepancies between the eras, but what are the eras really? Medieval this, ancient that. What do such terms matter when you're talking in the present day about fortresses and monsters? If I happen to remember anything about this night it will be the adjectives that spring to a writer's mind—garish, loud, surreal, absurd, affected, false, fantastic.

I consider this in less than a moment's time before tossing myself into the wonder.

If Lauren's still with me, I don't know it as I work my way to the nearest bar and order something gassy.

"Gin and tonic?" the Lady of the Lake says.

"That will do!"

"Or did you mean bubbly, like champagne? Come to think of it, maybe you want a beer and a Jager. You'll have plenty of gas in the morning."

"The gin and tonic will do, thanks."

Why something gassy? Does the stomach revolt against

this heathen display? I laugh.

No one's to answer. Or to ask the question. Gabe and Lauren have gone off to wherever they've gone, leaving me alone with the vampires. As I look around at the costumes, I wonder for a moment what it would be like to be the real thing. Would you attend these parties to laugh at the mortals? Indeed, why wouldn't you? It would be a great cover. *Withered body found at the foot of one of the guard towers with puncture marks on neck. Culprit believed to be a delusional psychotic among Vampire Ball attendees.* Yes, it would be too, too easy.

I let my thoughts go as one of the fanged faces appears before me, slowly sticking out its tongue. I see the tablet on it but am reluctant to accept the invite after what I've read recently about the local authorities wanting to stem the drugs coming in. It's only a moment, enough time to ask myself, *What the fuck are you talking about, Rod?* Then I'm sucking it out of her mouth, not caring what it is, though suspecting it's what I went to Amsterdam for in the first place—X.

Will they mix, the X and the H? Who the fuck knows? Vampire Balls only come around once a year. Enjoy them while you can!

"Come, cowboy," I hear behind me. "Let's go home and pretend to make love."

I turn and it's Lauren, but it can't be her, the party's only just begun.

"You don't like our little gathering?" I say.

"Just want to know more about you, that's all."

"What's to know? I live, I hurt, I fear, I write about it all."

"Exactly."

But as we head for the exit, suddenly Gabe is there, something of the look I saw earlier in his features. As he glares at me, he speaks to her. "I told you, Lauren, it's to stay in house."

"I don't know what that *means*!" she hisses.

"It means," he says as he continues to stare at me, "that this man can't help you. None of them can help you. Now get your ass back inside. That or leave with me. Those are your only options."

"Or *what*? What will you do, Gabriel? Who the fuck do you even think you are? I didn't ask for this shit."

"Didn't you," he says on a breath, shifting his eyes to her at last. "Didn't you, with all your questions during my myth lit class?"

I know it best not to enter into this, but can't help myself. "So you're an instructor at the university, Gabe? I'd never have guessed, as young as you look."

Seems he can't help himself either as he turns to me, snapping, "I'm older than you could possibly realize."

"*Gabe!*" fires Lauren.

They stare at each other, during which strange, ticktocking moment he seems to lose his thunder, to slowly, painstakingly resign himself to the futility of it. "Very well then, Lauren," he says. "You're on your own now. Don't come to me again with your mortal angst. I'm finished."

But it isn't over. His words have softened her. "Gabe… please. I must have a life. I cannot be under your wing forever."

"Where there is shadow," he says, "there is safety. Remember that as you cavort with your memories of yourself. Goodbye, Lauren." To me, he nods. "Take care of her, writer."

It seems he will be on his way with those words, but at the last moment he pauses, looking me directly in the eyes: "Take care of *yourself*."

Until this moment, as the gaze we share lingers, it has been merely weird. Alarming to some part of me, yes, but mostly amusingly dramatic. But there is something in his eyes, in their penetrating quality, that chills me through my opiate insulation.

"Just let him be," Lauren says. "Let us both be."

He nods again and is gone.

***

Outside it is cold. Wonderfully cold to my lightly clad body. Lauren shivers, but it might be a memory, the passage of a ghost across her person. The lights of the Neckar River, on whose slopes the castle sprawls, enchant and disillusion at the same. On the opposite side of the river, closer to town, Lauren unnecessarily tells me, it's the *Philosophenweg*, where Heidelberg's philosophers and professors have traditionally walked with their thoughts or the company of their fellows. What that has to do with this side of the river, with the here and now, I don't know. Lauren has grown philosophical. Melancholy.

She guides me down a narrow road to a path that leads to a parapet. The parapet is not connected to the main castle, but is rather an extension, like the property's outlying towers. It rests atop an earthen rampart, one of several tiers ascending to the fortress. The view afforded is made grander by the knowledge that I stand upon a piece of history. Standing on the brick structure, I think I should like to take off from it, though the rampart is scarcely fifteen feet high, if that.

As if answering this unintended call, a shadow suddenly descends on us from the right. I hear Lauren scream, see her lifted up as if into the crook of a wing as I'm falling, gasping, splintering upon the ground below.

Three

SCARS
October, 2014

I was on a cruise on the Mosel River when I saw her again. Summer was over, the wine fests were finished, and it was harvesting time for the vineyards on the steep slopes of the larger body of water into which my own beloved Kyll River, a stream really, emptied.

It was a dinner boat, with all the perks, and I was alone on the upper deck enjoying a random finger delicacy and watching the evening scenery when she seemed to simply appear beside me at the rail. I didn't say anything at first, and neither did she, but when one of us finally did speak, it penetrated.

"Now do you know who I am, Roderick?"

"Yes, for the love of God."

"When did you come to realize?"

"I don't know? When I was dreaming about seeing the bones stick out of my leg? Why does it matter?"

"Why does it matter that we spent the most mysterious and revealing nights of our lives together?"

"Yeah, okay, why does it matter that we did that, Lauren? It was seven years ago."

"Have you found someone in the meantime?"

I glared at her. "How could I ever find someone after what you did to me?"

"Did to you? As I recall, it was just the opposite. I did *not* do what you wanted me to."

I looked at the lights of Bernkastel on the far bank and mumbled, "Whatever makes you right."

She joined me in surveying the scenery. "After a week of it, you wanted to die. Gabe *commanded* me to kill you. But I could never have done it. Not after that week…"

"*Why*? What do I have left? My mortality? Please."

"You don't understand, Roderick. You didn't understand then and you don't understand now. How could I know you would become so… involved. After Gabe's doctor friend set the broken bones, we were supposed to be living again. Remember?"

"I really don't care, Lauren. Whatever they were, they were never games for me, don't you get it? I'm from Timbuktu, Louisiana. I'm a country boy at heart."

She looked at me hard. "You know that's not true."

I sighed. "Go away, Lauren. I asked for it once. I won't ask again."

"What if I told you I'm ready to give it to you? That Gabe's dead? That I myself killed him?"

Though something stirred in me, I didn't let it outwardly known. "I would say you are lying. You're the slave now that you were then. What do you want from me?"

Our gazes met, and I could have sworn I saw a tear form in her eye, though I knew it was not possible. "To be with you," she said softly. "That's all."

"You are a lying, fucking *bitch*, Lauren. You wanted a child, that's all. You admitted it to me in your heroin delirium that last day. Where is that child, Lauren? It's been more than a year since I last saw you. Why are you fucking *here*?"

"Rod, I was young then. Just a one-year-old baby. I didn't understand. I thought I still had that much humanity left. I'm so much wiser now. You have to believe me."

I smirked. "So you're alone, without a baby. Gabe's gone. And you've now come back to me to give me the gift you wouldn't give me before. How very pat *if you live in a goddamn fantasy*. I wanted that fantasy once. Now I don't care. I just don't give a shit. You should have killed me while the two of you were bleeding me for your pleasure."

She looked away but then immediately snapped her head back again. "Don't pretend you didn't like it. That you didn't get off on it."

"And that changes something?"

"It does. I mean… it *must*. I know there is a connection between us, Roderick."

"Yeah, the edge of a blade." I turned my back to her and lifted up my shirt. "Remember?"

"Oh, Rod."

"Oh, Rod. Oh, fuck you. Kill me now or go the fuck away."

"I won't kill you. But I will…"

"I won't ask for it. Never again. I won't give you an invitation."

"I don't need one," she said.

I saw it in her eyes, felt the thirst emanating from her, and held up my hands to ward her off. "Stay back, Lauren. You can't want anything but the pleasure now, you sadistic bitch. There are plenty of others on this boat you can feed on."

Breathing heavily, she drew back, looking off at the lights of the random German town that served as the harbor for this equally random boat. The shadow of loss, regret passed across her features. But I wouldn't feel sorry for her. I would never give her what she had failed to give me.

Composed again, she said, "It was Gabe. You can't imagine the power they have over you."

"They?"

"The ones who make us. Our masters."

"Because he made you what you are, he was your master? It seems to me you could have run, hidden, become invisible—"

"Ha! There's no hiding from them. There's nowhere to go after they've given you…"

"Given you what? Say it, Lauren. After they've given you *immortality*?"

"Don't be crude."

I laughed. "Crude. Now that's a fucking irony. Almost as ironic as the fact that none of us ever said the words, as though they were so unreal they might destroy the whole contagious fantasy. Drink your blood like you mean it, Lauren. You didn't have any problem feeding me my own."

To my surprise she seemed shaken by that. "No," she said. "No, that's not how it was."

I'd no idea what to make of this reaction, so simply waited silently.

"He… Gabe, I mean… he said it was *his* blood, that he was contributing his power to the conception. That I could later come back to finish the job. But not then, not while we were trying to make a baby."

I shook my head. "Did it never occur to you, Lauren, that all of this was to some purpose other than your own? That while you were looking for a baby, he was looking for something else through what was obviously a ritual of some kind?"

Her lips parted, began to quiver. "You mean… you mean Kawa?"

"*Kawa*? Are you kidding me? What the fuck is Kawa? Are you on drugs now, Lauren?"

"It's… it's just—" she stammered. "Just something that came up occasionally."

"And? What the hell is it?"

"You won't believe me if I—"

"*What the hell is it, Lauren*?"

She pulled back from me, uttering the words as though they were the unholiest of unholies: "Kawa is a rite of communion with Aerthryr."

"And what is this air-whatever?"

It was a whisper now: "Demon."

My mouth fell open. "Oh my *God*, Lauren. You *are* out of your mind."

"It's our world, Roderick. It's the world you practically begged to be a part of."

"I was a fool," I said.

"Because you don't believe in monsters?"

"Because I do, Lauren! I believe in the possibility of physiological aberrations. Hell, I'll even give you a whole physical species that's been roaming this earth, hidden to mortal eyes, since God knows when. But this. This notion of some spirit world is a lot harder to swallow than—"

"Blood? Than blood, Roderick? I'm finished talking. Be with us now."

Before I could react, she was upon me. As her fangs sank into my flesh, all I could think was, *Oh Jesus, this can't be happening, this can't be happening, this can't be happening…*

And it wasn't.

***

I woke abruptly. In a cold sweat and confused. A moment to get my bearings, to realize it had only been a dream, and then I was mumbling a prayer to the gods on the off chance that there did indeed exist spirit realms. How real it had seemed. But no, *thank the gods, no!*, it had never happened. That week of being high, it was in the hospital, not in the hands of those monsters. My heroin had been rawer morphine for my wrecked leg.

Which led me to wonder, had the incident at the castle even happened in the way I thought it had? It wasn't until weeks after the strange woman had visited me at the mill that the details had begun to emerge. I'd thought my leg had been mangled in a freak accident involving drugs and alcohol. Mightn't her suggestions have shaped later memories? And even if they hadn't, mightn't I as easily have slipped at the scene and fallen on my own?

Yet she'd been there at my house that night. And she'd also taken me to the Vampire Ball years before. Of that I was reasonably certain, as those memories had come back even before she'd left me in my lonely millhouse to contemplate my existence. Then again, how could I be sure of anything in this world? One moment, you're a guy with a bad leg and some regrets; the next, you're part of some supernatural or hallucinatory universe. What was there really to think about when nothing, in the end, could be known?

I went to the medicine cabinet and popped two of my pain pills and returned to bed. Don't let me back in there, into that dream again, I gently implored the gods. And within a few moments was out again.

***

"Rod? Baby? Can you hear me?"

I woke standing in front of a mirror, this girl from some past there to guide me.

"See these marks on your throat, Roderick? They will forever remain with you. Scars of what you were. Scars of what you are now. They are neither to be admired nor regretted. They are what they are. What you make of the change they represent is all that matters. These were the words Gabe shared with me, and for all his faults, they are meaningful words. Ponder them as you undergo the last of your transformation. They're all I have for you. All anyone could expect, considering—though I remain here for you throughout the process. No, not your master. Your friend and lover. Together, we'll mold our world. We'll change what it means to be immortal."

I heard her words, crystal as a bell. But my eyes were looking beyond her through the mirror, to the chair on which Gabe sat, the short end of a large wooden crucifix protruding from his chest. To my suddenly awakened senses, it was a perfect sort of symbolism. A Euro, Christian-mythos kind of kiss to anyone who cared. I hadn't believed in that aspect of it before, and I didn't now, even through these awakened eyes.

"Get rid of him," I said "What's wrong with you?"

"So you're coming 'round?"

"Enough to know we're lying to ourselves just like mortals do."

"And if the picture isn't what it seems?" came a masculine voice.

I turned to the tableau of which he was the centerpiece and for reasons an immortal can't explain, was not struck dumb by his resurrection.

"Gabe," I nodded, casting a glance Lauren's way.

"Are you tired?" he said. "You've barely been able to move, much less speak, these last few days."

"Days? Has it been that long?"

"We had to carry you off the boat, with a little help from a member of the crew."

"Where are we now?"

"Why, Trier of course. That's where you live, isn't it?"

"This… this isn't my apartment."

"No," he smiled. "We weren't that bold. We're in my rental on the Ehrang side. It's not much, but it's done okay so far. So how do you feel, soldier? Are you swinging from the trees yet?"

"I… I don't know. Getting there maybe."

"Good, good. We want you to feel as comfortable as possible, of course."

I didn't know what to say to that, so shifted to the rational angle. "Aren't you dead?"

"Have been for a good while."

"And all the stuff before? Was that intended to help me along somehow?"

"One could logically assume that, yes."

I felt alive and disoriented at the same time. "Which means?"

"Which means you're asking too many questions. Wondering too much. Here, let Lauren provide you with another drink and we'll explore it later."

And on and on and on it went until finally the morning light spilled into my bedroom and I found myself not burning in it, but merely waking to another, otherwise normal day, with my leg aching and my heart beating regularly, mortally, in my chest.

Four

TOXINS
November, 2014

The mobile rang as I was rushing to finish the day's work, the major having given the entire 52nd Services Squadron the Wednesday afternoon off before the long Thanksgiving holiday weekend. I ignored it at first, but after hearing one too many rings, finally picked up.

"Hello?"

"Rod?"

"Yes?"

"It's Valerie Rousseau."

It didn't click immediately.

"Don't tell me you've forgotten your former mother-in-law."

"No, of course not, Val. Sorry, my mind was on my work. How are you?"

"Well, I've been better. Which is why I'm calling. Danielle's been hospitalized. A snake bite, if you can believe that. She's been in the hospital for several days now, and they're not sure what's going on. Some kind of reaction to the venom. The snake wasn't identified—hell, she didn't even know she'd been bitten until after she got back from a camping trip with her boyfriend and his kids—so they used something they call a polyvalent antivenom. Doctor says there's no cause for alarm at this point, that weird reactions occur from time to time and just need to be treated carefully. But I thought I should make you aware of the situation."

She had my full attention now. "Yes, thank you so much for calling, Val. How is she doing? Is she okay?"

"She's weak. And has a rash around her neck, where the snake bit her—"

"Her *neck*? How does one get bitten in the neck and not know it?" I could feel my heart missing beats.

"I don't know, Rod. Knowing this boyfriend of hers, they were probably drunk or stoned and she was passed out. She says that wasn't the case, but how else to explain it? I know she's been taking tranquilizers lately. Valium, I think. It kills me how they prescribe those things like they're candy. But apparently her antidepressants hadn't been doing the trick, so they decided in their great apathetic wisdom to just numb her."

"Valerie, this is a bit much to take. Since when has Danielle been on antidepressants?"

"Do I really need to tell you that, Rod? Since you divorced her, of course."

"Jesus. I've told you before, she divorced *herself* when she had an affair. Look, let's not get into this. Will you please let me know if her condition worsens? Better yet, are you at the hospital now? Can I talk to her?"

"I'm in the car."

"Well, what's her cell number? Is it the same one she had before? I assume she's okay to talk on the phone?"

"Goodness, yes. It's not *that* bad. Here's the number. Ready?"

Ready being a relative term? I took the number and clicked off. Tried not to think of the implications, if there even were any, as I finished up my work and drove home to the rental I'd moved into in Trier after my landlord at the watermill had decided to let his granddaughter and her husband have my fairy tale.

The place was spacious, more than comfortable enough for me, myself, and I. The owner lived on the ground floor of the typically large German house; I occupied the second floor. Often he would ask me when I was going to get married so he could stop feeling guilty about taking the generous cost of living allowance I got from the government. Had I no shame, he said, using almost all that I was allowed as a single person? (How he knew how much I was and wasn't allowed, I didn't know, unless he'd gleaned it out of a former American tenant.) My standard answer to his question in all its permutations was, *I may live in Germany, Herr Orenstein, but as a federal employee I'm still an American taxpayer. This is my money, and I won't feel ashamed using it. Besides, what do you care? You'd rather have a brood of hellion children running around tearing up the place? Or worse yet, some party animal with friends?* He always smiled at that, teaser that he was.

I sometimes wondered what Lauren would have thought of this residence, where the pictures I'd framed in Heidelberg so much better fit the furnishings that had come with the place, courtesy of Frau Orenstein and her fine touch. Would she have been amazed by how the sepia in the mottled hues of the couch complemented the French-matted da Vinci that hung above it, centerpiece of the living room? Would she have marveled at how the Klimpt so matched the golden-brown Italian marble tiles? Though I'd not seen her since—when was it? at the watermill? the parapet at the castle?—I found myself, illogically, missing her at times. This afternoon was such a time as I ate a sandwich and watched some news before calling Danielle.

She answered on the third ring. "Hellooo."

It was more a drawl than a greeting. Which naturally concerned me as I let the volume down on the TV, focusing in on this woman with whom I hadn't spoken in years.

"Danielle? It's Rod. "

"Hi Rod." She sounded sleepy. Weak, as her mother had said. "I haven't heard from you in soooo long. How're you, baby. Are you coming to rescue me from the snakes?"

Baby? Was she drugged?

"Your mom called and told me what happened. Are you okay? How are you feeling?"

What might have been an attempt at a laugh came through. "Feeeeling? Feeling a little woused, that's how. I don't know what it put in my body, but it feels wicious. You going to come and give me the good medicine, Wod, like y'used to?"

"Jesus, Danielle. What have they got you on? And why? For a snake bite?"

"Snake bite. Yeah, that's what it was. A little boy snake with loooong teeth."

"What do you mean, Danielle?" Her words, along with the way in which they were delivered, chilled me, though I could not have said exactly why. "Where are you? What hospital? Are you still in Baton Rouge?"

"I'm here baby. Come and give me the medicine. I

miiiiiss you. Shhh! Don't tell Chris."

"Just give me the name of the hospital, okay?"

"Nurse! What's the name of this place?"

"The hospital? Our Lady of the Lake," I heard in the background. "Get that, Rod?" Danielle said. "King Arthur like. Come soon with the medicine, 'k?"

"Okay, Danielle. Can I speak to the nurse?"

But she'd closed the connection. Come give me the medicine, bye.

***

The medicine was sex. She'd used to playfully refer to it as that. Which probably took some of the sacredness out of making love. But it was just a flirt, a form of foreplay. Talking about sex in advance made her horny. This suited me just fine for a time. After a couple years of marriage, there was no sacredness left anyway. Eventually, however, my tolerance for her flirts wore thin, which is likely why she looked elsewhere for her medicine.

Strangely, hearing her talk that way to me again stimulated me. I ignored the sensation at first, dismissed it as perverse, unfair to her and unworthy of me, considering her situation. But the more I thought about her, the more aroused I became, and in the end I went into the bathroom and relieved myself of all the frustration, picturing her in her most decadent position while releasing tensions that otherwise had nothing to do with her.

Afterward, I thought about how long it had been since I'd had sex, or even masturbated. Who wanted me now after all, gimp that I was? But I knew that wasn't it, not really. I could perform; nothing had changed in that department. And on my good days I could almost entirely disguise my limp. Which made me, I suppose, an on-again, off-again cripple. One without the power to flip the switch.

Never mind, I thought as I got a beer from the refrigerator and turned on the TV. I found myself only half listening to the CNN story, however, as my thoughts drifted from Danielle and her circumstances to whether I should go out this afternoon or stay home and try to write (either of which would mark the first time in a while). I had plans for the holiday weekend. Tomorrow, after talking to family in the States, I was going to get in the Jeep and do a tour of the Mosel River valley and the Rhine Gorge. One-way, the trip from Trier to Bingen—by way of Koblenz, where the Mosel emptied into the Rhine— was only a couple hundred kilometers. But I'd be locating at inns along the way, spending the afternoons visiting castles and other attractions or just lazing on the river bank with a cold beer or a bottle of Mosel wine. The vineyards wouldn't be sporting that vibrant green color they did before the grapes were harvested, when their foliage literally carpeted the slopes, but there would still be the scent on the air.

But that was tomorrow. Today—if I could get up off my ass—would have the flavor of spontaneity, once a very close friend of mine. Yup, let's do it, I decided. And no use waiting. Anytime was a good time to walk around Trier's Old Town, nibbling on those greasy potato patties before settling in at a nice German restaurant for some *Jagerschnitzel* and Bitburgers.

Anytime was a good time to get away from the toxins of the nightmares and snake bites for a while.

***

As it turned out, freeing my mind wasn't a simple matter of finding diversions for myself. From the moment I arrived at the town center, the unwanted thoughts nagged at me. As I stood before the *Porta Nigra*, the massive, weather-blackened gate that served as the entrance to the Walkplatz and Square, I wasn't thinking about the ancient Romans who built the structure, but of a hospitalized woman with wounds in her neck—the neck I used to kiss. As I toured St. Peter's cathedral, it wasn't the lofty ceilings of its baroque interiors I considered, but what I should do if Danielle's condition worsened.

I'd experienced a foreboding when Valerie informed me of the situation, and the unease had never really left. Certainly not after talking to Danielle, though that conversation had disquieted me in a different way. A part of me said I was overreacting, that my fears were to do with past experiences, not present ones; and that Danielle was clearly not in any serious danger, her lethargic speech not-withstanding. However tempting it was to find meaning, to see *motifs* in the coincidences, they were still just a set of coincidences.

Rationally, I believed this. The trouble was containing the more fanciful thoughts, the ones that ran with perceived feelings that something lay underneath it all; and that the only way I might be able to get close to that something would be to take leave from work and fly to America to question Danielle, to look with my own eyes at those marks on her neck. What had that other French girl, the half-French, half-German one, done to me? Would she forever haunt me? Wasn't it enough that I carried her memory in my leg?

To my credit, I did manage to get a grip whenever my thoughts strayed too far, and was eventually able to go about my afternoon with a minimum of unpleasantness. I stopped for dinner at a place off the Square called *Der Schwarzwalder*, ordering *Jagerschnitzel mit Pommes und Salat*, my favorite German meal. Dipping the thick fries in the richly dark mushroom sauce and washing them down with a fine German *Pils* was the best experience in the world as far as I was concerned. When the waitress came around for my plate, I asked her to pass along my compliments to the kitchen, and ordered another beer. As I was resting back in my seat to watch the evening passersby through the window, my phone rang.

Had I been less relaxed, the foreboding might have returned before I actually heard the voice at the other end.

"It's Valerie again, Rod. The doctor wants to talk to you. I told him you had nothing to do with this, that you were in Germany for godsakes. But he's insisting. They've discovered Danielle's been taking Valium while in their care—I'm guessing now that that asshole Chris gave the pills to her—and they're none too pleased. She's gotten worse just in the hours since you spoke to her. When asked why she would risk her health that way while under medical treatment, she told the doctor to ask you. Kept murmuring some nonsense about you telling her to do it to 'make the transformation easier.' I tried to tell them that you hadn't spoken to her in years before that call, but—"

Another voice, its owner apparently having taken the phone from her, replaced hers. "Mr. Lachance? Yes, I'm Doctor Allen. I'm caring for your ex-wife. Mrs. Rousseau has explained the gist of it to you. I just need to ask you a couple of questions."

It took a moment to get my reply out because I was so stunned, I couldn't think. "Yes, of course. Whatever you need."

"Before this morning, when was the last time you spoke to Danielle?"

"Jesus. I can't even remember, it's been so long."

"Do you have a son, Mr. Lachance?"

"A son? What—" My heart was suddenly drumming. "No, I have no son."

"I ask because Danielle has this notion that your kindergarten-aged son visited her at the campground where she was staying when she was bitten—"

"What?" came Val's voice in the background. The rest was faint, but it sounded like, "You didn't tell me she said *that*?"

"Please, Mrs. Rousseau." Then: "Mr. Lachance?"

"I'm here."

Was I? Or was I remembering a drugged voice talking about *a little boy snake with loooong teeth?*

"Do you have any idea what Danielle could be talking about? I'm by no means ruling out that she's delusional, but she was pretty specific when she described the boy telling her he was there camping with his uncle Gabe."

Oh Christ. Oh Jesus, this can't be happening.

"Sir? Are you there?"

"Are you her medical doctor or a psychiatrist? What does any of this have to do with treating her for a snake bite?"

"Mr. Lachance, I'm only trying to ascertain whether we should be worried about more than a snake bite."

What? What could he be saying?

"If she has other problems, we have to take that into account when treating her. The Valium's caused enough problems on its own. Given that it could be interacting adversely with other chemicals in her body, I've never known a tranquilizer to produce these kinds of delusions. Tranquilizers shut the body down. They don't wake up the imagination like this. Particularly when a person's been taking the dosage she has. Which leads me to the main point of this conversation. Did you in any way, either personally or through another party, influence Danielle to take these drugs?"

"No, goddamnit."

"Very well. Thank you for your time—"

"Wait. I need to know if she's going to be all right."

"I can't answer that at this point."

A wail from Valerie in the background. I was surprised she'd kept it in that long, considering the content of the side of the conversation she could hear.

"Nurse, please take her out of the room."

"What room?" I said. "Are you in Danielle's room now? May I speak to her?"

"Hold a minute." A second or two passed before he continued. "Okay, we're alone now. Mr. Lachance, you cannot speak to Danielle. We haven't yet told Mrs. Rousseau, but Danielle is in a state of unconsciousness that very soon will be labeled a coma if she continues to fail to respond to stimuli. We considered gastric lavage—pumping her stomach—after locating the empty prescription bottle. But results from lab tests run earlier, when the nurse alerted me to her increasingly slurred speech, indicated that this would be a futile—and already risky in her condition—path to take. She'd been ingesting the tranquilizers, probably in increasing amounts, for days. To be honest, we're left wondering what previous diagnoses can now be attributed to what. It is a strange and difficult case, but we're doing everything we can for her, I assure you."

"I understand. But why haven't you told Mrs. Rousseau yet? She seemed more concerned about me than her daughter before you got on the phone."

"It is not that we have intentionally withheld anything from her. We cannot term it a coma until a certain amount of time has passed. Nor have we concluded definitively— if you can ever get that in medicine—that Danielle's state of unconsciousness is due strictly to an overdose. As far as Mrs. Rousseau is concerned, we're running tests—which we most certainly are, on an ongoing basis. I'd like to keep it that way for at least a little while longer. If we understand each other, Mr. Lachance…?"

I sighed. "Thank you for being forthright with me. Now let me ask you—is it time for me to start thinking about buying a plane ticket to the States?"

"That entirely depends on you, Mr. Lachance. You don't seem to have maintained a relationship with Danielle, yet I can see that you—"

"I'm asking you, Doctor, if there's the possibility that she will die."

"There is that possibility, yes," he said gravely.

"Likelihood?"

"Let me continue to be frank. We don't know what's wrong with her. We didn't know before. We know little more now. In my personal opinion, when considering the body of symptoms, Valium is a secondary player."

"And in your professional opinion?"

"Unfortunately, this is one of those rare cases where I'm forced to admit I've failed to establish one."

"Let me have your number. I'm getting on a plane as soon as I can."

Five

POOLS
Black Friday, 2014

As I sleep on the transatlantic flight, I am walking in the forested wetlands in which the campground is nestled. There are willows, cypresses, water elms, and hickories surrounding me. Cattails and alligatorweed and a thousand other plants in the freshwater bayou. I've been here before, or to some place very much like it, but names escape me. Is it a state park? A refuge? There are so many in Louisiana, who can remember every one they've visited?

This one is different, though. This one is home to the campground where my uncle… Gabe, was it? …used to take me. Yes, I do know this place better than the others, in spite of my memory lapse. There's nothing random or nameless about it after all, I realize. Its map is built into my constitution. It is a part of me, my childhood as a pre-schooler. How else could I be so easily following its trails through the marshes? I'm looking for something. A particular pool, it seems to me, among the many pools occurring around the inlets and outlets of the river that flows through here. Yes, there's something I must see at that pool, as I did as I child.

As I recall, it has a surface like a mirror. Captures the branches and leaves of the trees exquisitely. It might be a child's fantasy, true, but why am I here if not to prove the fantasy real? We've little enough time to dream in our adult lives. Why spend any of it trying to qualify what we've yet to discover again? As I pick through the small bodies of water I remember a feature of a book I read in middle school. Read again as a teen, and then watched in motion picture form as an adult. The Mirror of Galadriel, the author named it, after its keeper. A basin filled with water in which one might see the past, present, or future. Yes, this pool's like that one, though the boy who looked into it had never heard of Tolkien or his trilogy.

I sense it is near now. My uncle has led me here without actually taking my hand, as he will lead me to where the woman my father was once married to sleeps, sedated, on a hammock between the trunks of two live oaks. Is it now or then—who knows when you're the victim of your memories, for a pleasant change, instead of your experiences. Or is it the other way around as I step out of a thicket and finally see the pool shining like glass in the sunlight spilling through the canopy?

What is on offer, Galadriel? Can you at least guide me if you cannot, yourself, predict what I will see? She does not answer. For this is not her pool, it is mine and mine alone. An answer lies here. An answer to questions from another world. If it is not forthcoming, I shall conjure it up out of the depths of the glass. Invoke it, as Uncle Gabe has said he invokes. *Whisper his name once for every year of your former life. Five is a magic number. It was the number he chose for you when he allowed your virgin mother to bear you.*

"Virgin, Uncle? What does that mean?"

Among them it can mean unwed, undefiled, or innocent, the latter of which can be interpreted in different ways, depending on your patience and your interpretations of their tiresome morals and scripts. Among us it is less complicated. It simply means forever barren.

"What is barren?"

Unable to bear children.

"I don't understand."

Nor are you supposed to. Being a virgin yourself, you are to come into it like a cherub. Go now, to the pool and call him forth. We've work to do, young man. Remember his name. Pronounce it correctly lest we be deemed disrespectful.

I look upon the surface of the pool now, and I imagine I see him waiting. *Oh, glass, produce our master Aerthryr. Come forth, Aerthryr. Guide us, Aerthryr. Be among us, Aerthryr, as we do your duty. Aerthryr, we call thee, Aerthryr, come forth out of the depths that we may serve thee.*

I'm an adult, but I've had fangs since I was young. Young as I am now, Lauren.

Wherever you are.

***

Danielle was dead when I arrived, on Black Friday. As I left the airport, the first person I called was Doctor Allen, who delivered the news to me, adding that the body had already been moved to the funeral home. I tried Valerie, but apparently she was too exhausted with grief and incoming calls to answer. I could imagine her husband, a deeply religious man, saying Danielle was in God's hands now. But for her, it would be traumatic. She'd been a terror of love to her daughter when we were married. It couldn't have changed much since then.

Regardless, I had to go pay respects before I did what I knew I had to do, which was to visit the park where she'd been camping. The doctor hadn't had an answer to that. He'd learned from Danielle or her mother only that it was a state park. The boyfriend had conveniently never been around when the doctor was, apparently delivering the goods to Danielle at night, before visiting hours ended. Hopefully Valerie could at least point me in his direction. Maybe, just maybe, I could convince him to take me there. If he even gave a shit.

I did my diligent duty at the funeral home, inquiring as to when the body would be available for view and wrapping both parents in my embrace, feeling guilty for so many things, not least seeking information from them while they were here to take care of the details.

"Don't contact him," Valerie tearily said. "What good will it serve? You see he's not here now. He just doesn't care. Let it be."

"I'm not concerned about him or his feelings, Val. I just want to go to the campground. I want to be where she was when it happened."

"Valerie," said her husband. "Give him the number or address, whatever you have. He's a right to remember her however he wants. Roderick, at least, was good to her."

She gave me both, and with kisses to the both of them, I left.

He didn't answer my call as I sat in the rental car, prepared to pursue the thing to its conclusion right now, though I was lagging from the flight, with night fast approaching. I tried a second time on the phone I'd bought at the airport. This time there was an answer.

"Hello." It was a male child's voice.

"Hello, yes, is your father home?" I remembered the name at the last moment. "Chris. I'm looking for Chris."

"He's not available right now."

"Well, is he at home?"

"I'm sorry, I can't talk to strangers." And he clicked off.

You *may not talk to me*, I thought as I turned the key in the ignition. *But someone will, I swear it.*

I drove the fifteen miles to the rural address I'd put

into the rental's GPS and waited for a couple of minutes in the dark gravel area in which an old Ford truck was parked while I planned my approach. If he was the loser I envisioned, then God help him; I already had the tire iron at the ready and would gladly use it on him if he refused to take me to the site of the incident. If he half convinced me he wasn't the guy I thought he was, then I'd give him the option of putting his kids into safe hands before forcing him to accompany me. Thank God neither scenario played out.

When no one answered my knock, I turned the knob. The door was unlocked, which I supposed was no big surprise out here in the boonies, whether they were home or not. "Hello," I called as I entered cluttered interiors that reminded me of the house my grandmother had lived in all of her adult life before she died of pneumonia. "Anyone home?"

No one answered. Nor, now that I thought about it, had the Ford truck seemed other than a worthless relic where it sat outside listening to the nightly song of the crickets. Convinced that no one was home, I took the liberty of rummaging around, looking for anything that might be of use to me. I of course expected to find nothing. Who kept state park literature after the fact? But after a few minutes of digging through piles of bills and other miscellany, that's exactly what I found—a leaflet for what had to be the place I sought: Hickory Chip State Park. On the back of the brochure there was a small map showing the park's location. It was some thirty miles west of here, off the same state road that had led me to this house.

I stuffed the brochure in my back pocket and went to the car. As I was about to open the door, lights appeared through the trees that surrounded the long drive, which wound around a boggy area on its way to the house. A moment later the car itself appeared, blinding me with its brights before the driver, obviously seeing me, dimmed and then completely shut off the headlights while still rolling to a stop.

The only light to be had now was the porch light, which merely served its immediate vicinity. While I couldn't have identified the make of the hatchback as my eyes readjusted to the dark, it was evident to me that its windows were tinted. For when the driver turned on what must have been the overhead interior light after shutting off the engine, I saw only a faint, concealed glow. Some seconds passed—time enough for me to calculate how long it would take me to get to the tire iron lying under the front seat of my rental—before the driver's door came open. Why I felt danger was uncertain to me as a tall, thin man unfolded out of the vehicle, closing the door behind him. Perhaps because I, myself, had brought it?

"Hello," I said. "You must be wondering who this stranger in your driveway is?"

"We get them from time to time," he said. "What do you want?"

Cozy greeting, I thought as I decided not to scramble for excuses, but to put it out there exactly as it was. "My name is Roderick Lachance. I was married to—"

"I asked you what you want, not who you are. Spill it or get off my property."

I held the anger in check, but at the same time refused to mince words. "I want to know where you and Danielle were when she was bitten by the snake."

As he responded, the interior light came on again in the car. "Who is Danielle and what are you talking about?"

I wasn't sure which of the two instances to be more alarmed by—the light coming on or his denial of knowing Danielle. It was natural that he'd have his children with him, but the finality with which he'd closed the door had left the car vacant to my senses. As to his not knowing Danielle, well, that was another matter.

"I'm not in a very good mood, Chris. I've had a long flight and—"

"How do you know my name? Are you one of those asshole thieves from over at the Cranston place? Coming 'round introducing yourself to get a lay of the land? I'll fillet your ass like you do the game you poach."

The passenger door came open, and out stepped a woman whose face was turned from me as she folded her seat to let one, two, now three children out of the car. There was something disturbingly familiar about her as she closed the door behind the last child, a young boy who now stood staring at me while his siblings ran off toward the front door. I barely heard Chris's next words as her face finally came into view.

"I think it's time you climbed back in your car, stranger, and got your ass out of here."

"Never mind, Chris," said Lauren. "I know this man. Don't I, Roderick?"

I had no words. It must be another dream. That could be the only explanation for it.

"Cat got your tongue?" said the boy, displaying a smile in which I imagined I saw the flash of *two looong snake teeth.*

"Meet my son, Paul," Lauren said. "He was once Saul, before the conversion."

"Is—is he *mine*?" I stammered. Knowing the years didn't match up, but remembering the world they ostensibly existed in.

She looked at Chris, who was now staring across the hood at the boy.

"Chris has two children. I have one. Together, we form an episode of—"

"You never told me Paul had a *father*?" Chris said.

"Why of course he does, darling. What did you think? He materialized out of thin air?"

"You said he was a test tube baby."

"And so he was," she said pertly. "Test tube babies aren't immaculate conceptions in a bottle, love. But admittedly, I might have misled you a little. There was no fluid medium. I myself am the test tube."

"*What the fuck is going on here?*" I released. "What did you do to Danielle?"

"Judging by your concern, and if I in fact knew a Danielle, I'd say she's probably gone on to a better place."

Before I could absorb it, much less react, Chris came in again: "And this guy standing here right now—*he's* Paul's father?"

"I didn't say that," Lauren said. "Though you might say he was a… *facilitator*. Wouldn't you agree, Roderick?"

I'm going to wake up any second. Any instant now. This

isn't happening. None of it ever happened. I carry histories into dreams with me, and none of it, neither past nor present, is real.

"What about the future?" Lauren said to me. "Have you thought about that?"

She's not in my head. Except in the sense that I've created her. My mind conjured all of them up on a heroin-substitute trip gone bad. Yes, that's what happened. I was lying back on my bed in that student apartment in Heidelberg, a knock came, and then phoof! Existence as I knew it ceased to be.

"And yet, Danielle remains dead, doesn't she?" It was the little boy, flashing white again.

Shouldn't he still have baby teeth at his age, even in a dream?

"Who, for fuck's sake, is *Danielle*?" Chris demanded.

"Do you remember, Chris, when we watched *The Last Temptation of Christ*?" Lauren said. "Remember what the last temptation was? A trick of Satan's where Christ was offered the life of a mortal instead of dying on the cross as God's son and the savior of man? Do you remember the contradicting realities?"

He was clearly confused. "I guess. I mean I think so. I might have been high that night."

"Well, this *isn't* like that."

Upon which she turned and stared me directly, penetratingly, in the eyes.

"*Is* it, O Roderick, Keeper of Even Scarier Flames? In this story there are no contradicting realities, are there? You were offered the fruit and chose instead to father the serpent that did the offering."

"I *chose* nothing."

"Didn't you, you fiend? Didn't you call upon Aerthryr, himself, to assist?"

"Gabe did that! Not me."

"*Gabriel*? Ha! Who do you think you are if not that God-despising archangel? You were tired of delivering His messages to the mortals, so you decided to deliver a different one, with help from the other side. You made me, and then, with that high demon Aerthryr's assistance, you made our hybrid. That all of creation might laugh in His face. I know you, angel. It took some time, but I know you now. Flaunting yourself in your vampire outfit. Imagining that you, too, can be at least affiliated with mortality, if only in some vague, viperine way."

"Enough!" came a voice from behind me. I whirled, and there, in the flesh, stood Gabe. "We've toyed with him enough," he said. "Will you finish the job, Lauren, or shall I?"

"You do it, Gabriel. You've always done it best."

I'd turned back to her as she spoke, but I couldn't tell whether she was looking at him or me.

It didn't matter. I was in the car and driving again now, and it was only Gabe beside me.

***

We walked along the park's dark paths, lost in the cacophony of insects and frogs. I didn't know what I felt. How to feel. Who or what I was. I knew only that, whatever came next, I had already been transformed. I had tasted the fruit of the branch and been introduced to worlds without end. Did vampires exist? Did gods? Did

angels and devils? I didn't know. But I did know this: I was here, now, my senses alive to my environment. I knew that I was being led by a figure whose pale skin seemed to glow from some internal source in the darkness. I knew that he called himself Gabe and I called myself Roderick. And that we were headed toward a pool I had visited previously, and yet never in my lifetime. I knew that these lifetimes were ephemeral and strange, if they occurred at all. I knew sensation, finally. Or the perception of it. And perhaps that, in the end, was what it was all about.

As my thoughts broke up, dissipated among the flying insects, my guide suddenly turned to me, an earnest look on his face. "Let's have sex," he said. "Here and now, before it can never be known between us again."

"You feel that way about me?" I asked.

"I know you're straight. I know you're what most of your kind are. But you are a part of me, don't you see? Or soon will be. I saw how you made Lauren feel. I want to feel that way again, before it's too late. If you like I can come to you as a woman. It's within my power…"

"Do that, yes. Be a woman to me and I will be a man to you."

"Do you want me to be Lauren?"

"Yes! God yes!! Be Lauren, delivering herself to me with the fall of night."

"I did, you know." Becoming her even as he spoke. "I came to you, with the fall of night. And you partook of me even though you knew what I was. You gave yourself to me and I gave myself in return. And the rest of it—what's real and what's not, what's right and what's not—can any of it really matter in the embrace of such magic?"

"It doesn't," I whispered, accepting her mouth, her tongue, all the liberties of her as I flung her to the ground, ripping her pants off and turning her so that her ass was to me, and mounted her, freed animal that I was amongst the wild chorus of the bayou. I gave her all that she asked for and more as the juices of the fruit of the Tree of Mortality and Immortality flowed down my legs, my face, my very soul in this, its last dance.

When it was finished, when we'd cum a half dozen times between us, I felt empty, as I had as the masturbating pubescent. But the feeling would soon go, along with the guilt and all the other mortal concerns. We didn't speak about it as we continued along the trail. There was nothing to say that her now absolutely luminous flesh didn't already say. We'd paired in some interim between worlds, and that was the first and the middle and the last of it. Story, among the endless stories, told. Now was to find the next one among the dusty texts. Now, for me, was to find the secret that made our union such a thrilling, wondrous mystery.

And at last we have arrived. The surface of the pool, as the three of us gather around it, is as luminous as Lauren's skin. What must we call out of it to validate what has already been validated? The demon? The snake that bit Danielle? God Himself?

But no, as Lauren murmurs her invocations, I suspect it is something less crude than that. Something… fairer. Like the home I once lived in on the banks of the Kyll River. Like the home I once had with a wife who later learned she could not bear children and changed her view of the world as a nurturing thing to one of an indiscriminately punishing existence. I mourned her as I stood here awaiting my fate. She'd been something to me once, in my own failures as a human being.

Lauren, finished with her prayers, now turned to me. "You'll have to recite the name, of course. One time for as many years as you've been alive as a mortal. Thirty-three is a magic number. Wasn't it Jesus's age when he was tempted on the cross? All you've to do is welcome him, by name, up into your world."

"What name?"

"What name?" she said, frowning and smiling at the same time. "I'd have thought that obvious by now."

"Is it Aerthryr?"

"Aerthryr? Are you really talking about Aerthryr? The way is with you, Roderick, not myths and monsters."

"What name, Lauren? Let's have it done."

"Look into the mirror of the pool and you'll find it."

I did, and all I saw was my own reflection. Superimposed upon itself that many times.

"Don't waste it," she said as she sank her teeth into my neck. "It's what will speak for you when Judgment Day comes."

EPILOGUE
August, 2004

You look for the tomorrows, but somehow they never arrive as soon as you'd like. You've tried to talk to her, to reason with her, but there's no reasoning with a woman who treats sex as a pastime, a sport, and then finds herself devastated when she learns she can't conceive a child. You've told her it's okay, there are other ways, but she hasn't spoken to you since starting on the half-liter bottle of vodka that has put her in the state she's in now as she sleeps beside you, oblivious to your own restlessness.

"Danielle," you say aloud. "What is it you want from me?"

Though she is a rock where she lies, you can hear her saying, as she's done so many times before, "I want you to acknowledge that your writing gets you, gets us, nowhere. Find a real job, Rod. Be what a man's supposed to be."

It seems strange to you, mixing the two marital problems. But didn't she in fact, during tonight's hellish backlash, blame her barrenness on your writing? *If you put as much into the act of sex as you did your writing, maybe we wouldn't be having this discussion.* That she corrected herself almost immediately after making the statement did nothing to mitigate its effect. Indeed, the next words were worse: *God! And all along I thought it was you with the problem, with your forever limp dick.*

She's a sexual creature, your wife. You've always known it. You even enjoyed it in the early days. Yet lately you seem to only be able to forgive her for it. The two of you parted company some time ago—if not in practice then in spirit. Life came again when she started talking about having a baby. Though you were skeptical, you entertained the notion that maybe, just maybe, better tomorrows were on the horizon. What a fool you were to think so. Her cold heart is her barrenness. There's nothing external about it. You suspected it the day she brought home the Viagra. You know it with certainty now. You cannot please her. She's dead to your kind of emotion; it's her nature.

So you toss and turn while she sleeps. Wondering what's next in this wasted union...

***

"Lauren, sweetheart," I said as I got up out of bed and went to the bathroom to relieve myself. "You're going to be late for work." It seemed a strangely normal thing to

say after yesterday's news and the unpleasant evening that ensued...

I heard her turn, probably checking the clock. A moment passed before she spoke. When she did, it was completely devoid of warmth: "Wait, what did you say? Lauren? Who the hell's Lauren?"

"What? I didn't say that."

"Yes you did."

"Just a minute, babe." I flushed the toilet and washed my hands and face. When I stepped into the room, she was in a sitting position on the bed, looking at me darkly.

"Baby, stop," I said. "I must have been dreaming, that's all."

"I don't bring names back from dreams with me."

No, you just bring the eroticisms, I didn't say.

"Well?" she persisted.

"Well what, Lauren? You're making something out of—"

She threw the covers off her lap, leaped out of bed, and literally attacked me.

"I don't know what I'm saying, Danielle, I swear," I said as I warded off her blows. "It's last night. I had nightmares. I must still be fucked up over it."

"That's the lamest goddamn thing I've ever heard!" she screamed, still pummeling me. "Now I know why you can't perform. It's because you have someone on the side!"

"Baby, *please*. I swear to God I don't know any Lauren."

It took some time, but eventually she relented. I didn't kid myself into thinking it was because she believed me. On the contrary. She'd probably decided, yeah, okay, now I'm *really* free to pursue other interests. But where *had* that name come from, I wondered as she went into the bathroom, presumably to get ready for work. They still have to do that, don't they, after they find out they're barren? Get ready for work?

Weird Reflections

Weird Reflections

By Mike Davis

Photo courtesy of Mike Davis

The problem with reading Lovecraftian fiction *used* to be that there wasn't enough of it. Back in the day when I discovered a new Lovecraftian anthology at the bookstore, I didn't even think about it—I just bought it. Today, though, there are a plethora of Lovecraftian books on the market. Too many, really, for one person to read. That's what I call a good problem to have.

There are, in my opinion, two primary types of Lovecraftian fiction: mythos, and cosmic horror. Mythos refers to Lovecraftian fiction that is to one degree or another set in the universes established by H.P. Lovecraft, and make use of his tropes. Cosmic horror, on the other hand, does not rely on any of Lovecraft's creations, focusing instead on the themes in his work—most prominently, the insignificance of mankind.

Let me be clear that the terms "mythos" and "cosmic horror" are *my* way of differentiating between types of Lovecraftian fiction. You may disagree, and that's fine. Let me also be clear that I don't consider mythos fiction to be inferior to cosmic horror, because there are some very, very good examples of both.

On to those examples, then. Recently in the "mythos" category: The novel *That Which Should Not Be* by Brett J. Talley and the novel *Reanimators* by Pete Rawlik. I enjoyed both books immensely, and I can't imagine any Lovecraft fan who would disagree. The recent *X's For Eyes* by Laird Barron is—in my view—mythos as well. (I hear that *X's For Eyes* may be the first in a series; if true, we're all in for a horrifically good time.)

Three recent examples in the "cosmic horror" category: *Revival* by none other than Stephen King, *The Glittering World* by Robert Levy, and *The Visible Filth* by Nathan Ballingrud. Wonderful novels, all.

What *is* Lovecraftian fiction and what *isn't* can sometimes be a touchy topic with diehard fans. Some feel that for a book or film to be "Lovecraftian" it has to be set in New England in the 1920s and it must reference one or more of the gods of H.P. Lovecraft, cults, insanity, or all of the above. But I see "Lovecraftian fiction" as a large trunk, with "mythos" and "cosmic horror" branching from it, and perhaps even a third branch that I'll call "Lovecraft-influenced."

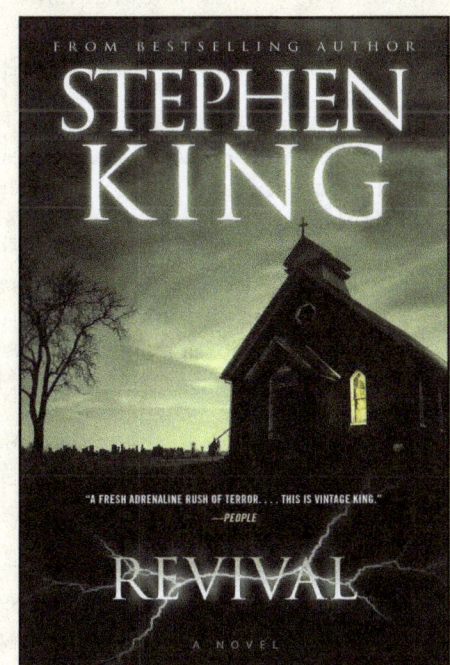

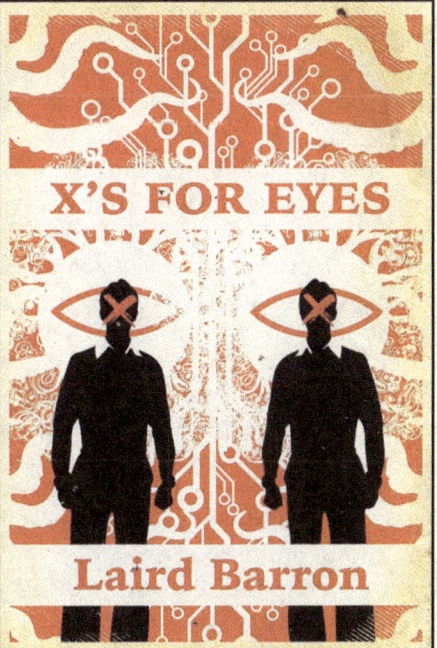

Debating whether something is Lovecraftian or not doesn't really interest me, but I do take exception to books, games, and films that name-drop Lovecraft's name, gods, or locations simply to call themselves Lovecraftian.

In addition to the titles listed above, I hope you'll allow me to recommend a few authors and books to you. Just a few. I'll continue to do so in the issues to come. Consider this simply a beginning.

Red Equinox, a novel by Douglas Wynne. I've been aware of Doug for several years now, and I had the pleasure of meeting him in person at NecronomiCon 2015 in Sesqua Valley.

Dark Energies, poems by Ann K. Schwader. Many consider Schwader to be *the* Lovecraftian poet working today. If you're into Lovecraftian poetry, pick this one up.

The Starry Wisdom Library, an anthology edited by Nate Pedersen. Something different... really different. I won't even attempt to describe it. Instead I'll just quote from the inside cover flap: "The greatest occult book auction of all time... the sale, of course, never materialized—as later events make obvious—but the book auction catalogue informs us of the cult's original intent and leaves for us

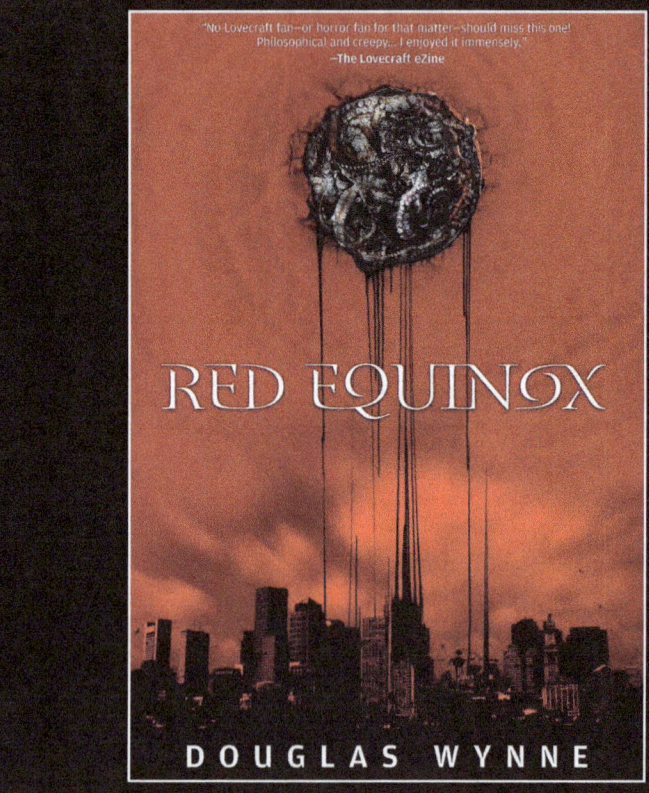

Providence. It was his recent novel *Red Equinox* that really grabbed my attention, though. Well written, creepy, and philosophical, it falls squarely into the mythos category.

Displaced Person, a novel by Lee Harding. This little novel will stay with you for a long time, if you can find a copy. Published in 1979, *Displaced Person* tells the story of a seventeen-year-old boy who slowly becomes aware that more and more people are ignoring him. The world becomes gray and soon he cannot interact with anyone. In his words: "We are all pawns in a game so vast we will never be able to confront the forces which control our destinies..." If that isn't cosmic horror, then I don't know what is.

The Revenant of Rebecca Pascal, a novel by David Barker and W.H. Pugmire. The atmosphere in this book is so rich, so wonderful, that I didn't want the book to end. And let me take this opportunity to say a few words about W.H. Pugmire: A self-proclaimed "Lovecraft fanboy," he, more than any other writer I know, epitomizes the spirit of Lovecraftian fiction. If you haven't read his work, you've got a lot of catching up to do. Just go to Amazon and type his name in the search box. Pick anything. Enjoy. Discover

an enormously valuable and fascinating piece of ephemera detailing the infamous collection..."

The Broken Hours, a novel by Jacqueline Baker. I'm not sure that this novel really fits into either of my categories... and that's fine. *The Broken Hours* was first published in Canada, and it proved nearly impossible to purchase a copy if you lived elsewhere. I'm happy to report that this book will soon be available in the US from Talos Press. As I write this, it's available for pre-order at Amazon. In 1936, Arthor Crandle accepts a position as a live-in assistant for an unnamed shut-in that he knows only as "Ech-Pi." He soon becomes aware of an ominous presence in the house...

The Gods of H.P. Lovecraft, an anthology edited by Aaron J. French. Honestly, I wanted to use another example of a recent mythos anthology, because the editor of this book also happens to be the editor of the magazine you're reading. But that's not a good reason to exclude it. With stories by Bentley Little, Christopher Golden, Laird Barron, Adam Nevill, Jonathan Maberry, you just can't go wrong.

I hope you've enjoyed this little stroll down eldritch lane. Join me next issue, for more thoughts on Lovecraftian fiction, film, and games. ◆

THE BLACK BARONY

DRAIN ME: VAMPIRISM IN FILM & LITERATURE

BY LAIRD BARRON

A Bloodsucker by any Other Name

Lestat consents to the world's strangest interview…
   Nosferatu levitates from his coffin…

A vampire queen dances a satanic dance of seduction in a hellish taproom…

Danny Glick hovers outside Mark Petrie's window, begging to be let in…

Jonathan Harker falls into the clutches of Dracula's brides…

A captain lashes himself to the wheel of a derelict ship while an unseen force annihilates the helpless crew…

The bloodstained pages from a young girl's journal tell a mournful tale…

A young girl crosses an apartment threshold, uninvited, and blood pours from her in sheets…

Jerry Dandridge contemplates his mortal rivals as he chomps an apple…

Such is the sweet music made by the children of the night as immortalized in many of our favorite movies and novels. I'm not exactly breaking the news that vampires have long been objects of terrible fascination. In days of yore, they served as bogeymen in children's bedtime stories and around tavern hearths and campfires banked in desolate regions. The "why" of vampirism's enduring popularity is almost as interesting as the subject itself. The bogeyman simply won't loosen its grip on our collective imagination.

Here in the West, our obsession can be traced to Bram Stoker's seminal novel, *Dracula* (1897), and the lesser known, albeit no less important, novella, *Carmilla* (1872), by Sheridan Le Fanu. Legends of the undead creature who preys upon the blood of the living has roots that dig deep into the folklore of many ancient civilizations. Be it the Greek Vorvolakas (I highly recommend Val Lewton's *Isle of the Dead* and its oblique take on the myth), revenants of the dearly departed who return from the grave and are heralded by a single knock at the door; or Slavic traditions which hold that Strigoi and Moroi share the traits of phantoms and shapeshifters; or the dreaded Aswang, a ghoulish shapeshifter said to haunt the Philippines since ancient times; vampirism is a subject that transcends culture and geographical boundaries.

The key word is "vampirism," the siphoning of a victim's essence, material or spiritual, by a predatory actor. Pop culture is satisfied to leave this dirty work to vampires in their various guises. It goes much deeper, however. The horror isn't confined to campfire tales or Gothic fantasies; the horror isn't subordinate to supernatural influence. Indeed, the mechanisms of vampirism are extant in the mundane world. Ask the swimmer who has peeled leeches from his or her flesh after a dip in the pond; ask the long-suffering spouse who undergoes a daily ritual of soul-sucking abuse that leaves him or her a husk of their former self; ask the fly as it succumbs to the spider's embrace; or the grasshopper whose innards are liquefied and then hoovered up an assassin bug's rostrum. Let us be clear, the horror of parasitical leeching is all around us, cloaked by numerous forms of camouflage, every moment of the day.

Presently, we'll focus mainly upon the traditional vamp, tied as the mythology is to the kind of overheated eroticism and stylized violence that stamps itself into our psyches, especially when it's encountered at a vulnerable age.

Open a Vein

From Stoker's *Dracula* to Anne Rice's *Interview with a Vampire*, and *'Salem's Lot* by Stephen King, to Justin Cronin's bestselling *Passage*, vampire literature has long been fertile ground for horror authors and filmmakers. The Rice and King novels were the big news during the 1970s and early '80s, alongside pulpier fare such as Brian Lumley's *Necroscope* series, and Robert R. McCammon's, *They Thirst*.

I had a brush with the *Tomb of Dracula* comics in my youth. One of my younger uncles was a maven of pulp paperbacks and comics and he'd pay us kids off with a stack of borrowed *Archie Digests, Amazing Spiderman*, and *Avenger* comics when we'd come around to pester him.

Carmilla
Joseph Sheridan
Le Fanu

Among those stacks of four color goodness, I caught the merest glimpse of a spread of the *Tomb of Dracula* issues. My mother swooped in to snatch that particular bit of gruesome fare before it could taint my malleable little brain. Too late, Mom, too late. The glimpses were enough to stick in my mind. Not so long ago, my colleague, John Langan, learning of my interest in the king of Vampires and the schlock (and not so) films and literature surrounding the brute, handed me the Marvel omnibuses that collected the magnificently transgressive work of Gerry Conway and Gene Colan, creators of the *Tomb of Dracula*. The line ran for around seventy issues and its plot became increasing baroque. I won't spoil it for you except to say, the writers made sure to reinforce the Count's credentials as a bona fide, dyed in the wool bastard.

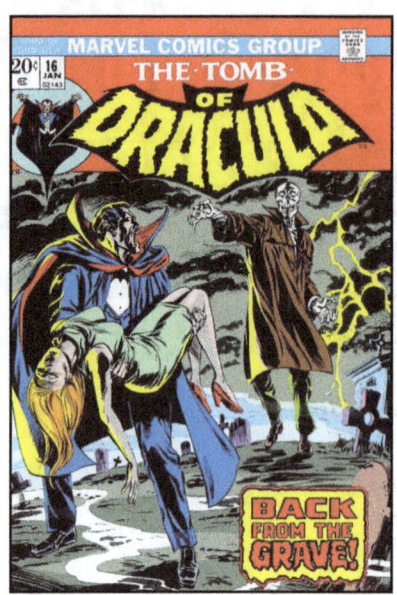

For connoisseurs of literary horror, I highly recommend the *Tomb of Dracula*. Other worthy takes on the vampires and vampirism you may or may not have encountered—*The Glow* by Brooks Stanwood (not strictly a vampire tale, but intimately concerned with vampirism); *Motherless Child* by Glen Hirshberg (eminently literary take on the vampire mythos with a *Thelma & Louise* vibe); *The Space Vampires* by Colin Wilson (space-faring energy beings feast upon the life force of humans, also a 1985 B movie); "The Third Always Beside You" (an MR James style story in John Langan's *The Wide Carnivorous Sky* collection); "The Power and the Passion" by Pat Cadigan (a story found in her collection *Patterns*); "All You Can Do Is Breathe" (a story by Kaaron Warren found in the Ellen Datlow edited anthology *Blood and Other Cravings*); "The Sea Was Wet As Wet Could Be" (a Gahan Wilson classic you'll have to dig for); Hans Rodionoff's modern classic, *Mnemovore* (a graphic novel series from Vertigo about a creature that devours memories); and Steve Niles' *30 Days of Night,* a siege tale set in the far north. One of the best pieces of literature to include Dracula (without explicitly naming him) and yet not classify as a vampire story, is Roger Zelazny's *A Night in the Lonesome October*. A tremendously fun novel that runs the great cast of monsters and villains from Hammer and Amicus (with some Lovecraft Mythos on the side) and runs it through a blender.

By Frank Langella's Claws

Nostalgia plays a role in the vampire-related cinema that has stuck with me over the years. Sir Christopher Lee's passing in 2015 means we've lost an actor who revived the greatness of the vampire myth and propelled it to the fore of modern horror films. Swaggering, smirking, devilish Lee will always be my favorite Dracula, above all the rest, including Bela Lugosi's interpretation which made him virtually synonymous with the arch villain. And yet, as a kid my nightmares weren't of Lugosi or Lee. Indeed, the bloodsucker who haunted me was Frank Langella.

The movie is John Badham's *Dracula*. The opening scene: nighttime aboard a freighter in the Atlantic. A storm rages and the seriously undermanned ship is headed for a rocky coast. Three remaining crew members struggle to jettison a cargo crate marked DRACULA. Frank Langella's monstrous hand bursts through the lid of the crate and tears the throat from hapless sailor Number 1. Sailor Number 2 is swept overboard by a wave. The captain, who has lashed himself to the wheel, is devoured by a massive wolf that presumably emerged from the crate. Numerous vampire movies existed prior to Badham's inversion of the Stoker classic, and I'd seen a few despite parental interdiction. Christopher Lee's portrayal of the dread Count is all aces in my view. But Badham's execution of that one scene of the clawed hand, is so visceral

and bestial; it reveals the truth behind Dracula's genteel demeanor and renders his essence in a manner that even the baring of bloodied fangs doesn't quite match.

Among the often overlooked gems is Cronenberg's *Rabid* with Marilyn Chambers cast as the sympathetic antagonist who possesses a uniquely disturbing method of draining her prey. Less of a gem, but canonical nonetheless, is *The Omega Man* starring Charlton Heston, a potboiler adapted from Richard Matheson's novel, *I Am Legend*. Both films deal with the implications of a vampiric plague and questions of good and evil that outstrip mere biological imperatives. Among the best of the new breed of gritty vampire tales was *Near Dark*. Doubtful that any of the horror movie faithful will forget the scene where Lance Henriksen and his evil clan descend upon a country bar. The extended tableau of carnage and cruelty possesses an operatic quality seldom rivaled in the genre.

Other films worth mentioning that might not otherwise ping one's radar—*The Hunger* (starring David Bowie and Catherine Deneuve); *The Addiction* (directed by Abel Ferrara); *Kuroneko* (directed by Kineto Shindo; and in fact, there is a treasure trove of Japanese vampire cinema to be explored); *Shadow of the Vampire* (starring John Malkovich, directed by E. Elias Merhige); *Martin* (directed by George Romero); *Cronos* (directed by Guillermo Del Toro); and *Marebito* (directed by Takashi Shimizu; and originally recommended to me by one of the finer critics of his day, Lucius Shepard).

It wasn't (and isn't) all doom and gloom. The latter 1960s onward saw the rise of horror comedies such as Roman Polanski's *The Fearless Vampire Killers,* which merges satire and pitch-black comedy in a scathing lampoon of the genre; *Love at First Bite,* a humorous inversion of the Dracula trope that immortalized George Hamilton; the deservedly lauded *Lost Boys*; and *Fright Night*, featuring the impeccable Chris Sarandon (in one of the finest Dracula-esque performances on record) as a vampire lord who invades suburbia to seduce and ultimately drain a bevy of local women. His diabolic machinations are opposed by an oafish, hormone-addled teenager and the decrepit host of a late-night horror show

(the eponymous *Fright Night*). Wryly self-aware, *Fright Night* manages to blur the line between camp and homage thanks to the wickedly humorous chemistry of Sarandon, William Ragsdale, Amanda Bearse, Roddy McDowall and Stephen Geoffreys. It remains a latter-day cult favorite. The 2011 remake does not do the original film any justice.

Terrible Mysteries

The tale of Count Dracula and vampirism in general owes its longevity to an aura of historical mystery. We shudder at the infamous exploits of Vlad Tepes and Elizabeth Bathory; we tsk-tsk at the antique customs of spiking the jaws of the deceased prior to burial or the old custom of lining the sill with garlic to keep haunts at bay. The power of myth may be diluted, and its popularity ebbs and flows. In the case of vampirism, the allure never truly diminishes; it simply changes shape and infiltrates broader aspects of pop culture.

A few years ago, novelist Paul Tremblay took John Langan and me on a walking tour of Salem, MA. Hawthorn's house was a treat, as were the various occult shops and tourist attractions. It's a lovely town with a rich culture and history. For me, the surprise hit of the afternoon was *Count Orlok's Nightmare Gallery*, a wax museum celebrating various movie monsters. Should you ever find yourself tooling around Salem, my travel advice is to cough up the eight bucks and take a stroll down a dark alley just off Memory Lane. Werewolves, madmen, ghouls, witches, and yes, vampires—Nosferatu, if my recollection serves.

During our tour of the gallery, one exhibit in particular caught my attention—an ornate ring that had once belonged to Bela Lugosi. Lugosi (and possibly others, including Christopher Lee) had worn it during his portrayal of Dracula in films during the 1940s. According to industry folklore, the ring has disappeared and resurfaced over the decades. More recently (1960s), the late Forrest Ackerman displayed it as a personal ornament for many years until bequeathing it to a young fan. Rumor has it, Ackerman commissioned duplicates of the original Ring of Dracula and that's what Lee and other actors have worn. Whether *Count Orlok's Nightmare Gallery* owns the real McCoy or a snazzy replica is an open question. I'm less concerned about what's apocryphal and what's not—the simple fact is, Dracula has inspired yet another, albeit minor, real-world mystery.

It is often said that vampire-themed stories (be it film or literature) is passé, and that nothing new can be done with it (or with zombies, werewolves, Cthulhu, etc.). As with any iconic mythos, there is a risk of saturation and enervation. While popularity may peak and fade in cycles, vampires aren't going anywhere. Count Dracula and his legions of offspring are embedded in the architecture of modern culture. All we can do is await the next innovation of the timeless myth and sink our teeth in.

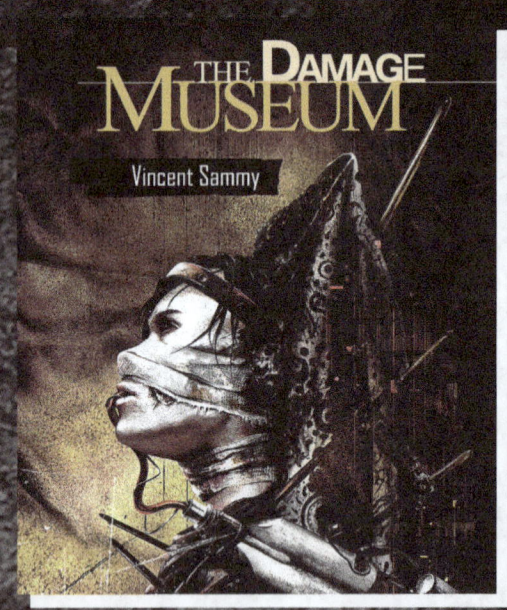

Photo courtesy of Stu Jenks

Dark Poetry: Linda Addison

CONSUMED, REDUCED TO BEAUTIFUL GREY ASHES

LINDA D. ADDISON

Linda Addison is an award-winning writer of poetry and fiction, working in horror, fantasy, and science-fiction. Since her first sale in 1994, she has published over 300 stories, poems and articles and is the Poetry Editor for Space and Time Magazine. Her collections *Consumed, Reduced to Beautiful Grey Ashes* (2001), *Being Full of Light, Insubstantial* (2007), *How To Recognize A Demon Has Become Your Friend* (2011), and *The Four Elements* coauthored with Marge Simon, Rain Graves, and Charlee Jacobs (2013) each won the Bram Stoker Award for Superior Achievement in a Poetry Collection, and she was a finalist in that category for her collection *Dark Duet* (2012) written with Stephen M. Wilson. She is a regular attendee and panelist at national conventions, and was the Poet Guest of Honor at the 2005 World Horror Convention. She will appear as a special guest at WHC 2016, and teach at Horror University at the Horror Writers Association's inaugural Stokercon in May. She is an annual participant and panelist at the Northeastern Writers Conference and will be honored as a NECON Legend this July.

Linda was the first African-America to win the Stoker, and appeared in the award-winning anthology *Dark Matter: A Century of Speculative Fiction from the African Diaspora* (2000) edited by Sheree Thomas. She recently added screenwriter to her resume, as she wrote a segment for the horror anthology film *Seven Magpies*. Conceived by director Lucy Cruell, this film will feature seven stories written by African-American Women, each directed by an African-American woman. The script has been finalized and is in pre-production with Rae Dawn Chong headlining the direction team. Linda is currently working on a science fiction novel and has a short story in the HWA anthology *Scary Out There*, edited by Jonathan Maberry. *Scary Out There* is scheduled for an August release from Simon and Schuster.

Born in Philadelphia, Linda now lives in Arizona, where she writes and edits.

Shadow Rainbow & Other Fragile Things
BY LINDA ADDISON

Red:

Quiet fluttered in her mind,

until the strangers came again,

with tongues of blood and faith

and prophecy, their language

a mutation of myth hardwired

in her primary brain.

Orange:

There were streaks in the stone,

like setting sun caught unaware.

Instructions: do not lose hope,

trust the story, dance when

no one is looking.

Yellow:

He was a dead end kid,

she was a Shanghai surprise.

She had a dead bone in her hand,

like a splinter in the mind

driving him mad.

Green:

It had no fear, growing,

taking in sun, rain, dropping

leaves, no fear, even when carved,

burned, crashed into, not

questioning what - who, knowing

without doubt, without fear.

Blue:

Meeting the unknown, to be part

of this world, to be part of any world.

Swirling in the wide open, meeting something

casually miraculous, peripherally discernible,

necessary & indeterminate & concrete.

Indigo:

The dark fairy tale began,

the shadows of Mount Semeru

where the portals of new born volcanoes,

dripped bitter nectar, flavored with

broken desire. The gods must be restless

inside the slippery craters, fragrant

with fate, loud with dim hope.

Violet:

Journeying thru flesh time, one

breath in a shadow-filled dream,

one in joy. Looking for mercy in the

tears you leave in your wake. Catch &

release the latest theory of perception,

allowing new myth to grow, integrating

molecular sensory input. Flesh clock winding

down. Dream tears easily tolerated, when Things

become enough, when even dreams end.

Nicholas Kaufmann

Whatever Happened to Solstice Young?

There are times, on dark nights when I'm alone, when the wind blows through the eaves of my house and sounds like a voice whispering my name.

A familiar voice. I suppose it should frighten me, and I suppose if I were anyone else it would, but it doesn't. Instead it gives me a strange kind of comfort.

It's not unusual for me to hear it while staying up late into the night in my living room recliner, grading my students' papers and sipping my evening tonic, a Balvenie DoubleWood on the rocks. If the dean of the university ever found out I drank while grading he would have a conniption, but how does the old saying go? What you don't know can't hurt you? Except I know that's not true. The wind likes to remind me of that.

When it whispers my name, it draws me back to long ago, to that terrible autumn of my youth, so defined by heartache and terror. It began with a simple childhood crush. It began with Solstice Young.

Luminous, with an effervescent smile that could chase the clouds from the sky and the ever-present fragrance of honeysuckle, hibiscus, and lemon—I loved Solstice Young with the wholesome, unconditional love only a child could have for an adult. In the fall of 1983, when the school year was new and the leaves had just started to turn the color of fire and saffron, I was twelve years old and Solstice Young was twenty-two. That ten-year gap might as well have been a chasm of eons, and had she not been the music teacher at my sleepy little town's school I likely never would have laid eyes on her. But I did, I saw her every day for third period, right before lunch, and it felt like a blessing. For a kid who excelled at the art of faking stomachaches to get out of school, that autumn was the only time I can remember actually being excited to go every day.

My love for her bloomed the first day I walked into her classroom, which was one of the smallest in the school. Even in 1983, music classes weren't given much respect. The administration and the school board always seemed on the verge of cutting its funding altogether. They hadn't yet, but in their twisted need to show their contempt they moved the music class to the smallest classroom they could find, a cramped, closet-like room where only half the ceiling lights worked. But somehow Solstice Young made the room feel so much bigger and brighter than it was. She festooned it with all kinds of musical instruments and tacked cardboard album covers to the walls: Fleetwood Mac's *Rumours*, *Led Zeppelin IV*, David Bowie's *The Rise and Fall of Ziggy Stardust*, Blondie's *Parallel Lines*, Roxy Music's *Avalon*, Duran Duran's *Rio*. We knew what music was back then.

At the time, I had never listened to any of those albums, although I knew Keith, my older brother, owned at least one of them. I remembered him coming home with *Rumours* one day, that unforgettable yellow sleeve art burning itself into my mind—a man and a woman holding hands in mid-dance, he with his leg up on a small ottoman, she circling him with her arms outstretched in almost mystical abandon. The man looked like everything I wanted to be when I grew up, dashing and debonair in his boots and vest like a bearded storybook pirate, and the woman—well, there was something about her that was very like the teacher standing at the front of the classroom.

She'd written her name on the chalkboard in a delicate, feminine script—Miss Young, with the *i* in Miss dotted by a smiley face she'd drawn. She wore a white cotton peasant blouse and a long, flowing skirt with a paisley pattern. Her dark blonde hair was long and streaked with highlights, with a single, braided strand that hung near her ear. A spray of summery freckles dotted the bridge of her nose and spilled onto her cheeks. Her big, blue eyes were bright with the enthusiasm of someone about to teach children for the very first time, the polar opposite of the jaded, tired, permanently annoyed eyes of those who have been teaching for years. I should know. I see those tired eyes in my own mirror quite often.

When Solstice Young smiled, dimples creased her face and it was like the sun was shining right on you. How I loved to make her smile. When I look back with the mind of a teacher, I can see how she humored us, laughing at all the students' corny jokes even if they weren't funny, and smiling as she listened to countless ridiculous questions and rambling, nonsensical stories. Even mine. But I prefer to remember it differently, to remember her smile as genuine, her heart so big it could encompass the whole class. That's how I want to remember Solstice Young now that she's gone. *If* she's gone.

I was too young at the time to understand what an unusual name Solstice was. I assume now that her parents were Beats or hippies, and given how she dressed and the way she spoke of musicians with the same reverence a preacher would when speaking of Jesus, that was probably the case. I didn't know anything about her except that she wasn't from our little town, where everybody knew everybody. This implied, astonishingly, that she'd *chosen* to come there after graduating from whatever university she attended. It meant she'd *chosen* to teach at my school, and to my feverish, lovesick mind that meant destiny had brought us together. All I cared about, all I lived for, was her attention. Even a table scrap was a meal to me. I raised my hand in class regardless of whether I knew the answer. I volunteered to transcribe notes from sheet music onto the chalkboard for her. I studied extra hard what words like *adagio* and *larghissimo* meant so she would see what a good student I was.

One night in early October, when I was in the family room reading a chapter on Italian Baroque composers, my father came in with a can of beer and shooed me to the far side of the couch. He plopped down where I'd been sitting, picked up the remote, and turned on the local news. There was no point in complaining about the interruption. Nothing came between my father, his post-dinner beer, and the evening news. The house could burn down and he wouldn't get up until the can was empty and the broadcast was over.

I tried to ignore the television, but the word *murder* caught my attention. I looked up from my textbook as the anchor reported that the dead body of a middle-aged woman, one Maisie Talbot of Fox Hill Road, had been found behind the bus station early that morning. Her throat had been torn open by a wild animal. The authorities were urging caution.

"Wild animal my ass," my father muttered, sipping his beer. "I bet it's one of those pit bulls they're always talking about on the news. One killed a kid a few months ago. You ask me, they should all be put down. That's what you do with vicious animals like that."

***

The next day in class, Solstice Young played Simon & Garfunkel's "The Sound of Silence" for us on the record player. As the haunting opening notes floated through the classroom, she said, "There's something so dark and seductive about the music, don't you think? And that first lyric, 'Hello, darkness, my old friend,' there's a resignation there, a giving up of one's self. But not out of fear. Out of love." She closed her eyes and sang along with the record without an ounce of shyness or timidity, swaying to the music like a charmed snake. "Take my arms that I might reach you," she sang out and hugged herself tight. Her blouse slipped off of one creamy, bare shoulder, but she didn't even care. She was a million miles away, and whatever she was imagining in that moment was hers and hers alone.

Afterward, the other kids laughed in the hallway about it. Even Craig Maberry and Bob Moore, my two best friends, thought it was weird, but not me. I thought it was magical. I felt like I had caught a glimpse of the real Solstice Young, the one no one else saw.

But as much as I wanted to impress her, I couldn't play music. I made such a mess of trying to perform *Hot Cross Buns* on the recorder along with the rest of the class that she had to come to my rescue.

"You've got your finger on the wrong hole," she said, gently moving my hand. "Here, put your finger on this hole instead. That's better, isn't it?"

Then, without warning, her cheeks flushed and she started laughing as if she'd said something funny. It was a different laugh from her normal one. This one was dark and full of secrets, and though I didn't understand what was so funny, the sound of it reached deep inside me and grabbed hold.

I stared at her hand on mine as I played the notes. The warm, perfect feel of it overwhelmed me. Her sleeve pulled back on her arm, and I noticed an angry-looking white scar along the length of her wrist, crisp and straight as if from a razor. The sight of it frightened me, but I forgot it a moment later when she squeezed my hand approvingly. I very nearly fainted. Surely it was a sign, a way of letting me know that she favored me above all the others, that somehow she knew of my love for her and returned it. It didn't matter that she moved on to Billy Mears next and did the same for him, I was still swooning from her attention, still inhaling the mystical fragrance that drifted in her wake like incense.

I didn't know if that combination of honeysuckle, hibiscus, and lemon was a perfume or soap or just her natural scent, but it was like catnip to me. When I smelled it in the hallways of the school I would slow my gait, hoping to catch even a glimpse of her.

***

Over the next few weeks, during my father's post-dinner beer and evening news sessions, I learned that more dead bodies had been found around town: at the bus station, near the garbage dump, in the alley behind the bars on Quinn Street. The victims were all women, and they'd all had their throats torn open like Maisie Talbot, but the police didn't think it was a wild animal anymore. They were certain now that it was the work of a human being, because all the victims had been drained of blood and no animal could do that, not even the pit bulls my father was so keen on blaming. Night after night, I watched the news reports with spellbound awe, until the anchor spoke two words that echoed in my head like a melody I couldn't shake: *serial killer*. It was a term I'd never heard before. Most everyone else back then hadn't, either. It was a new concept the FBI had come up with in the '70s, and the local police had taken it to heart. They determined that a serial killer was targeting women in our town, and recommended all women stay inside after dark until the killer was brought to justice.

During those same weeks, I hid my childish adoration of Solstice Young from everybody, including Craig and Bob, but somehow my brother Keith knew. He was two years older than me and attended the same school. He was also the cruelest person I knew. When we passed each other in the hallways at school, he would greet me with a punch in the arm, or stuff me into my locker, all to the delight of his cackling friends. But his favorite brand of torture was to throw my love for Solstice Young in my face every chance he got.

"I saw Miss Young's tits," he told me once, taking obvious pleasure in the shock on my face. We were in his bedroom. He had Pink Floyd's *Wish You Were Here* spinning on the turntable and there was still a pungent, herbal odor in the air from the joint I'd seen him toss out the window when I barged in on some business or other. I had surprised and embarrassed him by catching him in the act, and now he wanted to get back at me with these hurtful words.

"Shut up!" I yelled. My anger was quick and possessive. "You did not!"

"I did," he said, a merciless grin on his face. "It was just last week, in the hallway at school. She was rushing somewhere with an armful of books. She dropped one of them, and when she bent down to pick it up I could see right down her blouse. She wasn't wearing *anything* underneath. I saw *everything*. It was all right there on full display. *Everyone* in the hallway saw."

"Shut up!" I yelled again. I shoved him, and forgetting whatever business had brought me to his room, I ran into my bedroom and slammed the door. I threw myself onto the bed and cried into my pillow. I didn't know why I was crying, except that it felt as though my brother's story had sullied Solstice Young somehow, abused her in some way she didn't deserve, as if she were no different from the lewd naked women in the magazines Keith kept hidden under his bed. But she *was* different. She was special, and the way Keith had talked about her made everything feel thorny and wrong and ruined.

October was nearing its end. The foliage was gone, leaving behind bare trees like skeletal, grasping hands.

The grass faded to a lifeless brown. The air turned cold and bitter, and on some days it would sting your face if you didn't wrap up in a scarf. The hothouse bloom of summer was long dead, and everything was about to change.

***

On Saturdays, Craig, Bob, and I liked nothing more than to watch old black-and-white horror movies together and then run around in the yard pretending we were being chased by Dracula, or the Mummy, or the Wolf Man. Craig could run faster than any of us, faster than anyone. That boy could run like the wind. On days when our parents let us wander, we liked to go to the old cemetery on the edge of town. It wasn't in use anymore, and as far as we knew no one but us ever went there. There was even a chain on the gate, but it was too long to do any good. All we needed to do was push the gate open wide enough to slip inside. The gravestones were mossy and chipped, so old you couldn't even read the names and dates on them anymore. The grass and weeds were so overgrown they blocked your view sometimes, so that you'd push aside some tall weeds and find yourself staring at a stone angel whose face had worn away to nothing. It was the perfect setting for us to horse around in, laughing and shrieking and hiding from Frankenstein's lurching, stiff-armed monster.

But our favorite part of the old cemetery was the moldering, abandoned chapel that stood amid the graves. Its wooden walls had rotted through and were covered with clinging, brown weeds. Its roof had collapsed in places, and the spire had partially crumbled to leave only a twisted, mold-black arm that reached yearningly toward the sky. The three of us would watch the chapel from behind a row of graves, knowing the front door had fallen off its hinges ages ago and daring each other to go in. We were too scared to do it, of course, but it was enough just to imagine what the inside of the chapel looked like — dark, dusty pews draped with sheets of cobwebs; the altar probably smashed to pieces by beer-fueled older boys or else made home to families of mice, or better yet, thousands of crawling, chittering insects; empty holes where the stained glass windows had been, looming like the black eye sockets of a skull.

The sun sets early in October, and by the time we started back from the old cemetery it was already dusk. When we reached Main Street, we stopped to point and laugh at the young couple we saw kissing against the brick wall of an antiques shop. My laughter died away when I saw that the woman whose back was pressed to the wall and whose lips were pressed so passionately to someone else's was Solstice Young. My chest tightened and my stomach dropped to my feet. The man she was kissing was a little older than her, with dark hair and a stubbly jaw. He was dressed in jeans and a leather jacket over a Black Sabbath concert t-shirt. As he slid his hand up from her waist to twine his fingers in her hair, I saw he wore a big gold ring in the shape of an upside-down pentagram, that most metal of symbols. He looked exactly like the kind of guy parents didn't want their daughters dating, and so of course Solstice Young, who marched to the beat of her own

drum, was kissing him right in front of everybody. Right in front of me.

The man ended the kiss and began to pull away. She bit his bottom lip and pulled it with her teeth. When she let go, she looked at him with a devilish smile that seared itself into my mind. It bored down deep in me and awoke something I'd only ever felt before when sneaking peeks at Keith's hidden magazines. But even that delicious, furtive pressure had been only a shadow of the urgency I felt now in every beat of my heart. I watched, rapt and envious, as she took the man's hand and led him down the sidewalk.

"Who was that with Miss Young?" I asked, watching them vanish into the darkening twilight.

"That must be her boyfriend," Craig said. "I heard her talk about him before."

"When?" I demanded, prickly and defensive.

"Remember when I had to stay late at school for detention?" Craig said. I did. He'd hidden a piece of chalk inside Mr. Palmer's eraser so that it drew a line across the chalkboard when he tried to erase a geometry lesson. Mr. Palmer had been so angry he hurled the chalk across the room, shattering it against the far wall. Snotty little Jessica McCrum ratted Craig out and he got a detention. I felt bad for him having to be there with all the druggies, dopers, space cadets, and juvenile delinquents, but we all agreed the practical joke with the chalk had been so funny it was worth it. "When they let us out of the detention room, Miss Young was talking to Miss Nugent in the hallway. She said she met a guy who was new in town like her. I guess they've been going out for a while now."

Miss Young had a boyfriend! I railed furiously against the idea, tried to tell myself she didn't really like him, but I'd seen the way she looked at him. You couldn't fake that kind of longing. Believe me, I knew.

I went into a funk. I didn't want to get out of bed the next day, but it was Sunday and my parents dragged me to church. I didn't want to get out of bed on Monday, either. The idea of seeing Solstice Young was too much to handle, but my parents made me get up and go to school. I considered skipping music class, but once I smelled that familiar fragrance outside her classroom it lured me in, filling my head with promises that she wasn't dating that guy after all, that it was all a misunderstanding, that she was still...

Still what? Mine? But she wasn't. She never had been. I knew that, I wasn't crazy. I was just a pimply-faced kid and she was in her twenties. What did I think was going to happen? That we'd get married and live happily ever after like in some stupid story? I paused in front of the door as cold, hard reality weighed down on me, snapping my heart in half under its burden. Then I took a deep breath and forced myself to enter the classroom.

The first thing I noticed was that she looked different. Tired, paler, with bags under her eyes like she hadn't slept all weekend. I tried to feel indifferent about it, but instead I felt bristly and resentful. Even at twelve years old, I could think of things that a boyfriend and girlfriend did together that would cause them not to get enough sleep. She was spacey and uncoordinated throughout the class, forgetting what she was talking about, writing the wrong word on the chalkboard, telling us to read a chapter we'd already read. I supposed her mind was elsewhere. I supposed this was what love did to people.

It went on like this for several days. We moved up from playing *Hot Cross Buns* on the recorder to playing *When the Saints Come Marching In,* but I was still hopeless. It didn't help that I was distracted by jealousy. Solstice Young had to correct my fingers again, and like a trained dog my heart leapt to attention in her presence, but this time when she touched my hand her skin felt cold and clammy. As she moved my finger from the wrong hole to the right one—there was no laughter from her this time—her sleeve pulled back to reveal the scary white scar on her wrist again...and something else. There was another scar on her wrist, pink enough to still be new, only this one was in the shape of a crescent. It reminded me of the mark I'd left on Keith's arm when I was little and he was too rough with me and I bit him.

She leaned over to get a better look at my hands, and the neck of her blouse fell open. Remembering Keith's story and how bad it had made me feel, I looked away quickly, but not before I saw it. A second crescent-shaped scar on the swell of her breast. I thought feverishly of Solstice Young with her boyfriend's bottom lip between her teeth

Biting...

and the same urgent feeling I'd felt on Main Street came rushing back a hundredfold, an unbelievable pressure screaming for release. I thought I would go mad from it.

***

Every day she looked a little worse, her rosy skin turning white as paper, the brightness dulling in her eyes. Her hair turned limp and stringy. Sometimes she seemed barely strong enough to lift the textbook. But instead of feeling sorry or concerned for her, I grew angrier. This, I decided, was her punishment for betraying me. I wince now when I think about it, my white-hot rage that she had chosen, reasonably and correctly, a man her own age over a mooning child, but a broken heart clouds the mind and at twelve years old I didn't know any better. The changes came over Solstice Young so gradually that nobody else at school noticed, only me. She was my world, and I saw everything. If she needed help, if she needed someone to see what was happening and do something about it, then I failed her. That's something I have to live with.

But I don't think she did. I don't think she wanted that at all.

***

Eventually, Solstice Young stopped coming to school. We had a substitute music teacher, Mrs. Hanson, a stern harpy who always seemed angry to be there and whose pinched face and resentful sneer cured me of any further schoolboy crushes on teachers. No one knew what had happened to Solstice Young, not even the other teachers. With a killer on the loose everyone feared the worst, though no one said it out loud. I went into a funk even deeper and darker than before. Nothing mattered. The world could stop turning

and fall into the sun for all I cared. Solstice Young was dead, I was sure of it. Craig and Bob tried to get me to come play with them, but I refused. All I wanted was the safety of my bed and the comfort of my tearstained pillow. Finally, my parents told me it was either go play with my friends or be forced to see a psychiatrist, so I went with Craig and Bob, begrudgingly, to the old cemetery on the edge of town.

This time, when we dared each other to go inside the chapel, I didn't chicken out. I ran right in, not caring what I would find, not even caring if I died in a roof collapse or at the hands of the serial killer. Neither fate awaited me. The interior of the chapel looked like I had imagined it, full of dust and cobwebs and water damage from the holes in the roof. I was surprised, however, to find a thin metal cross still standing on the altar, badly rusted but upright. The sight of it brought my simmering anger to a boil. There was nothing good in this world. The cross was a lie. *Everything* was a lie. I picked up a rock from the floor, and with an angry shout I threw it at the cross. The rock knocked it off the altar, and the cross broke apart on the floor with a loud crash.

The sound brought my friends running. I don't remember what happened after that. My fury was too overwhelming. I found out later from Craig and Bob that I had fought them and yelled curses at them. They had to run and get my brother Keith, who came and dragged me out of there. I don't recall anything between throwing the rock and being at home again, listening to my parents whisper frantically about whether I was developing a nervous condition.

But as the days passed, they never found Solstice Young's body the way they did the other victims. This was a balm of sorts for my anguish. It meant there was a chance she hadn't died at the hands of a serial killer, that her final moments hadn't been filled with fear, a thought that had tormented me to the point of utter devastation. It left hope alive that she had simply skipped town with her boyfriend to establish a new life, safe and happy, somewhere else. That thought stung me with a fresh pang of possessiveness, but at least it meant she was alive. I could be happy for her, if nothing else.

The murders grew more frequent. The police found more bodies every day, and not just women anymore. Men and children had been added to the roster. "Children!" my mother had wailed, nearly collapsing in horror at the news. "What kind of a monster would kill children?" No one had an answer for that. Perhaps if they had, things would have turned out differently. As it was, it was only a matter of time in a town that small before the killer struck someone close to me. When you're a child, you think bad things only happen to people on the news. You think it can't touch you, but it can, and there's no way to prepare for it. It flattened me, pounded me into the earth like a hammer, when they found Craig Maberry's bloodless body in the woods near the school.

Poor Craig. Always the class clown, he'd been given a detention again, this time for making faces in Spanish class. It was hardly fair, he was only trying to make Abby Berger laugh because she was so scared about the killer, but rules were rules. It was early November and the sun had already set when detention let out. The police reckoned the killer got him on the walk home from school.

I was inconsolable. If the earth had opened up under my feet to swallow me, I wouldn't have fought it. I was a zombie at Craig's funeral. I couldn't look at anyone, not even Bob, who was just as shell-shocked as I was. It was a closed casket service. They couldn't reconstruct Craig's neck well enough to display the body.

The town put a curfew in place. No one was allowed outside after dark unless it was an emergency. But once Bob and I had recovered from the shock of Craig's death, we didn't let that stop us from coming up with a plan to honor our fallen friend. In secret, whispered phone calls we decided we would go to the old cemetery and write in chalk on the inside of the cemetery wall, where only the brave and the intrepid would see it, *Never forget: Craig Maberry was here first*. There was no way our parents would let us do this, of course. They hadn't been letting us do *anything* lately. So it would have to be done at night, after they'd gone to bed. It meant breaking curfew, but that didn't matter to us nearly as much as honoring Craig. With the fearless bravado of the young, which others might call foolishness, we agreed to sneak out of our houses at midnight and meet at the cemetery gates.

When the time came, I clambered down the trellis on the side of our house with a pocketful of chalk and ran full-speed through the empty streets toward the cemetery. It was freezing out, the coldest night of the fall so far, and my panting breath turned to clouds of vapor before me. A strange, cold fog wound through the streets and clung to the lampposts, diffusing their light into an eerie haze. When I passed the brick-walled antiques shop on Main Street, I thought suddenly of Solstice Young, and my heart ached at her absence. At the cemetery gates, I waited for ten minutes, shivering in the cold, but Bob didn't show. I figured he'd either chickened out or had been caught by his parents. But I was determined to complete our mission, with or without him.

Inside the cemetery, the fog enveloped the gravestones and turned them into dark, huddled shapes like a crowd of ghoulish onlookers. I was about to pull the chalk from my pocket when the sound of the chain clanking against the gate stopped me. I turned, thinking Bob had joined me after all, but the figure I saw through the veil of fog was too tall, the size of an adult. It was covered head to foot with gray funeral shrouds that made it almost indistinguishable from the fog around it. I ducked down behind a tombstone in terror, then peeked over the top. I held my breath so the vapor wouldn't give me away. No clouds of breath came from the shrouded figure, but they issued from a second shape that emerged from the mist beside it.

Bob.

Now I knew why he hadn't shown up. The shrouded figure had caught him. I wanted to signal Bob, let him know I was here, but I was too scared. I didn't want the figure to see me. But something was wrong with Bob. He wasn't trying to get away. His face was slack and expressionless. His eyes stared blankly into the fog. The shrouded figure reached over to put a hand on Bob's back, and something

glimmered on one of its pale fingers. A ring—one I'd seen before. A gold ring with an upside-down pentagram.

Bob was passive and compliant as the shrouded figure guided him into the old chapel. I released my breath and the vapor burst out of my mouth in a heavy cloud. For a moment I was too terrified to move, but I had to. It was Bob. I had to try to help him somehow.

I followed them, but it was like a dream. My feet wouldn't move as quickly as I wanted, and the cold, impenetrable fog was a wall holding me back. When I finally reached the chapel, I stayed just outside the doorway and peeked in. A thick odor of decay hung in the air. The shrouded figure was leading Bob toward the far end of the chapel where, to my horror, I saw a second figure waiting. This one was covered in gray funeral shrouds, too, but was smaller and slighter than the first. The taller one passed Bob wordlessly over to the smaller one. Bob's expression never changed, not even when the second figure stroked his face, pushed his head to the side, and bent its cowled head to his neck. I heard the sound of teeth ripping into tender flesh. Too terrified to move, I looked away, unable to watch, but I could still hear it. The slurping, sucking sound. I put a knuckle between my teeth and bit down. It was the only way to stop myself from screaming.

When the sound stopped, I dared to look again. Bob's lifeless body lay on the floor, his throat torn and glistening, his eyes open and sightless. I know there was no way I could have helped him, that I would have died, too, but the crushing guilt I felt upon seeing him like that has never left me. I watched as the second figure approached the first, and their shrouded faces met in a horrible kiss. The taller one took the smaller's arm, lifted its upturned wrist to its mouth, and I heard the awful sounds again.

This time, I didn't look away. A charge ran through me. Not of terror, but of something else, something carnal, as one shrouded figure bit the wrist of the other

Biting...

and drank from it, as if to share in the taking of Bob's blood.

The smaller figure suddenly turned its shrouded head toward the doorway where I stood. It was too dark to see inside the shroud, but the chill that came over me told me *it* had seen *me*. I turned and ran.

My mother had wanted to know what kind of a monster would kill children. I knew the answer now. Even through the confusion and the fear, I knew. Of course I did. How many old movies had I watched on a Saturday afternoon in which undead creatures rose from their graves to feast upon the blood of the living and turn a chosen few into creatures like themselves? But I'd never thought they were real, just actors who wore long capes and spoke with Eastern European accents—not *this*, not real creatures who could come to my town and kill people I knew. I ran, and when I remembered the cross that had stood tall and proud on the chapel's altar before I broke it, the cross that could have stopped or hindered these creatures if the stories were true, I was overcome with a despairing shame. My own careless rage had created a sanctuary for them. I'd given them a safe place to hide. Me.

I ran all the way home, climbed up the trellis, locked

the window behind me, and the bedroom door too, for good measure. I spent the rest of the night with the covers drawn up to my neck, sobbing for Bob and staring at the window. I waited for the shrouded figures to appear, convinced they had followed me home, but they never came. After an eternity, the sun rose again.

In the morning I told my parents I was going to stay home from school, and because they thought I was still in mourning they didn't argue. After my father left for work, and after my mother left to run errands with my assurance that I would be fine at home alone for an hour, I sneaked out of the house again. I returned to the old cemetery, but this time I went through the woods. It took longer, but I couldn't risk being seen on Main Street carrying a can of gasoline from our garage. My father's words echoed through my head like a drumbeat: *They should all be put down. That's what you do with vicious animals like that.*

I knew enough about these creatures to understand what had to be done, and since I was the one who had inadvertently given them a place to hide, it was up to me to do it. I marched into the old chapel, confident I would be safe in the light of day while the creatures slept in their hidden spots, and poured gasoline on everything, pausing only to note that Bob's body was gone. Standing in the doorway, I pulled from my pocket a book of matches I'd taken from the kitchen. I lit one, used it to light all the other matches still in the book, and threw the blazing matchbook into the chapel. It had been a dry autumn, and with the help of the gasoline the old wood went up fast. I didn't stick around to watch it burn. I couldn't risk getting caught. I ran and made it back home before my mother returned.

When my father turned on the news that night, I heard the chapel had burned to the ground. The police blamed teenage hooligans inspired to vandalism by heavy metal music, that all-purpose bugaboo of the 1980s, but no one was ever arrested for it. No one ever came to question me. I wasn't even on their suspect list. I never told anyone what I'd done, or why. When my parents told me Bob had been killed, that his body had been found discarded in a corner of the cemetery, I had to pretend I didn't already know and cry all over again. I did a pretty good job of it.

The murders stopped after that. The townsfolk theorized that the killer had moved away, or had died and was lying in the morgue without anyone being any the wiser. I grew up, graduated high school, and left town to attend a university where, inspired by my memories of Solstice Young, I studied to be a teacher. When I graduated, I focused on getting a job teaching at the college level. I wanted older students. I didn't want any twelve-year-olds mooning over me the way I had over her. It would have been unbearable.

Along the way I met women my own age, but no relationship lasted long. None of them measured up to my memories of Solstice Young. She was never far from my mind, even as the gulf of time between my childhood and adulthood stretched wider. Whenever the mood hit me, which was frequently, I would search for her name in newspapers, phone books, and, later, on the Internet, confident that any Solstice Young I found would be her.

After all, how many Solstice Youngs could there be in the world? But I never found anything. I never found out what became of her. On dark nights when I'm alone—and I'm always alone now, because no love runs as deep as first love—and the wind whispers through the eaves like a beckoning voice, I tell myself I still don't know. But I do. I do.

They say smell is the strongest sense that's tied to memory, and I have generally found this to be true. The scent of fresh-cut grass reminds me of Saturday afternoons spent running from imaginary monsters in the backyard with Craig Maberry and Bob Moore. (Had we known there were real monsters to run from, how foolish we would have felt.) The odor of dry, dusty earth brings back memories of our secret playground, where we would run shrieking with laughter through the tombstones. When I followed Bob and the shrouded figure into the chapel all those years ago, I smelled the stench of decay in the air, but I smelled something else, too, beneath it. The fragrance of honeysuckle, hibiscus, and lemon.

It makes me think about how there were two of those creatures in the chapel, not one. It makes me wonder who Craig, the boy who could outrun anyone, might have seen coming for him out of the woods the night he died. Someone he would have recognized. Someone he wouldn't have run from. A familiar face within the shroud.

They say what you don't know can't hurt you, but it can, and there are still so many important things I don't know. Was Solstice Young's boyfriend, he of the upside-down pentagram ring, the start of it all? I suppose if I were cursed to undeath for all eternity, I would want her by my side forever, too. She had that effect on people. Or was it possible they were turned by a third creature I never found?

I wonder sometimes if she was an innocent victim, or if it was a choice she made. Because despite her sunny exterior, there was a darkness to Solstice Young that I had been blind to as a child. She was a woman of contradictions, just like her name. After all, a solstice could be the longest day, or the longest night.

And then there's the biggest question of all: Were they in the chapel when I burnt it down? I didn't dare go back to look for bones. The murders stopped, it's true, but that didn't mean they were dead. Creatures like them aren't tied to a single location, a single town. They might have moved on.

The reason I wonder is that on some nights it's not just the familiar voice on the wind whispering my name that catches my attention. There's a familiar scent, too, a fragrance that slips tantalizingly between the window and its frame. It brings back memories of a young woman I thought had burned as brightly as the sun, but who had felt such despair that she had once dragged a razor down her wrist, who had stood before the class with her eyes closed and spoken unashamedly of how seductive the darkness was, and who might have given herself over to it in the end; a young woman I had loved so completely that I could forgive her anything. And whenever I smell it—*hello, darkness, my old friend*—I open the window and invite it in.

X

A Kirkus December 2015 Must-Read Speculative Fiction

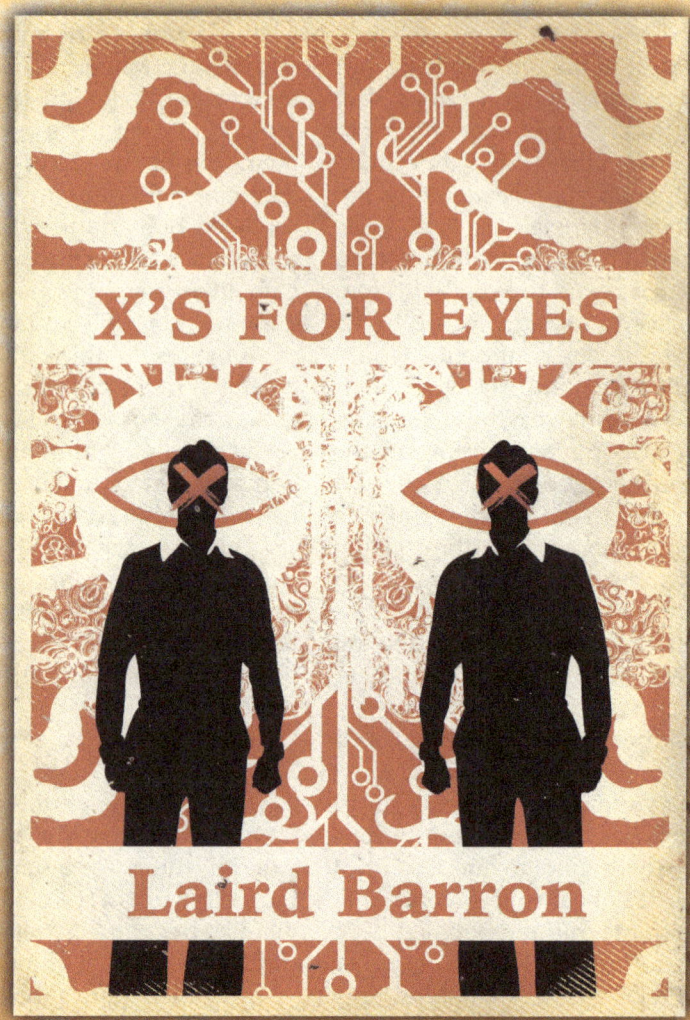

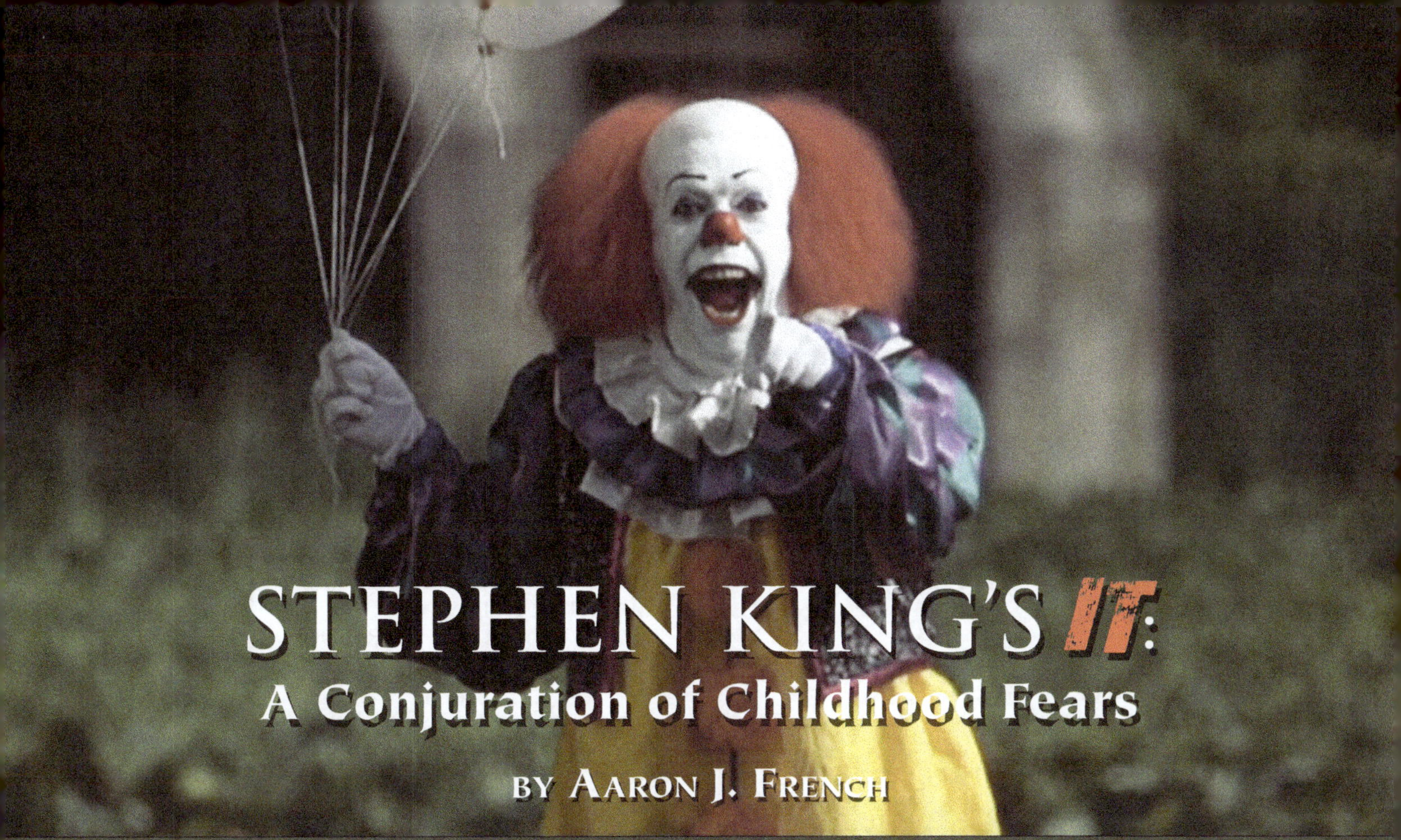

STEPHEN KING'S *IT*:
A Conjuration of Childhood Fears

BY AARON J. FRENCH

Warning: article contains spoilers

While my topic does not deal with this issue's theme directly—namely, vampirism—it does deal with the idea that hidden traumas are like psychic vampires sucking the life out of humanity's mental health. These vampires often take on the form of our worst fears, and sometimes, even, freaky diabolical clowns.

My first encounter with Stephen King's *IT* was when I was about seven years old. That was 1987. My stepmother was reading the book (about one year after its release) and I recall seeing the cover art, the claw in the storm drain and the newspaper sailboat drawing near it. The image fascinated me. When I asked my step mother if I could read the book, she told me no way, that it wasn't a book for children. Of course, this made me want to read the book more. This, her refusal, turned *IT* into something forbidden, a fruit which should not be tasted.

So I never actually read the book, not until much later. Instead, when the made-for-TV movie of the book appeared in 1990, directed by Tommy Lee Wallace, I sat glued to the television screen watching, as my VHS recorded onto a blank tape. The film aired in two parts. I recorded both of them then re-watched the film almost religiously over the next

ten years. It wasn't until I was much older that I finally read the paperback novel. Truly, it is not a book for children.

What's interesting is that King must have been writing this novel during the year I was born in 1980. He reported that it took him about four years to compose *IT*, and then there was the editing process and everything else that led to its publication in 1986; and then I finally saw the cover art in the hands of my stepmother in 1987, and four years later the TV movie came out, which I watched fairly regularly. Finally, my actual encounter with the novel when I was an adult. All this to illustrate how the book was constantly around me during my childhood and early life. Several of my horror writing colleagues have claimed that they, too, experience similar childhood associations regarding this particular novel by Stephen King.

There are layers I'd like to highlight as we proceed. The first is, King had a severe drug and alcohol addiction at the time he wrote *IT* (he's spoken about this openly) and was likely under narcotic influence through much of *IT*'s composition. He later detoxed during the revision process of *IT*. I believe he then eventually kicked his drugs and alcohol addiction completely. Additionally, in an interview with CNN he compared his writing to self-hypnosis, and said that having a daily routine helped him fall into a trance. Drugs

and self-hypnosis: a recipe for a mindbender.

Yet it is important because it relates to automatic writing, also called channeling, a practice that corresponds in some ways to writing fiction. Automatic writing is the process of putting one's self into trance (like King said),

picking up a pencil and then writing whatever comes into one's mind without thinking about it. The idea is that by writing this way, it is no longer the author speaking, but some other invisible intelligence (spirit, angel, demon) writing *through* that person; not unlike the Ouija board. Hence, channeling. Numerous famous esoteric authors have written books in this way, particularly H.P. Blavatsky (1831-1891) and Alice Bailey (1880-1949).

I'm comparing the processes King used in the beginning to write his early novels (i.e., trancing out with drugs and routinization) with the practice of spirit channeling to show that, really, they are not all that different.

Another layer I want to highlight is the psychological one. The plotline of the novel and the events regarding its main characters is equivalent to sitting through their own personal psychotherapy sessions. Freud had adopted what was to become known as "the talking cure," the idea that simply talking will eventuate in the discovery of hidden and repressed traumas within the unconscious. Freud also stressed what he called "free association," meaning the patient does the talking rather than the therapist. That way it is their *own* talking that kick-starts the healing process.

What Freud thought, and later Jung, was that a patient's current mental and emotional problems were in fact related to their early, repressed, childhood traumatic experiences—which the patient had repressed into the unconscious and completely forgotten about. The goal of "the talking cure" and of "free association" was to open windows on these unconscious childhood experiences,

shine the light on them and make them conscious again, then work toward reintegrating them (the latter was supposed by Jung alone, however; Freud, infinitely pessimistic, thought the best we could accomplish with psychotherapy was to become less anxious). The infamous "deadlights" of the creature IT in King's novel, shining out behind Pennywise the Clown and causing people who look to go insane, are an example of the light from these open windows shining down into the unconscious depth of the psyche. To look, to revisit childhood traumas, is to go insane, and only the strongest personalities can withstand IT.

In the words of Hermann Hesse:

MAGIC THEATER
ENTRANCE NOT FOR EVERYBODY
FOR MADMEN ONLY!

King clearly employs psychological concepts consciously when, for example, he writes: "Eddie did not need a shrink to tell him that he had, in a sense, married his mother." Eddie had had an overweight mother as a child who was always sick and smothering him, just as his later wife Myra does; and Beverly, with her abusive father, winds up with an abusive man; and so forth.

In *Six Phone Calls (1985)*, Mike Hanlon phones the other six of the Losers' Club to notify them IT has come back, to ask them to remember their promises to return to Derry. Mike never left Derry following that summer of 1958 when the Losers' Club battled IT using the Ritual of Chüd. However, the other six have gone on to new careers, new lives, and success. At the time of Mike's calls, they have completely forgotten IT as well as their childhoods in Derry, repressed them. And it's his call—his *talking*—that triggers the return of their traumatic, terrifying childhood memories, which start to assault and harass them mercilessly. For this is the *real* IT, the demon in the unconscious, the personal fears leftover from childhood, which we as adult work endlessly to ignore and repress.

One of the most significant descriptions of this happens after Mike calls Richard Tozier. King writes:

Oh Christ, that was nothing he wanted to know, not at this late date, but it didn't seem to matter in the slightest. Something was happening down there in the vaults [the unconscious], down there where Rich Tozier kept his own personal collection of Golden Oldies. Doors were opening.

And they're not records down there, are they? Down there you're not Rich "Records" Tozier, hot-shot KLAD deejay, and the Man of a Thousand Voices, are you? And those things that are opening… they aren't exactly doors,

or unleashes
ever afraid of.

are they?

He tried to shake these thoughts off.

Thing to remember is that I'm okay. I'm okay, you're okay, Rich Tozier's okay. Could use a cigarette is all.

They're not records but dead bodies. You buried them deep but now there's some kind of crazy earthquake going on and the ground is spitting them up to the surface. You're not Rich "Records" Tozier down there; down there you're just Richie "Four-Eyes" Tozier and you're with your buddies and you're so scared it feels like your balls are turning into Welch's grape jelly. Those aren't doors, and they're not opening. Those are crypts, Richie. They're cracking open and the vampires you thought were dead are all flying out again.

There is a principle in the occult world that runs: before one can begin on a path of self-development—i.e. working on one's inner psyche to achieve *unio mystica* (otherwise known as enlightenment)—one must first go to therapy. It's not really all that an unusual of a stipulation. Even in more conventional forms of religion, such as Christianity and Judaism, the priest, pastor, or rabbi functions as a kind of religious therapist, the person you go talk to about family problems, relationship problems, inner demons, sins, whatever. The idea is that such a figure can help you move past these issues on your way toward reuniting with and/or reaching toward God, or at least getting to Heaven.

The same idea is present in occultism pertaining to personal development, the first step being working on your own shortcomings and psychological traumas, before beginning any higher type of work. Usually, these traumas are located in the sphere of one's childhood, most times they are forgotten and must be "conjured" in order to revisit them consciously. King seems to be drawing from this occult principle in a very effective way when he describes the inner demons of the members of the Losers' Club, has the fears take on the forms of demons, and then has the characters remember

them and do battle with them consciously.

In occult development, religious mysticism, tantric training, etc., once the therapeutic stages are overcome, the pupil is ready for the real thing, a true spiritual experience, in the sense of William James in his *The Varieties of Religious Experience: A Study in Human Nature* (1902). The idea here is that the pupil, having worked out his/her inner turmoil, now possesses enough maturity to responsibly endure a direct encounter with the divine.

King observes this systematic progression, unveiling the *unio mystica* at the end of the book in one of *IT*'s most unusual and controversial scenes. In the sewers, after the monster has supposedly been defeated via the Ritual of Chüd, when the Losers' Club is lost and trying to find the exit, something extraordinarily shocking occurs. Beverly, the only girl in the group, decides that the way for the group to reconnect, and what's more in order to bind them all together eternally, is for her to lose her virginity by having sex with all six of her eleven-year-old male counterparts. This scene is described in highly vivid and poetic prose. On the surface, it seems like a perverted digression on the part of King, and perhaps it is.

However, if we take a close look at this scene, the more bizarre, almost random, and offensive it all becomes. But again, the IT is described as a being who is vile and offensive because it goes against norms. In feminist terms, this scene is unacceptable and appears as one male's (King's) repressive fantasy enacted within fictional narrative. There is a long tradition of King scholars who have attacked the author for, in their eyes, the misrepresentation of women in his books. Notable is a book titled *Imagining the Worst: Stephen King and the Representation* of Women, edited by Kathleen Margaret Lant and Theresa and published in 1998 by Greenwood Press for their Contributions to the Study of Popular Culture series. The book contains two articles concerning *IT*, both penned by women, which at times highlight, and at times attack, King's chauvinism and poor representation of the female sex.

The first article in the collection, "'OH DEAR JESUS IT IS FEMALE': Monster as Mother/Mother as Monster in Stephen King's *IT*," gives a balanced analysis. The second piece, "*IT*, A Sexual Fantasy," makes all the same points as the first article but with an oversaturated tone of anger and hostility. Thus, I will make the first piece my object of focus. This piece highlights the traumatic un-nurturing behavior of the mothers in the book, even the supposedly good mothers. The children of the Losers' Club, and the other

nature. There does not seem to be any pleasure throughout the whole act, in fact, and no clear orgasms occur either (except, perhaps, in Ben's case.) Instead, there is a lifting of the whole act into the world of innocence and imagination. So, we have two stark contrasts: the near worst form of sexual depravity (a pre-pubescent gangbang), and the raising of the sexual-physical pleasure to the spiritual via imagination and ritual.

This latter is the goal and practice of some Hindu tantric traditions and even in the occult ideas of Aleister Crowley. In ancient times, temples were places where someone, a male usually, went to have sex with the temple priestess in a ritualistic, religious ceremony. This is true of the ancient Semitic peoples and the mother goddess Asherah, against whom Yahweh had to continually incite his new covenanted followers—"stop having sex with her temple priestesses." By enacting a ritualistic temple sex ceremony, it was thought the two physical people—the priestess and the male—were actually replaced during the act by gods themselves, such as Isis and Osiris, or even Yahweh and Asherah. Psychologically speaking, a divine consummation occurred, resulting in the birth of a divine child. In the case of the Egyptians, for instance, it was Horus. Among the Jewish/Semitic, could this child have been the baby Jesus? In any case, whether consciously or unconsciously, King's over the top and unexpected coming-of-age sex scene bears a striking resemblance to these kinds of occult-spiritual ideas.

In closing, the goal of this short article has been to emphasize deep archetypal elements contained in Stephen King's *IT*, a novel which might be dismissed as merely that scary old book with the clown. As we have seen, there is so much more to the story. Not only does King confess to sinking into hypnotic trance when he writes—equating his work to a form of channeled writing—but he then also keenly

Derry children who became victims of IT, suffer traumatic experiences often because their mothers neglect them or leave them alone—or, in Bev's case, fail to intercept an abusive father. In the end, when the creature is revealed to be female—and *pregnant*—this becomes sufficient evidence for the author of the article that, on a symbolic level, the IT is really the evil mother, and therefore the novel is really about how "[t]he devouring bITch-mother can only be destroyed by masculine force, knowledge, and language in an exorcism or pre-Oedipal anxiety" (p. 120). This conflict is, for any male, necessarily hoped for in the "going to therapy" stage before advancing in occult development.

In the particular case of the novel *IT*, the conflict is largely from the male perspective, which is even why I myself have responded so strongly to it. I'm well aware of that. However, it is the identical template that is offered for women to enact a similar journey, because in reality the whole point is to confront one's childhood traumas as an adult and conquer/re-integrate them, regardless of sex. The novel *IT* is written by a male and emphasizes the male perspective, but the psychoanalytic journey for both men and women is, in its symbolic construction, relatively the same. After all, it is a *human* journey.

Nevertheless, the criticisms raised by these feminist scholars are totally valid and useful. But I contend it is only one part of the larger picture, in fact a low symbolic part, related to more material components: gender, survival, nurturing, and sex. I want to jump up a level on the symbolic planes to see the full magical significance of *IT*, a significance which is genderless and indeed can be, and has been, experienced by all. If we peer down from a higher symbolic vantage point, we can see that the scene of the "orgy" becomes even more strangely occult, almost bacchanalian, in that it represents an event of ritual magic. Indeed, the girl experiences no sexual pleasure but is actually in the process of imagining birds as each of the young boys penetrate her—establishing a connection with

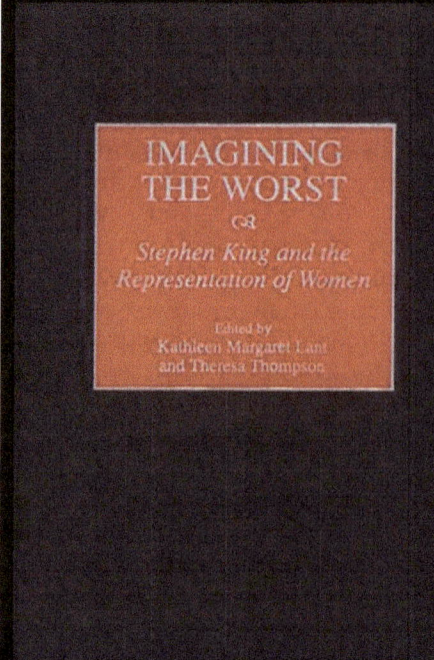

IMAGINING THE WORST

Stephen King and the Representation of Women

Edited by
Kathleen Margaret Lant
and Theresa Thompson

focalizes his novel around the repressed traumatic experiences of his characters, reawakening them, and then having them consciously do battle with them. Finally, the book's climax with a Rite of Passage involving ritual-like sex, and an experience of *unio mystica* with the divine-spiritual (perhaps represented by a cosmic turtle), elevates the story onto a higher imaginative plane. No wonder so many people have had such interesting responses to it. There must be more than merely "people being scared of clowns" going on here.

And, of course, there are my own personal memories in relation to this book, how the novel seemed to accompany me through the formative years of my early life. I don't think it would shock anyone to learn that much of my childhood was not unlike the traumatic events experienced by the young Losers' Club. Most people who get into the horror business, I think, are likely to have semi-conscious demons lurking around down there, which torture us. It's why we work so diligently to write them out into the light of our—and others'—conscious minds; King, by the way, has mentioned in several interviews that he is *willfully* doing precisely that.

So, the question one ought to be asking is: Is the IT of Stephen King's novel really just the IT of my own repressed childhood fears, lumbering around down there in the dark, waiting for a call from Mike Hanlon to be woken up?

Wait, what's that?

—I think I hear my iPhone ringing now…

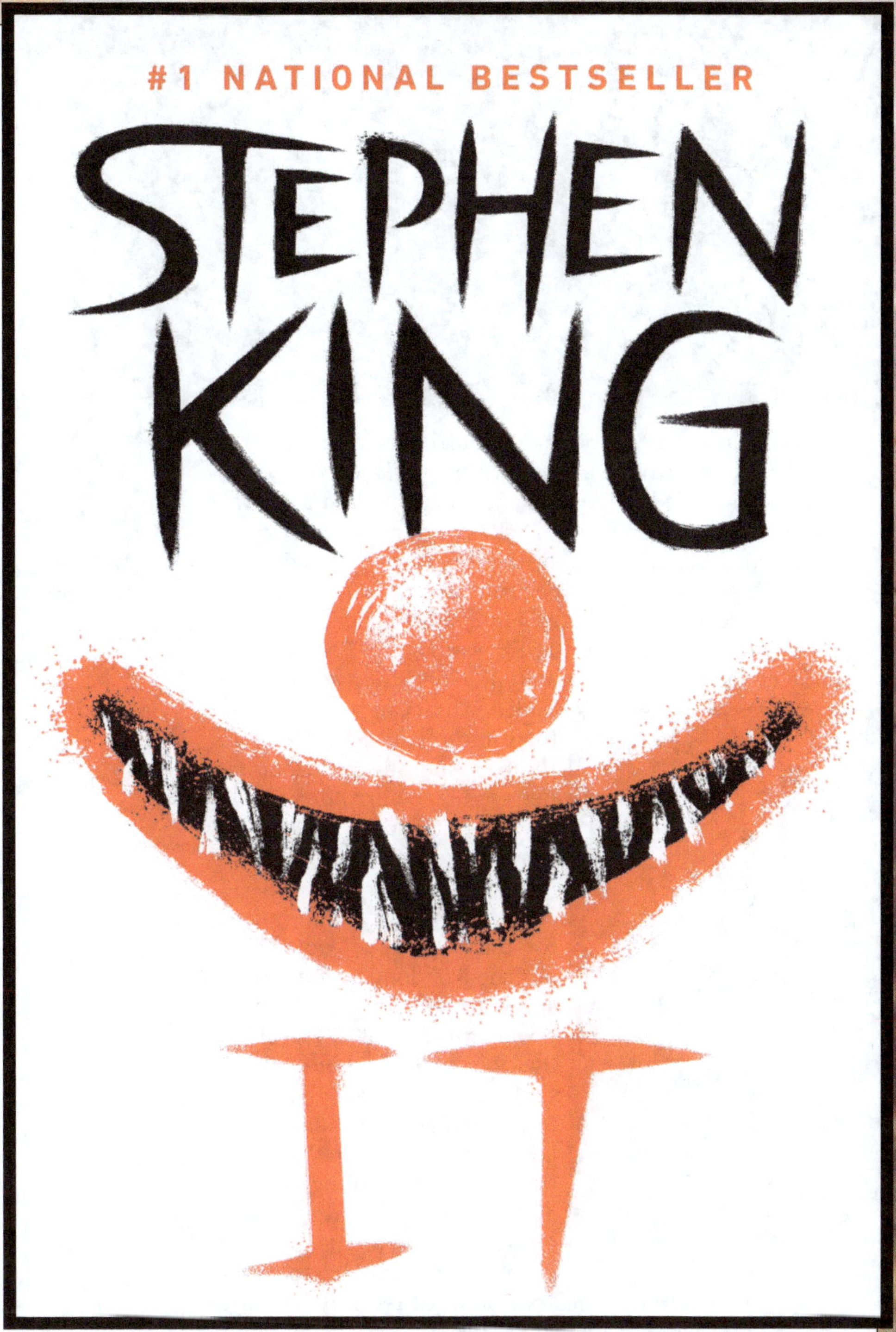

DARK ARTS:
KATHE KOJA

BY K. H. VAUGHAN

Photo courtesy of Rick Lieder

I t is difficult to describe the extraordinary creative force that is Kathe Koja. Her debut novel, *The Cipher* (1991) won the Bram Stoker Award and Locus Award and was nominated for the Philip K. Dick Award as well. Thirteen novels followed, including the Deathrealm Award-winning *Strange Angels* (1994) and Spectrum Award-winning *Under the Poppy* (2010). A prolific writer of short fiction, a portion of her stories are collected in *Extremities* (1997). Her adult fiction is noted for dark and graphic depictions of sex and

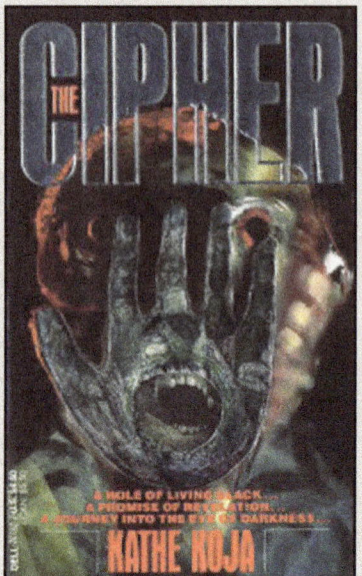

violence that can be disturbing for some readers, but in more recent years she has adapted her style to include fiction aimed at a young adult audience as well. Few authors can move seamlessly from NC-17 content to material more suited for the Scholastic Book Club, but she has done so with great success. Her young adult debut novel *Stray Dog* (2002) received the 2002 *ASPCA Henry Bergh Children's Book Honor*. *Buddha Boy* (2003) and *The Blue Mirror* (2004) were both listed as ALA Best Books for Young Adults, and *Kissing the Bee* (2007) received the Parents' Choice Award. In addition to writing, she is an accomplished editor, most recently helming *Year's Best Strange Fiction Volume Two* (2016) with co-editor Michael Kelly.

Koja is also the Founding and Artistic Director of Detroit-based *nerve. Nerve* is a performative art company that stages immersive production experiences somewhere between theater and literature. Each performance is site-specific and invites audience participation or interaction with no fourth-wall. People attending performances can choose less direct interaction with the cast, but the events invite curiosity and

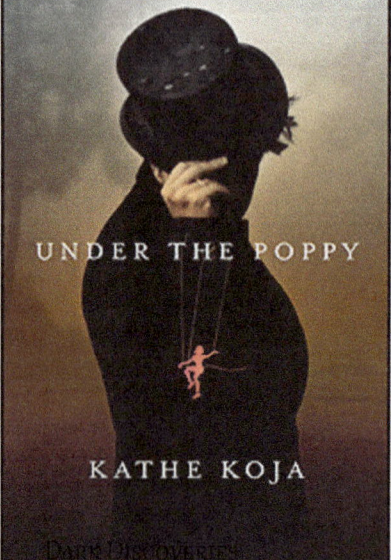

exploration. They are meant to be experienced, not simply seen. Asked about her creative philosophy, she says, "Nerve's mission statement really does sum up what I'm going for, every time out: *We define success as sensation. We take space and use it. We make consensual art. Our audience is everywhere.*"

Even the company's website (http://gonerve. com/gonerve/) is carefully designed to draw you in. It is visually lush, and tantalizes the visitor with glimpses that arouse curiosity. Although it tells you everything you need to know to find performances it teases just a little bit about what to expect. Past performances include

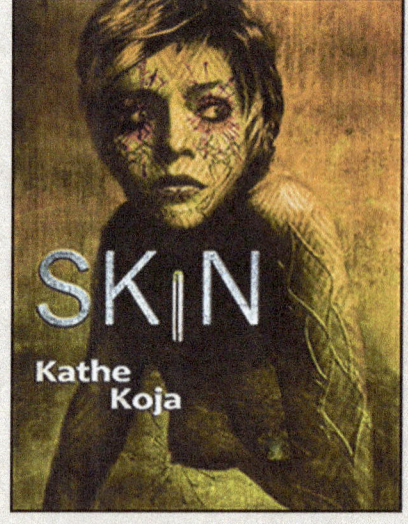

Under the Poppy, based on her novel of the same title; *The Heights*, adapted from Bronte's *Wuthering Heights*; *Faustus*, from Christopher Marlowe's novel; *Alice*, adapted from *Alice in Wonderland*, and most recently *Dracula*. Says Koja, "We came to *Dracula* from two chance comments—we were in the middle of *The Heights*, hanging out after the performance when Marisa Dluge said, 'I want to be a man.' And Rachael Harbert said, 'I want to be evil.' And the ceiling just opened up and I knew, OK, we're doing *Dracula*."

Dracula, which played in January of this year, invited the audience to attend a dinner

with the Count and Jonathan Harker at The Izzy, a Detroit art gallery. Vampires Renfield and Lucy attended the dinner as well. Audience members entered the performance uncertain of their role or outcome and, indeed, actor Chris Jakob (Harker) made a decision over the course of each performance whether he would flee or remain to be consumed at the end of the evening. I asked Koja about her use of space and the process of adaptation. Each production takes place at a different location and the location is an important character. *Faustus*, for example, was held at the historic First Unitarian Universalist Church of Detroit, with Reverend Roger Mohr taking the story as inspiration for one of his Sunday sermons between performances.

Nerve ensemble photo from FAUSTUS

Photo courtesy of Rick Lieder

Actors L to R are: Laura Bailey, Steve Xander Carson, Samantha Moltmaker

"The text always comes first, but the space is definitely another character to be respected and utilized as a fellow participant in the piece. And a nerve is made to deliver sensation, which could be interpreted as emotion or information, or both. Every piece is meant to be consensual in different degrees, or variables. Dracula was frustrating to some audience members because they expected more traditional interaction from the lead, they wanted Dracula to make eye contact, to speak to them, menace them… But this dinner is between Dracula and Jonathan Harker. The other two vampires, as much as they might have wanted to touch (or eat) the patrons, would respect Dracula's boundaries, and refrain. (They were pretty rough on the Brides, though, which is what the Brides were for.)

"I have to say that rereading the Stoker novel was an eye-opener, in that the propulsion was there in the narrative, but I found much of it to be useless in the way I perceived the heart of the story, which, if you strip away all the Christian moralizing, is really asking, 'Who gets to eat whom? Who's the meat here?' So that's how I adapted the novel into our script, with that question foremost."

Dracula enjoyed a run of six sold-out performances and *nerve* continues to build on its

Photo courtesy of the Divine Iguana

loyal and adventurous following of audience-participants seeking. Next up for nerve is an interactive recreation of Hieronymus Bosch's painting *The Garden of Earthly Delights*, scheduled for later this summer. As she prepares for this next theatrical effort, Koja continues to work on a new novel *Christopher Wild*, based on Christopher Marlowe, the famous poet, playwright, atheist, spy, and sexual revolutionary. Koja has a life-long interest in Marlowe and describes this work as, "Wit and sex and death and the turning wheel of centuries, as Marlowe moves across time, finding love and making enemies, always writing, always a rebel, always pursued, always himself."

Always pushing the envelope herself, Koja is taking an interactive approach with readers, allowing them real-time access to the novel writing process, including excerpts, updates, and notes as she moves forward with the book. How does she manage to balance and direct her creative energies?

"I work pretty much all the time. And I don't ever, ever work on stuff I hate."

In Marlowe, "the Muses' darling," Kathe Koja has her own Muse, and we, fortunately, have her.

Kathe Koja's site: http://www.kathekoja.com/blog/
Facebook page: https://www.facebook.com/kathe.koja

Painting courtesy Rick Lieder

GARY RAISOR

BAD BLOOD

A LESS THAN HUMAN TALE

PART 1

June 24th, 1976
5 miles west of Deadwood
South Dakota
just after sunset

Steven Adler looked at the Caddy's steaming engine with disgust. Cocking back his Stetson, he turned to Earl Jacobs. "Next time you steal a car, how about stealing one that works?"

"Whoa, take it easy there, pard," Earl replied, unperturbed. "She just needs a fan-belt."

"We're on the side of the road, in the desert. In the middle of the night. We should've taken the Chrysler."

"Screw that, the Caddy had an eight-track. CCR. I don't see the problem. We'll just hitchhike back to Deadwood." Earl fired up a cigar. "And maybe get us some Mexican on the way."

Steven shook his head. "You know I cain't do no Mexican. They eat those chili peppers, and that shit gets in their blood. Burns my mouth."

"It's my ass I gotta worry about." Earl doffed his own hat to fan away the steam covering the engine. "I eat a Mexican, an hour later I'm farting. Those hot ones, you know? That's why I don't have no hair on the back of my balls."

"I wouldn't worry 'bout it none. It's been two hours since I seen another car. There's only one way we'll be getting to town."

"Walking...?"

"You got it."

"In case you didn't notice, I got new boots," Earl protested. He pulled out a pint of *Dickel*, took a sip. "Those suckers ain't quite broke in."

"They will be."

"A car might come along, full of Mexicans. Fat, juicy, little Mexicans."

"No Mexicans. Put Mexicans from your mind."

Earl, looking disappointed, tucked the *Dickel* away and zipped up his ratty leather jacket. He put his hands over the engine for warmth.

"We can't take the road, anyway," Steven informed him. "A cop might come along, see the car's been stolen."

"So we're going to Deadwood? Cross country? On foot?"

"Yep."

Earl considered that. "There's snakes out there."

"Yep."

"Prairie dog holes."

"Yep."

"I could turn an ankle. I got awful weak ankles, you know."

"They'll be a lot stronger by the time we get to Deadwood. Grab the pool-cue cases and let's go."

Earl patted the fender of the Caddy, blew it a kiss. "You be good, baby. I'll be back."

With Earl humming *Run through the Jungle,* they set out.

"By the way, where'd you get those boots?" Steven said.

Earl grinned. "Mexican."

Deadwood, South Dakota
LUCKY BOB'S BINGO
ALSO THE VFW

Beneath the brim of his weather-beaten Stetson, Earl took in the parking lot, looking for anything out of the ordinary. Dead Wood about summed it up. Thunder rumbled, called attention to a few sullen clouds on the horizon. They were the only things moving, and even they looked too tired, too pissed off, to make the trek to town. Earl knew how they felt. For hours, he and Steven had waded through creeks, knee-high buffalo grass, climbed across arroyos and gulches, all while swatting at a cloud of deer flies kamikazing them.

Pausing, Earl lit up a smoke in hopes it'd keep the deer flies away. It didn't.

"I'm going in," Steven said. "I need to pee for about ten minutes. Then I need a drink and a game."

"Gimme twenty minutes. I'm gonna check out the parking garage, see what the transportation situation is." Earl headed off. Before he reached the parking area, he realized he also needed to drain the ol' lizard. Not out in the open. Deer flies weren't particular about where they bit.

There was a gas station on the corner with a sleepy Mexican behind the cash register. Without even looking up from his *HUSTLER*, the man handed over a key chained to a chunk of wood roughly the shape and size of two prairie dogs humping, and Earl headed for the restroom around back.

"The two-holer's okay. But don't do nothing in that first crapper," floated after Earl, "it runs over when you flush."

"It's okay. I got a log to hang onto." With those disturbing images in his head, Earl turned the corner. A couple steps later, he caught a whiff of something odd. Smelled like blood... but mixed in with another scent. Startled, he tested the air, but he couldn't locate either odor over the garbage stench. Then he heard flies. Not deer flies. House flies. They were clustered over by the trash cans where drink-containers, popsicle sticks, and half-eaten corndogs had spilled out.

Walking over, he saw there were a lot of flies. That meant only one thing. Something was dead. Maybe they got drowned by the toilet.

Earl eased aside garbage with the toe of his boot, gradually revealed a body. Puzzled, his eyes narrowed. At first he couldn't figure out what he was looking at. In the sodium yellow haze of the parking-lot lights, the mass of fur didn't appear real. The body wasn't much bigger than his hand, and it was so mangled, it was unrecognizable. Crouching down, Earl worked a popsicle stick under it where dried blood had stuck its head to the pavement. He gingerly turned the body over... and saw a baby jackrabbit. Or what was left of one.

The animal had been stomped to a pulp. Blood had spread several feet in every direction from beneath the hapless rabbit. Someone had stepped in that blood. Red footprints from running shoes trailed across the parking lot, growing fainter with each step.

Earl felt a surge of anger. Killing for no good reason infuriated him.

Staring at the remains, he sniffed the evening air again and his stomach did a slow looping lurch. A wet, musty, animal smell clung to the trash cans, a smell that had nothing to do with the dead baby rabbit or even the garbage.

It was as though some huge predator had sprayed the area, marking its territory.

Only thing, the odor was kind of human, too. He had smelled it only once before. By the Caddy—

—the one that'd left them stranded.

Earl felt the itch between his shoulder-blades. It took him a second to realize it was caused by his own cold sweat.

Staring at the busted crapper door didn't put Earl in a better mood. Bathrooms were supposed to stay locked. But this one was wide open. Someone'd sure been in a hurry, they'd damned near ripped the door off the hinges.

"Musta been the corndogs," Earl said to the buffalo watching him from across a fence.

Whoever had wrecked the door had used something heavy and sharp, and, when he looked closer, he noticed the gouges looked a lot like claw marks. Now that was odd, what kind of animal would force its way into a bathroom?

The deer flies made up Earl's mind for him. He entered, his footsteps clicking on the sweaty tile. The air was hot and stuffy in here, medicinal smelling, and it wrapped around him like a wool blanket. More sweat oozed down his back. Earl's hand rested on the pistol in his belt while he called out. That hand stayed there while he gave each stall door a hinge-rattling kick.

Satisfied he was alone, Earl stepped up to the urinal. That was when he heard the breathing.

Right behind him.

For some reason he couldn't specify, he didn't turn around. Not until he had eased out his pistol.

When he did turn, he saw he was alone. He looked at the pistol in one hand, his equipment in the other, and laughed shakily. His nerves were getting the best of him. No one could come up behind him on this tile floor and then walk out again without him hearing their footsteps. Could they?

Facing the urinal, he jammed the gun back into his belt and took a deep breath. He tried for calm as he went back to the business of trying to relieve himself.

No good. His equipment was locked up tight. He flushed the urinal, hoping the running water would help.

"Hey, mister." The voice was loud in the closed confines of the bathroom. "You wanna get your picture taken with a real Indian?" The words were so unexpected Earl damned near peed on his boots.

The voice came again. "Only cost you ten dollars. What do you say?"

"I say I'm kind of busy here," Earl answered.

"Doin' what, playin' with yourself?" the voice asked with a snigger.

Earl fought to hold his temper. "I don't think that would be any of your business, now would it?"

"Quit playing with that shriveled-up old dick," the voice said, "and give me some money. I ain't got all night here."

Really annoyed now, Earl turned and urinated on the floor. A sullen-looking Indian kid, who couldn't be more than seventeen, jumped back, barely avoiding the splash.

"You're the second guy that's tried to pee on me tonight," the teenager said, bristling.

"That oughta tell you something." Earl glared at the young panhandler, saw a chest and neck covered with scabs and dirt, but the shirt was what really caught Earl's eye. Fact was, he couldn't take his eyes off it. It was… pink. Neon, eye-watering… pink.

The kid caught Earl looking. "Quit starin', okay? The son of a bitch who peed on me hit me in the head and took my shirt. This one ain't mine. I found it in a trash can."

"Don't be modest, son. You're pulling off them male hooker duds just fine. So where's that camera at?" Earl asked. "That get stolen, too?"

"No, I figured I was gonna let you buy me a new one."

"And give you ten dollars?"

"Now you gettin' the picture, pops."

Beneath the one working fluorescent light, they eyed each other. Earl noticed there was something feral about the way the kid watched him. For several seconds, they both simply stood there, and the only sound in the place was the flies over by the two-holer. One landed on Earl's face. He didn't bother to brush it away.

The kid decided Earl needed some prompting on that money request. He pulled his weapon. "Come on, pops, let's go. I ain't got all night to mess around. Cough up that money, and maybe I'll let your stupid old ass walk out of here."

"That's mighty white of you." Earl eyed the kid's weapon. It was a sliver of glass from the busted wall mirror, seven maybe eight inches long, with one end wrapped in a handkerchief. The weapon might be makeshift, but it looked dangerous.

Earl spat on the floor. "I think I'm going to have to pass on giving you money."

"Why's that?"

"Because, son, you just crossed the line." Earl zipped up.

"What line?"

"The one that separates panhandling from armed robbery."

A flush of anger crept up the kid's neck. Earl assumed it was a flush since it was a little hard to tell on account of all the dirt.

"How about I cut you," the teenager said. "You ready for me to cross that line, old man?" The kid raised the mirror shard, and for a second the outside door was reflected in it. In that brief moment, Earl thought he glimpsed two yellow eyes staring in at them from the dark.

Before he could be sure, the mirror shard moved. Earl started toward the door to get a better look.

"Where you think you're goin', gramps?" The kid blocked the way. Glaring, wiping his sweaty face on the shirt, he pointed the shard at Earl's face. "I cut the last guy that messed with me. Cut him bad."

"Really." Earl sounded skeptical.

The teenager took a step closer and Earl caught a whiff of the handkerchief that made up the handle. It stunk.

"Jesus," Earl said. "What'd you do, wipe your ass with that rag?"

The kid, uncertain now, cocked his head at Earl. This wasn't going quite like he'd planned. All the people he'd robbed before would just hand over the money. They didn't talk his ear off.

Earl went to the sink and washed his hands, keeping an eye on the teen in the busted mirror. Most likely, Earl figured the young robber's plan was to render him unconscious with B.O., because the stench coming off the kid could peel paint, worse than the crappers, if that was possible.

In the meantime, the kid was growing agitated. "Come on, you crazy old fart, this is the last time I'm telling you. Hand over that wallet."

"I don't think so."

The teen lunged at Earl with the piece of mirror.

To the kid's surprise, Earl wasn't in the same spot as before. The young robber hadn't seen the old man so much as twitch.

"Now, son, I might be crazy," Earl said, turning to face the kid while he dried his hands, "and I might be old."

The kid started waving his makeshift knife around, like he'd meant to miss.

"But…" Earl fanned the air with his hat. The stink coming from the would-be mugger's vicinity was even more frightening now that he was moving around. "… and this is a big but, I cain't go giving you no money, son. Money's got to be earned. Or it ain't appreciated." Earl grinned. It didn't reach his eyes, though.

The young robber lunged again, and again. Each time his victim was in a different spot, causing the weapon to slice air. The kid's lower lip began trembling in frustration. He looked on the verge of crying. "Give me that wallet, or I'm gonna Kung Fu your ass. I got a black belt in karate."

"It's probably a white belt. You just ain't washed it in a while."

The mugger threw a roundhouse kick at Earl's head, which Earl dodged as easily as he had the other attacks. When the foot went by, Earl noticed the kid's running shoe had something stuck to it, something that looked like dried blood and some kind of fur.

Earl's grin vanished as realization came. "You're the son of a bitch who stomped that baby rabbit…"

"Yeah, so what? I'm gonna do the same thing to you, you stand still."

"Son," Earl said with as much patience as he could muster, "you're obviously lacking in respect for your elders. As well as personal hygiene. I could let all that go. Put it in the rearview and drive away. But I just can't get that baby rabbit out of my head."

"Yeah, you shoulda seen him," the kid said, trying to bait Earl, "stupid little fucker hopped right up to me. I guess he thought I was gonna give him something to eat." The kid sniggered. "I did, I gave him some shoe leather. He didn't much like it, though. I think it gave him a bellyache."

Before the kid could say another word, Earl grabbed the hand holding the weapon and slammed the teenager into the concrete wall with bone-jarring force. The impact caused shards of the already busted mirror to jump from their wall-frame and cascade to the floor in a rain of silver. With his other hand, Earl took hold of the teenager by the front of the pink shirt, lifted him two feet off the floor.

The young mugger's eyes gobbled up his face at this turn of events. Suddenly, without warning, the kid threw up. Something that resembled chunks of steaming, half-digested meat smacked Earl in the face and splattered onto the floor. It was disgusting and it damn sure didn't improve the smell in here, but right now, Earl didn't care. He held on, so pissed he could barely see straight.

The teen tried to wiggle loose. Earl applied leverage to some pressure points, twisted the hand holding the weapon. In less than a second, the glop on the floor had company—the kid's face. The handkerchief-wrapped weapon bounced off the far wall. Miraculously, it didn't break.

When silence at last descended, Earl stared down at the young mugger. "Breaking a mirror is bad luck, son. Don't you know that?"

The young mugger stared up at Earl with eyes the size of saucers. "Who the hell are you, mister?"

"Me, I'm just an animal-lover. Sometimes, to make ends meet, I might play some cards, hustle a little pool. Hell, one time I even played Bingo. But them old ladies are vicious." Earl tipped his hat back, took a deep breath. Which he instantly regretted. "What's your name, young rabbit-killer?"

"Fuck you."

Earl was mostly successful as he fought the urge to grind the kid's face into the slimed floor. He applied more pressure to the hand. The kid screamed.

"I don't get a name, you ain't gonna be abusing yourself for at least a week."

"Dwayne," the underage mugger stammered, trying to lift his face from the floor. "My name's Dwayne."

"That's a good solid Native American handle you got there, Dwayne. I thought it was something like 'He who does not wash.'"

The kid looked up defiantly. "What're you gonna do, call the cops, tell my dad?"

"Nah, we'll leave the cops out of this. I doubt your dad gives a shit what you do. Else we wouldn't be having this conversation."

"Then what're you gonna do?"

"Something your daddy should've done a long time ago." Earl eased Dwayne up off the floor, causing the bill of the teenager's baseball cap to catch the sink and tip forward, hiding the wide eyes.

"No sir, I'll tell you what you're gonna do," Dwayne informed him from beneath the cap.

"Dwayne, did you find some crack down there?"

"You're gonna let me go," Dwayne said. "You're not even gonna try to get me arrested."

"Why's that?"

"I'm sixteen and I'm Sioux. Fact is, you'd better take your stupid white hands off me right fucking now, or my grandpa'll have your wrinkly old white ass in a sling. He's the head of the tribal council. He's a lawyer, too." The teenager was quickly regaining his courage. He knew how the game was played; he'd been playing it since age eleven. There were rules. This stupid white man couldn't do squat.

Figuring he was home free, Dwayne tipped up his cap and let his familiar smirk appear.

"By the way," Earl asked, "where'd you get those marks on your chest?"

The teenager gazed into Earl's eyes and began speaking in his native Sioux, the smirk growing wider.

"You can leave my mother out of this," Earl answered back in Sioux.

The smirk on the kid's face vanished, to be replaced by sheer terror. Dwayne twisted loose and made a run for the door, leaving a handful of pink shirt in Earl's hand. The would-be mugger was a foot from freedom, but the tile floor was slippery from where he had up-chucked earlier. Down he went. His head made a loud bonking sound when it hit, sort of like a bowling ball when it smacked the lane too hard. His baseball cap now covered his entire face.

A muffled "Don't hurt me, I was only kidding" floated up.

"About the money or my mother?" Earl ambled over to the prone boy, continuing on like nothing had happened. "You know what, Dwayne, I don't give a rat's ass if your grandpa's Tonto with a fucking law degree from Harvard. Your butt belongs to me, tonight."

"Let me go, you'll never see me again. I promise."

Earl considered Dwayne's more than generous offer. "Let me see if I got this straight, tough guy. You just tried to rob me, then you tried to assault me, then you insulted my mother. And oh yeah, let's not forget you stomped a baby rabbit to death for no good reason—and you want me to forget all about it. Just let you walk—"

The teenager nodded.

Earl nudged the kid's baseball cap aside with a boot. The kid's eyes weren't quite focused. "Well, Dwayne, that wouldn't be very responsible on my part. You ever hear of that word, responsibility?"

The kid looked up at Earl like he was talking Greek.

"Well, you're going to." Beneath his calm exterior, Earl was still filled with rage. "Fact is, you're going to take responsibility for that rabbit out there. You killed the little guy. And now, by God, you're going to bury him. In fact you're going to give that little rabbit the best goddamned burial any goddamned rabbit ever had."

"You want me to dig a hole for a stupid-ass rabbit?" The teenager stopped short of laughing when he saw the expression on Earl's face.

The older man yanked him up off the floor, none too gently. Their faces were only inches apart. "No, you're going do more than dig a hole. Now listen up, Dwayne, this part's important. That little rabbit had himself a carrot. It was his favorite carrot. I think he'd want to be buried with it, don't you? It was all he had in the world."

"You're crazy, I didn't see no carrot."

"That's because somebody took it," Earl confided.

"Really." Dwayne was noncommittal.

"Yeah, I'm guessin' somebody went and dropped it down a crapper. Just to be mean. Probably some

karate-kickin', heavily armed, badass like yourself." Earl put an arm around the kid's shoulders, gave him a little squeeze. "Now I figure you'll want to do the right thing, and get that carrot back for the rabbit. Don't you think so, Dwayne?"

The kid pondered that statement for a few seconds before he reluctantly nodded. "Which crapper?"

"Good question. This is where it gets tricky. I don't really know." Earl rubbed his chin as he smiled at Dwayne. "The rabbit died before he could tell me."

"We're talking the two crappers here," Dwayne stammered, "not the row of port-a-potties out front, right?"

"Nope, we're talking about the whole she-bang. Every last one."

A look of absolute horror appeared on the kid's face. "Jesus, how am I supposed to find a carrot in all that crap, even if there is a carrot? There's gotta be ten or twelve of them nasty-ass things out there." Dwayne had tears in his eyes now and his lower lip was flapping around like a clothes-lined sheet in a high wind.

"There's sixteen, packed to the brim with shit. Just like you."

Dwayne ignored the jibe. "And you want me to look in every one?"

"Look? You wish. No, no, no, this is a roll-up your sleeves, hands-on kind of job. Here's what you're gonna do, son. You're gonna take your baseball cap and scoop out the crap. All the crap. Then you're gonna sort through it. That carrot'll be easy enough to find, since it's about the same size as my shriveled-up… well, you know what I'm talking about."

"I won't do it. You can't make me." Dwayne hung his head for a moment, then lunged at Earl with a piece of mirror snatched off the floor.

Earl caught Dwayne's hand. The boy fought, trying to cut him, while the two of them two-stepped across the slippery floor. They wrestled until Earl had no choice but to push the kid up against the wall. Only this time he pushed harder than he intended. Dwayne's hand smacked into the soap dispenser with a bang, shattering the piece of mirror in his grubby fingers into half a dozen pieces.

The teenager began screaming.

While Earl watched, red dots crawled out and jumped onto the floor like fire-ants spilling from their nest. For Earl, the world went suddenly gray. For the first time the kid was in real danger—

—because the sight, the smell, of blood was more than Earl could bear. He began looking at the artery pulsing in the kid's throat.

Grabbing hold of what was left of Dwayne's already ragged shirt, Earl fought to keep from giving into his lust for blood. He fell into the boy, smashing him into the wall again. The impact sent the few remaining shards of mirror spilling from their frame to the floor. Over the sound of crashing glass, a "Please, mister, don't hurt me no more!" reached Earl.

The words finally penetrated. He released the boy and took a wobbly step toward the sink, grabbed hold. His breathing had gone ragged. He splashed cold water on his face, fighting for control.

Dwayne, who had gone limp when his head had smacked the wall the second time, pitched forward like a pink sack of feed and again sprawled face first into a pool of urine and vomit on the floor.

Clutching the sink with both hands, Earl held on.

Finally, after five or six deep breaths, the gray receded enough he could see the kid struggle up and crawl into a corner, gazing up at him with eyes that had gone from frightened to terrified.

"Son, I was already having a bad day," Earl said, water streaming down his face, "before you came along. You don't want to piss me off anymore. You really don't." He made sure to keep his eyes off the boy's hand. "Stomping the shit out of that baby rabbit put a burr under my saddle, okay? Just nod if any of this is getting through, Dwayne."

Dwayne nodded.

"Alrighty then, we've got us a plan. You'd best wrap that hand. Time for you to get to work." Earl pulled a clean handkerchief from his pocket, well, cleaner than the one Dwayne had, and tossed it in the kid's general direction. "I'll be outside, waiting on that carrot. Don't make me come looking for you."

Earl lurched toward the door, praying his knees wouldn't fold. They didn't. He barely escaped the john before he realized he was going to throw up. Stumbling along in the dark, he tried to put as much distance as possible between himself and the rest room. He didn't want Dwayne to hear.

Even as he made for the fence, he knew he couldn't outrun his stomach.

On the other side, several buffalo had wandered over, looking for a handout. The animals were chewing their cud, eagerly pressing their wet noses up against the chainlink.

Earl braced himself, his stomach knotting. Before he could bend over, *Dickel* splattered the buffalo.

Across the way, the sound of Dwayne's puking echoed Earl's own. Earl couldn't help grinning between heaves. He hoped that little son of a bitch hacked up a lung. Along with a few toenails.

Earl's puking spooked the pair of buffalo and they wheeled around and took off across the pasture at a lumbering gallop. He watched them go. His grin went from mean to wistful. He'd thought coming back here would remind him of when his Lakota wife was still alive, bring her back to him somehow. Wakiya. Little Thunder. But this place only filled him with sadness, and all the wanting in the world wouldn't bring her back. Still, he had to admit this trip wasn't a total bust, he was having fun with Dwayne the rabbit killer.

Reeling away from the fence, he waited for his stomach to ease up. When it did, he just might go back in there and make Dwayne lick those crappers clean. He staggered across the parking lot, sinking to his knees beside a sign that warned against feeding the animals. With fingers that still had a few spots of Dwayne's watery blood clinging to them, he managed to fish out a cigar. Several shaky tries later, he even managed to get the damned thing lit. It smelled like the crappers, he smelled like the crappers, and he didn't care. Pulling cigar smoke into his lungs, he held it there until it hurt. Anything to take his mind off the agony in his stomach. His heart, well, that was another matter.

As he pressed his icy face to the warm smooth metal of the sign, he noticed howling had arrived on the night air.

Coyotes.

He listened to them, his stomach forgotten for a second. They were howling something fierce, as though something had spooked them. That storm coming must be a bad one. Or maybe they'd caught wind of some predator that had wandered into the area. But what kind of predator would spook a coyote?

For some reason, Earl thought of that strange smell over by the trash cans where he'd found the dead rabbit earlier. The hair on the back of his neck stood up.

A rumble came. Swiveling his head, which felt like it was mounted on rusty ball-bearings, he looked north across the valley, watching the lightning claw its way over the peaks, gutting the rain-swollen clouds in its way.

Earl counted from the flash. He was on four Mississippi when the thunder rolled in. That storm was still a long way off, but it was definitely headed in this direction. There was going be some wet asses tonight, his included, if he didn't get under cover. Right now though, he was too pissed-off to care. He put his back to the sign, stretched out his legs and eased his hat down over his eyes. Listening to the wolves, he waited for his stomach to unclench. In a minute or two, he'd get up and investigate. He just needed to rest his eyes.

Within a minute he was asleep.

***

A short while later, Dwayne staggered over, his injured hand wrapped in the clean handkerchief. It was the only clean thing on him. "Oh man," he said, breathing in the night air, "it sure smells a lot better out here."

"It did until you showed up. Move your ass down wind." Earl wanted to kick Dwayne's scrawny little butt some more, but that meant he'd have to get up. "How you comin' on that carrot?"

"Well," the kid said, digging in his pocket, "I didn't find no carrot. So far, I've dug out seventy-three cents, a comb, and a *Trojan* still in the pack." He held out the brown-smeared contents for Earl's inspection. "You want any of it? I washed the corn off."

"You trying to bribe me, son?"

"No," the kid lied.

Earl grinned. It was an evil grin. "See now, doesn't earning that money feel a whole lot better than stealing it?"

"No sir, I can't say it does," Dwayne answered, watching the distant lightning. "Stealing's a whole lot easier. Cleaner, too." He looked back at Earl, perplexed. "What if I can't find that carrot, you still gonna call the cops?"

"You'd like that, wouldn't you? Then you could call your grandpa, so he could trot down and get you out. No, son, you're on my work-release program, 'till I say otherwise."

"What's that mean?"

"It means your juvenile-delinquent ass gets released

when you find that carrot." Earl's eyes, gray and cold as creek ice, fixed on the kid.

The kid looked away. "I'm an oppressed minority, you know."

"You think that makes it okay for you to rob people?"

"You sayin' you never took nothin' that wasn't yours?"

"I took plenty that doesn't belong to me. Hell, I stole the car that brought me here. But then I never had no guidance growing up."

"What if I don't want no guidance?"

"Too bad. You know what, young rabbit killer, we might be looking in the wrong place for that carrot. See that old bull buffalo out there?" Earl pointed at the one taking a major dump. "I'm thinking whoever took the carrot might've fed it to that buffalo. How about I have you follow him around the rest of the night. Wait for that carrot to show up. What do you think?"

"I think I'll get back on them crappers."

Off in the distance, the coyotes continued howling. They still sounded weirded out. Earl didn't blame them—it had been one strange night all around.

The pain in Earl's stomach finally eased up. While grinding out his cigar, he noticed something moving around out there in the dark.

Footsteps were headed his way.

At first he thought Dwayne was coming back to whine some more about the carrot.

Only these steps weren't human.

Odd, he'd thought they were at first. His ears must be playing tricks on him because they belonged to something with four legs, not two. It wasn't no buffalo neither, the steps were far too light. Peering into the darkness beyond the parking-lot lights, he had trouble spotting his visitor against the white-washed concession stand. Only when the shape moved out into the parking lot could he tell what it was.

To his amazement, he saw what was causing the coyotes to act so weird. He was looking at a wolf... a white wolf.

Earl waited for it to come closer. At first the animal kept to the edge of the parking lot, as though afraid. It kept sniffing the air and looking around.

Earl held still and watched the creature come nearer, and all he could say was he'd definitely never seen its like before. Not only was the thing huge, it had the strangest eyes he'd ever seen. It wasn't that they were all shiny yellow-green when the animal passed under the sodium lights. That was normal. No, what spooked Earl was the intelligence he saw there. They looked smart, well, smarter than Dwayne, anyway.

The wolf limped across the parking lot and flopped down, as though it had traveled a ways. Tucking its paws under its chest, it gazed directly at Earl.

They regarded each other across the expanse of tarmac.

The wind caught some of the Styrofoam cups over by the trash barrels and pushed them across the lot, making a noise that sounded like whispering. The wolf watched the cups for a second then turned back to Earl. There was something otherworldly about the way the animal kept looking at him. It didn't appear rabid or anything. It was injured though, Earl had seen that right off, because it had favored its right paw when it had trotted over.

But why had it come here? And why did it keep on looking at him?

The only thing he could figure, the animal must have caught the odor of rabbit and had come over to investigate. That blood-smell would carry, the way the wind was whipping around tonight.

Still, he couldn't shake the feeling he was being visited by something that wasn't real.

Real or not, the wolf wouldn't stop looking at him

He decided to be neighborly and offer the animal something to eat. There was no need to waste Dwayne's dead rabbit. The wolf could get some good from it. The strange visitor was on the skinny side, as though it hadn't eaten in a while.

In a cordial voice, he asked, "Will you be dining alone?"

The wolf didn't even blink.

Earl took that for a yes. "Alrighty then, table for one. Thumper tar tar is our special tonight," Earl said, "courtesy of our chef, Mr. Dwayne. Thumper will be served on a bed of piquant *Slim Jim* wrappers, with a little bubble-gum and chewing tobacco thrown in for color. Piquant means savory, in case you're wondering. My wife taught me that. She was a lot smarter than me."

The wolf took its eyes off Earl long enough to give its butt a quick lick.

Grinning, Earl doffed his hat. "We're pretty informal down here at the road-kill inn. But I have to tell you, we generally try to discourage butt licking in the main dining-room." Earl wished he didn't have to get up. Groaning, he hauled his tired body off pavement that was still warm from the sun and tossed the baby jackrabbit at the wolf's feet. Then he went back over by the sign so as not to make the animal nervous. Or maybe it was himself he didn't want to make nervous.

The wolf lay there staring at him. It made no move toward the rabbit. Maybe the smell from the crappers had spoiled its appetite. God knows, it had certainly spoiled Earl's. He stared back at the wolf, waiting for it to do something. Anything.

It just continued lying there, alternating between licking its injured paw and staring at him. Once in a while, it would gaze around, sniff the night air, but its eyes always came back to him.

Was it waiting for him to do something?

After another five minutes or so, that staring game started getting old, so Earl chucked a rock in the animal's direction. Just to see what would happen.

The wolf didn't even flinch, let alone get up and run.

"Now that's damned odd."

So Earl seriously chucked a rock and Earl was a good rock chucker. Dust flew up inches from the wolf's head. Still it didn't move.

The animal refused to budge until Earl climbed to his feet. As Earl approached, the creature loped out into the buffalo grass. A few yards in, it stopped and looked back over its shoulder at Earl, its tongue lolling from its mouth.

"You want me to follow you, is that it?"

The wolf gave a short growl that Earl could only take for a yes.

"I'll be right with you." It was all Earl could think to say under the circumstances.

Before Earl headed out, he had to check on something first. He had to see how Dwayne was coming on the carrot search.

***

Dwayne was gone.

And less than half of the porta-potties had been emptied.

Earl briefly wondered about Steven, was his partner worrying about where he'd gotten off to?

"I hope you're only taking a break, son," Earl called out into the night, "cause I'll be back in a few minutes to check on you. I don't find your ass, you're gonna be learning a new profession—buffalo proctologist."

***

The wolf was moving at a ground-eating trot, drifting along with that peculiar sideways gait that wolves had.

An hour later, he and the wolf were still out in the middle of nowhere. The scenery, all crags and spires and Ponderosa pines belonged on a postcard, not under a man's boots. The terrain was treacherous as hell out here in the dark. Earl had already gone ass over elbows a couple of times and he'd been bitten by something that looked like ants when he'd sat down on a log to catch his breath. The bites were starting to itch like crazy. To make matters worse, if that was possible, the temperature was dropping, too. In fact it'd gotten downright chilly in the last hour.

He pulled up his jacket collar and stumbled on, digging at the ant bites.

"Where the hell are you going?" he bellowed at the wolf.

The animal just kept going.

***

After a bit they came to Bear Butte Creek. Earl loved that name, "bare butt" creek, and he said the name aloud a couple of times, grinning.

The wolf trotted across a fallen tree that spanned the rushing water. It disappeared into a grove of aspens on the other side. Earl looked on dubiously. The tree spanning the creek was at least four inches in diameter and appeared sturdy enough when he ventured out onto it. He took a few more steps. There were a few ominous groaning noises, but it held.

He'd almost reached the middle when a wind gust rocked him. Teeth chattering, he teetered, then regained his balance before edging forward some more. Another step and he overbalanced, caught himself. He grinned. Nothing to this, another ten or twelve feet and he was across. He took another step, trying to keep the wolf in sight.

A piece of the log bark crumbled under his feet. He listed to one side. Overbalanced, arms waving, it all seemed to happen in slow motion, he slipped off into the creek feet first, bumping his sore butt on the way down.

The water wasn't all that deep, just up to his waist. For a second, it actually felt good.

Until the cold hit.

Earl had labored under the illusion he was cold before—well, he'd only *thought* he was cold. This was a degree of cold that had gone unplumbed. This was like being plunged into ice. Everything from the waist down went numb.

He managed to grab hold of the log overhead or he'd have been swept away. As it was, he could barely stay on his feet. Pulling himself along, hand over hand, he reached the bank and that was when that damned wind came again and smacked his Stetson into the water. The hat took off like it had an urgent appointment downstream. He watched it bob along until it fetched up behind a boulder on the far side. That hat had been with him a long time. Wakiya had given it to him. She'd picked it up at Little Bighorn after Custer had been massacred.

No way he was walking without that Stetson.

Problem was, the hat was unreachable from the bank. Too steep.

The other problem, if he went for it, he'd have to turn loose of the tree he was holding onto. He didn't much like that idea. Still, as he stood here, he couldn't help noticing that water wasn't getting any warmer. Taking a determined breath, he set a course toward the other side and began slogging across the foaming water. He'd worked himself up a plan. He figured if he built up some speed, maybe even got himself a running start, he could make it to the other side. Do it on the slant, so to speak.

A couple of steps later, he couldn't help noticing there was a flaw in the plan. The current was stronger out here in the middle, downright fierce as a matter of fact. His feet began sliding along the gravel bottom. He turned back, tried to grab the tree. Too late. The current had him.

When he floated past the hat, he made a grab for it. And missed. Apparently he got the hat's attention. It took off after him as though it was trying to save him from the rapids waiting ahead.

Bouncing off eleven submerged rocks, eight logs, and a *Subaru*, Earl was deposited, battered, and damned near frozen, nearly a quarter of a mile downstream.

A few seconds later, the hat fetched up beside him. Grabbing hold of the waterlogged Stetson, he now knew why the local Indians called this stretch of water "Bare Butt" Creek. His jeans were down around his ankles.

Pulling them up, he took stock of the situation; nothing broken, that was good, one boot missing, along with his sidearm and his dignity. That was bad. Losing the sidearm. His dignity would recover. He looked up, saw the wolf standing high on a bluff, staring down at him with its pale yellow eyes.

Earl could swear he saw amusement there.

The way Earl saw this, his only real problem was he had ended up on the wrong side of the creek.

He had two choices; try to wade across, or go back to the log. He opted for the log.

The second time, he was half way across the creek when the log broke. There'd been no warning cracks or groans, it just snapped. On this trip down the creek he managed to miss most of the rocks and logs. But not the *Subaru*. Someone had stolen the tires. He hadn't noticed that the first time. A man had to be damned desperate for radials to wade out in water this cold.

The wolf didn't go with him this trip. Earl guessed the wolf figured he'd be back.

As he bobbed along in the dark, he thought maybe he'd open up a rafting business, since he was getting so familiar with this particular stretch of water.

A few minutes later he was again deposited in the pool below the waterfall and his hat sidled up to him like a dog looking for a pat on the head. He slogged out of the stream as fast as a man whose pants were down around his ankles could. "Dammit," he bellowed. "Dammit all to hell." He looked down. His other boot was gone now.

Pulling up his jeans, he looked around. At least this time he was on the right side of the creek.

Now, all he had to do was get up that bank that loomed above him. Slapping his wet hat on his head, he surveyed the steep incline. There were tree roots growing out of the dirt he could use to pull himself up.

On his fourth attempt, he reached the top. As he turned to give "Bare Butt" Creek the finger he stubbed his little toe. He spent the next thirty seconds or so hopping around and swearing. When he saw blood oozing from his mangled toe, he fought for calm. He'd almost regained it, until he stepped on a pine cone. One of those big gnarly ones, about the size of a hand grenade. He switched feet and hopped sideways into an entire bed of the things.

Now both feet were bleeding.

After all that exercise he needed to take a leak, but that was going to be a little tough. Apparently the part of his anatomy needed to perform that function was nowhere to be found. Cold, wet, his feet bleeding, his bladder about to explode, he limped back to where he'd left the wolf.

And it was, of course, gone. He wouldn't have expected anything else the way the night was going.

***

From the top of a dead-fall of trees, filled with slithering noises that sounded like pissed-off snakes, Earl scanned the valley below. He searched the rocks and scrub pine for any signs of white. He was pissed, too. This wasn't right. If the wolf was going to lead him out into country like this, it should damn well stay where it could be seen.

So far all he'd spotted were a few mule-deer and a pack of coyotes wandering around in the moonlight sticking their noses in every hole they could find. Mostly each other's assholes. Earl's teeth were now chattering like someone doing Morse Code on speed, and there'd still been no word yet from his dick or balls. He didn't know why he was trying to follow the wolf, all he knew was he'd chased the damned thing this far. No way he was giving up now.

Easing down from the dead-fall, Earl turned and saw eyes staring at him. He jumped back. His stubbed toe caught a limb.

When Earl's eyes quit watering, he saw the white wolf standing there. It had a live jackrabbit in its mouth. The white beast moved closer, and it was obvious it wanted Earl to take the rabbit.

"I don't need your help, I can get my own rabbits," Earl responded through gritted teeth, "thank you very much." He put his foot down and winced. That toe might be broken.

The wolf took no offense. It released the squirming rabbit and disappeared into the dark.

When the lightning flickered, Earl saw the animal had resumed its course. Due north. Right into the storm. That figured. Earl gazed down at his bare feet, then across the bramble-filled ground. There was a definite lack of enthusiasm in his step as he hobbled off into the night.

Where in God's name was the animal headed to in such a rush? They were on Bear Butte Creek, miles from anywhere. What could be so important way out here? The wolf seemed to know where it was going, though. "I got myself a wolf with a purpose."

The huge white beast looked back at him, as if to say hurry up.

"Aright, I'm coming, I'm coming." Earl hitched up his soggy, ice-cold jeans and limped faster. He just knew that toe was going to swell. Probably going to lose the nail, too. Already he could feel the thing throbbing like a bad tooth. He wished he had a dry cigar and some boots, but mostly, he wished he could find his dick. He really, really needed to take a whiz.

***

An hour and a half later, Earl was still grumbling when he caught up with the wolf at the backside of a parking lot. They were in Sturgis now. Across a stretch of pot-holed blacktop he saw signs announcing a pow wow was under way. Tents, tee pees, campers everywhere. Hippies mixed in with Lakota, Northern Cheyenne, Arapaho. The smell of weed floated on the night air. Now there was a peace pipe Earl wouldn't mind getting his hands on. Especially after the night he was having.

A couple of hippies, stoned, in handmade Indian apparel and feathers in their hair, staggered past. "Nice dog," one of them said.

Why had the wolf brought him here to Sturgis, of all places? Earl took a look at the rambling buildings. The wolf was ambling in the general direction of a casino. Nothing special here. This casino was like all the others he'd seen, flashing neon and quiet greed: Every Hand a Winner, Every Pull of the Slot Machine a PAY-OFF, if you believed the signs. As far as the cold, wet, footsore Earl was concerned, this had been a waste of boot leather—if he had boots. He cocked his bedraggled Stetson at a don't-screw-with-me angle and limped toward the main entrance, intent on finding a phone.

The wolf wasn't having any of that. It cut him off.

Earl wasn't happy at this turn of events. The wolf apparently wanted him to go to the parking lot. Maybe it had gotten him a job parking cars.

Earl took another step toward the main entrance. The animal showed him some teeth this time. Huge and sharp.

Suddenly pissed off, Earl was about to start chucking

some serious rocks when light glinting off metal in the parking lot caught his eye. The rocks fell at his feet. One of them hit his stubbed toe, but he barely noticed. What lay in front of him couldn't be... He moved closer, the cold forgotten. His swollen toe forgotten. The fact he could barely feel his lower extremities, all forgotten.

He gazed across the blacktop with reverence, trying to take in the majesty of it. Trying to convince himself it was real. It couldn't be. Only thirteen hundred and twenty of these bad boys had rolled off the assembly line, and that had been some time ago. Most were gone now. The few that remained were scarcer than hen's teeth and true love. This was the Holy Grail, with a V-8 and leather bucket-seats.

Earl couldn't breathe...

...because, not twenty feet away, nestled among

rumps were parked in front of him. Earl stared back at them, his mouth open. This night was getting stranger and stranger, no doubt about that.

The coyotes simply sat there, like furry little crackheads waiting for spare change, gazing at him with bright eyes, their tongues lolling from their mouths.

"Are you boys here for any particular reason?" Earl asked.

They looked around, sniffing the air.

Earl took a stab. "You wouldn't happen to be looking for a white wolf, would ya?"

Rapid sniffing now.

"Well, I hate to break the news to you boys, but your friend's gone." Earl swept his hand around the deserted garage. "So you might as well hit the road too."

the Fords, Chevys, and Pontiacs, and other hunks of bland American metal, sat the tastiest, most succulent automobile Earl had ever laid eyes on in all his years of car theft. As a matter of fact, he was getting himself a little boner just looking at it. Sometime in the last few seconds, his equipment had decided to slip back into town. It hadn't unpacked yet. It was just looking around.

He walked over, ran his hand over the car's silky skin, inhaled the scent of road dust and oil and leather.

It was a gas-guzzling Detroit wet-dream come true; a '59 *Cadillac Eldorado Biarritz* convertible. The thing was a sleek candy-apple-red torpedo, longer than a night in an El Paso drunk-tank. It was decked out too, with honest-to-god steer horns, naked-girl chrome mud-flaps on all four wheels, curb feelers, two pair of fuzzy red-white-and-blue dice dangling from the rearview, a Marilyn Monroe spinner knob on the silver-chain steering wheel. It even had a CB antenna. Most people didn't know how to properly accessorize a car. No, sir. Earl took his hat off with reverence. This kind of taste couldn't be bought, you had to be born with it.

Earl turned to the wolf to apologize for that earlier rock-throwing incident. He didn't get a chance. The creature had vanished.

In its place was a coyote. Even as Earl watched, more of them materialized from behind rows of parked cars. Within a matter of seconds, seven of their skinny, flea-ridden

They didn't move.

After a couple of seconds, Earl said, "Well, this has been swell, but I gotta get to work here. Breaking the law, you know..."

The coyotes continued watching him. He put a finger to his lips and shushed them, as he eased into the Caddy. "You boys keep your eyes peeled for casino security, okay? We don't want nobody getting trigger happy. Y'all can handle that, can't you? You're not too busy sniffing butts, are you?"

The oddest thing, they looked back as though they understood. Their grinning, staring faces were a trifle unnerving, but Earl wasn't about to let anything stop him from taking this car. He had to drive this Caddy. Even if only for a few minutes. He was about to connect the already dangling hot-wires beneath the steering wheel when he caught scent of something familiar. The odor seemed to be coming from the floormats on the passenger side. He leaned over and poked at the spongy dark rubber, touching wetness.

Even before he sniffed the finger, he knew he smelled human blood. Beneath the blood was that same odor he'd picked up back at the park. Human and yet animal-like. Uneasy, Earl was beginning to think that stealing this car might not be such a good idea after all. That maybe he might have to let this one go.

Before Earl could move, he heard a yap. The unexpected

sound sent his already nervous testicles to elbowing each other out of the way as they stampeded back up his butt. In coyote lingo, that had been a 'it's-time-to-haul-ass' yap.

Senses on full alert, Earl cranked his head up over the door panel and took a quick peek around.

The coyotes were gone. Every last one of them.

In their place were two people making their way towards him. He checked them out. They were an odd-looking couple. One was a tiny, barefoot Indian girl in pigtails holding a tan toy *Pooh Bear*.

The second member of the duo was the one who got Earl's attention.

It was a hatchet-faced cowboy, a dime-store, all hat, no cattle, dandy in a fringed suede jacket the color of butter, with greasy blonde hair down to his shoulders.

him again. Using the barrel of his pistol, he clubbed her to her knees before drawing a bead on the kid. As Earl watched, the cowboy snapped off a shot. Sparks flew up a few inches from the tiny running feet. The bullet ricocheted off the concrete, smacked into a Mustang, causing its alarm to go off. The cowboy fired again. Closer to the child's feet this time. The gunfire was seriously reducing that Mustang's resale value.

Another shot, and Earl realized this was some kind of sick game. The cowboy was missing the kid on purpose. He was torturing the woman. His sadistic efforts appeared to be working, because the woman climbed to her feet and came at him again. He hit her, harder this time. Her nose turned into a fountain and she went down in a sprawl.

The kid slowed when she looked over her shoulder and

And the coldest, deadest eyes Earl had ever seen. For a second, they seemed to reflect the lights in the parking lot.

Earl told himself he'd made a mistake. Had to be. Human eyes didn't do that. When Earl looked closer, he saw the left side of the cowboy's face was nothing more than one long, oozing furrow. The closer the cowboy got, the stronger that animal smell got.

The cowboy said something in a low voice that Earl couldn't quite catch and then laughed. The words didn't seem to be addressed to the kid, they seemed to be directed at someone out of sight.

"Okay, have it your way," Mr. Greasy Hair said. Walking around the kid, he didn't so much walk, as he strutted. With a smile, he slid an ivory handled .45 from a shoulder holster and pointed it at the tiny, pigtailed head. He then proceeded to make a show of cocking the gun. The sound of the hammer being thumbed back carried.

Before the cowboy could pull the trigger, a woman appeared. She tore into him. The woman was skinny, maybe five feet tall, but she was a hellcat who got her claws in deep. In a second, that first furrow in his face had itself a twin.

The kid just stood there, frozen. It wasn't until the woman did something with her hands that looked like signing that the kid bolted.

The cowboy watched the kid run. He didn't seem concerned that she might get away. The woman came at

saw the woman was bleeding.

Earl went for his pistol. Realized he didn't have one.

The cowboy gazed down at the woman in front of him with flat, emotionless eyes and stepped away to avoid getting blood on his boots. He re-cocked his piece, took aim. This time he shot the *Pooh Bear* out of the kid's hand. In a shower of stuffing, the toy jerked, hit the asphalt, a leg blown off. The kid stopped and came back. As she reached for the bear, the cowboy put another bullet in it.

Pooh jumped ten feet on his one good leg. Stuffing flew everywhere. Every time the kid reached for the bear, the cowboy put a bullet in it.

Earl had seen enough. Working feverishly, he sparked the Caddy to life, slammed it in reverse and backed out quick.

The cowboy's eyes came to life in the rearview when he saw the car bearing down on him. He squeezed off a shot that made the fuzzy dice on the rearview jump. A second later, Earl felt a satisfying, meaty thud as the rear bumper connected with flesh. The teddy-bear killer went airborne, landed on his back and skidded a good four or five car lengths. Without his gun. He looked faintly surprised as he fetched up against a red and white Bronco. As though it had never occurred to him that someone would run over him with his own car.

Struggling to his feet, the cowboy gave Earl a reproachful look before hobbling toward the .45.

The woman decided to go after the gun. She had a chance until the blonde dandy slipped a derringer from his sleeve. He fired and the small caliber bullet clipped the heel off her boot and down she went. That was some pretty fair shooting in Earl's opinion.

Pooh's insides whipped across the lot, pushed by the wind. The cotton batting blew past the cowboy in a flurry of white. He grinned as he moved through the swirling snowstorm toward his gun, looking as dapper as the *Marlboro* man in a Christmas ad closing in on the last scotch pine of the season.

To Earl's amazement, the blonde man started whistling.

Swinging the Caddy around, Earl realized there was no way to get to the woman and kid before the cowboy got to that .45.

As the hobbling cowboy reached for the gun, Earl goosed the Caddy. He intended to bump the guy again, knock him down, but somehow the car got away from Earl and one of the steer horns speared the man's fringed jacket. An instant later, the cowboy was going for a joyride on the grill. The joy part of the ride ended abruptly when the convertible fishtailed into a VW Microbus and slewed sideways.

Amidst a shower of broken glass, the cowboy slid off the steerhorn, like a booger on the end of a flicked finger, and went rolling. This time he didn't get up.

Earl stepped on the brakes, but there was oil everywhere. The car skidded toward the prone man. Earl felt a thump. When the Caddy stopped, Earl threw open the door and jumped out, saw he'd only hit a speedbump. He hadn't run over the guy. A sigh escaped him. He didn't know if it was relief or disappointment.

He moved around the Caddy, realized a tire rested on blonde hair. The cowboy was trapped.

Earl walked over, gave the son of a bitch a good kick in the balls. Just because.

That got the cowboy to stirring. Earl climbed back in the car and leaned on the horn, trying to rouse security. He didn't have much hope. If gunfire hadn't brought them, there was little hope a car horn would.

As the horn kept blaring, the cowboy began struggling, trying to work free of the tire. With a venomous look at Earl, he whipped out a skinning knife that appeared to be a first cousin to a machete and began sawing at his hair. In seconds he cut himself free.

Earl figured he'd better give this guy a little space. He backed up the car.

The cowboy came up shooting. Earl grabbed a handful of floorboard. Barely in time, too. A bullet punched through the windshield head high.

Staying low, Earl put the car in drive and hit the gas pedal. He smashed into the cowboy again and sent him rolling up across the hood.

When Earl risked a quick peek, he saw the gun was gone. But where?

The cowboy was one tough son of a bitch, he rolled off the hood onto the pavement, landing on all fours. He looked like a big yellow housecat that'd gotten his fur rubbed the wrong way. As he rose up, he began sniffing the air. Now what the hell was that about, Earl wondered,

watching him? Was the guy trying to catch a scent over the car's exhaust? Apparently he didn't get what he was looking for. The cowboy grinned, took a halting step toward the Caddy.

"Maybe we should introduce ourselves, since that's my car you're sitting in."

"This car," Earl answered, "is too good for an asshole who hits women and shoots at little kids."

The cowboy blinked in surprise at Earl's answer. "What do we have here, we got us a do-gooder?"

"That's right. You're under arrest."

The cowboy busted out laughing.

"What's so damned funny?" Earl yelled over the purr of the Caddy engine. "You don't mind me asking."

"Where's your gun, Mr. Do-Gooder?"

"Where's yours?"

The dandified cowboy studied Earl through the bullet-riddled windshield. His expression was amused. "Can I tell you something, Mr. Do-Gooder? I don't figure you'd mind, since you done snuck your nose in my business and all."

"Your business," Earl answered, "became my business when you tried to kill that kid."

"If I wanted to kill that kid, she'd be dead right now." The cowboy's painted-on grin was unwavering. "Are you going to listen or not?"

"Why don't you save your story," Earl said, "for somebody who gives a shit."

The blonde man looked at the tear in his jacket, then raised his lifeless eyes to Earl. "Today has been somewhat of a disappointment for me."

"What happened, the gay rodeo leave town without you?"

"A do-gooder with a sense of humor. I like that." The cowboy bent forward, peering beneath a parked car for his missing pistol like a tipsy bar patron searching for dropped car keys.

More disappointment awaited. No pistol. He hobbled on toward the next car.

In the meantime, Earl edged the Caddy forward, keeping pace with the blonde man. A sense of complete unreality had overtaken Earl. In his whole unnatural life, he'd only been shot at twice and one of those times had been an accident. He glanced around, trying to spot the woman and the kid.

They were still running, setting off alarms, searching for a car, any car, that was unlocked. The woman was yelling; the kid wasn't saying anything. She was busy stuffing *Pooh's* guts back in.

Across the way, a small crowd had emerged from the casino to watch the proceedings, but nobody seemed too eager to get involved. This bunch might not be smart enough to stay away from trying to fill an inside straight, but they damned sure were sure smart enough to stay away from the sound of gunfire.

Shuffling along, the cowboy dandy peered hopefully beneath the next vehicle. "Not too many folks know this, Mr. Car Thief, but a very important man died on this day. A great man. A hero to this great country of ours. It was a hundred years ago today that he rode off into history. I'm talking about Little Bighorn. June 25th, 1876—"

Still no gun.

"—so when I dropped by a town that bears this great man's name," the cowboy confided, "hoping that somebody there might remember a brave soldier who did his duty for God and country—what did I see?"

"My guess, some pissed-off Indians," Earl answered, "who did their duty for their God and country? No, wait. They did that at Little Bighorn."

The cowboy bent over to get his hat. That's when Earl realized the man was wearing a wig.

"Do you want to know what I saw, or not?"

"Tell me, all my hair's standing on end," Earl said.

The blonde dandy's voice rose a notch at Earl's dig. "Well, by God, I am going to tell you. It was Crazy Horse. Well, his statue, anyway. That sneaky red bastard's face is being carved into the side of a mountain, and it's as big as a house. Big as ten houses. And do you know what he's doing, he's staring down his nose on the great man's town, like the place was named after *him*. Do you have any idea how it feels, to see this insult done to one of our country's greatest heroes? Well, it hurt, that's what it did."

Finally, Earl figured he'd eased the Caddy close enough. It looked like he was going to have to tackle this crazy son of a bitch all by himself, sore toe and all. Earl started easing out of the car.

The cowboy appealed to Earl. "It's not right that the Sioux are still shoving that Little Bighorn thing up the great man's ass. They won the battle. He was the one who was killed, publicly humiliated, his wife left a widow." The blonde dandy took a deep breath, fought for calm. "You know what, screw all that. It's ancient history anyway. Where's my gun?"

Before Earl could reach him, the cowboy slipped over into the next row of cars.

Earl couldn't risk going after him. The guy might have found the gun. Jumping back in the Caddy, Earl turned the corner on squealing rubber and bore down on the blonde man again. It was tough going. This Caddy wasn't very maneuverable.

The cowboy still hadn't found his pistol yet. He was still looking around, tugging on his handlebar mustache, perplexed. Now he seemed to be talking to himself. "A man shouldn't hold onto a grudge, it's not healthy. Messes with your chi, knots up your colon. You have to let bygones be bygones."

Earl lined up the Caddy steer horns like the man was in the crosshairs of a rifle.

At the same time, the cowboy finally caught sight of his pistol and scooted under a Winnebago to retrieve it. The vehicle, roughly the size of a small barge, had Wisconsin plates and a bumper sticker decorated with smiley faces around the words, *"We're gambling away our kids' inheritance."*

"Well, shit," the blonde dandy blurted out a second later, "this thing's leaking oil. You can't get oil out of suede. This is coming out of somebody's ass."

Before the cowboy could make good on his threat, Earl realized he'd found himself some of that oil too. Spinning the steering wheel did no good, and neither did standing on the brakes. The Caddy wasn't going to miss that Winnebago. Earl braced for impact. Ten inches of steer-horns, backed by several tons of steel, slammed into the side of the camper, rocking the vehicle up on two wheels.

The horns went in deep. Earl held onto the steering wheel, his arms feeling like they were being punched from their sockets.

Thin yellow blood began spilling from the RV onto the pavement in pulsing gouts. It splashed the cowboy dandy's feet, causing a bellow of outrage. "These boots cost more than you made last year, Do-Gooder." Crawling under the next car, the cowboy dandy tried to escape the gas. He wasn't having much luck. He was on the downhill side.

Earl tried to back the Caddy up. He wasn't having much luck, either. The two vehicles were locked together. It would only be a matter of seconds before the blonde shooter figured out Earl wasn't going anywhere. Gritting his teeth, Earl put the gas pedal to the floorboard, his broken toe screaming. The air filled with the squall of burning *Goodyears*, which covered his scream of agony. The Caddy shimmied back and forth like a buffing machine on a glob of wax, but instead of leaving shiny in its wake, it was leaving black rubber and a cloud of eye-watering smoke.

"What are you doing to my car, Do-Gooder?" the blonde man asked.

Finally the '59 wrenched itself loose. Before Earl could get the car stopped, it rear-ended its brand new white brother across the aisle, sprinkling the pavement with more glass and chrome.

"Damn," the blonde man shouted, "I sure hope somebody's insured."

Apparently the new Caddy that Earl had hit was occupied, because it fired up. Its headlights popped on and it rammed Earl, knocking his car sideways as it pushed past and sped off into the darkness. Before the white car vanished around the corner, Earl caught a glimpse of the driver, a huge determined-looking Indian. He also saw two yellow eyes staring out at him through the darkly tinted glass. The eyes didn't look human.

If Earl had to say, he'd say they belonged to a wolf. A white wolf.

Before Earl could figure out what he was seeing, the odor of gas became stronger. He checked out the Winnebago. Gas was really pouring out of the huge RV, now that the horns were out. It was a mortal wound.

"I don't know why the hell you're poking your nose in my business…" The blonde man's voice floated out from beneath the vehicle, muffled, disembodied, filled with self-righteous indignation. "I've got a job to do here, and you're making it harder. You've left me no choice." He rolled out from beneath the Winnebago and trained his gun across the lot.

At first, Earl couldn't see what he was aiming at, then he spotted the child. She was crawling along behind a car, still picking up pieces of her bear. In a few seconds, she would be out in the open.

Earl leaned on the horn, trying to get her attention. She didn't seem to hear. Earl fumbled in his pockets for matches, before he remembered he'd gotten them wet in the creek earlier. He needed fire. Now. Desperately ransacking the car's interior, he spotted an overflowing ashtray. No matches, though. How the hell did blondy light his smokes?

The answer lay in the dash—a car cigarette lighter.

He punched it. In seconds the tip was cherry red. He flipped the hot metal into the gas on the concrete and flames sprouted. The Winnebago made a soft whoomph when the flames raced up to its tanks and climbed onboard. The sound was the sound a gas stove made when the fire first caught. Solid. Reassuring.

Earl heard an "Oh shit!" as the blonde dandy scrambled away from the RV and dove over a Pontiac with more primer than paint on it.

The RV burned calmly for a few seconds, then, as though it decided just burning was dull, it exploded. It wasn't a small explosion either; it was the granddaddy of all explosions. One of the RV's tanks must have been filled with fumes. It went off like a bomb.

Earl watched in awe as the vehicle surged forward, kicked in the ass-end by a huge foot of fire. The flames reached out for him and he came back to himself in time to duck. As it was, he felt the heat blow past at the same instant the explosion rattled his teeth.

More cracks appeared in the Caddy's windshield and pieces of glass embedded themselves in the seat like shrapnel while the glass on every other vehicle within a hundred feet was blasted out by the shock wave. The RV's front end smashed down onto the back of the Chevy pickup next to it. Pinned by the behemoth, gas poured from the Chevy's ruptured tank and pooled around the tires. More explosions erupted from the Winnebago's rear end, driving it forward with short rocking motions—it looked like a Clydesdale doing the deed with a Shetland pony.

Within seconds, the Winnebago climaxed in a fire-drenched explosion. More than a dozen cars were on fire now, their alarms bleeping for help. More pieces of hot, twisted metal rained down on the Caddy.

"God almighty, that paint job cost ten grand alone," the blonde cowboy screamed. "Fifty coats of lacquer, all hand rubbed." Outraged, he rolled out from beneath a van three spots over from the Chevy pickup and leveled his pistol at the child, who had emerged to watch the fire. His face, his clothes, were covered with black. When he cocked the .45, Earl yelled out, "How much is this gonna cost, asshole?" Earl took a piece of sharp metal that had landed in the car and began punching at the Caddy's upholstery, tearing holes in the custom-made leather.

The destruction was more than the cowboy could bear. He swung his pistol in the Caddy's direction, thumbed back the hammer.

Earl heard the bullet punch through the windshield as he grabbed more floorboard. Before the blonde shooter managed to squeeze the trigger again, Earl got a little help. The squashed Chevy pickup decided it'd had enough of its one-night stand. It too exploded, tipping its cumbersome lover over backwards. There was grinding of tortured metal when they uncoupled, and the smiley faces flipped,

turning to frowns.

The cowboy tried to get out of the way. He was quick, but not quite quick enough. The Winnebago clipped him. His expensive new boots came up off the pavement as he was thrown across several cars. He disappeared from sight. A second later he sprang up, arms windmilling, on fire.

His gasoline-soaked jacket wasn't helping matters any. But on the good side, it seemed he wasn't interested in shooting at anyone at the moment. The fiery cowboy did the right thing, Earl noticed, he stopped, dropped, and rolled. Unfortunately he rolled into the pool of gas by the Chevy. His condition went from bad to worse; he was now officially a human bonfire. The blonde dandy leaped to his feet and took off running. Streaks of flame, some as long as four feet, raced away from him. They hopped aboard more gasoline-soaked cars. He was a lighter, the cars were birthday candles. More explosions followed. The greasy black smoke that roiled up was thick enough to cut with a knife.

From the corner of his eye, Earl caught sight of a Jeep barreling into the lot. Drawn by the noise and smoke, casino security had finally arrived. They were greeted by an inferno. The first half dozen cars on fire had gone to twenty now.

And one blonde cowboy.

None of the security guards seemed too eager to get near the burning man with their hand-held fire extinguishers. Earl didn't blame them, not a bit. One guard, an older heavyset Sioux with a ponytail, stared closely at the burning man and fear crowded into his eyes. Backing away quickly, he shouted something to the other two men, something that sounded like ghost-walker.

Earl couldn't quite make out what else was said, because the heat from the fire caused the cowboy's dropped pistol to start shooting randomly. Bullets sprayed into the pavement, punched into cars. More alarms went off. The din, already deafening, grew.

One of the bullets smacked into the jeep. That was all the guards needed to make up their minds. They beat a hasty retreat.

The fleeing Jeep ran over a fire extinguisher. The stream of white foam that spewed out was jerky and sporadic, and a little on the brown side. The foam had about as much effect on the fire as a guy with prostate problems peeing on it. The cars burned on.

The cowboy, still on fire, made for the extinguisher like it was Niagara Falls.

In the meantime, Earl managed to catch up with the woman and kid and drag them inside the Cadillac. The kid had a death grip on the one-legged, gutless *Pooh Bear.*

Yelling for them to hold on, Earl ignored the agony of his busted toe and stomped the gas pedal. They barreled over the speed-bumps in a cloud of sparks and grinding metal, sideswiping several more parked cars. With pieces of the Winnebago dangling from its broken horns, the Caddy roared out of the lot, kicking up dust like a pissed-off Brahma looking for something else to gore.

To be continued…

WHAT THE HELL EVER HAPPENED TO...
S.P. SOMTOW

BY ROBERT MORRISH

Photo courtesy of S.P. Somtow

Somtow Sucharitkul, aka S.P. Somtow, is a true Renaissance man, having achieved notoriety not just in the field of fiction, but also in screenwriting, directing, composing, and conducting.

A descendant of the Royal Chakri dynasty, Somtow was born in Bangkok but while still an infant moved with his parents to England, where he was ultimately educated at Eton College and at St Catharine's College, Cambridge. Somtow returned to Thailand for five years during the 1960s, at which point he became a fluent speaker of the Thai language.

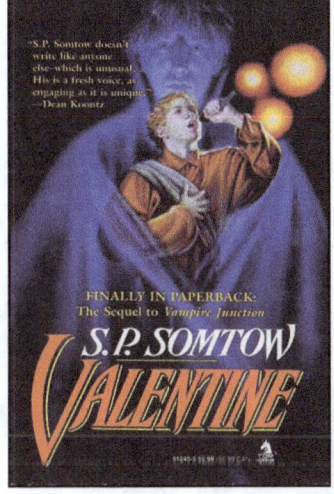

He first began publishing in the late 1970s in *Asimov's* and *Analog* science fiction magazines, and his debut novel, *Starship and Haiku,* appeared in 1981, winning a Locus Award for Best First Novel. After initially focusing on science fiction and fantasy work, Somtow authored the novel Vampire Junction, which went on to spawn two sequels, *Valentine* and *Vanitas*. His other horror work includes the werewolf/American West novel Moon Dance, the zombie/American Civil War novel *Darker Angels*, and the YA vampire novel, *The Vampire's Beautiful Daughter.* In the 1990s, Somtow also wrote and directed the cult horror film *The Laughing Dead* and co-wrote the Roger Corman-produced *Bram Stoker's Burial of the Rats* (1995).

Currently artistic director of the Bangkok Opera, Somtow made his first professional appearance as a conductor at age 19, and has composed six symphonies and a ballet, with the most recent, "The Snow Dragon," an adaptation of a fantasy short story he wrote, premiering in March 2015.

In addition to the aforementioned Locus Award, he won the World Fantasy Award for Best Novella in 2002,

and has been nominated four other times. He has won the International Horror Guild Award, the John W. Campbell Award, the American Horror Award, among others, and has been nominated for two Hugos and five Bram Stoker Awards. In addition, he was president of the Horror Writers Association from 1998 to 2000.

======

DD: Your 1984 novel *Vampire Junction*—concerning teen-aged rock singer and vampire Timmy Valentine, who seeks to deal with his past and his very nature by undergoing Jungian analysis—has been called "a major reworking of the vampire myth and one of the most original novels of the 1980s." It also spawned two sequels. What prompted you to take on the vampire myth? Had you previously read a lot of vampire novels? And did you write the first book with the expectation that there would be sequels?

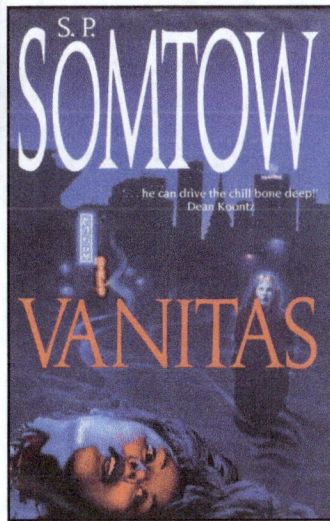

SS: What prompted me at first was simple crass commercialism. I could see that writers I knew who had been only moderately successful had erupted into bestsellerdom with vampires. I had loved vampires from childhood, because my mother never missed a Christopher Lee vampire movie—she was a rabid fan. I went to them all from an impressionable age, and did not close my eyes (my mother always closed them throughout the movie—I am not quite sure what she got out of them). It was when I had made the cold-blooded decision to do something commercial that I discovered myself congenitally incapable of treating the subject in a "commercial" way. I actually started to write the novel in the late '70s.

The music video was a new form and I thought it would be great to write a novel with rapid jump cuts, in the manner of MTV. I also thought it would be a lot of fun to include all the gore of those newly minted splatter movies, within the context of a literary novel. Finally, I was aware that Stoker's *Dracula* was very cutting edge when it came to sexuality, because it ultimately sensualizes necrophilia. I wanted to flirt with the last sexual taboos that could still make people squeamish, and by making the hero both thousands of years old and a child at the same time, I could write a novel that really disturbed people's moral compass. These three factors of course made *Vampire Junction* just about as uncommercial as it could be, and it was therefore rejected by thirty publishers, coming to light only years after I started writing it, when Susan Allison, Beth Meacham, and Ginjer Buchanan, who had been at different publishers when they first liked the book but could not pitch it to their bosses, all ended up working for the same publisher, Ace/Berkley. Between the three of them, they rammed it through. Absolutely no sequels in mind.

DD: In the first sequel, *Valentine*, Timmy spends most of the story crucified on a tree… which seems pretty gutsy and potentially off-putting to readers who wanted more of Timmy. Did you get any negative feedback along those lines from readers?

The second sequel, *Vanitas*, is likewise inventive in its approach and continues moving away from standard vampire fare/mythos, as Timmy winds up battling his doppelgänger "on the edge of reality." At what point did you know how you wanted to plot the two sequels? And did you feel any self-imposed pressure to "outdo" yourself with the second and third books?

SS: I'll answer both these questions in one sitting. I had years in which I tried to pitch various ideas to editors, and they would be sort of ho-hum, but if I ever said, "I'll do a sequel to *Vampire Junction*" they would all suddenly perk up. The two sequels were really conceived as one book, in which the real Timmy would step out of the mirror at the midpoint. But you know, all those other characters became interesting enough that by the halfway mark I had a book as long as the first one. So basically I had an attack of "GeorgeMartin-itis" there. When I handed in *Valentine*,

S.P. SOMTOW
VAMPIRE JUNCTION

'THE CLOSEST THING TO A NIGHTMARE EVER PUT ON PAPER!'
ROBERT BLOCH, author of *PSYCHO*.

MOON DANCE
A Novel of Terror

S.P. SOMTOW

I didn't really tell anyone it was the first half of a big arc. So after a few more unsuccessful pitchings, a few years later I was able to suggest another sequel, and a contract came almost by return. So by then, the early 1990s, there was a consensus that Timmy Valentine was, in a sense, iconic. But in attempting to sell this sprawling mythos to film or TV, which would perhaps have catapulted the books to another level, I was overtaken by a slew of much "safer" teen vampires. As for "pressure to outdo"— not per se, except from myself.

DD: After publishing 8 books under your given name, you began publishing under the pen name S.P. Somtow with *Vampire Junction*. I've heard that the publisher of that book, Donning/Starblaze, requested or demanded the pen name because they thought your given name was too unusual for a mass audience—is that the case? I've also read that, even though you were initially annoyed by the change, you seemed to later embrace the pen name by employing it for the reissues of some of your earlier works. Is that true or is there more to it than that?

SS: It was actually Ace who asked me to change my name. I really didn't want to, but they did have a reason. I think they stated succinctly, "Rednecks in Georgia need to be able to ask for it at the supermarket counter." Their words, not mine. The point is, I only want one writing name. That's why I changed it on my early books as well. S.P. isn't a pseudonym per se, it merely hides my other names under initials. The Thais do not change their name without an astrologer's guidance. I managed to do so without doing so.

DD: Your novel *Moon Dance* (1984) is set in America's Dakota Territory in the 1880s, interweaving werewolf mythology into that of the American frontier. How did you formulate the idea for this novel? Was it at all a hard sell to your agent or publisher, or did your earlier success provide you with the freedom to freely follow your muse? Did you ever consider doing additional werewolf novels, or did you say pretty much everything you had to say on the topic in Moon Dance?

SS: God that novel was so hard … I was so obsessed … I personally visited so many of the locations, I spent a lot of time learning the Lakhota language, though I've mostly forgotten it now. Everything they eat in the book is something I saw in a real menu from that period somewhere. I had never attempted something of this complexity and it took me about 6 years to write from initial concept to delivery of the ms. But the novel began with the train journey … the modern story that holds it together was added later. The TV series *Deadwood* is remarkably similar to my book, only without the werewolves. I always wonder whether they read it. Was the book hard to sell? No. In a way *Vampire Junction* had eased the pathway. I don't know if I have more to say on this subject or not. No one ever asked me before.

DD: You also explored the zombie mythos with your 1997 novel, *Darker Angels,* which employs a broad canvas with a Civil War background, a complex narrative, and features such historical figures as Lord Byron, Edgar Allan Poe, and Walt Whitman, along with passages intended to mimic their historical styles. This seems like an increasingly "gonzo" approach...how did the idea for this novel germinate? You were still publishing through Gollancz (UK) and Tor (US) at this point—how did they react to this novel?

SS: Gonzo indeed! The germ was a short story called "Darker Angels. I told Tor I would adapt it into a novel. It grew in the telling, but more like a babushka doll than like *Lord of the Rings.* It was essentially written in ONE very long sitting. I barely got up to eat. It didn't take six years. Once the dolls started opening up and revealing more dolls, I couldn't stop. Greg Cox, by then, was my editor at Tor. He called me and he said, "I read the book in one sitting." He asked for no changes. I reckon he liked it well enough. You could call it a tour de force in that I used the "Arabian Nights" technique and at one point was juggling six stories within each other. I couldn't have held it all in my head if I had had to do it over a long period.

DD: Your later novel, *Bluebeard's Castle* (electronically published in 2003 in the U.S., following its serialization in a Bangkok newspaper), went even further afield, being described as a simmering stew of "pop-culture and mythological references." How did this novel come together, both in terms of plot development and in being serialized in a Thai newspaper?

SS: I had had another novel, *Jasmine Nights,* serialized in the Thai papers as well. It led me to discover the art

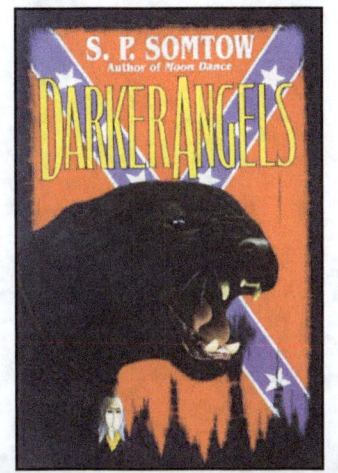

of having a cliffhanger every 2000 words and telling a story without knowing what was coming next. The Dickensian art. It involves giving your unconscious full rein. *Bluebeard* was altogether darker. I retitled this book "The Other City of Angels" because people in Bangkok are unfamiliar with the fairy tale.

DD: Looking back at works such as *Darker Angels* and *Bluebeard's Castle*, one could easily get the impression that you were starting to get bored with writing fiction, or at least restless with traditional approaches to fiction, and were looking to explore larger ideas and spread your wings further. Do you think that's an accurate assessment?

SS: Yes.

DD: Another indication of your broadening interests can be found in your dabbling in film-making during the 1990s, when you wrote, directed, and scored both *The Laughing Dead* and *Ill Met by Moonlight* (a non-horror work, based on Shakespeare's *A Midsummer Night's Dream*), and co-wrote *Bram Stoker's Burial of the Rats.* How did you get involved in film work? With regard to the two films that you wrote and directed, were you happy with the result? And what led you to exit the movie business after such a brief flirtation?

SS: With *The Laughing Dead,* many things were beyond my control. We couldn't afford experienced actors so there was a lot of variation in quality. The editor didn't realize this was a black comedy and was pulling it more towards a family drama, a mood that the script could not bear. I could re-edit it and it would be a lot snappier and wilder and funnier, if all the footage is still around. I could also make the acting less appalling in parts with some judicious workarounds. Maybe. I was thinking I could just do a sequel…

As for *Ill Met,* I need to cut 20 minutes from it and re-edit what remains.

What led me to exit? Frustration. I could never get anything off the ground and I was taking endless meetings. *Little Savages,* which is kind of "Lord of the Flies in Space" was written to take advantage of a spaceship set that a friend of mine had already built for some cheap movie years before. Porchlight greenlighted and then suddenly ungreenlighted it when the executive was fired. I had many other projects and the endless meetings, the whole Hollywood scene of hopes constantly raised and dashed, took its toll on me. At that point, back in Thailand, people were beginning to remember me as a composer, and so music was starting to pull me away from fiction.

DD: Over the years, you also tried your hand at young-adult genre novels, with titles such as *The Fallen Country* (1986), *Forgetting Places* (1987), and *The Vampire's Beautiful Daughter* (1997). Were these written primarily in response to market opportunities, or did you have a specific interest in YA books?

SS: I always loved YA novels and found many of them to be better written than the average adult light reading. Writers like Katharine Patterson were always some of my favorites. My most recent novel, the only one wholly written during my sojourn in Thailand so far, is *The Stone Buddha's Tears*, a book about children teaming up to bring down government corruption. I would love to do more young adult novels. They are very hard to do. I think when writers fail to write a good YA it comes from talking down to the audience. They know. They never let you get away with that.

DD: I was particularly struck by a description of your writing from the *St. James Guide to Horror, Ghost & Gothic Writers*, wherein Gary Westfahl says, "Most strikingly, Somtow has apparently managed to achieve the maturity and sophistication of an adult while retaining the innocence and sensitivity of a child, so that his fiction for children can seem unusually adult and his fiction for adults can seem appealingly childlike." Do you think that's a fair take?

SS: Very, very fair. Artists who say they have never grown up are lying. But we hide it well.

DD: Why did you largely move away from writing horror, and then later from writing fiction in general?

SS: One reason I am not financially successful is that I hate doing the same thing twice. To be a really rich novelist, for instance, it is essential to write the same book over and over again. Filmmakers, too. Writing was in a sense a very long holiday from music—in the '70s, my attempts to revolutionize music in Southeast Asia led to bafflement and burnout. Now I have to complete what I started before my clock runs out.

DD: When did you move back to Thailand? What led to that decision?

SS: I suddenly had an urge to enter a monastery.

When I got out of the monastery, 9/11 happened and I felt nervous flying, so I stayed for a while. Things kept happening to make me stay longer and I found myself selling my house in L.A. That is the short version. I have been doing a book about my stay in the monastery. It was illuminating and weird.

DD: Do you have much, or any, unpublished fiction? If so, what type of material, and dating from what point in your career?

SS: I have the beginning of a beautiful trilogy—fantasy—and the beginning of a fifth novel in the Inquestor series written. When someone gets interested enough, I'll finish them. The trilogy, by the way, is something very, very new. As for laundry lists … there has been demand for me to publish my dream journal (I post my dreams on Facebook, previously on a blog.) So, createspace to the rescue … that book should be out by the time this interview is published. Is it fiction? I don't know. I think of it as a kind of prose poetry, somewhat symbolist.

DD: Do you foresee yourself ever returning to more active fiction writing?

SS: Working on finding a window. Right now I am composing a ten-opera cycle. This dekalogy would by its very nature be the biggest work in all of performing arts in history, so it's a pretty big project (Wagner's Ring is "only" four operas). I am about to produce No. 5 (Dasjati.com for info).

I am republishing everything I have ever written to amazon via POD. It's actually now possible for the first time to get almost all my books, one way or another. I hope someone notices soon.

DD: If you had to choose one, which of your various creative endeavors would you most like to be remembered for?

SS: Puh-lease!!!! This is like *Sophie's Choice!*

I believe that in time, my career will be reassessed by critics and readers and it will emerge that I've done a lot of quite innovative things that will bear looking at in times to come. I hope I survive to enjoy the fruits of that :)

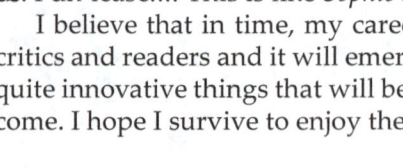
Painting of Somtow by Rachel Dionne

I confess: I had not read Tom Reamy.

Gene O'Neill gave me the book, sent it to me in the post. It's the only collection of Reamy's short stories out there, ranges from $30-60, used to new, on Amazon. *San Diego Lightfoot Sue and Other Stories* (1979) collects essentially everything Reamy had sold when he succumbed to his untimely (yet morbidly fitting) death while sitting at his typewriter working on a story for *The Magazine of Fantasy and Science Fiction*. Reamy also got one novel published. *Blind Voices* (1978). That one's a little easier to come by.

The introduction for the short story collection is "Embracing the Departing Shadow" by the one Harlan Ellison, in which Ellison brings both his warm sentimentality and heartless candor to Reamy's work—at times praising, at times dashing him. However, it does seem like Ellison is doing his best to remain critical and objective about a friend's work (never easy); on top of that, a friend who just tragically died (damn near impossible).

Reading the introduction, I am reminded of Ellison's overall wackiness and brilliance, but also that there is something uniquely magical in Reamy's fiction, in his abrupt passing, and chosen subject matter for stories. Ellison laments that there will be no more Reamy fiction, and I lament it too. Five stories in particular I found truly special: "Under the Hollywood Sing," "Beyond the Cleft," "Sand Diego Lightfoot Sue," "The Detweiler Boy," and "The Mistress of Windraven." These stories taken together represent some of the best that speculative fiction has to offer. The mood is often dark, and sometimes even graphic and a little vulgar, but overall there is a beacon of light shining through the plot, lighting on an unknown magic land. The endings of "Under the Hollywood Sing" and "The Mistress of Windraven," both rather unanticipated, showcase this turn very well. "Beyond the Cleft" reveals the horrors of children, and "Sand Diego Lightfoot Sue" and "The Detweiler Boy" are magical and poignant, two real gems giving us a glimpse into the human soul.

Based on these stories, I can only image what else might have come from Reamy's creative imagination. Great stuff, indeed. With Gene's help, we've gathered together some tributes for Tom from some of the people who knew him during his life. And he knew some interesting folk. Gene has also written a tribute piece of fiction, titled "A Faint Scent of Musky Lime," which wonderfully captures the feeling in Reamy's work. So, enjoy the tributes and Gene's new story and then please, go out and pick an old copy of *San Diego Lightfoot Sue and Other Stories*. You'll thank me later.

—Aaron J. French (editor)

~~~~~~

I met Tom when my family moved to Dallas in October of 1957. Brother Jim and I, age 16, got in touch because we had published 10 issues of a fanzine, *Void,* and traded them with Tom from Germany. Now we were nearby and soon met.

Tom was impressive—quietly competent, orderly, insightful—in marked contrast to many sf fans. I liked him and he encouraged Jim and me to pursue our careers in physics, which we did—Tom was more a precise engineer type. He had joined the local fan club, The Dallas Futurian Society, in 1953 at age eighteen. Tom edited the club's fanzine *CriFanAc* (a fandom term for Critical Fan Activity).

The wiki Tom Reamy entry notes, "With fellow Dallas Futurians Jim and Greg Benford, Reamy organized the first science fiction convention held in Texas."

We approached Dallas fandom warily, satirizing classic but agreeable 'fuggheads.' Here's the cover drawing for our fanzine, depicting a precise engineer type. He had joined the local fan club, The Dallas Futurian Society meeting, with my brother and I framing Tom, the big guy who's asleep—because our meetings were boring.

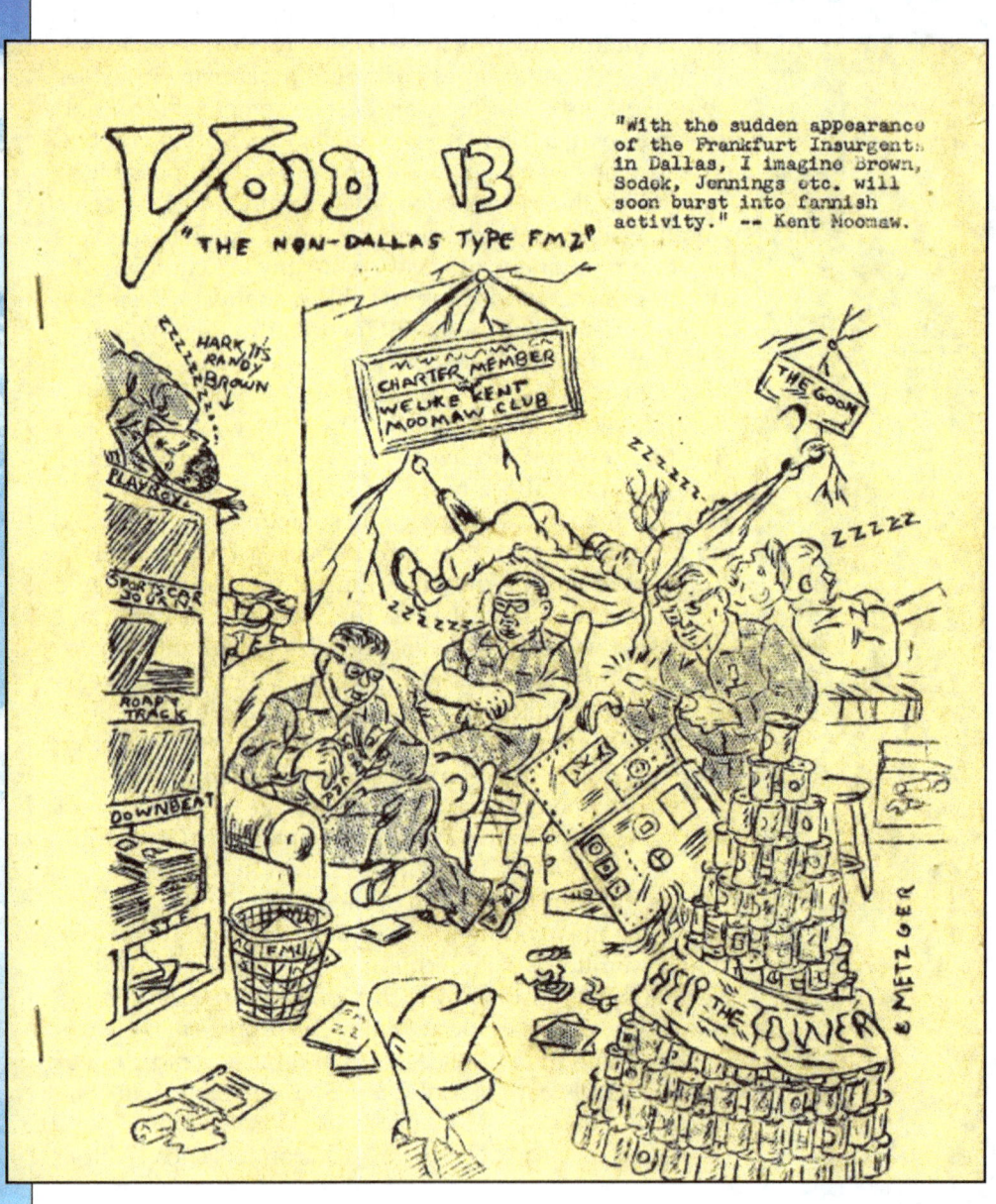

Still, Dallas fans were fun, and we helped with the first con in Texas, in Dallas 1958. (Having helped run the first German con in Wetzlar in 1956, this has got to be the most drastic transition in con-giving annals. We'd learned, though—and never worked on cons again.)

The club was continually active until July 6, 1958, when it expired by vote at the first sf con in Texas. The members disbanded their club as part of Southwestercon VI's business meeting. Tom had engineered that, to expel

an irritating guy by killing the club. (This gives the tenor of the times.)

His expertise at commercial illustration led to his becoming editor and publisher of a slickly produced, professionally printed fanzine, *Trumpet*. In the late 1960s Reamy also organized and became chairman of Dallas fandom's long-running "Big D in '73" bid to host the 31st worldcon; it failed. His exquisite offset-printed fanzine of the mid-70s, *Nickelodeon*, which didn't run for many issues, but did feature brief pictorials of nude male and female fans. He was very democratic about it, too, having one of each gender per issue. This was adventurous at the time.

All the while, Tom kept writing fantasy and sf stories, but not showing them to editors. Besides being a fine writer, Tom was also a very good photographer, and revolutionized convention program books with stylish layouts. He helped found the Turkey City Writer's Workshop, still running, and his stories started appearing. He gained much attention until his sudden death at age 42, just before his only novel appeared, the stylish *Blind Voices*.

He was a master of subtle dread and vivid description. A nostalgic sadness pervaded his work and he seemed on the brink of a major career—just as a heart attack struck him down.

Nearly 40 years later, I miss him still.

—Gregory Benford

~~~~~~~~~~~~~~~~~~~~~~~~~~~~~~~

I first met Tom Reamy at the organizational meeting of the Dallas Futurian Society (DFS) in December of 1953. A fan friend of mine Randy Brown was active in science fiction fandom (something I was not familiar with at the time) rounded up me and two other SF readers and got us to come to a meeting in south Dallas. Randy knew SF fans Orville W. Mosher (who had moved to Dallas to go to printing school) and Tom who had come to Dallas to go to art school. Randy, Tom and Orville talked up the idea of a citywide science fiction club. Tom and Orville were the only adults present, so about 20 teenage boys voted to form a club. Tom became the first president, Randy was vice president and Mosher somehow had the position of editor of the club zine.

In those days the club was meeting once a month, at first the Dallas Public Library. Later Orville Mosher made arrangements with the Eat Well Café in downtown Dallas and we met there for three years. As usual it was a chaotic affair; the only official business we conducted was electing club officers. I was president for two six month terms. The other was to bring books, paperbacks then, for auction which was supposed to finance club activities, outside of dues which were 50 cents a year. Mosher kept the books and the club zine would publish a rap sheet on all the scallywags who owed the club money, sometimes 5 cents! Orville soon became infamous for his officialness and drove fans away. The DFS had 60 members at one time, including a club Chaplin!

Tom Reamy finished his schooling and got a job at Collins Radio in Dallas in their graphics department. He must have done well because he rented a large house in Dallas where he kept a very large collection of books and magazines. Tom was an excellent artist but never really did a lot of independent work; he did turn out a lot of work for the graphics department at Collins Radio.

Tom would write short stories as a hobby and let us read them. Even as adolescents we keep telling Tom to send them to magazines, we could see he was good, but during this time he never did.

In 1958 Tom published two issues of the club zine *CriFanAc* that Orville, now with his own printing company, published in offset. I am thinking this is the first time any club zine had a graphics artist publishing a fanzine in this kind of format.

Tom with the help of Dale Hart, Greg and Jim Benford put on the first SF convention in Texas Southerwestercon VI. (I knew there was Southerwestercons before the one in Dallas, but I don't know how it got to be six!) The con was held at the moldy Dallas Hotel and held, mostly, in the ballroom at the top of the building. Our guest of honor canceled and since Tom corresponded with Marion Zimmer Bradley, who lived in Texas then, got her. To our surprise Forrest J Ackerman showed up. It was a ragged convention but fun. The DFS even had more fun the last day of the convention electing Orville Mosher president (he had never been) and voting the club out of existence.

In 1959 almost all DFS members graduated from high school and left town. I stayed in Dallas and me and a few DFS members used to meet at Tom Reamy's apartment, talk a little science fiction and then go to a movie. In the 1960s I remember going to hundreds of films. Tom was a real film buff and would write reviews of films. This was one of his motivations for creating *Trumpet*, the first 'slick' fanzine. This fanzine was nominated for a Hugo twice.

After I moved to Houston in 1966 Tom met some new fans in Dallas and worked with them on a new club and a convention. Sometime early 70's Collins Radio was bought and Tom was out of a job. He moved to LA, got into the movie business. I can remember in the late sixties Tom showing me a fine screenplay for a horror story about giant wasps, this was printed in a collection of screenplays as a good example, but this movie was never made. Tom started submitting stories and selling them. A little late but Tom finally got recognition as a writer.

Last time I saw Tom was in Kansas City, worldcon 1976, where he won the John W. Campbell Award for Best New Writer.

A note: below is an ad Tom did for a worldcon bid in 1959. This never happened but I did see a rework of this art in Tom's apartment in 1961 for a worldcon bid in Dallas for 1963, as far as I know that was never published anywhere.
—Al Jackson

~~~~~~

As I said in "Tom, Tom! A Reminiscence" (hard to believe it's almost 40 years ago now) I thought Tom was the best writer among all of us in the Turkey City bunch—us all starting to sell at the same time he came back from L.A. (to godforsaken Woodson, TX) finally made him start sending stuff out (Al Jackson said Tom could write like that in the '50s, but they could never make him submit the stuff)—he sold his first two stories on the same day (to Damon Knight and Robert Hoskins) and never looked back. His whole professional career (like Weinbaum's before him) was less than three years long. All those great stories and *Blind Voices* and half a dozen screenplays. *Blind Voices* was his novel from the same material as that of his screenplays, and, of course, it didn't sell until after Tom was gone, either.

—Howard Waldrop

I remember the first time I ever noticed Tom Reamy's name. It was in the September, 1974 issue of *The Magazine of Fantasy and Science Fiction*. Back then I read every issue with relish, and when I saw Reamy's name, it meant nothing to me.

I'm not positive but "Twilla" may have been his first published story and when I got to it in that magazine, I loved it. (I still have that issue of *F&SF* . . . I should go dig it up one day.)

At that moment, I had found a new favorite author and I couldn't wait to read more.

I didn't have to wait long. In the next few years, Reamy published a couple of dozen stories in magazines and anthologies. Wherever he published, I followed.

Of course his masterpiece was "San Diego Lightfoot Sue," published in 1975. That story won the Nebula award and he also won the Campbell award for best new writer that year.

Reamy had a unique style. Most of his work was dark fantasy, and it had a feeling of Bradbury or Matheson, but at the same time he stamped everything he wrote with his own amazing style.

I was stunned when I heard he died. There would be

no more stories like "The Detweiler Boy" or "Insects in Amber."

A year after his death, his one and only novel was published, *Blind Voices*. I read it and enjoyed it. It had the same magic as his shorter works, but it did feel like it was unfinished somehow. I read it several times over the next decade, and came to love the book, always reminded of the loss we had suffered.

In 1979, a second book was published. *San Diego Lightfoot Sue and Other Stories* was a wonderful collection of his best stories, although I'd read just about all of them before. It's still one of the best books I've ever read.

We only had him as a published author for a handful of years. I often wondered what amazing work would flow from his fingertips if he'd lived a full life.

I have no doubt Reamy would be thought of as a world class master writer. *Blind Voices* was published by Berkeley Putnam, a mainstream press, and it received very good reviews. Later novels would have been even better. Of that I have no doubt, but we'll never read those novels.

—John R. Little

Gene O'Neill
A Faint Scent of Musky Lime

unpublished books

I wish you could have seen me when I was fifteen, John Lee.
—Tom Reamy, "San Diego Lightfoot Sue"

I worked late Friday night at the San Francisco office, nothing to really go home to now that Nadia was gone.

After last Wednesday night's prodding, Nadia had finally packed up, and on Thursday morning she left my condo on Lake Merritt in Oakland. But she had paused at the door, called upon her distant Romany heritage and with a truly menacing scowl and scary throaty voice, she said: "Jack Johnson, you will never have another restful night from this day forth." After issuing her curse she dramatically turned her back and stormed out. The only thing that she left behind was her she-scent, lingering faintly on her pillow, on the bathroom towels, and on her cleaned-out side of the closet—a distinctive scent, its first smell always causing a tickling sensation in both my nostrils…

And, then, only a few minutes after she left the condo her *Chevy Volt* was broadsided by a hit and run driver and Nadia died on the way to the hospital.

I *should have* felt truly terrible.

She was a tall, gorgeous, dark-eyed woman, bright, talented, and creative. But she was plagued with a number of OCD-like rituals. Of course I could never follow all the strict rules governing almost every aspect of our lives together, including when we could have sex, which wasn't often. Her nagging me unmercifully grew more and more tedious. We argued and fought constantly. It had been that way almost from the start, over a year ago. I was a shy, socially inept nerd and very lonely, grateful that finally a beautiful woman had looked my way. In the early months, I conveniently dismissed what I chose to describe as her slightly *eccentric* behavior. Of course I eventually recommended professional help, which she ignored. I shouldn't have delayed the inevitable breakup by *trying* to be more tolerant and understanding. Because the reality was obvious that I'd made a terrible mistake: I was living with an often cranky and neurotic woman, who at the end I came to strongly dislike. It had been the absolute worst year of my life—a living nightmare.

When Nadia walked out of the door Thursday morning, I felt instant *relief*, as if I'd been released after serving a year at the notorious Alameda County Jail at Santa Rita. Truly grateful that she was gone from my life. I could care less about her half-ass Gypsy curse as she left.

Later that morning after I was notified about her accident, I did feel bad about her dying so suddenly, and even more than a bit guilty about initiating the breakup.

So, Thursday I took off from work and spent most of the afternoon with her older sister helping make the necessary funereal arrangements.

But tonight I had worked late at *Zaldivar, Kemper & Associates* to catch up, my team responsible for the graphic and written promotional brochure and other materials for *SoMa Bio-Logic Systems'* up-coming major drug release, *Interferox*—an innovative new immune system booster for cancer treatment. This was my first opportunity as a Project Leader, after being a senior tech writer for over six years at *ZK & A*; and I was truly sold on the probability of *Interferox* making an immediate and significant positive impact in the treatment of terminally ill cancer patients.

A little after seven o'clock, my stomach began growling.

I decided to leave the office on Howard Street and stop at *Fat Freddie's* on 2nd Street and grab a to-go green salad and an eggplant sandwich on flatbread, before continuing up to the BART station on 2nd and Market. I usually drove my *Fusion* back and forth to work, picking up riders at the Lake Street designated waiting spot in Oakland before crossing over the Bay Bridge to San Francisco. But after Nadia stormed out, I made a number of important promises to myself of immediate life-style changes, including taking the BART back and forth to work.

So the foot route over to *Fat Freddie's* tonight was not familiar. In addition, the fog was really thick and kind of disorienting. And passing no one on the mist-shrouded streets made the short walk rather eerie. Just after reaching 2nd Street and turning toward Market, the heavy fog swirled and then thinned enough to reveal a narrow alleyway. Where I spotted a sandwich board sign standing like a lonely sentinel at the mouth of the alley that read: **Unpublished Books,** and underneath that an arrow pointing down the alley. Now that's really an unusual name for a bookstore, I thought, almost an oxymoron.

I had been a fiction creative writing major with a minor in tech writing at San Francisco State. So, from assigned readings I was very familiar with the work of the late San Francisco Beat writer, Richard Brautigan, who mentioned in one of his stories the *Library of Unpublished Books*. But that was more or less a joke, like much of the other Brautigan weirdness. Staring at the name of the bookstore, I wondered if it too were actually a joke?

Intrigued and really in no hurry to get home, I took about six steps down the dark alley. There at the dead end cut into a grimy brick wall was this narrow bookstore door, with a dimly lit window barely wide enough to contain its name, written in a kind of Arabic-appearing script:

Unpublished
Books

After standing for a few seconds thinking about the possible meanings of the name, I decided it might just be a poor translation of *Rare Books*, published in very limited editions. Like a Taiwanese engineer's slightly off instructions in English. Or even our own local *All-Star Donuts*, which didn't quite make sense. But that explanation didn't feel exactly right, so I hesitated outside for another moment, leaning in closer and trying to get a better look through the dirty glass into the murky interior… with little success. Curiosity prevailed though, and I was finally drawn into the bookstore.

The instant after stepping in and glancing around, I gasped under my breath with surprise: "Wow!"

Because inside the narrow door the faintly lit interior was even stranger than its name suggested. I expected it to be a tiny niche bookstore of some kind, maybe fifteen feet by twenty feet or so. Certainly no wider than the width of the narrow alley. But no, this place was an *enormous* cavern, shelves and shelves of books from floor to a high ceiling, rows and rows disappearing finally in all directions back into the darkness. How could such a narrow front contain a bookstore of such immensity—?

That's when I spotted the suspected proprietor at the top of a book ladder, back at the edge of the gloominess. He must have heard me enter, even though there was no bell, or perhaps heard my whispered exclamation of awe, because he was staring directly at me with a wide grin. He seemed to parachute off and float down to the floor, not using any of the rungs… then disappear and reappear in front of me, all in the blink of an eye.

"Welcome to my bookstore," he said in slightly accented English, which I couldn't quite place. He was tiny, barely five-foot tall, with a wisp of a graying goatee, wearing black silken balloon pants and a loose long-sleeved embroidered white silk shirt with no collar—the embroidered black symbols, cut, and tailoring all unfamiliar. But perhaps the oddest thing was that he seemed ageless. He had the bright, dark eyes and white-toothed innocent grin of a child that contrasted dramatically with his gray hair and facial features, which were not exactly heavily wrinkled but definitely experienced. And his graceful, quick movements were almost supernaturally athletic. His overwhelming impression on me though was that he was actually a magical creature from a fantasy book—a wizard, or an elf, or maybe a djinn.

I partially gathered my senses together and mumbled hoarsely: "You call your place, *Unpublished Books?*" I gestured at the nearby shelves full of what looked like old, beautiful leather-bound books. Perhaps rare but obviously not unpublished.

He stared at me with a knowing look, then finally said: "Yes, I agree it is a confusing name. But, nevertheless, what we have here are really unpublished books and magazines of course." He chuckled. "But I will agree, a shop maybe named *Very Rare Books* would have been less confusing, even if it were false advertising. True?"

I nodded, acknowledging that name would've made more sense.

"But you see our name is one hundred percent accurate. These books are all unpublished fiction from the very beginning of each written language." He turned and gestured off into the apparent infinite murkiness. Then he turned back to me and stared with tented bushy gray eyebrows.

I was struck dumb by what he'd claimed. *All* these books were unpublished? And samples from every written language? It was mind-boggling.

Before I could recover though, he said something else surprising: "But I believe most of *your* fiction reading now is restricted to genre magazines. Am I correct?"

He was right of course. In college, I'd read lots of books. But I best loved short stories. And I'd even written a bit of short speculative fiction, submitting several stories to *Asimov's, Cemetery Dance, Dark Discoveries, F & SF,* and a few other publications with no success. Now, I only subscribed to *F & SF,* with the widest of range of all the print genre magazines, having reading time for only the one publication and an occasional book. Maybe now though with Nadia gone, I'd have more time to read at night after work. But I didn't mention any of this aloud to the tiny man. He somehow already knew *too* much about me.

He gestured for me to follow him along an aisle to the far right, and we trudged past rows and rows of books, until we turned up a perpendicular aisle into the also poorly lit magazine section. I squinted, scanning off to my left at seemingly thousands and thousands of issues of hundreds of various magazines endlessly disappearing into the darkness. Then he led me to a section containing strictly fantasy, science fiction, and horror magazines, before eventually stopping and saying: "Ah, here we are." He made an opened hand gesture toward a large collection of digest sized *F & SF* covers. I leaned closer and perused a few, not recognizing either the cover art or titles of any stories, although I recognized most of the writers' names, including four favorites: Philip K. Dick, Robert Silverberg, Kim Stanley Robinson, and Karen Joy Fowler.

"I believe you especially liked Tom Reamy's stories, many appearing first in *The Magazine of Fantasy and Science Fiction,*" the tiny man said, surprising me again with his apparent access into my private preferences, and pointing down at a specific cover of a copy of *F & SF.* There was Tom Reamy's name across the top, and a title: *A Faint Scent of Musky Lime*—the first of a three-part serialized short novel. I had never seen this title but it stirred an uncomfortable vague sense of something at the back corner of my mind.

Tom Reamy was one of my favorite writers. During his day he had been compared favorably to Richard Matheson. But Reamy was a much more transgressive writer, publishing in the early 70s. He reminded me of the old paraphrased Hemingway comparison of bullfighters and writers: *The good bullfighter fights in the terrain of the fighter; the great bullfighter fights in the terrain of the bull; and so it is with writers.* Tom Reamy was that kind of gutty writer, he never flinched or pulled a punch. His work often contained graphic violence and sex, but always as an integral part of the story. His Nebula winning novelette "San Diego Lightfoot Sue" dealt with a taboo sexual relationship between a thirty-five year old female artist, Sue, and her fifteen-year-old male model, John Lee. A beautiful, heart-wrenching, and ill-fated love story. Tom Reamy died in 1977 at 42, sitting at his typewriter, working on a story for *F & SF.* I'd read *all* of his thirteen published stories, the later ones first appearing in *F & SF,* and also his one posthumously published novel, *Blind Voices.* An unpublished short novella, "Potiphee, Petey, and Me," had been purchased for *Last Dangerous Visions* by Harlan Ellison, but LDV had remarkably not yet been released after being delayed for forty years. I had never heard of a Tom Reamy serialized short novel, nor did I recognize the creepy, dark alley illustration for it on the *F & SF* cover that the little man was now holding in his hand.

"Yes," I admitted hoarsely, clearing my throat. "I've read all of Tom Reamy's stuff, but I'm not sure I've ever heard of a copy of this particular story existing."

"No, this issue of *F & SF* like *all* of these others here is only available at *Unpublished Books.*" He held the magazine out to me. "Try this first part of the serial, which I think you will enjoy. If so, come back tomorrow night for the next copy of *F & SF*, which includes the second part of the serial."

I took the magazine, anxious to read the story. An unpublished Tom Reamy serial? It had to be some kind of fake. Still, I couldn't resist. "How much?" I said, figuring the price would be stiff.

The little man shook his head. "Nothing, now. If you enjoy the whole serial, we'll work out a *fair* price for you to own the three magazines. I trust you because I always get my due."

For a moment I took a closer look down at the little

in San Francisco, a highly competent nerd. I recognized a lot of myself in him. Even the guy's name was remarkably similar to mine, John Jackson…

Excerpt from Tom Reamy's ***A Faint Scent of Musky Lime***, **1st part**:

…Based on the recommendation of an acquaintance at work, John made his way over to North Beach to his destination on Broadway: The North Pole. *He slipped past the loud barker at the door front into the darkened club. A spotlight was focused on a skimpily clad, large-breasted, and platinum-haired woman, who was sliding her crotch up and down the lower part of a ceil-*

man, wondering if I were making a deal with some kind of an incarnation of the devil. I even shuddered at his last almost ominous words. But he just nodded as if privy to my suspicious but silly thought and smiled with his child-like eyes shining innocently.

I thanked him and took off into the fog.

It was late when I finally reached home in Oakland, but I couldn't resist immediately digging into the first part of the Reamy unpublished serial… If it was a fake, I sure couldn't tell. The lead character seemed typical Reamy—a common man, lonely and plagued with some socialization awkwardness. He was an engineer at a high-tech, dot com

ing-to-floor metal pole, smiling lewdly and leaving nothing to the imagination. John ordered a drink, but didn't sit up in the half-arc of seats pressing in close around the stage. He picked a table back farther in the dark. He watched the woman's bumping and grinding gyrations around the pole, the nearest spectators hooting and hollering in appreciation. The music finally stopped. And the pole dancer made her way along the edge of the stage near her sweaty and stirred-up fans. Many of the men were stuffing small bills into the top of her flimsy g-string. She acknowledged each tip by blowing the tipper a wet kiss. One guy stood up and leaned out to grab her, only to be quickly hustled away from the bar stage area by a pair of heavily muscled bouncers. John was fascinated by all this publicly displayed and sleazy sexuality—

"Hey, big fella, you ready for a private party," a slim brunette dressed in tight black shorts and a low-cut white silk blouse said in a sexy whisper near his ear, and then sat down at John's table. She smiled and waited.

"Ah, ah… sure," John said. This was actually why he'd come to The North Pole. His friend had described in glowing praise the sexy lap dances offered here by attractive young women.

The woman took John by the hand and led him to a private cubicle in the darkened back area of the club. As soon as she closed the door the woman pressed her sex against his thigh and in a throaty voice said: *"That will be fifty dollars in advance, hon."*

John clumsily dug out his wallet, ignoring the crow's feet and deep wrinkles in the woman's face now that she was so close. He was excited by her faint salty-sweet she-scent.

She tucked the bill into her bra, and then pushed him down into the cubicle's solitary piece of furniture, an armless chair. Without any other preamble, she easily straddled his lap, slowly sliding herself over the top of his now full erection. Then, she began to make abbreviated bumps and grinds on his lap similar to the movements of the pole dancer… Finally she began moaning in his ear: *"Oh, baby, baby!"*

At the height of her loud ecstasy, she reached down and clasped her hand over John's member, gripping it tightly through his trousers. Then, she made several jerking movements, until he closed his eyes and groaned.

The whole fifty-dollar lap dance was over in less than three minutes.

John quickly left the club, feeling ashamed, disappointed, cheated, depressed, dirty… and realizing that he was even lonelier than before journeying to the strip club on Broadway.

I think this ending of the first part of the serial was also very typical Reamy, and demonstrated a significant aspect of his work. Even though the story involved a socially-defined transgressive act just like the sex in "San Diego Light Foot Sue," Reamy developed it in such a non-flinching, compelling manner that nothing really *felt* terribly seedy or wrong. We understood John's neediness, which is revealed realistically. And his clumsy and fruitless search for love in a sleazy strip club made him a hapless but actually sympathetic character.

I sat the magazine on my nightstand and climbed into bed, glancing at the clock: 2:30. Way past my bedtime.

I immediately fell asleep.

But I was troubled by a dream obviously stimulated by the Reamy story—almost making me feel I was replaying a role in the story.

I found myself at *The North Pole*, sitting at the stage-side bar. I'd shooed away several lap dance invitations, but remained at the bar with a watery drink. I was watching an exotic Asian woman strip, her backside covered entirely with a colorful, fiery-eyed dragon-demon tattoo. She finally stripped down to tiny pasties on her nipples and a g-string that didn't quite cover her unshaven pubic area. Even though some of her bumps and grinds were crude, I still found her sexually exciting. As she circled closer, I pulled out a twenty-dollar bill. Spotting the apparent larger than normal tip, she squatted very near where I sat. When I leaned over the bar to put the bill in her g-string,

she reached out and pulled the back of my head forward a few inches until my face was pushed against her flimsy g-string. Then, she did a slow thrusting movement with her crotch.

I blinked, her strong perfume *not* quite masking the overwhelming smell of her swampy she-scent… and I recoiled backwards, gasping as if I had been pepper sprayed, almost falling off the bar stool.

The stripper giggled, and the men sitting at the bar on either side of me roared with laughter.

Embarrassed, I got up quickly and left the club—

At that point, I abruptly awakened from the dream, panting, my sheets tangled and sweaty. But, despite it only being a dream, the lingering feelings were similar to John's experience in the Reamy serial. I, too, felt ashamed, unsettled, and disturbed—a sense of being dirty and disappointed by my North Beach club experience.

The next night after work, I hurried over to the alley and *Unpublished Books*, to pick up the second part of the *F & SF* serial. The strange little man apparently anticipated my arrival and was waiting near the front door with the appropriate copy of *F & SF* in hand.

"Hello, John, glad to see you again," he said, handing me the magazine and shaking his head as I reached for my wallet. "No charge, yet."

I ignored the slightly ominous tone, and left.

Excerpt from Tom Reamy's ***A Faint Scent of Musky Lime, 2nd part:***

…John Jackson found himself walking down O'Farrell Street in the upper Tenderloin. It was just after midnight—the time of heavy buying and selling. He passed several painted ladies, their trade obvious from their similar appearance—high heels, tight vinyl shorts, low-cut blouses, and faces so heavily made up they almost resembled clown-like masks. But despite several being fairly attractive, John was too bashful to move close enough to talk to them. He finally tentatively approached a blonde. But by the time he sucked up his nerve to speak, the painted lady had taken another customer by the arm, leading the other man off into the night.

Then, someone touched John's shoulder and he turned to face her.

"Hello handsome, you have the look of a man needing some intimate company. True?"

She was tall, redheaded, dressed very similar to the other painted ladies, but much younger and her face was not so heavily made up and gaudy. It was not a look of innocence, her old eyes contrasting with her youth, but the woman appealed to John. Still, he felt too choked up to answer, just managing a bashful nod.

"Well, c'mon then," the young redhead said, boldly clasping his arm. "We'll go over to my place and get better acquainted."

They moved down O'Farrell and turned up Jones Street, John's heart thumping and his pulse racing with excitement. He'd really never been with a woman, although once a freshman girl had allowed him to fondle her breasts and rub her furry sex after he boldly kissed her at a fraternity drunken keg party in his senior year at USF. But she'd passed out before John had the opportunity to explore anything farther than touching. But this was going to be much different tonight, he knew.

John pulled up short after spotting the seedy exterior of the Hotel Reo, and the disreputable appearance of the crowd moving in and out of the entrance—most of them only a half-step up the social ladder from the homeless with their distinctive multi-layered greasy clothing.

His throat and chest felt tight as his initial sexual excitement quickly dissipated into a cold, sweaty fear. He was not about to go into that dump, and be trapped in some sleazy tiny room. Something terrible could happen to him.

He said: "No, I can't go in there."

The young painted lady turned, frowned, and said: "Why not?"

"I just can't," he said in a sheepish voice, unable to suppress a slight shiver.

The woman glanced at the Reo and then back at John. Then, she said: "Would it be better for you someplace maybe outside? I know a nearby alley where we can have some privacy."

He thought about it for a few moments, sucked in his breath, and finally nodded.

"Okay, let's go." Again she clutched his arm possessively, pressing her soft breast tightly against shoulder.

The alley was not only private, it was very dark. They made their way to the very end. The redhead pressed against him, backing him up near the brick wall.

"I can't wait, sugar," she said in a husky whisper, sliding her open hand down between his legs and pressing it firmly against his crotch. "But I need a hundred dollars before we can do the good stuff, you know." Then she deftly slid his zipper first an inch down… and then quickly back up.

John clumsily dug out five twenties from his wallet and pressed them into the girl's hand. A second later the money had disappeared down the front of the young redhead's blouse.

Then, she slid his zipper wide open, squatted, and provocatively wet her lips. But before going any farther, she pushed him gently backwards toward the wall. "Lean back, honey, and brace."

John leaned back into the brick wall, slightly off balance.

Something brushed against his ankles—

He froze with fear, after staring down at the clawed fingers reaching out from the shadowy wall and encircling his ankles.

Startled, I thought: *Move John! Run now!*

In the next moment though, I recovered my psychic identity, held the magazine at arm's length, and caught my breath. Taking a moment or two to completely recover my poise, I glanced over at the digital clock on my nightstand, which read: 3:15.

Remembering my dream right after reading the first part of the Reamy serial, I sucked in a deep breath of determination. I shook my head. No way that I was going to sleep now and take the chance of the second part of the story capturing me in another terrible nightmare. I decided that I wanted no part of those scary hands reaching out from the shadows of that brick wall.

So, I went to my writing desk, tapped on my iMac, and pulled up the mission statement I had been working on for the *SoMa Bio-Logic Systems* drug project. With some mental

effort I shifted from the Reamy story and was, after a few moments, totally involved with my own writing.

Even though exhausted because of no sleep, I couldn't get away from a full staff weekend meeting at *ZK &A*, which didn't end until late afternoon.

Finally, with a huge sigh of relief, I headed over to *Unpublished Books*. I had to find out what happened next to John Jackson. Did he escape those grasping hands reaching out from the wall… or not?

I have trouble finding the alley in the fog, which is extra thick tonight, almost like a great cloud has fallen to earth, engulfing me. After a minute or two, I realize I have gone way too far uptown, missing the entrance. So, I backtrack to where Howard met 2nd Street, passing a youngish painted lady trolling alone on the street, a scarf covering her hair. Then, at the corner, I turn around and head slowly back up toward Market Street, watching carefully. No alleys… Finally, almost at wits end, ahead I see the thick fog swirl and reveal the gaping mouth of the alley. But with *no* sandwich board sign this time. Instead, the hooker is standing there now and looking at me expectantly, after apparently watching me pass her by and then come back.

Emphatically, I shake my head and slip past her into the alley. I hurry to the dead end, where I stop in shock. There is no bookstore back here; there is nothing, except a grimy brick wall, which nevertheless *seems* really familiar even in the thick chilling mist… The light bulb finally goes on over my head and I snap my fingers. Of course! This place reminds me of the cover illustration and Reamy's alley description at the end of part two of *A Faint Scent of Musky Lime*.

Oh, man. I am trapped completely in Reamy's story… And almost simultaneously I remember the strange little man calling me *John* last night, realizing it probably wasn't a mistake on his part.

I am John.

Footsteps echo in the fog.

I blink and look back toward the dim streetlight framing the mouth of the alley. A shadowy figure is moving toward me, the young prostitute, slipping off her scarf, revealing her red hair. It is all coming together just like in the story. Frightened, I back away from her and shout: "I said *no*, stay away! Please."

I turn to flee from the redheaded woman, and smack solidly into the shadowy brick wall, stunning myself—

Before I can recover my senses, I feel the clawed fingers… clutching my coat, and dragging me into the chilling blackness of the wall.

A hand roughly cuts off my scream, smothering me.

But my last feeling as the blackness completely swallows me up is the familiar *tickling* sensation in my nostrils.

The darkened alley is left completely empty… except for a lingering faint scent of musky lime.

Playing with Vampires:
An Interview with Ken Hite and Justin Achilli

BY RICHARD DANSKY

Monsterhearts
a story game
about the messy lives of teenage monsters.

Tabletop roleplaying games have been awash in vampires from the beginning, and as the hobby has evolved, so too has the role of the befanged bloodsuckers. What were once unnamed antagonists in early Dungeons & Dragons books got dragged into the spotlight with Ravenloft's iconic Strahd von Zarovich. White Wolf's groundbreaking *Vampire: The Masquerade* took the next step, drawing on the romantic vampire mythology popularized by Anne Rice and her literary successors in order to turn vampires into tormented—and superpowered—protagonists. Since then, vampires have filled pretty much every possible niche in the RPG space. Two of the designers most responsible for the vampiric explosion are Kenneth Hite, creator of *Night's Black Agents*, and Justin Achilli, long-time creative hand on the tiller of the iconic *Vampire* brand. In this interview we discuss their takes on the rise of the vampire, how it stacks up against the zombie, and how they can still be relevant in a post-*Twilight* world.

Why are vampires so popular in the roleplaying space?

KEN HITE: Vampires are easily and by far the most powerful and evocative of the modern horror tropes—Dracula alone has been the subject of hundreds of films, TV shows, comics, and games. Even as early as Bram Stoker, the vampire existed at a powerful locus of race, sex, death, terror, fascination, magic, and bestiality. Any one of those ingredients provides charge enough; with all of those firing at once, the vampire is a semiotic atom bomb.

JUSTIN ACHILLI: The Big Three, in my opinion are:
- They're both relatable and alien: They look like us, but underneath that familiar veneer, they actually want to prey upon us. The human mind is inherently intrigued by perceived paradoxes.

- They suggest a rich history: Most vampire stories at least make references to things that happened A Long Time Ago, probably resulting in the vampire's becoming what she is. Since most popular myths assume immortality on the part of vampires, that's a compelling way to investigate the attitudes of the past and contrast them with the values of the present, whatever that present is in terms of the story.

- They project a sexual, sensual, or other social power: And power is an element that draws people to many fantasies. Whether the aristocratic take on Dracula to the lusty menace of "Carmilla" or *Byzantium* to the brutal fear projected by Count Orlok or the social brinksmanship of the television dramas like *Vampire Diaries*, vampires are powerful, and that power is often a metaphor for attraction or virility.

KH: You can shape the vampire's charge for sheer terror, for eroticism, or—as in games—for thrills of the roller-coaster sort. But that roller coaster still runs past terror and eroticism, which I suspect is what provides the fun. And of course, the immense amount of detailed, lurid, weird, and outright contradictory vampire lore out there in both mass and folk media makes working with vampires extra fun for research nerds like myself.

How can vampires thrive in a post-*Twilight* world, or have they ultimately been de-fanged as monsters?

JA: Much of this is cyclical. Dreamy boyfriend vampires are kind of like the late 60s psychedelic comedy Batman. They're an expression of the culture's current prevailing attitudes. The cycle will eventually return to the less implicitly beneficial vampire, and many subcultures—gamers included—already hold this different, and perhaps longer-standing interpretation of them. Some games even trade on the *Twilight* vampire interpretation, like *Monsterhearts*.

KH: Given that the *Twilight* series sold something like one-eighth of the books in America in their heyday, I think the appeal of the vampire is pretty solidly established. (There have also been four vampire movies with box office profits of over $100 million since then, and three or four TV shows about vampires greenlit.) If you're asking "how do you make vampires scary" or "how do you make adults interested in vampires" in a post-*Twilight* world, the answer (just like in the pre-*Twilight* world) is "write a scary vampire" or "write one for adults." For every jaded, dead soul who's "tired of vampires" there are dozens of new-fledged fans perhaps looking for a deeper bite than Edward Cullen's.

JA: Different games create different essential experiences for their vampires, and the gothic-punk interpretation of *Vampire* coincided nicely with the Zeitgeist of the 1990s when it first emerged. I expect White Wolf will spend no small effort updating that essential experience for the next edition when they undertake it.

Do vampires work better as protagonists or antagonists in a roleplaying context?

JA: It depends on the story you're wanting to tell. The vampire's motivation, not just the fact that he or she is a vampire, is what makes for a protagonist or antagonist.

KH: There have been successful works with vampire protagonists, so I can't say it can't be done. But the absolute core of the vampire legend is rape, and I think rapists work much, much better as antagonists.

JA: They make great antagonists because they exhibit certain characteristics that scare us, that we find repugnant, or because of the actions they inflict upon us. ("Us" being the erstwhile "them," since most vampire stories assume that a vampire becomes a vampire after having once been human.) They make good protagonists because vampires have implicit outcomes for their actions, built-in consequences that make for compelling primary or secondary conflicts around which the story can revolve.

KH: The amount of work you need to go to in order to make a vampire protagonist "the exception" could better be spent, I think, creating a powerful story around a believable, interesting, human protagonist: *Let The Right One In* is a great example. The other possibility is to try and create a kind of "denatured" vampirism that isn't murder and rape incarnate, but of course stories that dilute vampirism wind up being, well, denatured—thin and weak—right from the jump.

And that gets into the "rules" of vampirism, which always seem to be changing based on the needs of the plot. Garlic or no garlic, crosses or any religious symbol or no religious symbol—why do people keep changing the rules for bloodsuckers?

JA: Different stories told with different themes and intended experiences. The vampire is a tool in the writer's or designer's toolbox. The experience she wants to create defines that tool's properties and how it's used. The same could be said of a smoking gun. Sometimes the smoking gun is the murderous implement held in the villain's hand; sometimes it is the instrument of justice wielded by the righteous in a timely delivery of justice. If a story concerns itself with a vampire, that vampire means something in context.

With that in mind, what were the challenges of keeping vampires current in the gaming space?

KH: The biggest challenge was stepping up the more sedate pace of the traditional vampire story into the faster story beat of the modern spy thriller. This is where the action-horror genre—F. Paul Wilson or Robert McCammon novels, or *Aliens* or *28 Days Later*—came to my aid. (That said, an old-school vampire story fits very snugly into the rhythm of, say, a John Le Carré novel.) Once I kind of cracked that code, the rest tended to fit together pretty well.

So how would you describe *The Dracula Dossier*, and how does it tie in to the granddaddy of all vampire stories?

KH: The central conceit of *The Dracula Dossier* is that Stoker's novel is actually the redacted after-action report of the original 1894 British intelligence operation to recruit a vampire as an asset. The game comes about when

Stoker's original draft, annotated by three generations of MI6 analysts, falls into the players' hands, and they realize that MI6 is still trying to recruit Dracula—this time, as a deniable asset to kill terrorists. Stoker's novel, like a lot of 19th century fiction, is just bubbling over with loose ends, weird details, character moments, bits of setting, and so on that cried out to be "re-explained," in this case as evidence of his involvement with the espionage world. They also lend themselves well to providing plentiful leads for investigators in the present: What's on the site of Carfax now? Did Quincey Harker have any kids of his own? Are those Slovak river pirates still in business in the post-Soviet Balkans? Stoker's core story, and its core characters, were powerful enough that a 21st-century echo can still carry plenty of juice.

How, then, do you think a game like *Vampire: The Masquerade* has managed to maintain its cultural significance for a quarter of a century?

JR: People's cultures represent how they interpret the things that scare them. Over time, these change, because cultures themselves change over time. I have a pet theory that popular favor for vampires and zombies both look like sine waves, but they're out of phase. When our individual cultures fear single, powerful, persuasive individuals, vampires are the vogue monster. When we fear the masses of the Other, zombies are the culturally resonant monster. Peaks and valleys, but what scares us and how we represent it via popular fiction never quite disappears, especially when we use our folklore to personify it.

I think people always struggle with their own morality, and *Vampire* is a wonderful way to express and even exorcise some of those troubling questions. They allow us to challenge and provoke our societal assumptions. Storytelling as a relationship experiment.

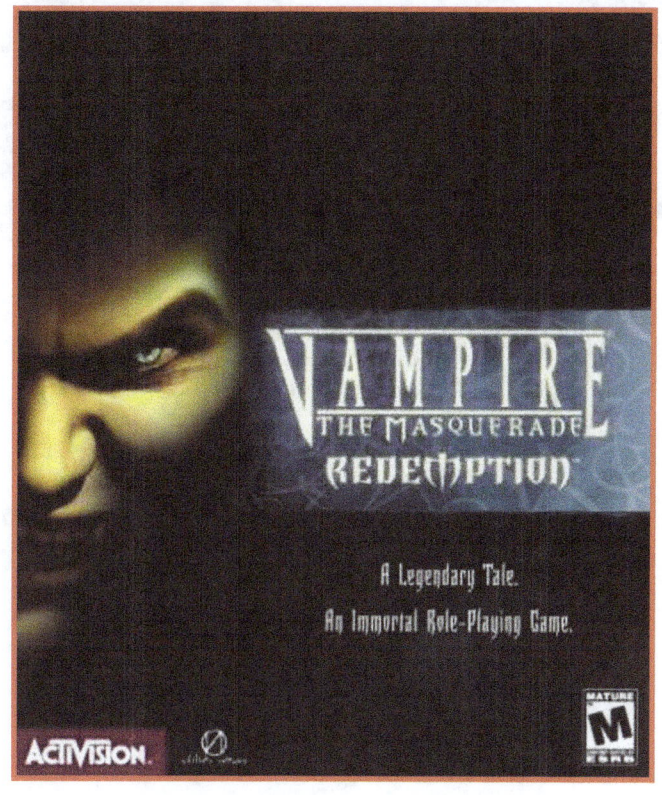

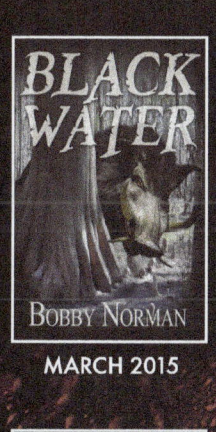

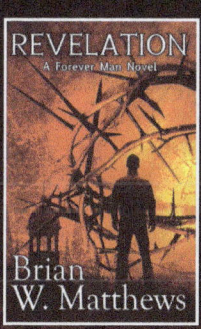

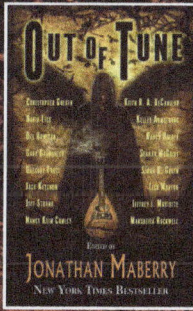

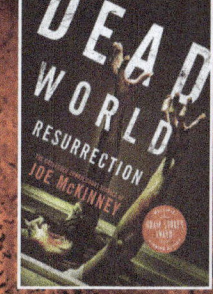

HELLNOTES

FICTION, MOVIES, AND ART
DEDICATED TO THE HORROR GENRE

THE HORROR
REVIEW

HORROR, SCIENCE FICTION
& FANTASY REVIEWS

JOURNALSTONE
YOUR LINK TO ARTISTIC TALENT

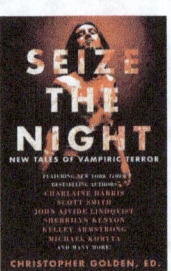

Seize The Night
Edited by Christopher Golden
Gallery Books
October 6, 2015
Reviewed by Mario Guslandi

Do you want to know a little secret? I'm sick and tired of vampire stories. I've had my share during the years and now I'm fed up with those bloodsuckers. Thus, I turned the first page of *Seize the Night* (**subtitled:** *New Tales of Vampiric Terror*) with a heavy heart.

I was wrong.

Unexpectedly, this new anthology (edited by Christopher Golden) provides an entirely new view about vampires: no longer romantic but as the deadly characters we remember them in countless variations from so many previous books. Here we have twenty brand new stories by a bunch of distinguished contributors, probing every possible uncovered aspect of the vampiric condition.

The overall quality of the included tales is more than satisfactory but, as always, some stories do stand out and deserve to be especially mentioned.

In "Paper Cuts," Gary A. Braunbeck offers an original take on the subject by contributing a story of "indirect" vampirism where books play a pivotal role. Always on the verge of implausibility the tale is, nevertheless, extremely enjoyable.

"Miss Fondevant" by Charlaine Harris is an excellent, gripping story of psychic vampirism featuring a creepy, evil schoolteacher bound to finally get her well-deserved punishment.

The talented Robert Shearman provides "Blood," yet another superb, puzzling and slightly Aickmanesque piece of fiction featuring a young seductress taking her aged teacher on a trip to Paris where increasingly odd events take place.

Finally, I'd like to single out Laird Barron's "In a Cavern, In a Canyon." It's an outstanding tale graced by an extraordinary narrative style depicting a subtle, ominous type of hidden vampirism.

So the secret is out: long live the vampires.

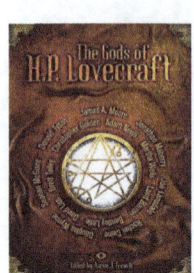

The Gods of H.P. Lovecraft
Edited by Aaron J. French
JournalStone
December, 2015
Reviewed by Michael R. Collings

Much has been said recently about Howard Phillips Lovecraft.

A fair amount of it has been stridently negative.

He has been ridiculed for his facial features and disparaged for beliefs inculcated in him as an adolescent, although they became less strident as he matured.

His style has been castigated as "lugubrious" and "turgid"—both, curiously enough, words he would have appreciated for themselves. His stories sometimes seem to have little or no plot; descriptive, atmospheric darkness or evocative weirdness suffices instead of actions and resolutions. They likewise often have little in the way of fully-rounded characters; and when they do, the characters frequently seem rather like each other, which is understandable since most of them derive from "the ancient, lonely farmhouses of backwoods New England; for there the dark elements of strength, solitude, grotesqueness, and ignorance combine to form the perfection of the hideous." ("The Picture in the House," 1921).

On the other side, he has been rightly acclaimed as the originator of a particular branch of horror literature that has endured for nearly a century and that, if anything, is as prevalent today as it was half a century or more ago. Few authors have been honored with an eponym-creating suffix: Chaucerian, Shakespearean, Miltonic, Swiftian, Byronic, Dickensian, Faulknerian, Heinleinian are among them. Each word defines a specific sub-genre, a kind, with a well-defined sense of style; characteristic vocabulary; narrative structures, both macro- and micro-; themes, approaches, and contents. Simply to say the word conjures a complete vision of a clear-cut sort.

Among horror writers, Lovecraft is the premier example. Lovecraftian horror or Lovecraftian supernatural horror conjures a vision uniquely linked to his name and diligently expanded upon by generations of fans, followers, and imitators.

In part, his influence stems from those elements some

readers and critics choose to disparage. Yes, his style can seem overblown and pretentious, especially for readers conditioned to post-Hemingway curtness and directness; readers of his own times, perhaps more familiar with the conventions of eighteenth-century prose than we are, would have responded more positively to his elegant constructions, his labyrinthine periods, to sentences whose formation are almost as much a contributor to meanings as his words. His vocabulary might be abstruse, but it is always accurate. And his landscapes at times become virtual characters. To take an example, here is the second paragraph from "The Picture in the House":

> *Most horrible of all sights are the little unpainted wooden houses remote from travelled ways, usually squatted upon some damp, grassy slope or leaning against some gigantic outcropping of rock. Two hundred years and more they have leaned or squatted there, while the vines have crawled and the trees have swelled and spread. They are almost hidden now in lawless luxuriances of green and guardian shrouds of shadow; but the small-paned windows still stare shockingly, as if blinking through a lethal stupor which wards off madness by dulling the memory of unutterable things.*

The movement from "Most horrible of all sights" to "the memory of unutterable things" twists and turns through three complex sentences, carrying readers through time and space and sanity.

Beyond this, though, Lovecraft achieved something few writers have attempted. He created a cosmos inhabited by beings—mortal and immortal—so far beyond humanity as to be almost incomprehensible. For lack of a better term, the most enduring of them touch upon being gods; and the most horrifying neither care about humans nor are hostile to them, but are absolutely and utterly, coldly and completely indifferent to what happens on this miniscule planet.

Perhaps more than anything this cosmicism explains Lovecraft's perennial influence. During his lifetime, friends and fellow-writers helped themselves to his universe, inventing whole pantheons of lesser gods to bolster his originals. The tendency to borrow and to augment continued until his death in 1937 and beyond, manifesting itself most recently, perhaps, in characters appearing in role-playing games.

Underlying all of the accretions, however, and warranting their existence, are Lovecraft's gods. Some are so well known that their names come with ready-made mythologies: Great Cthulhu, the most prominent, the most expansive, the most hideous of monsters; Yog-Sothoth, almost reborn into this world through his grotesque son in "The Dunwich Horror": the "far Daemon Sultan" Azathoth; and Nyarlathotep, the "crawling chaos." Others are less familiar but equally capable of stimulating nightmares and beneath them writhe scores of additions by August Derleth, Clark Ashton Smith, Abraham Merritt, Brian Lumley, and dozens more.

Still, there is the core.

That core is the focus of *The Gods of H.P. Lovecraft,* edited by Aaron J. French and featuring twelve stories exploring possibilities implicit in the Cosmic Mythos. The volume is a paean not only to the imaginations of the writers involved—which are as wide-ranging as they are unpredictable—but to the richness of Lovecraft's initial creations. Each story takes as its starting point with one of Lovecraft's cosmic entities, however precisely or vaguely defined in his stories, and develops it into something new, something integrally tied to modern audiences, something that transcends imitation or mere replication to move farther into the unknown.

Some are set in distinctly Lovecraftian landscapes, as is Joe R. Lansdale's "In the Mad Mountains," a tale of the Elder Things set in a landscape desolation, of ice and snow, of star-head things and tentacular monsters. Although a later story, it expresses one of the themes implicit in the Mythos: As a character is swept into the mouth of a resurgent creature, gigantic and impossible, "'Why?' she yelled to the wind and water. 'I am nothing. I'm not even an appetizer'"—the nothingness, the less-than-nothing-ness—of humanity in the face of the Old Ones.

Others start in more familiar settings and from there trespass dangerous borders that are better left uncrossed: Brett Talley's "The Apotheosis of a Rodeo Clown," which begins in California's Owens Valley and from there follows its circuitous trail into madness and into the realm of the toad-like Tsathoggua. Or Douglas Wynne's "Rattled," which moves across America toward the Mojave Desert, the Valley of Fire State Park, and the resolution to a mysterious death years before, and a confrontation with the serpent-god Yig.

In between are stories that move seamlessly from one kind of tradition to another. Jonathan Maberry's story of the Night Gaunts, "Dream a Little Dream with Me," also stars a werewolf-detective, Nazi treasure-hunters from the Thule Society, an Ogre, and a secret entrance to Lovecraft's Dreamlands. Bentley Little's "Petohtalrayn" begins by linking evidences of a mysterious Dark Man with historical disappearances, Mayan myth, Christian missionary journals, and lost tribes.

Perhaps the most evocative of the stories is Adam LG Nevill's "Call the Name," a stark creation of an Earth nearing annihilation, as the last of four generations of women, all plagued by premonitions and insanity, must watch as her worst dreams develop around her…as humanity inadvertently prepares the way for the return to the surface of the submerged citadel R'lyeh and its dreaming god, dead Cthulhu.

Rounding out the volume are: Martha Wells's "The Dark Gates" and Yog-Sothoth; Laird Barron's nightmarish tale of time-travel, "We Smoke the Northern Lights," and Azathoth; David Liss's "The Doors that Never Close and the Doors that are Always Open," and Shub-Niggurath; Christopher Golden and James A. Moore's "In Their Presence" and the Mi-go, Rachel Caine's "A Dying of the Light" and the Great Race of Yin; and Seanan McGuire's "Down, Deep Down, Beneath the Waves" and the Deep Ones.

It is a tribute to the power of Lovecraft's cosmos and the fertile imaginations of the storytellers that none of the tales sound alike, none of them are cookie-cutter representations of conventional expectations of things-Lovecraftian. Each develops its own tone, its own way of interpreting creatures that have—in literary terms, at least—taken on lives of their own over the last near-century.

In addition, the volume becomes a compendium of Lovecraft's Others through commentary on the deities by Donald Tyson, several pages at the end of each tale outlining the backgrounds, locations, powers, and attendants of each god. Prefacing each tale is a black-and-white interpretation of the relevant god or, when physical descriptions are too vague, of a key event within the tale.

In all, *The Gods of Lovecraft* is beautifully produced and beautifully rendered, offering "Searchers after horror" a multitude of "strange, far places" to haunt.

<><><><><><><><><><><><><><><><><><><><><><><><>

Ashley Bell
Dean Koontz
Bantam
December 8, 2015
Reviewed by Marvin P. Vernon

In Dean Koontz's new thriller *Ashley Bell*, we are introduced to Bibi Blair, a 22-year-old author with a critically acclaimed book to her name. Her life looks like it is just getting started until she finds she develops a rare, and especially vicious, form of cancer. There is little to no hope that she can be treated effectively, yet she wakes up in the hospital the next day in total remission. Through an odd form of divination, she discovers the reason she was miraculously cured: to save the life of a teenage girl by the name of Ashley Bell.

With that idea, Dean Koontz takes us into a whirlwind supernatural/science-fiction thriller that we have not seen from him since *Watchers* or *Lightning*. There are all the usual Koontz gimmicks: sadistic villains, deadly cults, a taste of the paranormal and a resourceful young innocent throw into chaos; thankfully in this one he kept the noble golden retriever at minimum sweetness level. Yet this is the first in a very long time that I did not think Koontz was sleepwalking through it. The author takes an intriguing premise and makes it complex and befuddling in a good way. Bibi Blair is one of his best characters and one whose full importance and talents are very slowly revealed. The story only spans a few days, yet the 600+ page narration plays with it, adding important reveals from her past and vague characters whose roles are not clear until the information is needed. Much of the tension, and pleasure, comes from Bibi's own thought process as she puts together the clues to her new purpose and evidently the surprise turn near the end.

Recently I reviewed *The City* and stated it was a change from Koontz's usual, yet I criticized it for not being different enough. Here we have the author going back to the horror thriller that made his reputation but finding new ideas and ways to express them that will keep even the stalwart Koontz reader interested. *Ashley Bell* is not the usual roller coaster ride of a thriller – there are times it feels a bit slow, but the attentive reader will realize that those slow parts often provide the most important materials to the mystery. Sometimes Koontz's characters can feel a bit thin but Ashley Bell may be one of his best since Odd Thomas. I have purposely stayed away from revealing anything but the bare bones because every detail is important and knowing it in advance may take some of the pleasure out of the reading.

So what we have in *Ashley Bell* is Koontz's most interesting novel since *Odd Thomas*, and one of his best since *Watchers* and *Lightning*. If you have soured toward this prolific writer in the past, it is time to check him out again.

<><><><><><><><><><><><><><><><><><><><><><><><>

nEvermore! Tales of Murder, Mystery & the Macabre
Edited by Nancy Kilpatrick and Caro Soles
Edge Science Fiction and Fantasy Publishing
July 1, 2015
Reviewed by Michael R. Collings

As a newly transferred junior in college, I worked as a student assistant in a Survey of American Literature course. After hearing the professor outline the readings for the semester, I approached him and asked whether the students would be reading Poe—not coincidentally, I had just finished my first go-through of Tales of the Grotesque and Arabesque and was eager to find out more about him and his stories.

No, I was told. The class would focus on writers for a more refined palate. Interest in Poe among students should have waned by the time they were sophomores in high school. No, there would not be time for a writer such as Poe.

In his defense, the professor was a deeply-read scholar in the period I had chosen as my emphasis—The English Renaissance. He became my advisor, my mentor, and my friend. And, back in the distant days of the mid-1960s, Stephen King and others had not yet re-imagined dark fantasy, transforming a minor sub-sub-genre (if even acknowledged as that) into a vehicle of relevance and versatility, so the slight might perhaps be forgiven.

Later, I found graduate professors more amenable to Poe and began discovering what a powerful voice he had been in American literature. Far from being merely a scribbler of sensational stories and sappy verses, he is arguably one of the greatest nineteenth-century influences on modern fiction. He invented the detective story before the word detective appeared in English. He helped formulate the modern short story, not only directly but indirectly, through French symbolists who imitated him and were in turn imitated by early twentieth-century writers. He helped establish the critical vocabulary for discussing modern literature. He helped change the rhythms and directions of verse. He was a capable editor and an extraordinary hoaxter.

Kilpatrick and Soles' Nevermore! Tales of Murder, Mystery & the Macabre demonstrates how pervasive, how extensive, how profound Poe's influence is among modern writers of supernatural and weird fiction. Twenty-odd stories based on a single nineteenth-century writer might be expected to explore similar paths, exploit similar vocabularies and narrative structures, and, in the least successful cases, sound distressingly the same.

With Poe, however, there is always something new to be investigated, whether it be his physical landscapes (often as important as his characters), his psychological insights into abnormal states, his studies of obsession and madness, or his emphases on love and loss, grief and sorrow, self-destructiveness and death. And there is even room for a bit of a hoax now and then.

When these possibilities are coupled with such accomplished writers as Chelsea Quinn Yarbro, Christopher Rice, Lisa Morton, Nancy Holder, Richard Christian Matheson, William F. Nolan and Jason and Sunni Brock, Tanith Lee, Margaret Atwood, David Morrell and a dozen other estimable talents, the results display the remarkable talents of all involved…including Edgar Allan Poe.

The collection begins with landscape: Yarbro's "The Gold Bug Conundrum" pits a treasure hunter in a decrepit house, seeking the still-hidden secret to Poe's tale, and the forces of nature that oppose him. Barbara Fradkin's "The Lighthouse" neatly blends isolation, loneliness, fear, and a hint of the supernatural set in a world fraught with war and death.

Kelly Armstrong's "The Orange Cat" concentrates on obsessive characters—human and feline; while Margaret Atwood's "The Eye of Heaven" constructs a fantasia of terror around a single, superficially innocuous image. Richard Christian Matheson's "133" raises the art of Poesque retribution and revenge to chilling levels. At the opposite extreme, Thomas S. Roche's "The Masques of Amanda Llado" shows that even within Poe's framework of terror and horror there is the possible of humor, no matter how macabre.

The final segment, David Morrell's "The Opium-Eater," seems to break with the protocols of the collection—it is set in pre-Poe England and includes Thomas de Quincey, William Wordsworth, Samuel Taylor Coleridge and others in a story of a series of seemingly unrelated, horrific deaths. The point is that, just as Poe influenced generations, so he was influenced. The complex web of cause and effect; the injuries, willful or unknowing, inflicted by characters upon others; the power of grief and loss in distorting survivors' lives; the ennobling and disabling power of love—all point directly to elements integral in Poe's best stories. Nevermore! Tales of Murder, Mystery & the Macabre performs an excellent service in warranting Poe's modern reputation as a master of letters and a continuing resource for ideas, images, and emotions.

The Dream Beings
Aaron J. French
Samhain Publishing
January 5, 2016
Reviewed by Alex Scully

The Dream Beings, the latest novella from Aaron J. French, opens with action. We are immediately drawn into a ritual style murder, but we quickly learn this is no "typical" crime. Bizarre clues are left at crimes scenes. There are horrific injuries to the victims, and a sinister, secret world emerges from behind the worlds.

French often writes in the classic Lovecraftian vein, and The Dream Beings fits into this style wonderfully. Phrases such as "soul eater," "herculean movement," and "vibrational atmosphere" create that haunting longing that Lovecraft captured so beautifully. French's characters long for answers, but the truth comes coated in that sheen of terror of the unknown that Lovecraft mastered so well.

Our protagonist, Jack Evens, has a gift, if it can be called as such. This "gift" cracks the veil, thus allowing an unnatural, albeit necessary, awareness into places humanity has yet to breach. Reality slips as this veil between worlds shimmers, and ultimately fails. Using the most basic principles of String Theory, French weaves a complex tale of multiple Lovecraftian dimensions. Evens is a psychic into other worlds; frightening, mysterious worlds. Creatures so unthinkable live within a whisper's breath of us. They want us, but for what? Read on to find out.

The Dream Beings is an excellent Lovecraftian story. French captures Lovecraft's sense of the monstrous while at the same time, very effectively creates his own voice and style within the genre. The concept of multiple dimensions alone will stir the imagination long after the novella is finished. The Dream Beings is a chilling, thought-provoking tale of monstrous proportions.

Midian Unmade: Tales of Clive Barker's Nightbreed
Edited by Joseph Nassise and Del Howison
Tor Books
July 28, 2015
Reviewed by Tim Potter

Fans of Clive Barker, his book Cabal and film Nightbreed will find numerous stories of interest in the new anthology, Midian Unmade: Tales of Clive Barker's Nightbreed.

More than twenty authors contribute original short stories to the volume that expands upon Barker's own work. Their stories run the gamut from fantastic to forgettable in a book that succeeds more often than not. While adding new characters and situations to the Nightbreed mythos, the collection still manages to revisit some of the most interesting characters and locals from the classic book and movie.

Joseph Nassise and Del Howison serve as editors and have collected a wide range of very different stories. Nassise starts things with his preface about his personal experience with *Cabal* and his obvious love for the story. One of the only disappointments from *Midian Unmade* is the introduction by Clive Barker, which is reprinted from 1989's *The Nightbreed Chronicles*. The actual introduction is fine, but it feels dated and serves only to put Barker's words into the book.

"The Moon Inside," by Seanan McGuire, is a solid start to the fiction. It tells the story of Babette, a teenage member of the Breed, who has visions connecting her to Lori who travels the world with Cabal searching for a new Midian. The tale nicely establishes a world after the fall of Midian, one where the slaughter and destruction of the Nightbreed and their underground home has become the stuff of urban legend, known to the public, but not in all of its secrets. Babette is researching Midian when she comes into contact with a Seattle teen and his friends. The friends are playing at being monsters, and it becomes clear that some of the Breed are playing at being teens.

Kevin J. Wetmore's "The Night Ray Bradbury Died: A Tale of Lost Midian" is equal parts lovely and absurd. The idea of Drummer, a member of the Nightbreed who does not speak, becoming the drummer for a GWAR-like costumed metal band is just too over the top to work. The story, however, is redeemed by the ending which is as subtle and emotional as the beginning is crazy.

Kurt Fawver contributes the dynamic story "The Kindness of Surrender," which explores the idea of the Breed having to do things they hate because they are compelled to do it. This story is full of death caused by Asteria, but the author makes the reader feel for Asteria and see the tragedy in her existence. It also explores how the Breed are a minority group and what diversity really means. This story powers through from beginning to the deftly plotted ending and is one of the finest works in the collection.

"Pride" by Amber Benson also turns the idea of monsters on its head, blurring the divide between good and bad. Nancy Holder's "Another Little Piece of My Heart" revives original *Cabal* characters Eigerman and Ashbery. "Lakrimay" by Nerine Dorman, "Cell of Curtains" by Timothy Baker and "A Monster Among Monsters" by Stephen Woodworth and Kelly Dunn are also stand-out stories.

The pinnacle of the collection is found in stories written by Weston Ochse and David J. Schow. Ochse's "The Devil Until the Credits Roll" is about Rook, a member of the Breed who resides in a cave in the Tora Bora Mountains of Afghanistan, and Dobler, a CIA operative who knows all about Midian and the Nightbreed. The story adds the element of the Breed to armed warfare and explores their possible use as weapons. Schow delivers with his "Collector," the story of a member of the Nightbreed who exists just getting by day to day, collecting recyclables to sell for a bit of cash. The Collector doesn't even know her own name until she comes in contact with another Collector, Jexelle, who teaches her what being a Collector is really all about.

The collection is not just memorable for its great stories, but also for its lack of any truly poor stories. There are a few stories that are flat and don't stick with the reader, but the read is smooth all the way through. For those unfamiliar with the mythos, *Midian Unmade: Tales of Clive Barker's Nightbreed* isn't very accessible, and though a few stories may resonate, most of the content will lack context and easily confuse. On the other hand, fans of Clive Barker and the world of *Cabal* and *Nightbreed* will find this a terrific read.

Wolf Land
Jonathan Janz
Samhain Publishing
November 3, 2015
Reviewed by Tim Potter

The latest release from Jonathan Janz, one of the genre's most consistent authors of horror fiction in the last few years, comes *Wolf Land*, a deep dive into classic werewolf lore. Though modern and utilizing new ideas, the book fits squarely into the generally accepted mythology of the werewolf. There are only a few likeable characters, though there are more than a few unlikable characters, and this plays out well as the story moves along. 'Likeable' and 'werewolf' are not two identifiers that usually go well together. These are brutal werewolves, driven by violence and other sins and negative emotions. The only criticism with the book is something that is just as easily a positive for some, in that the action is dense and constant and certain sequences go on for quite a while, arguably too long.

Starting in 1202 and moving ahead to 1883, the prologue tells the story of the beautiful Antonov sisters and their eventual journey to the United States. From there the narrative jumps ahead to the present with a group of friends and former high school classmates preparing for their ten-year reunion. At an informal gathering a week before the proper reunion things go horribly wrong. A bonfire party in the woods becomes a slaughter when a werewolf attacks the party-goers, leaving many dead, numerous wounded and a few transforming to werewolves themselves. Who becomes a monster and who doesn't, who can control their animal urges and who remains a fragile human are the elements that drive the rest of the story forward.

The characters are very genuine and well rendered. While almost all of the players are not likeable, there are a few that are very much people the reader will want to cheer for. And likability isn't the metric for creating successful character, one could argue, but whether or not the reader cares what happens to the character, good or bad. With complex characters like Savannah, Weezer, Joyce, Glenn, Melody and Short Pump, the reader will want each character to face a specific outcome, be it happily-ever-after or violent evisceration.

Jonathan Janz is a talented writer whose prose stands out among his peers in any genre and that ability is on display in *Wolf Land*. It is always a pleasant, easy and intelligently written work that shows an impressive ability to convey scenes of action and chaos. Some may find that the action scenes occasionally last longer than they should, but even the lengthy scenes are a joy to read. This work is lighter on dialogue than much of the author's prior work, which is disappointing, but when dealing with werewolves dialogue is naturally not going to be plentiful.

The climactic battle is set in a local amusement park called Beach Land. Blood splatters from roller coaster to water park, heads roll from the Roof nightclub to the haunted attraction The Devil's Lair, and werewolf mayhem never lets up in this success of a gore-fest.

◇◇◇◇◇◇◇◇◇◇◇◇◇◇◇◇◇◇◇◇◇◇◇◇◇◇◇◇◇◇◇◇◇◇◇◇◇◇

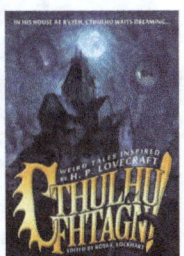

Cthulhu Fhtagn!
Edited by Ross E. Lockhart
Word Horde
August 15, 2015
Reviewed by Matthew Scott Baker

These days, if I hear the word 'Cthulhu,' my ears perk up and my salivary glands kick into overdrive. It seems I simply cannot get enough of the tentacled Old One, in any shape or form. As such, I'm a huge sucker for Cthulhu fiction. I never tire of seeing where authors can take this beloved (if such a word is applicable here) Lovecraft creation. Today, I am honored to present *Cthulhu Fhtagn!*, a collection of dark stories that Lovecraft himself would be thrilled to read. If you are a fan of terrifying short stories, this is a book you will want to pick up immediately.

For those of you not versed in Lovecraft, the words 'Cthulhu' and 'Fhtagn!' are uttered in a chant in his famous 1926 story *The Call of Cthulhu*. Many scholars believe the phrase refers to the dark god sleeping or waiting…but editor Ross E. Lockhart has a different theory. According to information shared with him in a dream, the term actually means Cthulhu's House, or more precisely, 'the house of Cthulhu.' While I'm not sure about this translation, I am positive the stories within this tome are excellent in every way and worthy of your attention.

The stories in *Cthulhu Fhtagn!* are carefully constructed and well fleshed out. Most are written in a style similar to Lovecraft's own: lengthy exposition that is interjected here and there with dialogue. This is not a negative, either. In fact, it is a nice homage to the legendary icon who many consider to be the founding father of the modern horror fiction age.

I enjoyed every story in this collection, which is a rare feat. Most anthologies I read usually have a couple (if not more) of stories that were just so-so, but every tale in *Cthulhu Fhtagn!* is entertaining and kept my interest. This is a true testament to the talent contained within these pages.

One of my favorites is "The Lightning Splitter" by Walter Greatshell. In this story, a man's new home contains a hidden passage to a horrifying place. Unfortunately, once you find this secret location, your life will never be the same. I love how this tale played out, as I didn't see the end coming.

Cthulhu Fhtagn! is a major win for me, and I highly recommend it. The authors work hard to continue Lovecraft's dark legacy, and their commitment shows in the excellence of their stories. The book is available now in a variety of formats, so give it a look.

◇◇◇◇◇◇◇◇◇◇◇◇◇◇◇◇◇◇◇◇◇◇◇◇◇◇◇◇◇◇◇◇◇◇◇◇◇◇

The Leper Window
Frazer Lee
Samhain Publishing
October 6, 2015
Reviewed by Marvin P. Vernon

Daniel Gates is hired to deliver a demonic book called the Choronzon Grimoire. When it is found, a page has been torn out of it. He is sent to North Wales to retrieve it, but he is not the only one who wants to find it and take hold of the demonic secrets told in its writing. He discovers a dark secret about the town where he is sent and why the book may be more dangerous than anyone realizes.

That is the bare bones of *The Leper Window* by Frazer Lee. It is a good story of demonic horror limited by its brevity of 50 plus pages. The author appears to have an expert grasp on this type of tale and understands the traditional roots surrounding its telling all the way from Machen to Campbell. I was caught in the tale immediately and enjoyed the author's distinct yet descriptive style. Lee has a good sense of atmosphere and uses the old Welsh countryside and history to good advantage. In fact, I wished he used it more since I felt there was a much longer story aching to get out. But overall I really enjoyed it. I have never heard of a leper window before this. A quick search told me that they were actual fixtures in medieval churches used for a particular purpose. The town and church in Lee's story seems to be fictional but the way he instills these fixtures is quite intriguing, as is how he merges the history of the demonic book with the end of his tale. It is this type of detail that kept me engrossed in what some readers might classify as an old fashioned tale of horror.

The Leper Window is an interesting and creepy work that entertained me for an evening. One might call it mainstream and subdued in style yet it packs an eerie punch in the end. I suspect *The Leper Window* may be an appetizer to steer you to his longer novels. If that is the case, it is successful as I plan to check out his other books soon. ◆

HELLNOTES
FICTION, MOVIES, AND ART
DEDICATED TO THE HORROR GENRE

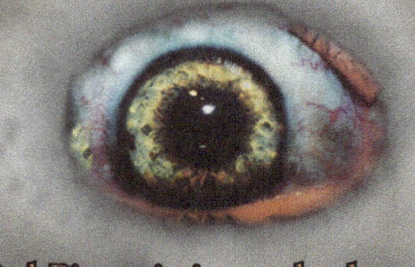
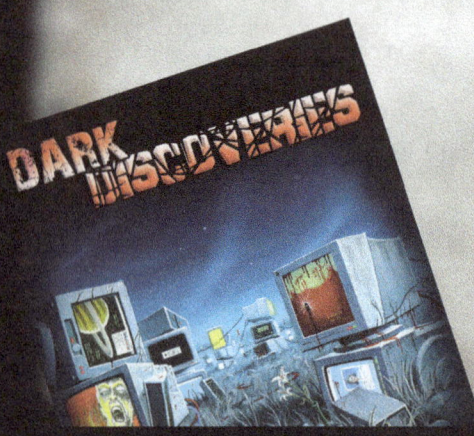